SHARDS OF FROST
The Mercury Pack Series, Book 5

SUZANNE WRIGHT

ISBN: 9781078288767

For the person who thought to invent electronic reading devices—having so many books at my very fingertips is just awesome. I salute you.

Anyone who has read Untamed Delights, the last instalment of the Phoenix Pack Series, will have read the eight-years-later-final-chapter. In terms of timeline, Shards of Frost doesn't begin after Untamed Delight's final chapter; it begins six months after Mila and Dominic's mating ceremony.

Hope you enjoy Eli and Casey's story!

CHAPTER ONE

Sitting on the stool at the corner post of the boxing ring, Casey draped her arms over the ropes and took long, steadying breaths. In all the years she'd been coming to The Den, she'd never lost a fight. Not once. In fact, she'd defeated each of her past opponents in the first round. That consistency made her a favorite among the spectators who placed bets on who, and in what round, a fighter would win.

Casey could sense that said spectators were getting restless tonight. Why? Because it was approaching round *three*.

Shame made her gut roll. Not because she was losing, but because she was losing on purpose.

Go down in round three, Casey. Round three. I have a lot of money riding on this, so do not disappoint me. Don't fight badly or it'll be obvious that the fight is fixed—just let your opponent get some good licks in, don't put as much strength behind your blows, and then fake a knock-out. Simple.

As the words replayed in her head, Casey caught the eye of the bastard who'd spoken them. Ignacio Rodriguez—Alpha cougar, drug dealer, and sociopathic motherfucker—was standing among the crowd with his cronies, watching her carefully.

Now yeah, okay, it was worth noting that he wouldn't come knocking on her door for cash if her drug-addict brother didn't do a disappearing act whenever his debt became too high. And, yeah, maybe she was stupid to keep paying off those debts for Miles. But he was her brother; if the debt wasn't paid, Ignacio would hurt him—*bad.*

Shit as it was, she couldn't go to her Alpha for help. Miles was under the protection of the pack, despite not being an official member. But if she told Adrian that Miles was once again on drugs, the Alpha would live up to his threat and withdraw that protection. Then Miles would be more vulnerable than ever. In that sense, her hands were tied.

1

Of course, Ignacio was fully aware of that and took advantage of it. So long as the debt was paid, he didn't care who the money came from. Sometimes, though, she got the sense that he liked taking it from her; liked that he could push, manipulate, and corner someone as dominant as Casey—it was like a power trip for him.

This time, though, he hadn't been placated to hear she'd pay him in instalments. No, he'd had the bright idea that she could pay off the four-hundred dollars in one swoop if they fixed her fight—which was why she hadn't wiped the floor with her opponent the way she normally would. And in the next round, she'd be expected to fake a defeat. The thought twisted her gut.

It only made it worse that *he* was there. Eli Axton. Everyone in The Den knew of him, considering he was the most savage fighter there. Brutal. Pitiless. Cold as ice. He never winced or flinched or cowered. Never gave any quarter or showed any mercy. Casey *loved* to watch him duel.

She also loved getting a glimpse of that magnificently muscled body ... Broad shoulders. Solid chest. Badass tattoos. Big hands that were probably exceptionally skilled at making a girl come—he just had that air about him that said he knew his way around the female form.

He was truly sinfully, achingly good-looking. Especially with that full carnal mouth, the sharp cheekbones, and the well-defined jaw dusted with stubble. Depending on how the light hit his hair, it could look anything from pale bronze to ash brown.

His appeal went deeper than the surface, though. Eli throbbed with a dark dominance and barely restrained sexuality that made a girl think all kinds of dirty thoughts. Then there was his air of unshakable self-assurance and how unapologetically male he was ... Yeah, he sure packed a sensual punch.

Casey knew with every bone in her body that he was out of her league. Hell, he was out of her solar system. More experienced. More secure in himself. More everything. Keeping up with the amount of game he'd bring to the table would be a struggle for any female.

And now he was watching Casey through those cool, sharp eyes the color of weathered oak. Eyes so piercing, they could see through any mask or lie. She could literally *feel* the heat and weight of his gaze; *feel* it pulling at her.

She'd never fought in front of him before, and it was just her luck that he'd come to The Den tonight. She had enough pride that it rankled Casey to know he was watching her "lose," particularly since she admired and respected him as a fighter.

The bell rung.

"Round three!" the umpire called out.

Shit. Standing, Casey rolled back her shoulders. Her gaze flicked to Ignacio, who smirked, the piece of shit. Rage churned inside her, making her blood boil and her fingertips prickle.

The bastard had introduced her brother to drugs, got him "hooked," dragged Miles down so low that her brother didn't see a way to pull himself back up ... and now Ignacio wanted to drag Casey down too. Why? Because that was what twisted people did.

God, she couldn't do this. She just couldn't.

Honor and integrity were important to her. If she threw this fight, if she let Ignacio take those things from her, she'd hate herself afterward. And it might even encourage him to demand other things of her in the future, like to throw her pack's soccer game or to do certain "favors" for him. She'd spiral deeper and deeper down the rabbit hole until there was no way out—a little like Miles had.

She needed to make a stand here and now. Needed to communicate that she wouldn't be his lapdog; that he would never rule or own her.

His eyes narrowed in warning, as if he suspected she didn't plan to "cooperate," as he'd put it. Well, he'd be right to suspect that. She'd pay off Miles' debt, but she wouldn't lose pieces of herself in the process.

Determination welled up from Casey's toes to the top of her head as she strode to the center of the ring. The breeze coming from the ceiling fan fluttered over her skin, ruffling her T-shirt and lifting her bangs. Her mink stood tall, bracing herself to shift and lunge if needed. The animal hadn't liked or understood why Casey was holding back during the fight, and she was sure as hell happy that Casey no longer intended to do so.

Her opponent licked her split lip. "You're not gonna win this one, Frost."

Casey stared at the fox shifter. Sasha Flint was a good fighter—there was no doubt about it. But she'd never have gotten this far in the fight if Casey had truly let loose on her. Apparently, she'd made the same mistake as Ignacio and had forgotten one thing: Casey was no one's bitch.

She swiped out her claws, slashing Flint's face. Casey didn't give her a moment to react. She rammed her foot into the female's ribs and then slammed her fist into Flint's solar plexus, knocking the breath right out of her.

Adrenaline pumping through her veins, Casey attacked from all angles—punching, kicking, slashing. And the spectators lost their damn minds.

The fox recovered fast from her shock and retaliated hard. She came at Casey with claws, fists, and elbows. She was strong. Sneaky. Went for every weak spot and injury. But Casey was lightning fast, and that had always given her an edge in a fight.

Casey ducked, weaved, and dodged. Flint still landed plenty of blows, and they all hurt like a motherfucker—the female had a mean right hook. But Casey had long ago learned to push past pain. She'd also learned how to *deliver* maximum pain, even if it meant fighting extra dirty, and she did exactly that.

Flesh tore. Blood dripped. The scent of pain permeated the air.

Both females growled, hissed, grunted, and cursed.

Soon, their breaths came fast and shallow, but they didn't slow down. Didn't lower their guard or give any openings. Just continued to fight fast and dirty. Casey's mink stayed close to her skin the whole time, anxious to join the battle and defend her.

Flint, the sneaky bitch, shackled Casey's wrist and yanked hard, trying to dislocate her shoulder. *Oh, the fuck no.*

Casey peeled back her upper lip and swept out her leg, knocking Flint clean off her feet. The female hit the ground hard, and then Casey was on her. One hard blow to the fox's temple was all it took—she was out cold.

Knuckles stinging, muscles quivering, Casey stood upright. She felt the burn of many superficial wounds and knew she had to look a mess. Flint looked no better—especially with blood matting her hair and what appeared to be a fractured cheekbone.

Panting, Casey lifted her head and glared at Ignacio, who stood among the cheering spectators, his eyes flinty and cold and gleaming with a promise of retaliation. She let a smile curve her mouth, daring him to do his worst. And she had absolutely no doubt that he would.

As a juvenile, Eli had been forced to brawl in an illegal fighting ring. It had been *nothing* like The Den, where shifters went to simply blow off steam and sharpen their combat skills; where there were rules, healers, and a no-kill order. No, the fighting ring had been inhumane.

He'd been repeatedly pitted against humans, feral animals, and fellow shifters. Each duel had been a fight to the death, and no one had given a single shit whether you were there willingly or not. In a place like that, you learned to be quick. Vicious. Cunning. Learned to switch off from your moral compass for just a while. It was the only way you could kill night after night. The only way to survive.

While forced to duel in that fucked-up pit, he'd seen a lot of good fighters come and go, just as he'd seen many good fighters compete at The Den. But *this* female ... he'd never seen anyone move the way she did. Casey Frost was *explosive*. Could go from naught to sixty in a fucking nanosecond. She moved with blistering speed and a savage, no-holds-barred style as she went at her opponent with laser targeted strikes.

Seriously, she was fucking hardcore. There was raw power behind every pitiless punch, kick, blow, and block. In his experience, a fighter's strikes were often less accurate if they moved too fast. Not with Casey. Her timing and precision were faultless.

She wasn't all about speed and ruthlessness, though. She fought smart. Kept up the pressure. Didn't fall for her opponent's tricks. She didn't just use her limbs, no, she incorporated her entire body into the fight. Twisted this way and that way, always smooth and fluid like the moves were ingrained in her. She also used her claws and teeth like they were weapons—slashing, biting, and stabbing.

He'd gone to The Den to distract himself from the shameful bitterness that curdled in his stomach. Receiving news that his cousin from another pack had recently found his true mate should have been welcome. It wasn't. Although it made him an asshole, Eli couldn't help but resent that yet *another* person had met their mate while he remained alone.

He'd stood back and watched as each of his pack mates and friends met their match. In most cases, they'd found their true mates. In other cases, they'd imprinted on someone. In every single case, they were utterly content. Although he was happy for them, he couldn't help envying them.

One might have thought that Eli would be reluctant to find his true mate, considering he'd watched his mother crumble to pieces after the death of her own until she was a shadow of her former self. But although he'd seen the mess that a broken true-mate bond could leave behind, Eli had always longed to find his predestined mate. And that longing now plagued him day and night.

It wasn't that he was unhappy. He had a good life. He was part of a tight-knit, powerful pack. He was Head Enforcer, and it was a position he enjoyed. A position that suited him and his highly dominant wolf, who would never have coped with a lower rank. Also, his mother, siblings, and nieces were part of his pack—not every shifter had that luxury. So, yeah, his life was good.

Still, he always felt that something was missing. It was the same feeling you had when you attended a party where a person important to you was absent from the large crowd. It might be just *one* absent guest, but the lack of their presence made a huge difference. Eli carried that feeling with him wherever he went, whatever he did.

Each time he witnessed another mating ceremony, it fucking hurt—they were the times when he felt the absence of his own mate so much more acutely. She should be right there, at his side, where she belonged. But he didn't have a clue where she was or even if she was waiting for him. For all he knew, she'd chosen to imprint on another male. While he could never begrudge his true mate any happiness, the thought still clawed at him.

Maybe it was selfish of him to want to find her so badly. It wasn't like he was a prize. Eli had done a lot of bad things. The kind that marked a person's soul; that ate at it until the edges were frayed and jagged. He hated that he would go to her that way, but he needed her.

His wolf was equally eager to find the other half of his soul. Being surrounded by mated pairs day-in day-out had soon begun to make the beast feel … sort of pushed out, as if he now hovered on the periphery of their pack. As if he didn't quite fit anymore.

Lonely, the wolf constantly prowled and brooded and vented at Eli, swiping out with his claws. The beast was in a perpetual foul mood and craved the company of his mate so much that he showed no interest in any female who crossed his path. But when the wolf had caught sight of the mink in the combat ring, he'd instantly stopped prowling. And now he was utterly still, absolutely entranced by her.

Eli couldn't blame him. Even before she'd started to fight, something about her had snagged Eli's attention. Something elusive. Elemental. He couldn't quite put his finger on it. Then she'd started to move, and he hadn't been able to look away for even a second. All that strength and power she possessed was seriously fucking hot.

Fire, he thought. Casey was like fire. Untamed. Fierce. Intense. Uncontrollable. And Eli wanted her. Suddenly, the thought of blowing off steam in her bed held far more appeal than blowing it off in that ring.

As his wolf watched her melt into the crowd, he urged Eli to hunt her down. Well, he'd get his wish.

Eli deeply suspected he wasn't the only one who'd be following her. It had been obvious to him that she'd initially held back during the fight with the fox, and he hadn't understood why. Then he'd seen the looks she exchanged with Ignacio Rodriguez, and he'd suspected the bastard had told her to throw the fight—it was something the cougar had done before with others.

Really, it surprised him that Ignacio had dared to tangle with her. No one picked a fight with a mink. Why? Because an entire pack would seek vengeance for the harm of just one of their own, and since a single pack could contain hundreds and there was literally no way to mink-proof your territory … yeah, it was just best for all if they were left well alone.

One would think that mink shifters were weak while in their animal form, given how small they were. Not at all. Like their animal counterparts, they were ferocious, bloodthirsty predators who were remarkably strong. Hell, they could carry prey up to four times their own body weight—sometimes more. And they had a stare that even he found disturbing.

Eli thought of them as ninjas. Stealthy. Cunning. Moved with blinding speed. Killed quickly and quietly. If a mink was stalking you, you'd never know it.

Those sleek little furballs hunted for sport and killed for the mere thrill of it, leaving behind mangled, beheaded carcasses. Carcasses they usually macabrely piled on top of one another. Because why wouldn't you?

Alphas constantly sought alliances with mink packs. It was pointless. Minks rarely agreed to alliances, refusing to be "used" as armies. Plus, they didn't do war. They either settled the matter on a one-to-one basis—usually by pitting their best fighter against that of their enemy—or they descended on their foe's pack in the dead of night, decimating its number in a matter of minutes. It depended on just how badly you'd pissed them off.

Eli had to wonder what kind of leverage the cougar had over Casey that he felt comfortable fucking with her. There was really only one way to find out.

Inside the restrooms, Casey quickly cleaned the blood from her skin and checked the state of her wounds. Some were ugly looking, but they'd heal by themselves within the hour; she didn't need the help of a healer.

Once she'd retrieved her purse and jacket from the metal locker she'd hired for the evening, she slipped out the back door into the cool night. It didn't come as a surprise to find Ignacio and his four cronies gathered in the parking lot. She stopped a few feet away from them, keeping her expression carefully blank.

As usual, Ignacio's dark, shoulder-length hair was slicked back into a ponytail. Even as he stood there looking every inch a fucking CEO in his tailored suit and gleaming black shoes, his predatory nature was perfectly apparent. There was a distinct darkness about Ignacio.

She'd met some seriously cold people in her life, but *this* male … he was a whole other level of callous. Those black, dead, reptilian eyes could give even the bravest person a soul-shattering chill—especially when he fixed that malignant stare on you as intensely as he was fixing it on Casey.

It was crazy that he could ooze charm and draw people in even as he possessed that cobra look. She wouldn't go as far as to call him inherently evil or anything, but he sure seemed to lack that certain something that made a person … well, a person.

Ignacio Rodriguez could be a cruel son of a bitch. And he was evidence that "cruel" wasn't always curt, gruff, and aggressive. Cruel could be polite. Cruel could be softly spoken. Could have a mate. Could smile and laugh and act understanding—though the latter was mostly to toy with you. But it was always ready to strike, and it would strike hard.

Right then, she had the feeling that Ignacio was done acting "understanding" toward her cause. Would he hurt her? Maybe, since he knew she couldn't go to her Alpha for help without revealing *why* Ignacio was on the scene. His usual MO, though, was to target the relatives of those who'd wronged him. The only close family she had was Miles.

His typical forms of retaliation often went along the lines of giving people what he called an "acid shower" or stripping them naked and leaving them in a metal cage for days. Hell, he'd even once poured molten silver into someone's eyes.

Casey doubted he'd go too far with her. No, he'd want to communicate his displeasure, but he wouldn't leave any injuries that wouldn't be healed by the morning—he wouldn't want her pack mates seeing her marked for the same reason that no one messed with a mink shifter.

He let out a long sigh, like he was disappointed in her. "You confuse me, Casey," he said, his voice pitched low and soft. "Why would you turn down the chance at paying off your brother's debt in one hit? Why drag this out for yourself?"

"You'll get your money," she said.

"But now I'll have to wait, and that is an issue for me."

"That ponytail is an issue. This is just a hiccup."

His mouth twitched in amusement. She'd been giving him shit about his ponytail from day one, refusing to show any fear, since he'd only exploit it. Ponytails might look good on some guys, but the look didn't work for him.

"It is a shame your brother is not as strong as you. He would not be in this position if he were." Ignacio crossed to her with slow, sure steps. "I think you will agree that I have been gentle with you, Casey."

Gentle? Nope. He might not have physically hurt her, but he'd been playing with her like a cat with a mouse, finding amusement in making her dance to his tune.

"I respect your strength, I respect that you are so loyal to your brother," he went on. "I have a sister your age; you remind me of her in many ways. This has made me reluctant to hurt you. Especially as I like to look upon that pretty face of yours—it would displease me to mar it. But I worry you are not grasping how bad this situation can get for you." Those black eyes glittered for a moment. "I am not the kind of man you should fuck with."

No, he wasn't. But he also wasn't the kind of man you let manipulate or rule you. She'd *had* to make a stand tonight.

He softly skimmed the tips of his fingers along her cheekbone. "Do you not grow tired of always cleaning up after Miles?"

Fuck, yes, but … "He's my brother."

"And so you will continue to protect him. Admirable. But who will protect you when I take a blade to your flesh as a message to him? Tell me that."

Lightning fast, he whipped out a knife. She fluidly wrestled it from his hand and put it to his throat—a move she'd mastered at the age of sixteen.

His men edged closer, bodies tensed to spring. Ignacio? He chuckled, the weirdo. She had the sense that he'd simply been toying with her again. A little like a lion giving a gazelle a fighting chance because it made the killing all the sweeter.

"Balls of steel. Lower the knife, Casey."

"You could back away and leave instead." But she knew he wouldn't. As an Alpha, he'd stand his ground.

"You've displeased me enough as it is. You don't want to make this even harder on yourself. Oh, you could attempt to kill me right now, that is true. And I believe you would. But then my men would take you down."

"They could *try*."

He smiled. "Such strength and defiance. You know, if I were not already mated, I would take you as mine. You will give a man strong sons one day." His smile faded, and his face hardened to stone. "Now, lower the fucking knife."

There was a ripple of unease in the air as someone stalked out of the shadows to her left. She barely glimpsed the newcomer in her peripheral vision, unwilling to look away from the threat in front of her.

The corner of Ignacio's mouth canted up just a little. "Eli," he greeted simply.

Eli? *Great.* Just great.

The wolf hummed. "Five men against one woman," he said, his voice so deep and gritty that it practically oozed testosterone. "I have to say, Ignacio, I don't like what I'm seeing here."

"Walk away," Ignacio told him, his voice soft and lazy. "This female and I have a few things to settle."

"Walk away? Hmm, that won't work for me."

Annoyance flickered across Ignacio's face. "This is not your business."

"I'm making it my business. Tell your cats to back off and give the female her space. You know I can take them down, Ignacio, so it would be stupid to test me. Really, you should know better than to try trapping a mink anyway. Especially this one. I have the feeling she can kill you easier than she can breathe—blade or no blade."

Ignacio clenched his jaw. "You do not want to interfere here," he warned silkily.

"I don't hear you calling off your cats, Ignacio. This confuses me."

"As I said before, this is none of your—"

"I heard you the first time. Now call. Them. *Off.* The only thing stopping that female from slitting your throat is that your cats would attack her. If I take them down, there's not a damn thing to stop her from ending you right now."

The tension ratcheted up as the cougar held his gaze, unwavering. Then Ignacio slowly lifted his hand and flicked it back slightly. His men backed away.

Ignacio looked at her, his eyes glittering. "Run to the wolf, let him protect you," he taunted. "I must say, it surprises me that you would hide behind another."

"I have a blade to your throat, I wouldn't call that hiding." Casey took a slow, casual step back and then held out his knife to him.

Mouth twitching in a dark amusement, Ignacio took the blade from her. "We will see each other again soon, Casey."

"Stay away from her, Ignacio, or you and I are going to have problems," Eli warned, but the cougar didn't respond.

Casey watched as the cats walked to a black Audi without a backward glance. Only once the car smoothly drove out of the lot did she turn to face Eli. His eyes followed the Audi even as he slowly stalked toward her, his muscles rippling and flexing, each step sure and deliberate. Damn, he was too much uber hotness for her to deal with.

Her pacing mink paused. Pushed closer to her skin. Eyed him closely. *Purred.*

As his scent of cinnamon bark, spicy cloves, and a dark masculinity surrounded her like a blanket, her hormones went into a frenzy and all her feminine parts did a little cheer. Moreover, her mink purred again and did a languid, flirtatious stretch.

His gaze finally snapped to hers. That was when everything went tits up. An electric, irrepressible, blindsiding force crashed into Casey's mind and wrenched at her psyche like a magnet. She winced, breath catching in her throat as a visceral, all-consuming, unbearable need flooded her body and battered at her soul. Her nipples tightened. Her pussy clenched. Her nerve-endings went haywire.

God, she needed to fuck. Hard. Fast. Rough. Needed *him.* Needed her mate.

Oh, hell.

As a pair of hooded, unusually pale hazel eyes met his, Eli felt like someone had punched him right in the gut. Seriously. His breath almost gusted out of his lungs. At the same time, a terrible hunger snaked through his system—thickening his blood, heating his skin, and making his cock harder than it had ever been.

His wolf lunged for her with such force that Eli almost stumbled. *Shit.* He took a deep, steadying breath and got a lungful of her scent. *Fresh peaches, vanilla cream, and raw sensuality.* It was like a slick, warm fist curled tight around his dick, and he wanted more of it. Wanted that scent filling his lungs and clinging to his skin.

Eli's blood thrashed in his ears as the primal hunger built and built … until the only thing he could think of doing was pinning her to the ground, burying himself deep inside her, and fucking her until she was addicted to his cock.

And as he watched her cheeks flush, her eyes glaze over, and her breaths start coming hard and fast, he knew she was having the same struggle. Knew she was … "Mine."

She put a hand to her stomach and almost doubled over, as if the hunger pounding through her was just too much. In a flash, he was there, pulling her flush against him.

"Shh, breathe," he said, curving his hand around her nape. "Just breathe."

She stared up at him, struggling to regain her composure, her eyes begging

10

him to do *something*. Helpless against that silent plea, he kissed her. Sank into the moment, into *her*. Poured himself down her throat. Drowned in her taste.

Eli took that mouth like it belonged to him, licking and biting—because it *was* his. He relished every moan and whimper she fed him as she ground against his cock, as mindless with need as he was.

Wrapping her braid around his fist, he angled her head how he wanted it. Her hair was as sleek and dark as wet seal-fur, and he could just imagine having it spread over his thighs as she swallowed his come.

Intellectually, he'd known the mating urge was intense and overpowering, but nothing could have prepared him for the sheer force of the insistent, pressing, violent hunger that hammered at him, driving him to possess and claim and mark. Fuck, he *had* to have her right there—

Not safe, a voice in his head whispered.

That whisper somehow reached him through the fog of red-hot lust. Ignacio was gone, but he could circle back or send one of his cats after her. She was too exposed there, out in the open. Too vulnerable. No, Eli couldn't claim her there. He needed her safe more than he needed to take her.

Scrounging for some measure of control, Eli pulled back and took a series of deep breaths. Her lips parted, her eyes dazed, she looked adorably off-balance. He caught her face with his hands and drank in every feature, every curve, every line, every freckle. *Mine,* he thought.

"I've been wondering where you were." And now he'd found her. His mate. The other half of his soul. "How far do you live from here?"

She licked her lips. "Five minutes away."

"I'll drive us there in my SUV. I can't fuck you here, but there's no damn way I'm not claiming you tonight."

SHARDS OF FROST

CHAPTER TWO

Pretty much in a sensual daze, Casey didn't object when he literally picked her up and set her on the passenger seat of an SUV. Moments later, he was sliding onto the seat beside hers and then they were driving out of the lot.

"Where are we headed?" he asked, his voice thick with the same relentless arousal that beat at her.

She swallowed around her dry throat. "Do you know where Craven Pack territory is?" He just nodded. "I live above the bakery on the border."

Her territory was much like a gated community. Among the streets of houses and apartment buildings were a school, an infirmary, a rec center, and the headquarters for her soccer team. Surrounding the housing estate was a great deal of land and wooded areas complete with rivers and lakes.

Many breeds of shifter shopped at the pack's stores—all of which were situated just outside the large iron gates of the community. Although her pack rarely encountered trouble from outsiders, the enforcers lived in the apartments above each of the pack-run stores so that they were near the border in case—

A wave of unbearable heat swept over her again, making her pussy clench and her nipples throb. Letting her head sag forward, Casey swore and gripped the edges of the seat hard. Jesus, this was bad.

A warm hand palmed her nape. "You're okay. Just breathe."

She *was* fucking breathing. She was also burning up inside. Her body raged for his, not just for satisfaction—no, it demanded *him.*

Casey could sense his beast pressing against Eli's skin, watching her. Yeah, she'd heard that his wolf always liked to make its presence known. Her mink was just as bold. Right then, the animal was hanging close to the surface, wanting at her mate.

Soon, they were pulling up outside the bakery. Eli followed her up the iron staircase at the side of the building that led to the upstairs apartment.

Her hand was shaking so badly he took her key and unlocked the door for her. Then they were inside, and he was kicking the door shut behind him. She only made it two steps before he was on her.

Growling low in his throat, he backed her into the wall and shoved his cock against her; it was long, fat, and rock hard. His eyes were locked on her with the lethal precision of a sniper rifle, and they glittered with something dark that made her blood heat and her mink quiver with anticipation.

"Now I'm going to claim what's mine," he rumbled. "You won't be able to move after I'm done with you."

Eli took her mouth, needing more of that sweet, addictive taste that seemed imprinted on his soul. Egged on by his wolf, he greedily took what he craved—licked at her tongue, nipped the corners of her mouth, sucked on each lip. Feasted on her until his head was spinning and his cock felt so impossibly hard it ached like a bitch.

Nothing had ever felt better than having his mate's body pressed to his, her scent filling his lungs, and the heat of her pussy practically scorching his cock through his jeans.

The mating urge still had a firm grip on him, but he'd managed to find enough semblance of control to battle the drive to just rut on her with no thought to anything but claiming her. No, he'd make this good for her.

Needing to feel more of that butter-smooth skin beneath his hands, he clawed off her jeans and panties, scoring her flesh slightly. He smoothed his hands up her thighs to cup her ass. "So soft. But this skin won't be so flawless by the time we're done here. I want to mark you. Bite you. Scratch you. Maybe even bruise you just a little." Her pupils swallowed the color in her eyes, and he almost groaned. "You like the idea of being all marked up, don't you?"

She tore off his shirt and splayed her hands on his chest, letting him feel the prick of her claws. "You won't be the only one marking their territory." And then she raked those claws down his abs, drawing blood.

Snarling, Eli slammed his mouth down on hers again. He rocked his hips over and over, grinding against her clit, delighted by her little gasps. All the while, he squeezed that tight ass he had every intention of fucking at some point.

He'd known plenty of women, had had a lot of great sex. But not even during the hottest of those fucks had he felt anywhere near as good as he did right then. Everything was just so much more intense with Casey. Like she'd woken up nerve-endings that hadn't before been active; ones that responded only to her.

Casey almost scowled when he pulled his hips back slightly, but then she heard a zipper lowering. *Thank God.* He pressed his cock against her pussy and, oh shit, she could feel it—so warm and hard—throbbing against her clit.

"I bet you taste as good as you smell, don't you?" He dropped to his knees and nuzzled her pussy.

"No, I need—"

"Shh, I'll give you what you need soon." Eli parted her slick folds with his thumbs. "I'm not leaving this apartment until my come's deep inside you." He lashed her clit with his tongue.

Breaths sawing in and out of her, Casey kept her palms flat on the wall behind her as that wicked tongue devastated her pussy—licking, swirling, flicking, probing, and generally driving her insane.

God, she needed more. Needed him inside her. Needed his *come* inside her. And she knew her body wouldn't give her a minute's peace until she had it.

"Eli." It was a demand for more that vibrated with hunger and desperation.

Standing, he lifted her leg and hooked it over his hip. "I've got a feeling I'm going to find myself addicted to your taste."

Casey gasped as he swiped the smooth, thick head of his cock over her clit and between her folds. Again. And again. And again. "In me. *Now.*"

"Not yet." Eli clawed off her tee and bra. He sighed happily at the sight of her breasts. "Hmm. I'll be fucking these soon."

To Casey's utter delight, he didn't cease swiping his cock through her folds while he squeezed and plumped her breasts, occasionally pinching, twisting, and plucking at her nipples until the taut buds were throbbing with both pleasure and pain.

But it was the whispers that really hit Casey in her core—whispers of how much he needed her, of what filthy things he wanted to do to her, of how much he craved the feel of her mouth around his cock.

Her pussy felt so empty it hurt. Casey almost whimpered. "Stop torturing me."

Eli bit her lower lip, deliberately leaving a print of his teeth there. "You ready to be fucked now, Casey?"

"You know I am," she rasped, throat dry. He hoisted her up and inched the thick head of his cock into her pussy—and, God, that felt amazing. But he didn't thrust inside. Instead he drew one of her throbbing nipples into his mouth and suckled. Head falling back, she slid her fingers through his hair. "Seriously, stop with the torture."

He blew over her wet nipple. "I'm going to come inside you, make you mine. You want that, don't you?"

Her mink hissed, out of patience. "For God's sake, yes. *Fuck me.*"

He arched a brow at her. "You know what I want."

Yeah, she did. She'd just hoped she wouldn't have to give it to him. She wasn't sure *how* she knew what he needed from her—the knowledge was somehow instinctive.

"The longer you keep me waiting, the longer I'll keep you waiting," he said. "That's how it'll work. So, what will it be?"

Licking her lips, Casey gave him her throat. With a growl he slammed her down on his long, thick cock, stuffing her full. A whoosh of air gusted out of her lungs. God, it burned as he stretched her, but she didn't care. She could only marvel over how utterly possessed he could make her feel with just the sensation of his cock filling her, throbbing against her inner walls so that she felt every beat of his heart.

Eli's eyes fell shut. *Finally*. He was finally inside his mate, right where he needed to be. Jesus, she felt so damn hot and tight, it was almost too much.

He licked over her pulse. "Gonna mark you right here, so I can watch your brand throb every time your pulse beats." Eli slowly withdrew, groaning as her inner muscles clutched and fluttered around his cock. "Who do you belong to, Casey?"

"You. And you belong to me," she snarled.

"That's right. You don't let anyone else near this tight little pussy, Casey. Not a single soul."

Then he was powering into her—oh God, yes, this was what she'd needed—filling the room with the sound of flesh slapping flesh. It only made it hotter that his firm grip on her ass held her still, forcing her to take the pounding he gave her. Happy to just hold on for the ride, Casey fisted his hair and dug her heels into the base of his spine.

His pace was furious as his cock sliced through her over and over, stroking her clit each time, winding her so tight Casey felt like she was stretched on a rubber band. This wouldn't be a slow build up, she knew. No. Her release was going to hit her out of nowhere—she could sense it.

Eli uttered a curse. "Never had a pussy this fucking sweet." He wasn't going to last. He'd make it up to her later. Would worship every inch of her with his tongue, teeth, and hands. Right then, he needed to possess her. Stake his claim. Fuck her so hard she was mindless to anything except the need to come.

"Mouth," he bit out, slamming hard and deep into the scorching hot pussy that belonged solely to him. "Give it to me."

Casey pressed her mouth to his, moaning as his tongue sank inside. He kissed her over and over, pouring hungry growls down her throat. Greedily ravished her until she was arching, bucking, and clawing at his back.

She smelled both his blood and her own, and she knew they'd each left several deep brands. That thought only made her hotter. God, she was so close …

She tore her mouth from his, panting. "Harder, Eli." Eyes dark with naked want, he set his mouth into a merciless slash and gave her what she asked for. Every thrust was as possessive as it was brutal. Her pussy couldn't seem to get enough—it was squeezing and rippling and weeping around him.

He snarled. Grunted. Cursed.

She moaned. Whimpered. Breathed his name.

And then she felt it happening.

"Yeah, that's it, come for me, Casey. Drain every bit of come from my cock."

She shattered, swept under by the shockingly forceful orgasm that made her eyes go blind and trapped a scream in her throat. Sharp teeth sank into her neck just as his cock slammed deep once more, pulsing and shooting jet after jet of come inside her.

She felt him lick and suck on her bite, knew he was leaving an irrevocable mark. She chose that moment to leave her own, biting down on the crook of his neck, tasting blood.

Sapped of energy and floating in a post-orgasmic daze, she slumped against him, shaking with little aftershocks. Truly, her limbs felt like noodles. Well, he *had* told her that she wouldn't be able to move after he was finished with—

Her eyes flew open as a sharp pain lanced through her head and chest, making her breath catch. Her vision briefly dimmed and blurred as her world tilted. Then the pain receded, and there was only the mating bond. Surprisingly strong for two people who barely knew each other, the bond vibrated with emotions. Satisfaction. Contentment. Awe. Calm.

Her mink sprawled on the floor with a yawn, happy and serene despite that the bond wasn't yet complete. It would take certain *steps* to help the bond progress, and those steps could differ from couple to couple.

Casey weakly lifted her head from his shoulder. The look of pure languid satisfaction on his face would have made her feel smug if it weren't for the fact that he'd done all the work. Damn her mate was delicious. God bless fate. "Hey," she whispered.

His mouth curled into a warm, lazy smile. "Hey. You good?"

"Can't feel my legs. Other than that? Super." She slanted her head. "You?"

"Well, let's see … I've got my mate wrapped around me, our bond is alive and strong, and she just made me come so hard my knees shook. Yeah, I'm good, baby." Eli kissed her softly, sipping from her mouth, loving her taste.

He'd claimed his mate. The knowledge settled into him, trickling through his system like thick, warm honey and gifting him with a peace he'd never thought he could feel. It had all happened so damn fast that he should have been finding it hard to process. He wasn't. Nothing had ever felt more natural than the feel of her soul bonded to his.

It didn't matter that he hadn't officially met her before today, he *knew* her on a level he couldn't quite explain. Strands of emotions had already formed between them. Affection, respect, tenderness, and protectiveness—they were all there.

She'd chased away that loneliness that had plagued his soul for too long, warming all his cold spots, soothing every frayed edge, and filling every empty space. Never in his life had he truly felt balanced until right then. "How's your mink doing?"

"Oh, she's lazing right now, quite content. What about your wolf?"

"He's happy. He wants to lick you all up and have some time with your mink. So do I." Eli also wanted to get a good look at the claiming mark on his neck—it pulsated and stung, just like the other brands he could feel marring his skin. They made his wolf rumble a growl of contentment.

Eli breezed his thumb over the claiming bite on her neck, brimming with self-satisfaction. He intended to fully relish the time it took to get to know her. He was in no rush. The bond was humming with life between them. Casey was going nowhere.

"Hold on." As soon as she curled her limbs around him, Eli said, "I want to take you again, but next time I want to do it in your bed." He didn't need to ask where it was, since the open-plan apartment was tiny. She'd clearly tried to separate the space into "rooms" by using different shades of paint for each one—magnolia for the living area, apricot for the kitchenette, bright white for the bedroom area.

She'd also used a tall shelving unit as a divider between the living space and small bedroom area. She didn't have a lot of furniture, so the place didn't look cluttered. Really, given that shifters didn't do well in enclosed spaces, it was a wonder that the apartment didn't drive her crazy, despite that it was warm and cozy.

Eli carefully settled her on the bed, shed the rest of his clothes, and then slid in beside her. She wasn't small, but she was petite against his larger frame. He liked that, though he couldn't really explain why. He just dug it.

Lying on his side facing her, he drank her in. She was truly beautiful with her bewitching eyes, extremely fuckable mouth, satin-soft skin, and delicious yet delicate curves. She also had a … presence. An energy that was gritty, earthy and *commanded* attention.

Nothing had ever enticed him the way she did. Everything about her incited his senses and drew him in. Her scent, her taste, the feel of her skin—all of it was perfect.

"I was starting to think I'd never find you." He pressed a soft kiss to that plush mouth he had all kinds of plans for. "You were worth the wait."

Casey felt her lips curl, *feeling* his sincerity through their bond. She could also sense how relaxed and at peace he felt, and that both warmed and reassured her.

She hadn't realized how very alone she'd felt until the mating bond roared to life, connecting them. With her family, it had always felt like she was on the outside, watching a show unfold; she'd never felt a part of them. She had her soccer teammates and fellow enforcers, of course, but it wasn't the same as having someone who was indispensable to you.

She'd only ever been truly close to her maternal grandparents, who'd taken her in when she was just fifteen. Both had long since passed on.

"So, is there a male in your life who'll now need to be warned off?" he asked *far* too casually.

Goosebumps swept across her fresh. "No." Dread suddenly filled her as she asked, "Were you dating anyone?" He simply shook his head. And the world was a fabulous place once again. "It feels wrong that I don't know much about you other than your name."

"I'm Head Enforcer for the Mercury Pack," he said, gently removing her hair tie so he could unravel her sleek braid. "My brother, Nick, is Alpha male. My mother, Kathy, and my sister, Roni, are also part of the pack. There are eighteen of us in total. There'll be nineteen once Ally has her baby. She's the Beta female. Her mate, Derren, has been so extremely overprotective since she fell pregnant that he's driving her crazy."

"Wait, I've heard of your pack. It owns the Velvet Lounge, right? I went to the club once with my teammates. There was a woman singing there—she's amazing. Her voice is all smoke and soul."

"I think you mean Mila. She mated into the Phoenix Pack, which is closely allied to mine. She's also a pallas cat, like my pack mate, Madisyn."

"Those little felines might be cute as a button, but they're plain crazy."

His mouth kicked up into a smile. "I won't deny that. Madisyn sure keeps Bracken—that's her mate and one of my pack's enforcers—on his toes." Eli combed his fingers through the silky mass of Casey's hair. He could just imagine bunching it in one hand as he took her from behind. "You said, 'teammates.' What do you mean by that?"

"I play for my pack's female soccer team. Minks *love* soccer; it's kind of our thing."

"Yeah, I heard. The females were long ago banned from playing in the pros, though, because they tended to attack the referees or opposing team, right?"

"That's right. So, now the female teams play against those from other mink packs. Each year, the six US teams compete against each other, all financially chipping in to cover the prize fund."

"What position do you play?"

"I'm a forward. The teams take turns hosting the event. It's our turn this year, so all the games will take place on my territory."

"What's the prize?"

"It's often different each time—it can be anything from a team all-expenses-paid vacation to a year's supply of luxury chocolate. All minks have a *major* sweet tooth, so the latter was a favorite of the past prizes. This year, the winning team will receive twenty-five grand, which will be distributed among the players. But it's never really the promise of a prize that motivates us. The win itself means far more to minks than anything else—we're highly competitive and *hate* to lose."

"I can relate," he said with a smile. "So, has your competition started yet?"

"It will soon. Whenever the games approach, our coach puts us through ten weeks of high-performance training, which basically involves an endless amount of soccer drills, sprints, and workouts so grueling that they make you want to die. We're now on week nine. After training is over, the teams will draw straws to see who plays against who, and then they'll eliminate each other over qualifying rounds. Those that come in first and second will then play in the final."

Casey's team, who called themselves the California Hounds, had won quite a few tournaments. The Orlando Seals, however, often bested the other teams and took home the prize. They were damn good, but the high-and-mighty females also loved to rub their win in the faces of the other teams and talk smack about them.

Miles' ex-girlfriend, Sherryl, had switched from Casey's pack to the Seals' pack a year ago, and she was now a member of the Seals' soccer team. This would be the first competition during which Sherryl would play against the Hounds, and what a fucking shitty situation *that* would be.

"I'm intrigued about what kind of player you are," said Eli. "You're a powder keg in the combat ring." He fully intended to be at every one of her games, supporting and cheering her on. He had the feeling that she was as aggressive on the field as she was in the ring.

"I'm also an enforcer."

"Yeah? Well, things must be pretty hectic for you." In fact, Eli would be willing to bet her days were a lot more eventful than his. He was Head Enforcer, sure, but there were *hundreds* within her pack, and her territory was far larger than his.

Now okay, yes, Eli had to worry about attacks from outsiders and people invading his territory. Mink shifters rarely had such problems, since people tended to leave them be—a smart move. But ... "I'd wager you have far more issues to resolve each day than I do. Talk me through the type of stuff you have to do."

"I mostly patrol the streets and borders of my territory. I also answer the calls that are made by my pack mates—reports of vandalism, accidents, drunken brawls, overloud music, and so on and so on. Minks are highly strung, temperamental creatures who can get into an argument over just about anything. But we're also quick to resolve issues, and we don't hold grudges against pack mates. Some days are calm, but those days are few and far between. I'm used to it. I've been an enforcer since I was seventeen."

Eli's brows lifted. "That's pretty young."

"I always knew I wanted to be one. I was sixteen when I asked my Alpha to let me train for the position. Adrian's a throwback to the years where women didn't take on what he considers 'masculine roles,' so I wasn't the least bit shocked when he said no."

"But you didn't let it deter you."

"No. I badgered him and badgered him for months until, just to humor me, he agreed to put me through the enforcer training. He'd fully expected me to fail. In fact, he hadn't thought I'd last the first day." But Casey hadn't failed. She'd worked her butt off. Put her body through the ringer to strengthen it. Had done everything the trainers asked of her. Mastered every skill and form of combat they insisted on teaching her.

"Even though I exceeded Adrian's expectations, he kept claiming I wasn't 'up to standard yet.'" She snorted. "He simply hadn't wanted a female enforcer in his ranks. His old Betas intervened on my behalf, claiming I was ready. Adrian relented eventually, muttering that I had no quit in me."

Eli smiled, pride flaring deep in his belly. God, she had so much grit and drive in her, and that appealed to him on a very primal level. Casey Frost knew who she was and what she wanted out of life, and she had no compunction about going after it. He admired and respected that. Admired and respected *her*.

He also loved that she had a highly competitive streak he could fully relate to. That was going to lead to a lot of fun in the bedroom.

She bit her lip. "I guess we're going to have to decide which of us is moving packs at some point."

"There's no rush." Eli wasn't gonna lie, he hoped he could make her fall in love with his territory. He'd switch packs if she couldn't be happy within his own, but he'd always found his territory somewhat magical. If they *did* stay on Craven territory, they'd need to get another place, because he could never live in this apartment.

He glanced around the bedroom area. "I wouldn't have thought a shifter could function living in such a small place."

Casey sighed. "Yeah, I guess it's fair to say I have pretty tight quarters. But size isn't the only thing that matters and … Wait, I didn't just say *tight quarters*, did I?"

Unable to stifle a smile, Eli cleared his throat. "You did, baby, yeah."

Casey groaned. "I should probably warn you that I have a mortifying tendency to accidentally spout out sexual innuendos. But we'll ignore that."

His lips twitched. "All right."

"I should probably also warn you that I've never been good at relationships."

"Neither have I," he admitted. "Or maybe I just wasn't fully invested in my past relationships because those women weren't you. We'll find our way."

She nodded. "There are no hard and fast rules, so there's no sense in us obsessing over the ins and outs of everything. But since being closed off can have a deep impact on the bond, we should also take a long, hard look at …" Trailing off, she cursed. "See what I mean about the innuendos? Just scrap the last few seconds from your mind."

His shoulders shaking, Eli dipped his head and pressed a kiss to the hollow of her throat. "My pack mates are going to be very anxious to meet you." Especially his siblings. His mother? Kathy might be weird about it, especially since she disliked pretty much all breeds of shifter that weren't wolves. Which meant it would probably be best if Casey wasn't there when he first told Kathy about her.

"I have a lot to do tomorrow—including soccer practice and enforcer stuff," she told him. "But I'll be done by five."

"All right. How about I pick you up at six and take you to my territory for dinner?"

"You sure you wouldn't rather give your pack some time to get used to the idea of you being mated?"

"Fuck, no. I want them to meet you. I want you to meet them. And if I don't take you, the females of my pack will harass me until I do. Especially Shaya, the Alpha female, since she's not the most patient of people. You'll like her, and she'll definitely like you."

"Are you close to your family and pack mates?"

"Yes, though I think some people might find it hard to believe that me and my sister are close. We constantly play pranks on each other and take sibling rivalry to a whole other level. We've been that way for as long as I can remember. She's a tomboy with an IQ that would intimidate most people. She's also an enforcer, and highly dominant."

Eli paused to trace the tattoo on Casey's side with his finger. The cluster of red roses was incredibly vivid and detailed. He loved that a sparrow wearing a top hat was nestled among the flowers. His mate had a streak of whimsy in her. "My brother, Nick, is like most Alphas—thinks he's always right, wants everything to go his way, and is hyper-protective of the people he cares for. He and I get along well. My mother ... I've got to be honest, I think she might irritate you at first."

Casey's brow creased. "Why?"

"Kathy was once a very open, trusting person. But after my dad died when I was just a kid, she changed. Became harder, colder, less accepting of people. She feels threatened by change, and she tends to stick her nose in places where it doesn't belong.

"Don't get me wrong, she's a good person. She'll kill or die for those she loves. And people respect her because she didn't let go after her mate died, didn't fall into a well of self-pity; she fought to live for Nick, Roni, and me. We're grateful to her for that. But it doesn't change that she can be a major pain in the ass when she chooses to be."

"If she tries sharpening her claws on me, I won't sit back and take it. You should know that now."

"Baby, I wouldn't expect you to take it. Not from her, not from anyone. I just wanted to warn you that she probably won't make a great first impression on you." Eli tugged her a little closer. "Tell me about your family."

Casey inwardly groaned. She didn't like talking about them, but she couldn't exactly blow off the question when this was *her mate*. "My parents, Ira and Gayle, mated when they were eighteen. My dad is human, and my mother is a latent shifter. Honestly, I think Ira might have fought the pull of the mating bond if she hadn't been latent—he doesn't like shifters much. He was beaten by a gang of jackals when he was eleven. Beaten *bad*."

Eli cursed. "Jackals can be cruel little fuckers."

She nodded. "Ira didn't want to live on pack territory, so he convinced Gayle to live as a human. My brother and sister are both latent like her, which means my dad can pretend they don't possess shifter blood. But with me, he doesn't have that luxury. I was thirteen when I shifted for the first time. He hit the roof. Threatened to throw me out if I ever shifted again."

Eli's eyes flashed wolf. "He *what?* Tell me your mother spoke up for you."

"Gayle rarely contradicts her mate. She just told me to never shift near or inside the house, so I spent more and more time at pack territory. Despite that my mom left, the Alpha always considered her, me, and my siblings to be unofficial members, so I was welcome to visit whenever I wanted."

"When did you move here?"

"When I was fifteen." She licked her lips. "Me and my dad got into a fight, which wasn't unusual. He said some pretty shitty stuff, and then he grabbed me by the throat. My mink rose just enough to take a hard swipe at his face, her claws out. Ira *freaked*. And for the first time, he looked truly scared of me."

A growl rattled in Eli's chest. "He should never have fucking touched you that way."

"No, he shouldn't have. He told me to get out and never come back, but I'd already decided I was leaving. While my mother was busy trying to calm him down, I packed my shit with my brother's help. Miles then gave me a ride to pack territory. I've been living here ever since."

"Do you still see your parents?"

"No. Miles told me that Ira forbid him, Mom, and my sister from contacting me. Miles was the only one who disobeyed that order. To be truthful, Dad never liked me anyway. I was a disappointment from the start. Both my siblings were child prodigies, you know. Emily's a walking calculator. She has all kinds of degrees in mathematics, and she got the first of them when she was *six*. Miles is a violinist. He started playing when he was two, and he mastered it after only five months of training. That's no exaggeration.

"Me? I'm not academic. Or musical. Or 'gifted' in any area other than sports, which he doesn't consider relevant. I'm not bitter that I'm not a genius, so please don't think I am."

"I know you're not, I'd sense it through the bond if you were bitter."

"I never minded that I wasn't a prodigy. I just minded that *my father* minded. He and Mom put all their time and attention into my siblings, supporting and encouraging them. And I'm not saying they shouldn't have. Child prodigies can be a handful."

"But you needed that time and attention, too."

Her nose wrinkled. "Not really. I just needed my father to not make me feel 'less' simply because I wasn't a genius. His disappointment in me bloomed into full-blown disgust when he realized I could shift.

"Really, Emily's the only child that Ira feels any pride in now. Not just because she's super smart. She's always fallen in line with what he wanted, always met his expectations. In short, she reflects well on Ira. Makes him look good to the outside world, which is important to him."

Another growl built in Eli's throat. Her sense of isolation fluttered down their mating bond. Ira had succeeded in making her feel like an outsider in her own family, the bastard, long before he'd tossed her away. Well, now she had Eli. She'd never be or feel alone again. "Does your sister share his view of shifters, even though she's part shifter herself?"

"I don't know. Emily is somewhat haughty and self-involved. She wasn't nice *or* mean when we were growing up. I was sort of inconsequential to her. But when my mink surfaced, she changed. Became distant. I could never tell if she was just adopting my father's views or if she was jealous that my animal had surfaced when hers hadn't."

"Was Miles jealous?"

"No, though he's disappointed that he's latent. He's different from Emily. Cocky, sure, but also fun and quick to laugh. A sensitive soul. He spoke up for me if Ira went too far. He snuck me treats whenever I was confined to my room. Helped me with my schoolwork."

Her brow furrowed as she added, "But he retreated into himself after his girlfriend—who'd also been one of my teammates—Sherryl, ended the relationship. See, the stirrings of an imprint bond had been there. It meant that the separation wasn't easy on him. It gave him bad headaches and mood swings. It also made him slightly depressed.

"He withdrew from everyone. Disappeared for days at a time. I heard he was hanging out at shifter bars, but I didn't think much of it. I don't know at what point he started taking drugs—he was never specific about it. I only know that Ignacio gave him drugs for free at first."

"He got Miles hooked on them."

Casey nodded. "My father has disowned him, just as he did me, so my parents won't help him. I'm really all Miles has. He never contacts me, though. You hear of addicts lying to and stealing from their relatives, but Miles ... it's like he just wanted to cut everything out of his life that reminded him of Sherryl—even me. Or maybe it's that he just can't face me, ashamed of how low he sank. Maybe it's both, I don't know."

24

Eli smoothed his hand up and down her back. He now understood the reason for her unwavering loyalty to her brother. Miles was the only member of her family who'd never made her feel like she wasn't good enough for said family. He'd stood up for her, he'd brought her to a place where she was safe, he hadn't tainted the surfacing of her mink, and he'd kept in contact with her up until his own life fell apart. The rest of her family? They were fucking useless, as far as Eli was concerned.

He kissed her shoulder. "My dad was hard on us, but not in a shitty way. He was just all about tough love. He taught us that second best didn't count, which might be why I hate not winning."

"I'm sorry that you lost him." Casey slid her hand over the intricate, tribal tattoo that not only spanned the left side of his chest but also covered his left arm. There was another tattoo on his right bicep; the face of an old, mechanical clock blended with a chess board on which a few pieces sat. Casey swiped her finger over the small numbers that had been tattooed just beneath the clock. "The date and time of your dad's death?"

"Yeah. He was a master chess player. And if it looked like you might just manage to beat him at it, he'd swipe the board."

She chuckled. "Miles used to love playing chess when he was a kid."

Able to *feel* her pain as if it were his own, Eli kissed her, wishing he could take it away. He could feel sympathy for Miles, despite that he couldn't condone the mink's way of coping with his pain. But he really didn't like that her brother had lumbered her with his baggage. Well, she'd no longer be dealing with the Ignacio situation alone.

Just the bastard's name was enough to make his wolf snarl and pace. It had recognized the powerful predator in Ignacio; had seen that said predator had locked its sights on Casey, and he wanted to hunt the cougar down.

"How much does your brother owe Ignacio?" he asked. Her expression shuttered. "How much, Casey? I can't help if you don't talk to me."

"I can handle this myself. Really."

Yeah, he'd figured she'd say that. "You have no idea how dangerous that cougar is. You lost him money tonight. He'll add that to your brother's debt, and he's not going to give you the option of paying it off a little at a time. You embarrassed him. You defied him. And then you put his own blade to his throat."

"I know, I was there."

Smart ass. "He's going to want his pound of flesh." Eli was surprised that Ignacio had let things get that far outside The Den. Eli had waited in the shadows, ready to intervene if the cougar moved to harm her or ordered his cats to do so for him. But the Alpha had seemed content to merely toy with her, which made absolutely no sense to Eli … unless the cougar had simply been drawing the whole thing out for his own amusement.

"I appreciate you wanting to help, but it's my issue to deal with."

25

"You're not dealing with it alone, and that's that." Eli tensed as her eyes briefly flashed mink and he saw the animal's annoyance. He *really* didn't want to tangle with her mink. For one thing, he had a sentimental attachment to his nose and fingers. Minks would bite right down to the bone, and they weren't always keen to let go. Two, trying to pin it down would work about as well as trying to baptize a cat.

Still, he wasn't prepared to drop this matter. He rubbed Casey's arm. "I know you think you're protecting your brother by paying his debts, Casey, but you're not really helping him. If he doesn't have to face up to his mistakes, he'll keep on making them."

"Would *you* leave the fate of someone you cared for to Ignacio?"

Hell, no. He sighed. "Tell me how much Miles owes him."

Casey didn't know how, but his voice … it seemed to reach inside her, *pull* at her, compel her to obey. She didn't think he even realized it. No, she got the sense that it was just part of the sheer force of his personality—a personality so big and powerful that it was almost like a weight, and it battered at her defenses.

He might not be a born alpha, but he was close enough for it to count. Going toe-to-toe with him would be truly like coming up against a brick wall. Good thing for her that she'd never been a pushover.

He nipped her chin. "Tell me."

"You're used to getting your own way, aren't you?"

"My mom always said I had a one-track mind. When I want something, nothing will distract me from going after it."

"Oh, I see. You live in Eli's World. A place where it's always sunny and warm and everything goes how you want it to go. Awesome." Hell, Casey herself was somewhat single-minded—she owned that. But it seemed that Eli had her beat by a landslide.

She got the feeling that he'd be ten times more demanding than any of her exes were. This wolf was someone who would take and take and take, leaving a girl feeling wrung dry, unless she could somehow make herself stand up to be counted.

"My world is a good place to be, that's true. Especially now that you're finally in it." He brushed his mouth over hers. "Tell me, Casey. I get that we don't know each other well and it may feel strange to trust me with this, but I'm your mate. You don't have to deal with this shit alone anymore. I'm here now. I protect what belongs to me, I keep it safe—it's my right. Don't try to take that away from me. Let me help you with this. You'd say the same thing to me if the situation was reversed."

Unable to argue that, Casey sighed. As his mate, she saw it as her right to defend and protect him, so she could hardly deny him this. "Four-hundred dollars. It's not about the amount for Ignacio. It's the principle. Miles doesn't always leave me to take care of his debts. Sometimes he pays them. Other times he disappears so well that not even Ignacio can find him."

Eli twisted his mouth. "I'll pay Ignacio the four-hundred. No, don't argue, just listen. I will pay it, and I will make it clear to him that it will be the last time you take care of Miles' debts. I'll also make it clear that if Ignacio comes at you in any way, he'll deal with the kind of blowback from which he'll never recover."

"If you want to talk to Ignacio, fine, but the only way you're handing him the four-hundred dollars is if I give that money to you."

"All right."

She narrowed her eyes. "I mean it, Eli."

"I know you do." Eli closed his hand over one perky, creamy breast and gave it a possessive squeeze. It was enough to make her nipple bead. "I have no idea how you can get your skin this soft."

"You're trying to distract me," she accused.

Of course he was. Eli skimmed his fingertips over the folds of her pussy. "You sore?"

"Not in a bad way."

"Good. Because I want you again." Eli rolled her onto her back. "This time, we'll take it slow."

CHAPTER THREE

Casey woke five minutes before her alarm was due to go off. She always did. Her internal body clock operated like ... well, clockwork. Still, she always set the alarm just in case, and she never rose until it went off. She liked to spend those minutes just lying there as the sleep-fog cleared from her brain. That morning, she intended to spend those minutes snuggled into her mate, who was presently wrapped around her like a clinging vine.

God, she was mated.

It was a little surreal. In just one evening, her life had changed. Before, she'd only really had herself to think about. Her days had been dedicated to her enforcer-role, and her loyalty had been mostly toward her Alpha.

Now, she was part of a couple—something she hadn't been good at in the past. But it was no simple relationship. Her soul was *bound* to this male. Her loyalty would always be primarily to him. He had access to her emotions, which probably should have felt at least a little uncomfortable, considering he was a practical stranger. But he didn't *feel* like a stranger.

Her mink didn't take to people easily; there were few that she trusted. Like Casey, she felt more at ease with Eli than she ever had with anyone else. Not just physically, but emotionally.

Both woman and animal sensed that although there might be times in the future when he'd do or say something that would hurt them, he wouldn't *purposely* cause them any pain. Would never betray them, tire of them, or leave them for another. How could they *not* feel one-hundred percent safe with him?

And how could Casey not feel damn lucky to have this lethally sexual male in her bed?

When he'd said they'd go "slow" the second time around, she'd thought he meant he'd take her soft and easy. She hadn't thought he intended to indulge in a very long, thorough exploration of her body that seemed to go

29

on for hours. He'd left no part of her untouched. Had discovered every hot spot she possessed. Had licked, bit, scratched, and kissed her until she was a quivering, whimpering mess.

Then he'd fucked her, and there'd been nothing slow about it. His pace had been feverish. His thrusts had been rough and deep. And she'd come so hard she'd lost her breath.

He'd woken her sometime in the night and then, just as rough and furiously, he'd taken her all over again. And she'd totally loved every second of it.

Her alarm went off, snapping her out of the memories. Casey grabbed her cell phone and swiped her thumb over the screen to switch off the horrendous noise. He stirred behind her and pressed a soft kiss to her nape. Before he could work his magic on her body and lure her into staying in bed, she slipped out of his hold and edged off the mattress.

He frowned. "What time is it?"

"Six-thirty," she said, digging a sports bra, tank top, and shorts out of her drawers.

"Why in the world would you get up this early?"

"I'm going for a run."

Watching his mate dress, Eli felt his frown deepen. For one thing, he preferred her naked. For another, he preferred her in bed. "A run? You do this often?"

"Every morning apart from Sundays, yeah."

He groaned. "Just when I was beginning to think you were perfect ..."

She snickered. "Go back to sleep."

Instead, he flicked back the covers. "I'll come with you."

"The running track is inside the gates of my territory, I'll be quite safe."

Probably, but Eli wanted to be at her side whenever he could. Not just for her protection, but because he liked being with her. Liked being able to touch and smell and hold her whenever he wanted.

Standing, he curled an arm around her waist, hauled her close, and kissed her hard. "I'm coming with you."

"So, you have spare clothes with you? Because I kind of ruined your tee last night. I don't think you want to go running in jeans anyway."

Well, he kept a spare set of clothes in the trunk of the SUV. But they'd get sweaty if he wore them while jogging, and then he'd have nothing to wear after his shower. "I'll go running in my wolf form."

"That won't get people's attention *at all.*"

"You'll need to tell the pack you're mated now anyway. It's not like you ever intended to keep me a secret." He palmed her ass. "You look hot in these shorts. All I want to do is peel them off you."

"Maybe later. Now if you're really set on coming with me, you'd better get ready, because I don't dawdle."

He kissed her and then, with a mock sigh of annoyance, disappeared into the bathroom. Once he'd done his business, he headed to where she was sat on the sofa, slipping on her sneakers. "Be warned that my wolf won't like other males being close to you, especially since the mating bond hasn't yet fully snapped into place."

"I know, I know. But you don't need to worry—a running track isn't a place where guys try to pick me up."

He grunted. "Good."

He shifted so wickedly fast that Casey felt her brows shoot up. "Impressive." She petted the huge, powerfully-built, gray-white wolf. He licked at her jaw and rubbed against her, scent-marking her. "Well, aren't you an imposing sight. Seriously, does Eli give you steroids or something?" The wolf gave a playful bark. Nodding, she stood and said, "I agree: Time to go."

The track circled the housing estate within the gates, never crossing over into the surrounding woods or land. Her teammates often jogged whenever the annual competition came around, but not as often or as far as Casey. She'd always pushed herself and her body hard—she didn't know any other way.

She'd been working her ass off, intent on securing her place as a starter, which meant she'd be one of the players who were on the field from the very beginning of each soccer game. And she'd be thoroughly pissed off if all that hard graft came to nothing.

The wolf kept pace with her the entire time she ran. Didn't once leave her side—not even to sniff at a bush or pee on a tree. Since it was so early in the morning, she didn't happen across a lot of people. Those she *did* see ... yeah, they did a whole lot of staring. She greeted them oh so casually, as if it were totally the norm to have a wolf shifter at her side. A few people tried calling her over, but she just kept moving. There didn't seem any sense in introducing them to her mate when he was wearing his animal's skin—the wolf wouldn't exactly be able to talk to them.

Back at her apartment, Eli shifted back into his human form and followed her into the shower. After soaping her down and washing her hair, he took her from behind while she kept her hands plastered to the tiled wall. He also delivered one hell of a bite to the back of her shoulder. Her mink had never liked guys being so territorial with her, but the animal rather liked how roughly possessive Eli could be.

Clean and dressed, they went to the kitchen. He froze, looking adorably confused. "Where's the coffee machine?"

Leaning against the counter, she said, "I don't drink coffee."

He looked at her like she'd told him she was a secret member of the Manson family. "You ... you don't drink coffee? When? When don't you drink it?"

"Oh, like, ever."

He just stared at her. "You're joking."

"Nope." But she was rather enjoying his reaction.

"How can you get up at six-thirty most mornings and still function without drinking coffee?"

She gestured at the bottle she'd just taken out of the fridge. "I prefer smoothies. Sometimes fruit juices. They provide a lot more energy than caffeine."

He did a slow blink. "I really don't know what to say to you right now."

"If you need coffee that badly, you can get one in the bakery downstairs. It opens at seven every morning, so you're covered." He looked so relieved she had to laugh. "Come on, I'll come with you. I could really do with a Danish pastry right now."

An hour later, Eli pulled up in the parking lot outside the main lodge. Normally his wolf would relax on reaching their territory. Not today. The further away Eli had driven from Casey, the more the beast had snarled and snapped his teeth.

Eli let out a heavy breath. It shouldn't have been so hard to leave her. It wasn't like she was in any danger on her territory. But their mating was so new that he wasn't quite secure in it yet. Being away from her made him edgy, and he suspected that that would only worsen as the day went on.

Every instinct he possessed urged him to remain at her side. Not just to guard her, but to reinforce their bond. The link wouldn't strengthen until they got to know each other better and deepened their emotional connection. He didn't properly know her, so he couldn't yet claim to love her, but the seeds of that emotion were there. Everything he *did* feel for her was so intense and consuming that she cast a huge shadow over every female who'd come before her. And that was as it should be.

Eli slipped out of the SUV and headed for the main lodge. The three-story, timber-framed building housed the Alphas, their pups, and Kathy. The other members resided in varying smaller lodges that were dotted around their expansive territory.

With its earthy colors, spacious rooms, comfy furnishings, and rustic tone, the main lodge had a very relaxing, welcoming feel to it. Especially the large open-spaced living, dining, and kitchen. The pack often gathered there throughout the day, so it was a constant hub of activity until after dinner when most people headed to their own homes.

He was quite sure they'd be shocked to hear he was now mated. Although they'd be happy for him, they wouldn't like that there was a chance he'd leave the pack. Eli had felt the same when the others mated—it was only natural, since they were such a tight-knit group. The loss of one could affect so much.

Their pack was very insular, but Nick would be happy for Casey to join purely because she belonged to Eli. The others would welcome her just the same, but they'd also be slightly wary. When you had such a small group of people, the addition of another person could shake the dynamics in a major way.

Casey would never be content to lounge around, doing this or that. She was far too dominant for that. She'd need a place in the hierarchy. Eli didn't doubt that his brother would see the benefits of having Casey as an enforcer, especially since she wouldn't require any training. The pack already had five enforcers—Roni, Marcus, Bracken, Zander, and Jesse—but there was always room for more.

Roni was the most dominant female within the pack, though Ally was a close second. His sister was also one of the best fighters—Eli should know, since he'd trained her himself. Casey, however, was even more dominant than Roni, and she could probably wipe the floor with his sister in a matter of minutes.

There was a chance that Roni wouldn't like having such an addition to the pack. And if Roni didn't like it, her mate—by extension—wouldn't like it. Marcus would always back Roni, just as Eli would always back Casey. And that meant Eli could end up at odds with his sister. He really didn't like the thought of that.

The porch steps creaked beneath Eli's feet as he climbed them. He pushed open the door and walked through the country-style kitchen, past the dining area, and then into the living room. With the bulky chairs and sofas, there was ample seating, but some of his pack mates preferred to sit on the shaggy rug near the stone fireplace—just as Harley and Madisyn were doing right then.

The living room had a very cozy feel, especially with the throw pillows, artsy display shelves, potted plants, and the framed pictures that lined the walls and mantle. The only people absent were a mated pair, Kent and Caleb, and the Alpha's pups. The little girls' laughter and squeals filtered in through the open windows. Eli suspected they were having fun in the outdoor play area set back from the lodge.

Jesse saw him first. "Well, look what the cat dragged in. I stopped by your lodge to see if you ..." The enforcer trailed off as he caught sight of the brand on Eli's neck. "Is that what I think it is?"

Shaya's head snapped around to face Eli. "What? What is it? What am I ... *Oh*. Wait, you found your *true mate*?" The shrill note to her voice woke a pregnant Ally.

Eli stepped further into the room. "Yes, I found her. Knew she was mine within seconds of meeting her. The mating urge hit us hard, and we claimed each other last night."

Standing, Shaya glanced behind Eli. "Well, where is she? Tell me you're not making me *wait* to meet her. You know how I hate to wait."

Eli snickered. "She'll be coming here for dinner. You can all meet her then. And I expect you to be nice."

Blowing out a breath, Nick stood and held out his hand. "Well, congrats."

Eli shook his brother's hand and accepted the well wishes that came from the rest of his pack mates. As he'd anticipated, they were happy for him but also seemed wary about what would come next—particularly his mother, whose smile was somewhat strained.

Ally studied Eli. "You feel a lot steadier to my Seer-senses."

"I was just thinking that he looked it," said Bracken. "You've always been kind of unflappable, Eli, but there's a ... restfulness about you that wasn't there before. Like every bit of turmoil inside you just went still."

Probably because that was exactly the case. "Being the last unmated pack member was getting to me and my wolf. If I'm honest, it was eating at us. What made it worse was that I couldn't be sure I'd find her, or that I'd even instantly know she was mine if I did. And then there was the possibility that she'd imprinted on someone else. It all messed with my head, and I wasn't in a good place. Then there was her."

Bracken's gaze briefly slid to his own mate. "Yeah, I get it."

"Tell us about her," urged Harley.

And then several questions were hurled at Eli at once from various people ...

"What's her name?"

"Where did you meet her?"

"How old is she?"

"Is she a wolf?"

"Does she want kids one day?"

"Is she dominant or submissive?"

"Does she have any food allergies?"

Eli raised his hand to stop the flow of questions. "Her name is Casey Frost. She's twenty-seven. I met her at The Den—she fights there sometimes. She's an enforcer for her pack, and she's strong as fucking hell. Even more dominant than Roni."

His sister's eyes widened. "Really? Well, now I'm super intrigued. What pack is she from?"

"The Craven Pack," replied Eli, relieved that Roni didn't seem bothered by the idea of having a female around whose level of dominance exceeded her own.

Marcus frowned. "That's not a wolf pack, is it?"

"No," said Eli. "Casey's not a wolf. She's a mink."

Zander gaped at him. "You're kidding."

"Wait, there are mink shifters?" asked Gwen, the only human in their pack. She was also mated to Zander. "That is *awesome*."

Kathy shot to her feet. "It's far from 'awesome.'"

Eli's brows snapped together. "Why is that?"

Kathy spluttered. "Maybe because they're the psychopaths of the shifter kingdom. And cannibals. Did you forget that part? They'll kill and eat each other."

Nick sighed. "Mom—"

"Are you sure she's your true mate, Eli?" asked Kathy. "There's no mistake?"

Eli felt his face harden. "I'm sure."

Kathy flapped her arms. "I just can't believe fate lumped you with a mink."

Madisyn shrugged one shoulder. "I like them."

Smiling, Bracken snorted at his mate. "You would. They're as bloodthirsty as your kind."

Kathy perched her hands on her hips. "But whereas pallas cats are crazy, minks are just rampant, indiscriminate serial killers."

Shaya cast her an exasperated look. "Do you have to be so dramatic? Really?"

Kathy blinked. "*Dramatic?* It only takes for you to hurt one of them— just one—and their entire pack, which often totals *hundreds,* will descend on yours in a fury. Crossing a mink means you get to experience the meaning of wholesale massacre."

"If they were bigger, they'd rule the world for sure," said Madisyn, smiling. "And pallas cats would totally help them do it."

"Well, I'm glad you've found your true mate, Eli," declared Derren. "It doesn't matter what breed she is; what's important is that you're happy. Isn't that right, Kathy?" It was more of a pressurizing statement than a question— it had no effect.

Kathy pushed her hair out of her face. "I think it's possible that you're wrong about her being yours, Eli. As you said, it was getting to you and your wolf that you hadn't found your mate. I've known males your age to start panicking that they're never going to find their true mate—they can be so eager to do it that they'll easily mistake a strong attraction for a true-mate situation. Think about it, Eli. *Really* think about it. Just because you're sexually attrac—"

"And we're done," Eli cut in.

Kathy's lips thinned. "But—"

"No." Eli slashed a hand through the air. "You had your say. I listened. Now the conversation is over. And make sure you don't repeat any of that shit to Casey. Think what you want, but don't offload it on her."

"I'm entitled to my opinion," Kathy clipped.

Nick sighed. "Be honest with yourself, Mom. Your problem isn't that Casey is a mink. Not really. It's not even that you simply hate change. You found it difficult to be happy for me and Roni when we found our mates, and that's because you know what it would do to us if we lost them. You've been through the loss of a mate, you came out the other side of it, but you didn't come out of it whole. You don't want that for us, and that taints this for you. But you can't let it taint things for Eli."

Some of the bluster left Kathy. She sniffed. "I have a few things to do."

Nick watched her hurry out of the room. "She'll be fine, Eli. Don't let this put a downer on finding your mate."

"Nothing could," said Eli. "On the subject of Casey, I need you to ask Donovan if he can track someone for me."

Nick's brow furrowed. "Who?"

"Her brother." Eli told them about the business with Miles and Ignacio. "Miles has now gone into hiding, and Casey says he's damn good at it."

Nick twisted his mouth. "Well, that explains it."

"Explains what?"

"Why I got a call from Ignacio literally minutes before you arrived. He wants to meet with me today, and he asked that you be there."

Eli narrowed his eyes. "Fucking did he now?"

"My guess is he wants to talk you out of involving yourself in this situation with Casey."

His wolf snarled. "There's no chance of that happening."

"When he hears she's your mate, he'll know that. It should be enough to make him back off. He's a cold motherfucker and he's strong, but you could take him. And if a Head Enforcer defeated him, his pride members would lose respect for him. Some would challenge him for the position of Alpha. He won't want that. As for her brother, I'll talk to Donovan. If anyone can find Miles, it's him."

"What time do we need to leave for the meeting with Ignacio?"

"Noon."

That meant Eli had time to tidy up his lodge—he didn't want it looking a mess when Casey arrived. First … "I'll go say hello to the girls," he said, referring to his nieces. "I'll meet you in the parking lot at noon."

Eli headed outside and strode over to the play area, where Caleb and Kent were monitoring the pups. The mated couple did a double-take at the sight of his claiming mark, and then they were practically bouncing up and down in delight. He was just telling them about Casey when the pups spotted him.

"Uncle Eli!" Eleven-year-old Cassidy dashed over, making her long, blonde ponytail swing from side to side. "I had a *knowing* about you earlier, and I just *knew* you were going to bring a woman here to meet us."

He smiled at the little Seer, who often had visions and knowings about her pack mates. "I'll be bringing her later. Her name's Casey. You'll like her."

"Is she your girlfriend?" asked Willow, tilting her head. With her red curls and pixie facial features, the ten-year-old looked a lot like her mother, but she had Nick's green eyes.

"No, she's my mate." Eli told both girls about Casey, sure they'd welcome her. They were wide-eyed to hear she was a mink.

Given how close the pups were, a stranger would never guess that Cassidy hadn't come to live with the pack until she was four. Nick and Shaya had adopted the little girl from the homeless shelter for lone shifters where Madisyn worked. Cassidy had foreseen that she would join the pack. Unlike Ally, she had more knowings than she did visions.

Saying goodbye to his nieces, Eli headed to his lodge and tidied up the place, which mostly involved decluttering and then tackling his laundry.

As promised, he went straight to the parking lot at noon, expecting to find Nick and whichever pack mates were coming to the meeting. There was only Zander, who was sitting in the driver's seat of the SUV.

Eli slid into the front passenger seat. "What's the delay?"

"Nick and Shaya are arguing," said Zander. "He told her that he wanted her to stay behind."

Eli winced. Highly dominant, very unsociable, and annoyingly tyrannical, Nick was pretty much the opposite of his mate. Shaya was a bubbly, impish, warm soul who had an enviable ease with people. But she also had a wicked temper, and Nick had a terrible habit of prodding said temper—especially when he insisted on her skipping meetings for her "safety." That kind of overprotectiveness didn't fly with Shaya.

"Well, they need to hurry, or we'll be late." Eli snapped on his seatbelt. "Was it just me or did Ally look really pale earlier?"

Zander grimaced. "It's not just you. Derren said her morning sickness is bad and she's not sleeping well. I think it bothers her more that her abilities are playing up. It means we're relying on Cassidy for warnings of danger— she's just a kid, she shouldn't have that kind of shit to worry about."

"Cassidy once told me that she likes the visions, even if they're not always good," said Eli. "But when she reaches Ally's age and has foreseen dozens upon dozens of bad things happen—some of which she wasn't able to prevent happening in real life—Cassidy might feel differently."

Eli had never envied either female their ability to foresee the future. Especially since their visions never felt like visions. To them, it seemed real; they truly thought those things were happening. Ally had once seen Shaya die in a vision, and she'd believed it to be true right up until she snapped out of the vision.

Zander tapped his fingers on the steering wheel. "Have you told Casey about this meeting with Ignacio?"

"No, because she'd insist on coming along. I don't want him near her. I saw the way he was with her last night, Z. He enjoyed playing with her—I'm not going to give him another chance at it."

"I don't blame you, but she's not going to like that you went without her."

"No, she won't. She'll be pissed at me. But better that than she's in the general vicinity of someone who wishes her harm. She can handle him. I just don't want her to have to."

Zander flicked up a brow. "Does that mean she can handle you, too? You're not an easygoing wolf."

The corner of Eli's mouth canted up. "Oh, yeah, she can deal with me just fine. There's so much grit and fire in her."

"She's your match."

Eli nodded. "Yeah."

"Nothing like Jen, then?"

Eli almost did a double-take. Fuck, that came out of left field. People rarely mentioned Jen. It wasn't that she was a no-go subject, it was just that he and his family had different opinions about why Eli's relationship with her had ended. He felt to blame for the fuckup. His family felt that the blame belonged solely to her.

Forcing a nonchalant shrug, Eli said, "We weren't what the other needed. I was too much for her." Even at the age of eighteen he'd been pushy, demanding, and overprotective. "I drove her away."

Jen hadn't been as strong-willed as Casey, but she'd had spine. She'd stood up to him, she'd pushed back when he pushed too hard. Until she didn't. Little by little, the fight had started to leave her. She'd become someone who rarely questioned him, let alone defied him. And then she'd walked away, claiming he'd "broken" something in her.

Really, he hadn't thought of her much over the years until Jesse brought Harley to their pack. The margay not only bore a resemblance to her, she was just as musically talented.

"I never met Jen, so I can only go on what Nick told me," said Zander. "I happen to agree with him; I don't think you were too much for her or that you drove her away. I think she just wasn't the person she showed you in the beginning and that she gave up on you because, despite being a dominant female, she was mentally weak. She tossed the blame at your feet because she didn't want to admit to that weakness."

Twisting his mouth, Eli turned his gaze to the window. For a long time, he'd been convinced that he'd crushed the spine, and it had fucked with his head in a major way. But looking back, he had to wonder if his family was right. Had to wonder if she'd simply showed Eli the defiance and spunk that she'd thought he wanted in a female. Maybe, in truth, she'd always been a more pliant, easygoing personality.

At this point, he didn't see that it mattered much to either of them anymore. She was happily mated with kids now, and Eli had finally found the female he'd been waiting decades for—all was well in both his and Jen's worlds.

"So, you recognized Casey as yours at first glance?" asked Zander.

Thankful for the change of subject, Eli replied, "It wasn't so much at first glance, though I think my wolf did recognize her instantly. When I was up close to her and our eyes met … then I knew."

"It took me a little while to realize Gwen was mine. What's it like? The feeling of recognizing your mate that quickly, I mean."

Eli blew out a breath. "She slammed into my consciousness like a fucking freight train. My mind, soul, and body reached for her. The mating urge took hold, I claimed her, the bond formed … and then it was like everything just clicked into place."

"Is it weird having such a strong connection to someone you don't know?"

"Not at all. I might not know everything about her, but she doesn't feel like a stranger. How could she? She's part of me."

"Well, I'm happy for you. I'm just hoping it doesn't dredge up bad shit for Shaya and Nick."

Eli frowned. "What bad shit?"

"They knew at first sight that they were mates, but Nick walked away. I know he had his reasons and she later forgave him. But seeing that you did the opposite when you found *your* mate … well, it might bring back Shaya's hurt."

Fuck, he hadn't thought of that.

"Not that that's your problem, and I truly don't think Shaya would make it yours. She'd hide any pain she felt so that she didn't ruin this for you. I'm just hoping that what Nick did isn't still a sore spot for her, or she'll later be upset with herself for letting her own pain interfere with how happy she is for you." Zander tipped his chin at the rear-view mirror. "We have movement."

Moments later, Nick, Shaya, and Bracken were sliding onto the rear passenger seats—Shaya looked smug, Nick was grinding his teeth, and Bracken wasn't bothering to stifle an amused smile at what was no doubt Nick's expense.

Zander switched on the ignition. "You all ready?"

"Ready," Shaya confirmed, flicking her red spiral curls away from her face.

The tires crunched as Zander drove along the dirt path that ran between tall, regal, claw-marked trees. Once they crossed the border of their territory, he asked, "What do we know about Ignacio? I've never met the guy."

Nick hooked an arm around Shaya's headrest. "He's a cougar. A few years back, he left the Buxton Pride and mated the daughter of the Rotunda Pride Alphas. It was mere months after the mating that her parents stepped down from their positions and made Ignacio and Dahlia the new Alpha pair."

"I heard it was an arranged mating and that Dahlia's father, Glenn, promised Ignacio in advance that he'd make him Alpha," said Eli.

Nick nodded. "Donovan, who has a contact within Ignacio's pride, told me the same thing."

Zander frowned. "Why did Glenn choose Ignacio as a mate for his daughter? Arranged matings are often political. From what little I know of Ignacio's old pride, it's small and has very few alliances."

"True," said Nick. "But what Glenn needed most in a son-in-law was someone who wouldn't be whatsoever bothered by Dahlia's sidepiece. Said sidepiece is a submissive cat she's been sleeping with for years; a cat too quiet and subdued to run a pride. The only way she could be Alpha female was if she mated with someone strong enough to run the pride alongside her, but she wasn't willing to give up her lover."

"Ignacio obviously decided he wouldn't care that the mating would basically be a façade," said Shaya. "Then again, becoming an Alpha meant he could give his old pride the alliances it needs to survive in the cutthroat world of shifters. It's understandable that he'd find that so important."

"I initially thought that was why Ignacio agreed to the mating," said Nick. "But when he met with Glenn's allies to be sure the alliances wouldn't be broken by the change in leadership, Ignacio requested that they each sever their alliance with his old pride."

Shaya's head jerked back. "Why?"

"Ignacio said it was weak and rotting from the inside," Nick replied. "Said it was only a matter of time before a more powerful pride came along and tried to take it over. He didn't believe his old pride was worth going to war for."

"*Is* it rotting from the inside?" she asked.

"According to Donovan, yes. It's full of alcoholics and drug addicts, and the members are constantly fighting among themselves. They're not a unit anymore. The Alpha lost most of his alliances because he refused to back them up in battle, claiming his pride was so small it wasn't needed. But the real reason he refused is that he doesn't have enough control over his members to force them to fight. And why would a bunch of drunks, addicts, and assholes care to fight for another pride?

"Donovan's contact also revealed that Ignacio's father, Reeve, is the Buxton Alpha's younger brother. Reeve was allegedly always jealous and bitter that his sibling had the position of Alpha. By all accounts, though, Reeve is too weak to ever rule. He also likes to smack around his mate when he's drunk. Reeve also used his fists on Ignacio. The rest of the pride turned a blind eye to it all, even the Alpha."

"That explains why Ignacio hates them," said Shaya. "They all sat back and did nothing."

Nick nodded. "It gets worse. Ignacio's mother tried to suffocate him when he was just a baby. Said she was trying to save him from Reeve, certain he'd hurt the baby just as he hurt her. She never tried to harm Ignacio again after that, but she also didn't stand up to Reeve and protect her son."

"So Ignacio didn't just want out of his pride, he wanted to be an Alpha so that he could lord it over his father, who'd always wanted that position. It also enabled Ignacio to cut the pride off from their alliances, leaving them vulnerable the way he was vulnerable growing up," Shaya surmised. "I have to feel sorry for the kid he once was. But the adult he's become? Dealing drugs, delivering torturous punishments, messing with our Casey? Nah, I got no love for him."

Our Casey. Yes, Eli thought with a curl of his lips, she was theirs. And with any luck, he'd one day be able to convince her to officially become part of their pack. First, he needed to get rid of this fuckhead who'd been playing games with her.

SHARDS OF FROST

CHAPTER FOUR

No one spoke much throughout the rest of the drive to the marina, where Ignacio had asked to meet. After Zander parked in a nearby lot, Eli slid out of the SUV and was greeted by the briny scent of sea water and the prickle of heat coming from the sun.

"A smart place to conduct a meeting," said Shaya. "Relaxing. Pretty. Popular. Makes the whole thing less formal, which can make it easier to get people to lower their defenses."

"It's also crowded, so there's a lesser chance that any fights will break out if things get heated," said Bracken.

They all turned toward the pier and walked toward the long row of cafés, restaurants, and shops. The boardwalk creaked beneath their feet as they headed to their destination, passing families and couples.

White, gleaming boats of various sizes idled in the water near the pier while birds circled overhead, ready to swoop down. Some boaters were hauling fishing paraphernalia onto their boats; others were rinsing the decks with water hoses.

Flags snapped in the breeze. Water lapped the boat hulls. Nylon ropes creaked as they pulled taut. Music played low in the various eateries.

Finally, the wolves reached the café that Ignacio had chosen as a place to meet. The cougar in question sat at an outdoor table with one female and two males. All four stood when the Mercury wolves approached.

Ignacio saw Eli coming and curled his lips into a small smile. Recognizing the cat as the male who'd threatened his mate, Eli's wolf lashed out with his claws, wanting to slice open the bastard's throat. It took everything Eli had not to lunge at him.

Ignacio nodded at Nick. "We've never met officially. I'm Ignacio Rodriguez, this is my mate, Dahlia." His gaze slid to the redhead at Nick's side. "You must be Shaya." After the Alphas exchanged greetings, Ignacio gestured at his other cats. "On Dahlia's left is our Beta, Deon, and on my right is our Head Enforcer, Tyson."

Nick inclined his head. "On Shaya's right are two of my enforcers, Bracken and Zander. I believe you've already met my Head Enforcer, Eli."

Most people eyed Bracken warily, considering the dark reputation he'd earned after hunting, torturing, and killing the anti-shifter extremists responsible for his family's death. No one blamed him. In fact, they respected him for it. Still, Bracken tended to make people nervous. And Eli could see that the enforcer had that effect on Dahlia, Deon, and Tyson.

Ignacio, however, was too busy staring at Eli to pay Bracken any notice. "Ah, Eli," said Ignacio. "Glad you could make it."

Eli did nothing more than incline his head, shifting his angle slightly so that the bastard would get a good look at Eli's neck.

The moment Ignacio's eyes dropped to the claiming mark, they hardened to stone. Pure stone. The cougar's nostrils flared as he drew in a breath, and then those dark eyes slammed on Eli's. "Casey."

"Yes," Eli confirmed, surprised by just how pissed the cougar appeared to be.

Ignacio's smile was brittle. "You think lying that she's yours will be a good way to keep her safe from me? How admirable of you."

"Casey's mine—don't doubt that for a second."

But it was clear that Ignacio *did* in fact doubt it.

"Why don't we sit down," proposed Shaya with a forced smile.

"Good idea," said Dahlia. Tall and lithe, she looked like she'd just stepped out of a fashion magazine. Designer clothes. Shiny accessories. Expensive jewelry. Ridiculously high heels. Sunglasses perched on her head, pinning back her wavy blonde hair.

Before finding his mate, Eli might have given the Alpha female a second look. He was too full of Casey now, like she was inside him, filling him, leaving no room for anyone else.

"Dahlia's father, Glenn, spoke very highly of you," Ignacio said to Nick once they were all seated.

Splaying a possessive hand on his mate's thigh, Nick sighed at the cougar. "You called for this meeting. What do you want?"

Ignacio pursed his lips. "I would imagine your brother told you what transpired last night between myself and Casey."

"He did," said Nick.

"That saves us some time." Ignacio's lips thinned as the waitress appeared. No one ordered anything, so she quickly left.

"I'm guessing you hoped to convince me to butt out of the situation," said Eli. "As you can now see, that's never going to happen." He tossed a brown envelope on the table. "Your money. Now you stay away from Casey. She's done paying her brother's debts."

Ignacio didn't even look at the envelope. "Oh, I agree that she shouldn't—she's not really helping him, and it isn't fair to her. But … I'm a businessman, Eli. If there is a debt to be paid, I will go where the money is. In this case, the money is rarely with Miles."

"That's not her problem," said Eli.

"True, but it means I have no option other than to—"

Eli growled. "You stay. Away. From Casey."

The other cats fidgeted, uneasy. Ignacio, however, sat utterly still.

Dahlia spoke, "Let's all remain calm. Eli, it is understandable that you would insist that Ignacio keep his distance from your mate. And we appreciate that you'd pay this debt for her brother. But you must see that the situation isn't quite as simple as we'd all like it to be. Casey put a knife to my mate's throat. You really expect that to go unpunished?"

Oh, apparently Dahlia felt that she should avenge Ignacio for the sake of appearances. What a fucking joke. If she thought they were kidding anyone that their mating was anything other than a façade, they were wrong. "You want to take my mate on? By all means, challenge her to a duel. See how that works out for you."

Dahlia gave him a somewhat condescending smile. "I'm an Alpha female, Eli."

"But not a born alpha, and you're nowhere near as strong as she is. You don't believe me? Ask your mate. He knows the truth. He knows you wouldn't stand a chance against her." He looked at Ignacio, daring him to deny it. The cougar didn't, which earned him a hiss from his mate.

Eli tipped his chin at the envelope. "Take it, Ignacio. I wasn't kidding— that's the last payment you'll get. Casey's done cleaning up Miles' messes for him."

Drumming his fingers on the circular, metal table, the cougar tilted his head. "Is that her decision … or yours? I've known Casey for a while now. I know how protective she is of her brother. I know there's very little she wouldn't do for him. If she wants to continue being Miles' savior, there isn't a single thing you will be able to do about it. That female is far too strong for anyone to ever govern her." He sounded as though he respected that.

"She's agreed with me that this is the best cause of action for all concerned."

"Even knowing that if she doesn't pay his debts in future, Miles will pay them in blood?"

"I've got an easy solution for you: Don't give him any drugs."

The cougar inclined his head slightly. "Yes, I suppose that is the simplest solution."

"This isn't just about her brother's debt," Dahlia cut in, a bite to her tone. "She has to answer for what she did."

Eli glared at her. "Are *you* going to make her answer for it? Because I can tell you now that there'll only be one outcome—she'll take you down so effortlessly that she'll weaken your stand with your pride. I can't imagine why you'd want that."

The female pressed her lips together, her cheeks flushing.

Eli sliced his gaze back to Ignacio. "We're done here. You have your money—take it and go. Forget about Casey. I don't think I have to tell you what I'll do to you if you go after my mate. I have no limits when it comes to her. None. I don't care who you are, how many people you have at your back, or how well protected you think you are. If you go near Casey again, I will find you, Ignacio, and I will kill you. Don't doubt that."

Ignacio's mouth curved into a mocking smile. "How could I, when you've made yourself so perfectly clear?" He pushed away from the table, and his mate and cats followed suit. "Congratulations on your mating, Eli. Do be sure to tell Casey that I wish you both the best."

Dahlia gave the Mercury Alphas a hard, insincere smile. "Thank you for meeting with us."

Once the Rotunda cats were out of hearing range, Bracken spoke, "I wouldn't say Ignacio fears you, Eli, but he knows you'd kick his ass. And he won't be interested in letting that happen. Having said that, I can't say for sure that he'll keep his distance from Casey. He weirdly doesn't seem to want to."

Nick twisted his mouth. "He doesn't believe that you and Casey are truly mated, so he won't expect you to be as fiercely protective of her as you are. That means he might still go after her."

Eli had had the same thought. "I don't think I'll have to kill him, though."

"Why not?" asked Shaya.

"Because if he ever went at my mate, she'd kill him herself."

Standing in her team's locker room, Casey ground her teeth as she read the text message she'd received from Miles' friend, Fjord: *No idea where your bro is. Sorry Case x*

The two males had been best friends since they were toddlers. Fjord stupidly felt guilty that he couldn't "save" Miles from himself. But she understood … because that same senseless guilt nipped at her. Ugh.

She placed her phone in her locker, regretting that it didn't have a door she could slam shut. The lockers ran along the perimeter of an oval space that gave the room a "huddle" feel. The team logo was dramatically displayed on the ceiling. There were also tribute lockers to honor past players.

Sitting on the integrated wooden bench, she pulled up her cleats, each movement sharp and stilted. She loved her brother. She really did but, God, he needed a good bitch slap.

Beside her, Emma eyed her curiously. "You look like you want to ram your foot into someone's face. It would be best if you didn't do that on the field again. Coach won't buy it was an accident if you do it twice. What's wrong? Is it Preston?" Emma asked, lowering her voice, referring to one of the assistant coaches. "He keeps shooting glares at you. I don't think he's happy that you're mated. Did he say something? Send you a bitchy text that was overflowing with jealousy?"

"He has no reason to be jealous, he has a mate of his own." A mate who happened to be Casey's cousin.

Emma snorted. "You're not dumb, Frost, you know he only started dating Mallory because you refused to give him more than a one-night stand. He wanted to hurt you and make you green with envy."

"That was over a year ago. He cares for her."

"He does *now*. But initially, he was just using her. I don't think he expected anything to come of it. Nobody did. Mallory's boyfriends were never in the picture long—she always got bored so quickly."

Although Casey had been equally doubtful that the relationship would last, she *had* considered telling Mallory about her one-night stand with Preston. But how did you tell your cousin that, hey, the guy she really liked was only using her to hurt another female? She and Mallory didn't get along, true, but Casey hadn't wanted to upset her.

Emma had discouraged her from saying anything, pointing out that—being highly vain and so sure of her sexual appeal—Mallory wouldn't have believed *any* male would pursue her just to hurt another woman. No, she'd have accused Casey of trying to stir shit out of bitterness that she'd lured away some of Casey's boyfriends.

After far too many hours agonizing over it, Casey had eventually decided not to say anything. Keeping the one-night stand to herself had seemed harmless when she'd been so sure the relationship wouldn't last. But it *had* lasted, and the longer she'd gone without telling Mallory, the harder it was to say anything. Then Preston and Mallory had imprinted on each other, and he'd *begged* Casey not to tell her.

The only person other than Emma who knew of the one-night stand was Sherryl, since she'd paid Preston a surprise visit just as Casey was leaving his house that night. Sherryl probably would have blabbed about it if she wasn't good friends with Preston, considering how much she seemed to hate Casey.

"Although he's happy with Mallory, he never likes hearing you have a guy in your life," Emma added. "So, no, I don't think he's taking it well that you're mated. Surely you can feel him glaring daggers at you. It's starting to piss me off."

Yeah, Casey could. "Ignore him. I do."

"If it isn't Preston that's bothering you, what has you so wound up?"

"It's Miles. He's done a disappearing act again."

"And he left you to clean up whatever mess he made." Emma sighed. "I want to call him a selfish asshole and a bunch of other names, but he's really not a bad person. He's just …"

"Miles. He's just Miles." Lost. Aimless. Wounded. Far too sensitive for his own good.

"Well, maybe Eli can help you with this. I *love* that you've finally met your mate. Have you told Adrian yet?"

"Nope. I intend to do that after training."

"Okay, everyone, listen up," Coach Donahue called out. Clad in her red and blue jersey with matching track pants, she stood beside the team's healer, Dennis.

A total softie, Dennis was always on standby during practices and games. But the rule was that healers could only help during games if the player left the field and sat out the rest of it. The rule made sense since, otherwise, the game would be repeatedly paused, and a lot of time would be taken up by players being healed.

"I don't have to remind you that we have our first game next week," Donahue went on, fists perched on her hips. "As Emma likes to say, shit just got serious. I've pushed you girls hard during practice, but now I'll be pushing you harder—and I expect nothing but everything you've got and *more*. Before you all start whining at me to tell you who's been picked as starters, we'll get it out of the way."

Mentally crossing her fingers and toes, Casey stayed very still as Donahue spoke one name after another. She knew the other forwards would want it just as much, but most were younger than her. She'd earned her spot; had worked harder and longer than they had. She deserved—

And then she heard her name. Doing a victory dance in her head, she exchanged a smile with Emma, whose name had also been called out.

Emma poked her arm. "I told you you'd be picked. You don't listen to me, I'm not sure why that is."

"Well, when you insist on doing weird shit like making 'lost dog' posters and putting a photo of a hotdog on it—"

"I *did* lose one once."

"—you sort of make it hard for me to really heed you in anything. It's truly a good thing that you now have a mate to keep you out of trouble. I got tired of that job."

"You were shit at it."

Casey frowned. "Hey, I saved you from getting arrested multiple times."

"But not *every* time. Slacker."

Smiling, Casey snorted. "Fuck you."

Donahue gave a hard clap. "Okay, ladies, let's get moving."

Everyone filed outside onto the wide, rectangular field. Casey's tension slipped away as the oh-so-familiar scents of freshly-cut grass and warm earth swirled around her. Even the muffled, distant sounds of busy traffic, car horns, and engines rumbling were so much the norm here that there was something comforting about them.

After years of playing on the pitch, Casey knew it as well as she knew the back of her hand. She didn't even need to glance at the white lines that defined the boundaries of each area of the turf. No, they were imprinted on her brain.

Casey took a swig of water from her bottle and then, like the other girls, placed it near the sidelines. She rolled back her shoulders. God, it was hot. The sun pricked at her skin.

As a tall, wiry shadow fell over her, she looked to see their team captain, Kristin, throwing her dark curls into a messy knot. The mink was an excellent midfielder who always did them proud. Until she lost her shit and lunged at someone. For a skinny female, she had some *serious* power behind her punches. No one on the team had been given more red cards than Kristin. The midfielder found a strange kind of pride in that.

"We're going to win this year, Frost," said Kristin. "I can feel it."

"Just try not to get red-carded at the games, yeah?"

Kristin grinned. "Can't promise anything."

As always, Donahue led practice, though her assistants chipped in here and there. She barked and yelled instructions, throwing out the occasional insult if someone wasn't trying hard enough—the insults only ever spurred the team on.

They did jump squats, push-ups, dips, sit-ups, lunges, and ran sprints until Casey's muscles burned and sweat beaded her skin. The baking heat didn't help. Before long, her uniform was so damp with sweat it clung to her body.

Midway through practice, clouds passed over the sun, casting shadows across the field and giving the players a slight reprieve from the scorching rays. The reprieve was far too brief. The sun was soon beating down on them again as the team executed high intensity ball-touch drills. After that came a short five-on-five game—Casey's mini team won.

Tired, hot, and sore, she was more than relieved when Donahue announced that it was time for their cool-down. That amounted to a light jog followed by some static stretching exercises that mostly concentrated on the calves, groin, hamstrings, quadriceps, and lower back. Only then did their coach blow the whistle, signaling that practice was over.

"Thank God," muttered Emma.

"Yeah," sighed Casey. All she wanted was to get clean, dry, and spray on some deodorant.

Breathing hard, she dabbed her face with the bottom of her jersey as they headed inside. Back in the locker room, Casey shucked her uniform, nose wrinkling at the grass and dirt stains, and quickly hit the showers. She winced as the hot water beat at her turf burns, but the spray felt good on her sore muscles.

No one ever bothered asking Dennis to heal the burns. As shifters, they healed quickly from minor injuries anyway. Plus, his gift could take a lot out of him if used too much. People preferred for him to deal purely with *real* injuries so that he didn't later feel burned out.

Clean, she wrapped a towel around her and headed for her locker. She didn't bother trying to shield her body as she dried off. Shifters were used to being nude in front of others, so they rarely suffered from body-consciousness. Plus, the team were so tired, sore, and hungry that they often really didn't care about anything but getting clean and dressed so they could munch on some food.

She pulled on her clothes, surrounded by the hissing of deodorant cans, the whir of hairdryers, and the laughs of her teammates. When everyone was dressed, they sat on the benches while Donahue switched on the wall-mounted TV and spent the next fifteen minutes replaying clips of video footage from practice. She pointed out where players went wrong, where the team's weaknesses were, and dished out lectures to those she felt had let themselves or the team down. Such fun.

Once Casey was ready to leave, she pulled a granola bar out of her duffel and slung the bag over her shoulder. "Bye guys," she called out before biting into the bar.

She'd barely made it a few steps outside when Preston came prowling around the side of the building and stalked toward her, his eyes cold.

"You couldn't have called Mallory about your *news*? You don't think it's shitty that your cousin is going to hear about your mating via gossip?"

Casey frowned. "You say that like she'll care either way. It's not like me and her are close or anything. If I recall correctly, *I* heard she'd imprinted on *you* through the grapevine."

"You two might not be close, but she does care about you."

"That's unlikely, but whatever."

"It's true. And she's going to be upset when she hears you're leaving the pack."

Casey's frown deepened. "Who says I'm leaving?"

"In case you haven't noticed, Eli Axton is a wolf, Casey. He'll want you to transfer to his pack—wolves don't like living amongst other breeds of shifter. He didn't warn you about that? I'll bet there are a lot of things he hasn't told you. I've heard plenty of rumors about Axton and his pack. Some are good, but a lot are bad. Letting someone you barely know *claim* you … Fuck, Casey, you're smarter than that."

Her mink hissed. "I don't know at what point you reached the conclusion that this is your business, but it's not, so back the fuck off."

A muscle in his cheek ticked. "You can't be pissed at me forever, Casey. I'm sorry if it feels weird for you that I'm mated to your cousin now, but you should have made your peace with it at this point."

Casey could only stare at him. "You think I'm mad that you mated Mallory? Really?" He had to be kidding. Seriously. He *had* to be.

"You've been upset with me since the day I first started dating her."

"No, I was upset about the *reason* you started dating her. Mallory didn't deserve to have you use her like that."

"And I regret it. Believe me. I hate that there's this big secret between me and her. Honestly, it's a wonder the imprint bond ever fully formed. It took a while. *You're* going to have the same problem with your true-mate bond."

"Say again?"

"It's not such a bad thing to let people in, Casey. But you're set on keeping everyone at a distance. Look, I get it—your family isn't worth shit, and being disowned like that would give anyone trust issues. I can understand why you stuck to shallow relationships and ruined anything that even had the possibility to become more. But how can you ever expect your mating bond to fully snap into place if you're set on leaving everyone before they can leave you?"

Okay, that made her spine snap straight. "I don't abandon people. I'm loyal to the people in my life. I'm there for them whenever they need me. Playing amateur psychologist doesn't suit you." She was a private person and found it hard to trust, sure, but she didn't keep people at a distance or fear being disowned again.

"You never let guys get close to you. You told them it was because you were waiting for your true mate, but that was just an excuse to hold them at bay. How you expect to fully bond with Axton when you're scared to let people in, I have no idea."

She could only gape at him. "You really don't know me at all, do you?" She shook her head. "I have to go, I'm starting my enforcer shift soon."

"Casey—"

She slammed up her palm. "We're done." She sharply skirted around him and walked en route to her Alpha's house.

Preston was wrong about her in so many ways. She didn't expect people to leave her just because her parents and sister had shunned her. No. The way Casey saw it was that if they could so easily toss her aside, they'd never loved her in the first place and weren't the kind of people she needed in her life.

She'd never been good at relationships, no. But she was so used to people treating her like an outsider that she never really knew what to do with anyone who tried getting close. At the same time, though, she'd always craved a connection with someone. Had always wanted what her grandparents had—a bond true and deep. A partner whose love and acceptance wouldn't be conditional.

She'd fallen short of every standard her father had. Even before he'd discovered she could shift, she'd never been "enough" for him. He'd nitpicked at her constantly. In his eyes, she'd always been too much of this or too little of that. To put it simply, Ira had never seen any real value in his youngest daughter.

That had stopped hurting her a long time ago, though, because she'd come to see something else. Ira had taken such a natural dislike to her merely because he couldn't control or manipulate her the way he could her sister and mother. He resented Casey's strength. Resented *her*. It was Sherryl who'd pointed that out.

Sherryl.

Ah, she'd been the typical frenemy—someone who pretended to be your friend but was more of a rival. Casey hadn't associated with her until the female joined the Hounds, so she hadn't known Sherryl well. Donahue had asked Casey to take the new player under her wing, so she had. Sherryl had climbed up Casey's ass shockingly fast, lavishing her with praise and flattery. Casey had sensed it was fake, but she'd thought the other mink was simply trying to secure her friendship.

When Sherryl had asked for private soccer lessons from her, Casey had obliged. Then Sherryl had wanted Casey to "recommend" to Adrian that he give Sherryl an enforcer position. Adrian, however, didn't believe the female had what it took. She'd then accused Casey of convincing him not to grant her the position; she'd maintained that Casey selfishly wanted to be the only female enforcer. Sherryl later apologized profusely, but that had only been for show.

Sherryl's sickly-sweet act stopped then. Oh, she continued her "friendship" with Casey. But she also constantly made passive-aggressive jabs, tried treating Casey like her own ATM machine, and only came around when she wanted something. Oh, and Sherryl did like to make sarcastic, cutting remarks that were always immediately followed by, "What, I was just kidding! You take everything so seriously."

No pushover, Casey always called her on her shit. The other mink would then apologize, and they'd move on, because Casey wanted peace and coherence within the team. Besides, Sherryl wasn't a horrible person. She could be fun and encouraging, and she'd cut down anyone who talked smack about any of her teammates—even if that teammate was Casey.

Sherryl was also hugely protective of her family; never had a bad word to say about them. She simply did not make a good friend. Didn't seem to know how to have a balanced friendship. And, well, Casey couldn't help but feel sorry for her. Sherryl's true mate had died when he was a child, and Casey figured that would mess anyone up.

Still, she had not been a happy bunny when Sherryl later started dating Miles. She'd tried warning him that Sherryl could be quite the backstabber, but he liked to see the best in people—a trait that was admirable but often caused him pain.

Sherryl had seemed to care for him, though. She'd made him happy. And it had obviously been real, or they wouldn't have almost imprinted on each other—the beginnings of the bond had been there. But then she'd dumped him, claiming she felt like bonding with him would be betraying her deceased true mate.

No matter how many times Casey had told her that she wasn't to blame for Miles' subsequent downward spiral, Sherryl couldn't bring herself to believe it. Nor did she believe that Casey and the pack didn't blame her.

Basically, Sherryl had projected all her self-blame onto everyone else, and then she'd pushed them away and transferred to another pack.

Late one night a few months later, Sherryl had called and—drunk off her ass—given Casey an earful of shit. She'd spouted a lot of hurtful comments, laughed at how much of a joke Casey's family was, even accused her of sucking Adrian's dick just to get the position of enforcer, and proudly admitted that she'd slept with some of Casey's exes *before* those relationships ended. How mature.

Even though the friendship hadn't been real, Casey probably should have felt betrayed. But the one good thing about being riddled with trust issues was that you expected people to fuck you over, so it didn't always hurt when they did.

Casey knew herself well enough to know that despite being sure she *could* trust Eli utterly and completely, it wouldn't be so simple for her to *believe* it with every fiber of her being. She also knew her habit of getting touchy whenever anyone tried dismissing or crushing her strength could be an issue—he was an extremely dominant male, after all, and liked to have his own way. But they could find a balance, so Preston could just fuck right off with his dumbass presumptions.

Reaching the Alpha's home, she knocked on the door. Like the other houses so deep into the estate, it was pretty as a picture, especially with the colorful garden and the flowerpots under the windows.

It was Adrian's Beta, Clare, who answered the door—the female was often there, since she and Adrian had been dating for a short while.

Clare smiled. "Casey, it's nice to see you. Come in." The Beta stepped aside to let her pass. "Adrian's in the yard putting the new barbecue together. He's planning on inviting all the enforcers around here for burgers later. Will you be able to make it?"

Following Clare into the kitchen, Casey said, "Sorry, no, I'll be busy. I just came by because I have some news." She pulled her collar aside to bare her claiming brand.

Clare's mouth fell open. "You found your true mate?" It was a shocked whisper.

"Yep."

Clare's face lit up. "This is amazing news!" She hauled Casey into a tight hug. "Oh honey, I'm so happy for you." She pulled back, practically bubbling with excitement. "What, when, where, how? I want to know *everything*. Oh, we should throw a celebratory—"

"No," Casey insisted. She liked parties well enough, she just didn't like parties that included hundreds of drunken minks. They never ended well.

The kitchen door swung open, and Adrian strode inside. His lips curved as he spotted Casey. "Afternoon. How was soccer practice?"

"Good, thanks," said Casey.

He grunted. "Now, what's this I heard about you running with a wolf this morning?"

"Casey has *the best* news." Clare elbowed her. "Go ahead, tell him."

Casey bared her claiming bite again.

Adrian blinked. "Wow." Shaking himself out of his stupor, he pulled her into a hug. "Congratulations. Who is the lucky bastard?"

"His name is Eli Axton, he's—"

"The Mercury Pack Head Enforcer?"

"That's the one."

He let out a low whistle. "I've heard he's ... intense. That wolf has the kind of reputation that make grown men shiver."

"He's a wolf?" Clare's face fell. "Does that mean you'll be leaving us?"

"I don't know what it means yet." Casey shrugged. "We'll have to see."

"No matter what, this is great news." Clare squeezed her hand. "I'm happy for you."

"I look forward to meeting him," said Adrian. "I'm assuming he'll be at your game, so I'll see him then, if not before."

Casey nodded. "I have to go. You guys enjoy your burgers."

Back at home, she did a few chores and then started her enforcer duties. Her shift was fairly uneventful, since she was patrolling the border as opposed to the busy estate. After it was over, she returned to her apartment and changed into a smart, casual get-up of white blouse and black pants. She figured dinner at Eli's territory would be an informal affair, but she wanted to look like she'd made an effort.

She wanted Eli's family and pack mates to like her or, at the very least, simply be happy for him. She'd seen how ugly it could get when families didn't take well to someone's mate. Gayle and Ira were a perfect example. Gayle's parents despised him, but although she'd been close to her family, she'd chosen Ira over them when he gave her an ultimatum.

Casey was sitting on the sofa watching TV when there was a hard knock on the door. Standing, she sank her toes into the fluffy, white rug that was the same color as the cushions on her cream, upholstered sofa and then crossed to the front door. Opening it wide, she found herself staring at well over six feet of pure muscle, tanned flesh, and raw male power. And there went her ovaries. *Poof.*

Eli stood tall and proudly erect with his shoulders back, gut sucked in, and an assertive stance that made several words spring to the forefront of her mind. *Dominant. Powerful. Self-assured. Dauntless.*

His powerfully built body was utterly still as he watched her with that sharp, penetrating gaze—a gaze that was currently glittering with so much heat that her stomach clenched painfully. Sexual tension flickered to life, thick and hot. It made the air crackle and her hormones go a little haywire. Her mink let out a highly contented purr.

"Well, hello," said Casey as he slowly walked inside with a predatory grace, sucking the air out of the apartment with just his very presence.

"Hello to you, too." Unable to fight the soul-deep urge to touch her, Eli caught her face in his hands. It had been a long-ass day that had felt more like a fucking week. The hours had ticked by so damn slowly it was close to agonizing. She'd dominated his thoughts the entire time.

"Missed you," he said softly. Missed her taste. Her scent. The feel of her skin. Missed those unusual eyes that were framed by thick lashes dark as soot. "Gonna need to feast on this mouth just a little."

He didn't kiss her, he devoured her. Held her close as he took and took, wishing he could crawl inside her. Loving that every cell, every bone, every hair on her head belonged to him. Was *made* for him.

He'd driven to her apartment with his cock hard and his blood hot with excitement, itching to get his hands on the thing he'd been craving since the second he left her. When she'd opened the door, his gut twisted with a ferocious, sexual need that made him want to slam her onto the nearest surface and fuck her raw. If they weren't scheduled to have dinner with his pack, he'd have done exactly that.

Pulling back, he brushed his lips over hers, satisfied by the flush on her cheeks and the spice of need in her delectable scent. A scent that would be mixed with his own once the mating progressed—he couldn't wait for that.

He also couldn't wait to introduce her to his pack. He wanted to take her to his lodge, show her the kind of home they could have, let her fill the space with her scent. "What did you do today?"

"Soccer training. Patrol. Visited my Alpha to tell him about you. Adrian is pleased for me, as is his Beta female, Clare. And now you and I need to leave before I make us late by wrestling you to the floor and riding you like a pony."

He groaned. "I love your honesty. I have no objections to you riding me."

She stepped back. "Oh no, this is the first time I'll meet your pack. I won't make a very good impression if I don't arrive on time. The riding you like a pony thing—we can put a pin in that, okay?"

"I'm holding you to it." He gave her one last kiss, waited for her to slip on her shoes, and then led her outside with her hand in his. "Do you have a car?"

"Nope. I can drive. I just don't own a car because it seems pointless. I rarely leave my territory, since everything I need is here and these stores sell just about everything." Once inside his SUV, she clicked on her seatbelt and asked, "So, how did your pack react to the news of you being mated?"

"They're happy for me." He switched on the engine and pulled out onto the road. "All the adults are mated, so I think it was just as hard for them to see me alone as it was for me to see them moving forward with their lives. Now that I have you, they don't have to worry about me anymore."

"So your mother's okay with this?"

He hesitated. "Not exactly, but that's nothing personal to you—she just has some shit to work through." He squeezed her thigh. "I'm sorry, baby. She just needs time."

"You don't need to apologize for her. And don't worry about it. Out of all your pack mates, only one disapproves. I'll take that as a win." Casey frowned. "I heard today that wolves don't like living among other breeds of shifter. Is that true?"

Eli stroked her thigh, knowing the real question was ... "Do I want to leave my pack? No, just as I'd imagine you don't want to leave yours. It's natural. But it's more important to me that you're happy. If you don't feel you can be happy living on my territory, we won't—it's that simple. We don't have to make any decisions now."

She gave a slow nod. "Okay. So, what did you get up to today?"

"After I told my pack about you—and they're really looking forward to meeting you, by the way—I accompanied Nick and Shaya to a meeting with Ignacio."

"The fuck? *Ignacio?*"

He winced. "Yes." Eli braced himself, anticipating a rant that would be totally justified. But she didn't say another word. And when he flicked her a sideways glance, he saw her staring at him in a truly unnerving way that made him itch to cup his balls protectively.

Before he knew it, he found himself rambling. "He called Nick earlier today and asked us to meet with him. The only reason I didn't tell you was that I knew you'd insist on coming along. I didn't want to give Ignacio another chance to play mind games with you. I wanted him to get the message that I wouldn't allow him to ever again go near you—he wouldn't have heard that warning if you were sat within a few feet of him.

"Be mad if you want, baby, but you wouldn't want me anywhere near a female who meant me any harm; you'd want to deal with that shit yourself. You'd *need* to do it, woman to woman. I didn't do anything today that you wouldn't have done in my position."

Again, Eli braced himself for a verbal rollicking. It still didn't come. And that made him far more nervous than he would have expected. Stopping at a red light, he looked at her. "Yell at me if you need to. But say something."

She took in a long breath. "I get why you didn't want me there," she said, her voice pitched low, soft, menacing. "And I'll let it slide this one time. But if you ever again make the decision *for* me of where I do or don't go, we're gonna have the kind of problems that result in you crying like a bitch while cradling your broken kneecaps. You got me?"

Eli swallowed. "It has to make me twisted that my cock just jerked."

She snorted. "Light's green."

Feeling like he'd dodged a bullet, he shifted gears and drove on. Well, he'd learned one thing from this—his mate didn't shout or lose her shit when she was angry, she went very quiet and still. He'd have to watch for that.

SHARDS OF FROST

CHAPTER FIVE

Throughout the remainder of the drive to his territory, Eli launched dozens of questions at her, wanting to know more about his little mink: What did she do to unwind? What was her favorite movie? Had she read any books recently? What places had she traveled to? Was there a particular place she'd always wanted to visit? What trend did she struggle to understand the existence of?

As they crossed over the border of Mercury Pack land, she frowned at the building on their right. "Why does a motel sit on the edge of your territory? Does it belong to your pack?"

"Yes. After our neighboring pack fell apart, we claimed the land. Instead of moving onto it, we kept it separate and built the motel there. My human pack mate, Gwen, runs it with the help of a mated couple, Kent and Caleb. My entire pack wanted to be present at dinner to meet you, so some Phoenix Pack wolves are manning the motel reception desk tonight."

"I've heard plenty about the Phoenix Pack, particularly that the Alphas are a special brand of crazy."

His lips twitched. "They'd be the first people to tell you that's true." Reaching the parking lot outside the main lodge, Eli whipped the SUV into a free space and switched off the ignition. "We're here."

"That's not a lodge, it's more like a rustic mansion."

"So people often say." He squeezed her hand as a flicker of anxiety traveled down their bond. "You don't need to be nervous."

She shrugged. "I want them to like me," she gruffly admitted.

Warmth bloomed in his stomach. He liked that this was so important to her; liked that the opinions of the people in his life mattered to her. He got the feeling that Casey rarely let the opinions of others matter. "Ready?"

"As I'll ever be." She slid out of the vehicle and stared up at the lodge.

Rounding the SUV, Eli took her hand in his and led her up the porch steps. Entering the kitchen moments later, he saw that everybody was gathered at the long table.

Everyone other than his mother, he realized a second later.

They all stood as one to greet Casey, staring at her with avid interest. No one would like to be under that kind of scrutiny, but she didn't squirm or fidget or avoid anyone's eyes—not even when his Alphas approached. She stood at his side like she had every right to be there, which she did.

Eli draped an arm over her shoulders. "Casey, these are my Alphas, Nick and Shaya."

"It's good to meet you both," said Casey.

Nick inclined his head. "My brother's been waiting a long time for you. I'm glad you finally found each other."

"Eli's been brooding all day because he wanted to go see you," said Shaya, her eyes twinkling.

Eli frowned. "I was not brooding."

Shaya snorted. "You were. A lot. It was sad."

"Let's get the rest of the introductions out of the way," said Nick.

Casey kept an easy smile on her face as the Alpha male gestured at each of his pack mates, stating their name and what—if any—position they held within the pack. She received smiles, nods of the head, and little waves. All seemed welcoming enough. One person was suspiciously absent: Kathy.

Her mink pushed to the surface, taking the measure of each of the strangers. Slightly distrustful, the animal kept her muscles bunched tight, coiled to spring. Although she was impressed by the power that pulsed from the Alpha male, it also made her antsy.

Once the introductions were over, Willow turned to her mother. "Can we eat now? I'm *starving*."

Shaya stroked her daughter's curls. "Sure, let's eat."

Casey soon found herself sitting at the table, wedged between Roni and Eli. He scooped various foods out of the bowls and platters to pile them onto her plate, ignoring her comment that she could do it herself. Conversation came easy, and there was a lot of teasing and laughing. Still, a sharp tension filled the air … as if everyone was bracing themselves for something. Like Kathy charging into the room, raring to spout shit.

Personally, Casey didn't think the woman would bother. Kathy had clearly wanted to communicate her disapproval, and she'd done that just fine already.

"I heard you're an enforcer," Ally said to Casey. "That's good. If you move to our pack—and I'm hoping you will—we'll have another enforcer in our ranks."

Nothing like a bit of pressure to make a girl feel awkward. Casey just smiled.

"I've never met a mink before," said Jesse. "But I heard lots about them.

Do your inner animals really do a war dance like weasels do?"

Casey pursed her lips. "Well, that depends."

"On what?" asked Jesse.

"On whether we're in the mood to toy with our food," said Casey.

Madisyn chuckled. "My cat kinda likes playing with hers."

Bracken nodded. "Especially voles, although she kills them *before* she plays with them. Usually."

Shaya lifted her glass, studying Casey. "You're not full shifter, are you? I can always tell."

"I'm half shifter, too," said Harley.

Casey looked at the margay cat. "I recognize you from the Velvet Lounge. You perform there, right? It's a nice place. A little bluesy in style."

Gwen raised a hand. "I said the same."

"Yes, I play the electric violin," said Harley. "I also run the place."

"Does your pack own any businesses other than the club and motel?" asked Casey.

"No." Shaya sipped water from her glass. "I've been trying to convince Nick that we should open a salon next to the motel. Maybe also a diner. A movie theater would be good, too. Me and the girls went to see the new James Wan movie last weekend."

"I went to see that with my friend, Emma," Casey told her. "It started off slow. But then things began to move a little faster and the tension built, so I was wound tight. Nearly screamed at one point. And the climax was pretty good and ..." She trailed off as she realized just how that had sounded. And no, she didn't miss the smiles that people were struggling to hide ... or that her mate was shaking with silent laughter. "I'll just stop there."

Ground, swallow me.

It didn't.

Walking inside Eli's lodge a short while later, Casey felt her brows lift. *Nice.* Although it was only one-story high, it appeared to be pretty spacious. And it definitely had that rustic look going on. Oak flooring. Weathered, log furniture. Wood-paneled walls. Wooden beams on the high ceiling.

The leather recliner near the brick and stone fireplace had been angled toward the large TV. There was also a leather sofa that, like the recliner, was such a deep brown it was almost black. The soft hunter-green cushions and fake fur rug gave the place a cozy feel. A mix of white and different shades of gray, the rug made her think of a wolf's coat.

The folded, dark brown faux blanket resting on the arm of the recliner caught her eye. Not just because it looked luxuriously soft, but because it was the typical color of mink shifter fur.

Pointing at the blanket, Casey turned to Eli. "When did you get this?"

He stalked towards her. "I've had it for about two years. Shaya bought a bunch of different colored faux blankets and offered them to the pack. I was going to pick one that matched my rug, but then I saw this and had to have it—couldn't even explain why." He framed her face with his hands. "Maybe some part of me knew what you were."

Eli rained soft kisses all over her face, loving how her body molded itself to his. She fit right there against him, like that groove had been made just for her.

His wolf relaxed, satisfied that his mate was in his domain. Content that she was where she belonged. The animal would be pissed when she left; wouldn't understand why she hadn't simply moved in. For now, though, he was at peace.

"Haven't stopped thinking about you all day." Eli sipped from her mouth, lightly flicking her tongue with his own, taking her taste inside him. "The things I could do to this mouth …" He speared his fingers into her hair, fisted it tight, and snatched her head back. "I want it wrapped around my cock, Casey. I want to blow my load right down your throat."

She let out a sigh as he kissed along her neck. "It's good to have dreams."

His lips curled. Yeah, he knew dominant female shifters gave oral sex in their own sweet time. He righted her head and nipped her lower lip. "Those dreams will become reality one day soon, Casey."

"Oh, I see you're back in Eli's world, where everything goes your way. Cute."

"*You're* my world, baby."

Casey just about melted at that. Yep, that puddle of goo on the floor was her. Even her mink was touched, and the animal was a hard-assed bitch. Casey splayed her hands on his chest—it was packed with so much muscle she almost shivered a little in delight. "I'll bet no one would believe me if I told them you could be sweet."

"I wasn't being sweet. I was being honest."

"Which was sweet."

"Not sweet. Just frank. I'm determined to make sure you never doubt how important you are to me."

"Like I said, sweet."

He playfully snapped his teeth at her. "You're going to be a pain in my ass, aren't you?"

She shrugged one shoulder. "It's only fair, since you'll be a pain in mine."

"In a number of ways," he agreed, palming her tight little ass. "There's a good chance I'll drive you crazy." Like his wolf, he was a territorial bastard, so he'd always known he'd be uber possessive of his mate. Known he'd hold her close, determined not to lose her the way his mother had lost her true mate. No dominant female would fail to bristle at that kind of behavior. Casey would be no exception.

She was far too dominant and independent to let him wrap her up in cotton wool and tuck her away someplace safe, where the world could never harm her—and yeah, he'd do that in a heartbeat if he thought she'd let him get away with it. Perversely, he liked that she wouldn't. Liked that she'd refuse to allow him to steamroll her.

"Drive me crazy?" she echoed. "Why?"

"I don't have to tell you that I'm not an easy man, Casey. I'm pushy and stubborn and selfish. I'll want more of your time and attention than I'm entitled to."

She narrowed her eyes. "You're warning me that you're going to be clingy."

"Clingy? No. Overprotective and all up in your space, demanding everything you've got? Yes."

"So, clingy." She circled the claiming bite on his neck with her fingertip. "Just know that I'm no pushover, Eli. I might cede some control during sex, but I won't do it outside the bedroom."

"Believe me, I *like* that you're someone who'll push back. Like that you're strong, confident, and know exactly who you are. It means I don't have to worry that I'll crush you."

She tilted her head. "And why would you ever have such a dumb worry?"

"I told you, I'm not an easy man. There was once someone … It didn't end well, Casey. I was too much for her."

Her nose wrinkled, and he got the sense that she didn't want to hear about the females in his past. "Or she just wasn't enough for you. Whatever the case, it doesn't matter. What happened between you and her … that was then. This is now. And I'm not her."

"No, you're not."

"I'll be no easier to handle than you'll be, you know."

Oh, Eli had no trouble believing that. He kissed the hollow beneath her ear. "You were a good girl for me last night. Gave me your throat. Came when I told you to. Followed almost every order I gave you. 'Almost' is fucking astounding when the female in question is as dominant as my baby is." He took her mouth, need rising inside him as memories of their claiming flashed through his mind.

Her own hunger rose to match his, spicing and warming her scent, inciting his wolf. Eli slowly peeled off her top and tossed it aside. "I'll give you a tour of the lodge later." Right then, he needed to touch and kiss more of that soft skin.

Eli perched himself on the wide arm of the sofa. "Come here." He saw the struggle on her face, knew her natural instincts would be prodding her to challenge him. She took a long, deliberate breath, and the tension in her shoulders fell away. His wolf rumbled a growl of approval.

Eli hummed as she came to stand between his spread thighs. "That's my good girl." It took serious strength for such a dominant female to fight that reflexive urge to challenge orders, but she'd done it. He loved that she wouldn't defy him for the mere sake of it.

Flicking the front clasp of her bra open, he brushed the cups aside and filled his hands with those silky-soft breasts. "Perfect." And so very *his*. He latched onto her nipple and sucked hard.

Inhaling sharply, Casey grabbed his hair and arched into him. Damn, but he was good with that mouth. A mouth that felt even better when pleasuring … other places. She put a slight pressure on the top of his head. "Heaven is further south, Eli." He let out a deep, throaty chuckle that made her stomach clench.

"I'm happy where I am. For now."

Gripping his shoulders, Casey held on as he licked, flicked, bit, and suckled her nipples. Sparks of pleasure shot to her clit, which only made her pussy burn for more. She gasped as he raked his teeth over one taut bud. "Would you stop playing with my tits!"

He lowered the zipper of her slacks. "They're not yours anymore, baby. They're mine. Just like this"— his hand delved into her panties and cupped her hard— "is mine. There's not a single cell in your body that doesn't belong to me." He bit down on her nipple just as he sank two fingers into her pussy. "Hmm, nice and wet."

Casey moaned as he pumped his fingers in and out of her. The heel of his hand rubbed her clit with each thrust, winding her tight as a drum. He hooked his fingers and stroked her sweet spot, and she felt her orgasm bubble up. Then the fucker slowed his pace. She hissed. "Eli—"

"What do you need?"

"Your cock."

"Where do you want it?"

She jerked as his finger pressed on her sweet spot. "My pussy."

"Then that's what you'll have." Eli withdrew his fingers. "Strip. Now." He whipped off his own clothes as she shed her own. "Good. Get on your hands and knees right there on the rug."

The order made her stiffen slightly, but she battled the drive to fight him and did as he asked.

"So good for me." Eli kneeled behind her and draped his body over hers. He caught her earlobe between his teeth. "Have you missed my dick, baby? Do you want it inside you again?"

"Yes," she hissed.

"Then what are you gonna give me?"

Casey bit back a curse. It was such a simple physical movement, but there was truly nothing simple about giving someone your throat. It was a complete surrender, an offer of trust. And although Eli had her trust, it still wasn't so freaking easy to push past her dominant instincts—instincts that balked at the very idea of her submitting in such a way.

Honestly, her mink didn't like it much either. The whole thing hadn't been so hard during her claiming, because the mating urge had taken hold, sucking rational thoughts and inhibitions from her head.

He scraped his teeth over the back of her shoulder. "Casey."

She sucked in a sharp breath as she felt the thick head of his cock pushing inside her. Stretching her. Causing the most delicious burn. Yes, she needed this. Needed—

He pulled back. She hissed, curling her fingers into the rug. *"Eli."*

"You want my dick back? Then show me just how bad you want it. Remember how this works: If you make me wait, I'll make you wait."

Casey swore, sensing he meant it. With a grind of her teeth, she tilted her head, exposing her throat.

He slammed his cock home, knocking the breath from her lungs. Fuck, she'd forgotten how thick he was. He didn't give her a second to adjust. Just pounded into her like he was caught in a frenzy, his fingertips biting into her hips. His snarls and grunts mingled with her moans and the sound of flesh smacking flesh.

No one had ever fucked her the way Eli did. They'd never been so forceful or unrelenting. Never taken her with such raw sexual aggression. Even as he ruthlessly rammed his cock so deep it hurt, Casey threw her hips back to meet each thrust, wanting more.

"That's it, give me that pussy."

A burning hot tension coiled inside her—a promise of divine pleasure that was so close yet so far. One touch to her clit would be enough to set her off. She couldn't wait, couldn't take anymore.

Seeing her hand reach toward her clit, Eli brought his palm down sharply on her ass. "No. When I want you to come, I'll tell you to come." He spanked her again when she would have argued with him, loving the way her ass turned such a pretty shade of pink.

Planting one hand on the floor near her own hand, he draped himself over her, still slamming hard and deep. He growled low in her ear. "Do you know how hot it is being inside this pussy, knowing it was made for me?" He wrapped her hair around his fist and pulled hard. She hissed, and her pussy rippled around him. "You like that? You like how I fuck you?"

She only groaned, throwing her hips back even more frantically.

Eli mercilessly hammered into her, feeling his control beginning to shatter. His senses were filled with Casey—her raspy moans, the sway of her tits, the succulent scent of her need, and the tight, scorching hot clasp of her inner muscles. It was all too much, and it left him feeling drunk. Drunk on *her.*

As her hot pussy tightened and superheated around his cock, Eli knew he couldn't hold on any longer. "Now you can touch your clit." Her hand slid down her body, and then a moan flew from her mouth just as her inner walls fluttered around him. "Come, Casey. Come all over my cock. Yeah, that's it."

Even as a scream tore from her throat, Eli locked his arm tight around her stomach and pounded harder into her rippling pussy again and again and again. Then his release pulled him under. He bit out a harsh curse as he jammed his cock deep one last time, shooting jet after jet of come inside his mate.

Breathing hard, he pulled out of her and lay on his back. She instantly melted into the rug, her eyes closed, shaking with little aftershocks. He dragged her on top of him and kissed her hair. "You good?" He got a soft grunt in response that made his mouth quirk.

Happy to simply lay there with her, he danced his fingers up and down her sleek back. He'd already committed every line and curve of her body to memory. He loved touching her, loved having her all warm and limp and sated against him.

He also loved that his pack mates had taken to her so easily. He was pissed at his mother for missing dinner with the pack, though—well-aware that she'd done it just to express her discontentment. He was also well-aware that she was expecting him to seek her out and confront her, but Eli wouldn't credit her shitty behavior with any form of attention.

"I'm gonna fall asleep if you keep on petting me," Casey slurred.

"We can hit the sack soon." Watch TV in bed, relax, and then he'd take her all over again before they settled. "But I have a request first."

"What?"

He nuzzled her hair. "I want some time with your mink."

"Do you have protective gloves lying around?"

"She won't hurt me."

"Much."

"She won't. Just as I'd never hurt her." He squeezed Casey's nape. "Come on, you've had time with my wolf. Let me see her."

Casey lifted her head. "You certain? Because, honestly, I'm not sure how she'll behave toward you. She sees you as hers, and she acknowledges that she's yours. But, well, she's a moody little bitch, Eli. She can be vicious as hell. I truly can't guarantee that she won't bite you if you make a wrong move. And no, I can't say what constitutes a 'wrong move' to my mink. It all depends on her mood, which changes every hour."

"I already know minks are temperamental creatures. I won't touch her if it doesn't look like she'll welcome it. I just want to see her. She'll never feel truly comfortable with me if she and I don't build up a level of trust, will she?"

"Well, no, but I don't want you to lose a finger."

"I'll be careful with her. I promise. And then afterward, I'll let my wolf out so they can have some time together. She'll like that." He patted her ass.

"Come on, I want to meet her." She stood with a sigh. And as Eli got a good look at his mate's body, his cock jerked. "Or maybe we can wait until I've taken you again."

Casey snorted. "One-track mind. You, um, should probably put your pants on. She has a habit of climbing people's legs, and I don't think you want her getting close to your bare cock."

"Fair point." Eli rose from the rug and pulled on his jeans. "Ready when you are."

"Good luck." And then Casey shifted.

Mouth curling, Eli stared down at the little mink. Sleek and short-legged, she had a long, slender, muscular body covered in the most luxurious fur. He wanted to know if her rich, glossy, blackish-tawny coat was as silky as it looked, but he didn't dare invade her space. That would only earn him some nasty bites.

He very slowly crouched down and murmured, "Hey there."

Her small dark eyes locked on his, and she was looking at him … well, like he was prey. He wasn't gonna lie, that unblinking, unwavering stare was somewhat unnerving. She seemed calm enough, though.

"Cute little thing, aren't you?"

With a low hiss, she lashed her black-tipped tail. The move wasn't so much aggressive as a message that he'd better tread carefully.

"I wouldn't hurt you," he softly assured her. "I want to stroke you. Pet you."

She slanted her head, blinking. He wondered if Casey was communicating what he wanted to the little mink.

"I'll let my wolf out so he can play with you. I just want to give you a little stroke first. You're safe with me."

A bit of the starch left her spine—probably at the promise that she'd get some time with his wolf. Yeah, he'd figured that might spur her into giving Eli a chance. She bounded forward three steps. Honestly, she moved so fast, he almost jerked in surprise.

"Closer, gorgeous."

She leaped onto his thigh and stared up at him, nose wrinkling.

"That's it." He gave her back a gentle stroke, and she arched into it like a kitten. "So soft." He petted her with long, soothing swipes of his hand from her neck to her tail. All the while, he whispered sweet nothings to her, injecting a little purr into his voice.

She made little clucking sounds, seeming content. So he blinked in surprise when she suddenly jumped down and looked up at him, expectant.

"Oh, I've had my allotted time, have I? Fair enough." He stood, shed his jeans, and then opened the front door so that their animals would be able to go outside. "Please don't lay waste to the wildlife." Because, yeah, minks would kill for sport.

Eli pulled back, allowing his wolf to surface.

The mink sniffed at the large gray-white wolf. Purred as she recognized his scent. He circled her, gently rubbing against her. She scrambled up his back, gave the back of his neck a playful nip, and then leapt to the ground. She scurried outside with a clucking sound. The wolf followed.

They spent hours exploring his territory. The mink bounded and zigzagged across the ground with a darting speed, easily keeping pace with the wolf. He kept close even as she climbed trees, swam in the river, darted into burrows, or raced into tunnels in pursuit of prey.

When it was dark, they returned to the lodge. Feeling the pull of sleep, the mink curled up on the rug. Just as tired, the wolf curved his powerful body around hers, keeping her warm. Protecting her as his instincts demanded.

It took mere minutes for them to fall asleep.

CHAPTER SIX

Catching sight of the figure standing outside the Hounds' HQ a week later, Casey felt her stomach sink. Up until that point, her veins had been buzzing with anticipation at her upcoming game. Now, agitation spiked through her system. They hadn't spoken in a very long time. And if Sherryl's smirk was anything to go by, she wasn't here for a friendly chat.

Sherryl had probably come with the rest of her team to watch the Hounds play against the Ohio Wildcats. Anyone could watch providing they paid the fee. The mink teams often attended the other games, looking for weaknesses in the players they'd soon be up against.

Tightening her grip on the strap of her duffel, Casey kept her expression neutral as she came to stand before Sherryl. Her mink snarled, wanting nothing more than to scalp the backstabbing bitch and rag out a chunk of that pink, pixie haircut.

She'd lost weight since Casey last saw her. And not in a good way. Honestly, Sherryl looked like a harsh wind could blow her over.

She also looked … strange. It was hard to describe. Her body language seemed casual and relaxed, but she was giving off a weird, dark vibe that made Casey's hackles rise. And the look in her eyes was just … *wrong*. They were glassy. Unblinking. Alive but somehow dead. It was like looking right at an amped-up junkie as they contemplated whether to fuck you up now or later.

Miles had looked at Casey like that once, and that was *before* he'd turned to drugs. She'd been consoling him after his breakup with Sherryl, and he'd turned on her so quick her head had spun, but it hadn't been *Miles*. Not really.

The couple hadn't imprinted on each other, but the threads of the bond had been there, and the abrupt severance of those threads had fucked with his emotional state in a major way. Could it also be fucking with Sherryl?

"I suppose I should be congratulating you on your *mating*," Sherryl spat, her arms folded, her mouth set into an acidic smile.

The bitter note in her voice was no surprise, considering Sherryl had never stopped pining for the true mate she'd lost as a child. She'd let it twist her up inside; seemed to embrace the pain, even.

Casey sighed. "Is this shit really necessary?"

The other female tapped her chin. "I wonder what your mate would think if he knew you'd fucked your cousin's mate. He'd probably be even more disgusted than Mallory would be. Hmm, maybe it's time she knew the truth. Out of curiosity, will you fight back when she comes at you? Or will you take the pounding you deserve? The pack would turn against you if they knew, you know. They would. Just like they turned against me."

This crap again? "No one turned against you, Sherryl. Not until you joined another soccer team, anyway. Some consider you a traitor now." In fact, every Hound would happily stomp on the bitch's head. "The only one who blamed you for what Miles—"

"*Don't* say his name."

Again, Casey sighed. "I'm done here. Move out of my way. I have shit to do."

"Like go see your mate?" Her eyes glittered with something dark and cold. "Why should you get to have everything when I don't?"

"You're really going to be dramatic now? You're a starter for the Seals, and you're an enforcer for their pack; you have what you want."

"But not my true mate."

"That doesn't mean you have to be alone. You're *choosing* to be." Tragic as it was, many shifters lost their mates—they didn't all sink into a well of bitterness and self-pity. They didn't all begrudge others happiness or wear their pain like a badge. "Now, I really am done with this conversation."

"Oh, you are?"

"Yeah. I got bored five minutes ago."

Sherryl's upper lip curled. "You always were a high-and-mighty little whore. I'll bet Mallory would agree with me on that when she hears the truth. And she will hear it." When Casey didn't react, Sherryl raised a brow. "You think I won't tell her what I know?"

"Oh, I think you'll tell her. I think you'll get a perverse joy out of it." Because any jealousy that Sherryl had once felt for Casey had substantially intensified since Eli came into the picture. And now that dark emotion was intertwined with spite, resentment, and scorn. Sherryl would gladly see Casey suffer just as she was suffering, which was why ... "It'll be the same perverse joy I'll get out of beating your skanky ass to a pulp for hurting my cousin just to get to me. Because that's what will happen. You know idle threats aren't my thing."

"It won't be *me* who'll have hurt your cousin. Her pain will be on *you*."

Okay, that much was true. But it would hurt Mallory even more if she were to find out from *Sherryl*—a person who would delight in telling her. Which meant Casey would have to be the one to do it. But how did you tell your cousin you'd once slept with her mate? "Preston will hate you if you do this."

Sherryl's eyes flickered, and her sour mask slipped just a little. She and Preston had been a couple once upon a time. They no longer cared for each other *that way*, but they were good friends. Sherryl made a dismissive sound. "He'd get over it."

"No, he wouldn't. And you know it, just like you know he'd never forgive you. So think very carefully before you go running to Mallory with little tales. You stand to lose something, too." With that, Casey headed into the building.

Instead of going straight to the locker room, she went to the break room where the staff often hung out. Just as she'd expected, Preston was there having coffee with Dennis.

"Can I speak to you for a sec?" she asked Preston.

His brows dipped. "Sure." He walked into the hallway and closed the break room door behind him. "What's wrong?"

She licked her lips. "We need to talk—me, you, and Mallory. We have to tell her." She didn't have to explain what she meant by that, since there was only one thing they were keeping from her cousin.

His eyes widened. "*What?* No! No, Casey, she doesn't need to know."

"Sherryl was waiting for me outside the building. She's threatening to tell Mallory."

He scoffed. "She's just calling your bluff, trying to ruffle your feathers, hoping it will put you off your game."

Possibly, but ... "I doubt it was just that. I think hearing that I found my true mate might have knocked her over an edge that I didn't even realize she was dangling on."

"Edge? She's not crazy."

"Not crazy, no, but also not emotionally stable. There might have been only the strings of an imprint bond between her and Miles, but the separation still messed him up. Maybe it messed with her head too and we just didn't see how badly."

"*I'll* deal with Sherryl. She won't say a damn thing."

"I'm not so sure—"

"I am. Just say nothing, Casey. Mallory can't know what happened."

Casey rubbed at her nape. "If she finds out from Sherryl—"

"She won't. I promise."

"You're that positive you can keep Sherryl quiet?"

"Yes. Trust me, I have this. Now go get changed. Don't let her psych you out. That's all she's trying to do."

While Casey would love to believe there was nothing more to it than that, she wasn't so certain he was right. But as she headed to the locker room, she pushed Sherryl to the back of her mind, refusing to let the female's presence shake her focus. There was no room for distractions on the field. None.

It was a little over an hour later that the team gathered into a huddle on the sidelines of their turf while Coach Donahue gave them her usual pep talk—her voice steady, brow furrowed, feet planted. The players drank in every word, standing solidly, their jaws set in determination.

Stomach fluttering, Casey stayed very still, ignoring the way her muscles quivered with the urge to get out there and *win*. Adrenaline coursed through her, readying her and sharpening her senses.

She didn't feel edgy with nerves, though. She felt calm. Prepared. Determined. Positive. Bloated with the same sense of purpose that always filled her before and during a game.

It would be no easy win. The Ohio Wildcats were damn good, and they always gave the Hounds a run for their money. Last year's game had ended in a draw. Not this time, though. No, this time, the Hounds would kick their ass.

Knowing that Eli was out there watching and supporting her gave her that extra *oomph*. It fed her desire to win so that she could make him proud.

Casey shared a look with Emma, who bounced on her toes, her face deadpan, her eyes glowing with both anticipation and a little hint of viciousness. They exchanged grim, bloodthirsty smiles.

Coach rubbed her hands together. "We have this, girls. We have this. Now go kick their collective ass."

Sitting on the bleachers, Eli watched as Casey's team set off at a jog, positioning themselves on the field. He couldn't help but stare at his mate. Right then, she radiated confidence, ferocity, and an almost animalistic need to win. His wolf bared his teeth in a feral grin of approval.

Roni glanced at the large gathering of spectators that were focused on the field, their expressions sober, their bodies tense. "The minks really are taking this seriously, aren't they?"

"Hmm," said Shaya. "It ain't no friendly game for the love of the sport."

"Minks are *very* serious when it comes to soccer." Marcus dipped a hand into his popcorn and tossed a few pieces into his mouth. "I like these seats. Never sat on a front row at a game before."

At Eli's request, Casey had reserved seats for him, Roni, Marcus, Nick, and Shaya. Eli hadn't asked them to come, they'd *demanded* to come along. She was family to them now, and they wanted her to know it. Eli would have invited Kathy if she wasn't still pretending Casey didn't exist.

He hated that his mother couldn't be happy for him; hated that he couldn't share his happiness *with* her. He might have only known Casey a week, but she was everything to him. He couldn't imagine ever not waking to the sight of her right there. Just the thought of it made his stomach harden.

Each morning they had breakfast together at his lodge or at her apartment, they moved around each other with total ease. They had a rhythm already, like they'd known each other for years.

Roni offered Eli some of her popcorn, but he shook his head. "Still pissed at me, huh?"

Marcus frowned. "Why would he be pissed at you? What did you do this time?"

"Oh, she only taped a harmonica to the grill of the SUV," said Eli. "I was driving Casey here. Every time the SUV hit forty miles per hour, it set off the fucking harmonica. The wailing sounds were downright painful. I almost called for road assistance—that would have been embarrassing as all hell. Seriously, Roni, can't you be normal for, like, a day?"

Roni lifted a brow. "Says the asshole who put lubricant in my hand sanitizer bottle!"

Eli shrugged. "I'm sure you and Marcus found some use for it."

"Children, children, let it go for now," said Nick. "How long has Casey been playing for her team, Eli?"

"Since she was fifteen," Eli told him. "And yes, I have considered that it will be hard to get her to switch packs if it means she won't be allowed to play for her team anymore."

"As long as you've considered it," said Nick.

A whistle was blown, and both teams exploded into action. Eli forgot about his pack and focused solely on his mate.

Casey always seemed to be in motion. Jogging. Running. Tackling. Feinting. Her every move was fast and fluid and skilled.

Really, her speed was incredible. There was truly no other word for it. She didn't *pick up* speed. She shot into a sprint like a bullet zooming out of a gun. Moreover, she played with a controlled aggression that had to be somewhat intimidating for the opposing team. His wolf fucking loved it.

She focused on that game with a concentration so intense it was like nothing else existed for her. Her eyes hardly ever left the ball. She went after it again and again in the same fierce, determined way a predator ran down its prey. Once in possession of the ball, she kicked, dribbled, volleyed, headed.

She never tried to dominate the game. She created scoring chances for her teammates and passed the ball when she needed to. But if she could get off a shot, if there was a decent chance she could score, she wouldn't hesitate to try.

The spectators could sure make some noise—catcalling, barking encouraging remarks, chanting the names of players. They all seemed to love it whenever the players got rough with each other, which was often. Not just tripping people up. There was head-butting, heels slamming into people's insteps, elbows ramming into the back of heads—all *seemed* accidental of course, but they weren't.

The Wildcats' goal keeper was damn fucking good, but not good enough. Only twenty minutes into the first half of the game, a hard kick from Casey sent the ball zipping through the air and into the corner of the net.

Eli was on his feet before he knew it, cheering as loudly as the rest of the spectators. Her team lost their damn minds—rushing at her, lifting her in the air, practically roaring with triumph. Casey's gaze flicked to where he and his pack mates stood, her eyes bright with joy.

And then the teams went at it again.

The Wildcats were skilled and sneaky—a good combination. But Casey and her teammates seemed to preempt their cunning moves. Time and time again the ball came sailing toward the Hounds' net. Time and time again her teammates were there, shielding the ball from the keeper and either blasting it downfield or passing it on.

Still, the Wildcats managed to score a goal just before half-time, which pissed Eli off. His pack mates, who'd been completely sucked into the game, whined and bit out curses.

Casey didn't look at him or the other spectators when she left the field for the break. Nor did she even so much as glance in their direction when she returned. Her head was completely in the game.

The second half went a little slower, but the teams still pushed themselves hard. They were tiring, though. And he knew the baking heat had to be getting to them.

A fight almost broke out at one point; it took Casey and two of her teammates to drag the team captain away when she would have dived at an opposing player for *breaking her nose*—something that wasn't considered a big deal, apparently, because the ref only issued the offending Wildcat a yellow card. Even as the Hound's captain snapped her nose back into place, she spat at the other player.

Hearing Roni threaten the referee for not red-carding the Wildcat, Eli smiled and said, "You do know he can't hear you, right?"

His sister just snarled at him.

The referee blew the whistle, signaling for the teams to resume playing. Through their bond, he could feel that Casey was hot and tired. But she went after the ball just as aggressively as she had in the beginning. Kept on tackling and kicking and passing the ball on. It finally paid off, and she scored another goal. Again, Eli was on his feet, pride flooding him. A Hounds midfielder scored another goal shortly afterward, and the game finished 3-1.

Smiling like loons, Casey and her teammates exchanged hugs, high fives, and ass-slaps. They also shook hands with the Wildcats—even those who'd delivered some exceptionally dirty fouls. Then again, the Hounds had committed enough fouls of their own.

"Casey's damn good," said Nick. "Every inch the predator when she goes after the ball."

Marcus nodded. "She oozes confidence in general. But when on the field, it's the kind of unshakable self-belief that even I find intimidating."

Smug, Eli smiled. "Yeah, my Casey's the shit." The scent of a male mink drifted into his personal space, and his wolf stilled. Eli turned and found himself face-to-face with a bulky, middle-aged guy who was *all* alpha. "You must be Adrian."

"I am. Behind me is my Beta female, Clare. And I'm guessing by the comment you just made that you're Eli." He held out his hand. "I wanted to introduce myself to you and your pack mates and congratulate you on your mating. Casey's a keeper."

Eli shook the Alpha's hand. "I agree. It's good to meet you both." He introduced them to his pack mates. Of course, Adrian and Nick did a little dumb Alpha male posturing, to which Shaya rolled her eyes.

Eli glanced back at the field to see his mate sprinting to the front row of the stands, grinning. He leaned over the barrier, caught her around the waist, and lifted her just enough to plant a kiss on her mouth. She was all sweaty and flushed, her eyes fevered with joy and triumph. And he wanted to straight up fuck her right there.

"Congratulations on your win, baby." He brushed his nose against hers. "I'm proud of you. You're like lightning on that field."

"Totally," agreed Roni, who then proceeded to give a quick, succinct commentary on how incompetent she believed the ref was.

Adrian congratulated Casey, adding, "Didn't fail to notice how you *accidentally* almost snapped off the arm of the midfielder who flattened Kristin. Good move."

She snickered. "Thanks." After Clare and Eli's other pack mates had finished congratulating her, Casey turned to him and said, "I need to go shower."

"All right. I'll meet you in the parking lot." Eli pressed a kiss to her mouth and set her on her feet. "Don't be long."

She gave him a brief wave and then followed her team off the field.

"Who's that?" asked Roni.

"Who's who?" Eli tracked her gaze, frowning as he noticed a skinny, pink-haired female glaring hotly at his mate. "Yeah, who the fuck is that?"

Clare sighed. "That would be Sherryl. She used to be part of our pack and played for the Hounds. She also dated Casey's brother, Miles."

Casey had mentioned her once. She hadn't, however, mentioned that Sherryl seemed to hate her guts. He made a mental note to ask Casey about it later.

"So, tell me, Eli," said Adrian. "You planning to move Casey to your territory?"

He'd anticipated that the Alpha would throw that question at him. "I'm planning to do whatever will make Casey happiest."

"Even if that means moving here and living among minks?" asked Clare.

"As long as she agrees to move out of that large room she calls an apartment," said Eli.

Adrian chuckled. "I think that can be arranged. It's good to see that your family members came along to support her today. She doesn't have that same support from her own family. You know, her mother was once a force to be reckoned with. But she let Casey's father emotionally beat her down over the years. He only did it because he felt threatened by her strength, just as he does by Casey's. But I won't have that worry with you, will I?" It was a question that held a threat.

Ignoring the amusement that he could feel emanating from Roni, Eli replied, "No, you won't."

Adrian clapped him on his back. "Excellent."

Walking toward the parking lot with her teammates, Casey rolled back her shoulders. Feeling pumped from the team's win, it was easy to ignore the tightness in her muscles and the heaviness in her limbs, but she knew from experience that she'd no doubt crash sometime within the next hour. She needed food first. The post-game smoothie she'd had in the locker room had done little to ease the gnawing sensation in her stomach.

Casey's heart jumped as she spotted Eli leaning against his SUV. She couldn't help but smile. She'd initially been determined to shove him out of her mind as she played, but it was impossible to do that when she could *feel* him.

She'd felt his pride when she scored, felt his anger when the opposing players got in her face, felt his frustration when the Wildcats' goalkeeper blocked the ball.

It should have been distracting. It wasn't. It was like he was with her, experiencing the whole thing right alongside her. That had been both comforting and invigorating.

They hadn't spent a single night apart over the past week. Sometimes they slept at her apartment, but mostly they'd stayed at his lodge. He'd done his best to make her feel comfortable there, even bought her a juicer. So she'd bought him a coffee machine to keep at her apartment.

"Well, damn, look at those muscles," said Kristin, her gaze on Eli. "I don't think there's an ounce of fat on that body."

"He's only got eyes for you, Casey," said Emma. "I'm guessing that's Eli."

"Yeah, that's him. I'll introduce you, but please don't get weird. Oh no, don't pretend you don't know what I mean." Clenching the strap of her duffel tight, Casey walked toward him. His eyes raked over her, bold and hungry.

That slow, intense perusal made her stomach clench.

He tugged her to him, and she let out a happy sigh as his arms came around her, enfolding her in his warmth. Even exhausted, her body reacted—stomach flipping, pulse quickening. Her mink pushed against her skin, wanting to rub up on her male and scent-mark him. "Thank you for coming."

Eli's brow furrowed. "Where else would I be?"

"Aw, dude, you're being sweet again." She quickly introduced him to her teammates, hoping the two females would behave like, you know, normal people.

Kristin tilted her head. "What size shoes do you take?"

"Your aura is black with a few muddy shades of red in it," Emma told him. "Makes me think of a tee I bought last month that has a red-bellied black snake on it. You ever seen one of those? They don't have teeth or fangs, which I think is pretty sad."

Because that was *totally* relevant. "I'll see you guys tomorrow," said Casey.

Emma shrugged. "So long, wolfman. See ya later, Case."

Kristin put a fist to her heart. "Peace out, people."

Eli watched the females walk away, his brow creased. "They're ... interesting."

Casey snorted. "Yeah, that's a word for them."

Looking down at his mate, Eli brushed her bangs from her face. He could sense through their bond that she was tired. If *he'd* spent ninety minutes doing a series of walking, jogging, backpedaling, running, and exploding into short bursts of speed, he'd be exhausted as well. "You ready to leave?"

"Yep." She glanced around. "Your pack mates already left?"

"Yes. They were very impressed by you and your team. Willow and Cassidy really wanted to come, but Nick wouldn't okay it."

"My pack wouldn't have hurt the pups, but I can see why he'd be nervous of his girls being surrounded by hundreds of minks."

Eli kissed her forehead, silently thanking her for being so understanding. If the situation had been reversed, *he* wouldn't have liked that her family didn't trust his pack around their young.

Smiling at the sound of her stomach rumbling, he patted her ass. "Come on, let's get you back to your apartment so I can pamper you."

"Is that what they're calling it now?"

"Pamper as in feed, massage, and relax with you. I'd much rather fuck you so hard you scream until your throat's raw, but that will come later." He wanted to get some carbs and protein in her first. She needed to replenish her system. So when they arrived at her apartment, he insisted that she sit at the small, round dining table while he made dinner.

"You really don't have to feed me," she said.

"I want to."

"I can help—"

"Just sit, woman. I want to feed you."

She huffed. "Fine. What are we having?"

Instead of responding, Eli raided her cupboards and fridge, pulling out a garlic clove, olive oil, breadcrumbs, pork mince, wholegrain spaghetti—

And then it hit her.

"Meatballs," she guessed. "You're making spaghetti meatballs."

"I am," he confirmed, grabbing the rest of the ingredients.

"Who taught you to cook?"

"My mother. She's big on her kids being independent."

Bracing her elbow on the table, Casey rested her chin on her hand and quite simply enjoyed the sight of him in her kitchen. His hands moved so fast they were a blur as they chopped, scored, grated, and stirred. Soon, he was adding several perfectly proportioned meatballs to a frying pan.

"I'll bet your mink's happy that your team won today," he said.

"She's smug as all shit. A little like you are every time she purrs for you." They let their animals run together at least once every two days, and Eli always insisted on having some private time with her mink before the run.

"Your adorable mink is one mean little thing—she bites my wolf if he steps a foot wrong, keeps him in line. But she's nice to me."

"She's nice to you because you won't let your wolf out to play with her if she's not."

"She likes me," he insisted, using a hand-held blender to smooth the tomato sauce he'd made. "And she likes it when I cuddle her, though she pretends she doesn't. The purrs give it away."

Her mink sniffed haughtily. "How was Caleb today? Mad at me?"

Eli frowned. "Why would he be mad at you?"

"Oh, I don't know … maybe because my mink chased his wolf clean across the clearing and scared him so bad he tried to climb a tree just to get away from her. Wolves don't climb trees, so that was dumb. Minks *do* climb trees, which made his choice of refuge even dumber."

"He was laughing about it this morning. Said he never would have thought something that small could move that fast. His wolf knows better than to cross onto the land surrounding people's lodges, but he's a nosy fucker who can't seem to help himself. We let him get away with it because he's harmless, but your mink didn't know that. She saw an intruder and she chased him off. No one's mad about it."

"Not even Kathy?"

"If she is mad, she didn't say so. Or, at least, she didn't while I was there." Having added the meatballs to the sauce, he left them to simmer and then set about cooking the spaghetti. "She'll come around eventually. She just needs to feel that she's made her point."

"I think it's killing her that we haven't called her on her shit. Is it wrong that this amuses me?"

"No. I say get your kicks where you can."

"I tend to get my kicks at The Den, just as you do. If you tell anyone I'll deny it, but watching you fight *totally* revs my engines."

Eli felt his mouth curve. Some of the females in his past had been put off by the way he chose to "wind down," especially since he shed every little bit of civility when he fought. But not Casey. Hell, she liked brawling just as much as he did.

"I could say the same to you," he told her. "I've wanted you since the second you threw your first punch at the fox."

"Here you are being sweet yet again."

His brows snapped together. "That wasn't sweet."

"It was to me. But back to you … You know some really good moves. Who trained you? Was it Nick?"

Eli hesitated. He'd received training, sure, but he'd learned his savage style of combat in a hard school. "I learned from lots of people." It wasn't untrue.

"From what I heard about your pack, it didn't form until a little over a decade ago. Where were you before that?"

"You could say we moved around a little."

"How come?"

Again, he hesitated to answer. His life story was no fairy tale, and he didn't want to darken the good day she'd had. But he also didn't want to lie to her. She made a point of being completely open to him, even when it was difficult for her. He'd be an asshole if he didn't give her that same courtesy. Their bond would never progress otherwise.

"It's not a pretty story," he warned her.

"Yeah, I guessed that by the look on your face. Tell me."

Stirring the softening spaghetti, Eli began, "When we were part of our childhood pack, Roni was attacked by a gang of humans. One tried to rape her while the others egged him on—one was even recording it."

"Motherfuckers."

"Yeah. Nick intervened. Although the other humans tried to subdue him, wanting to force him to watch, it didn't work. He maimed two of them badly and killed the one who'd tried raping her. He was sent to juvie for it. He was only thirteen at the time."

Casey straightened in her seat. "Jesus."

"You'd think the pack would have rallied around Roni, wouldn't you? They didn't. The backlash was bad. Some kids teased her, some insisted she really was raped, and one prick even spread bullshit versions of the assault around. Said prick also made copies of the photos taken of her injuries and then plastered them all around the territory."

"Bastard," she spat. "Why would he do sick crap like that?"

"Nolan was a piece of shit. He was also pissed because the court case earned our pack the attention of anti-shifter extremists; they looked for dirt on the pack, and they discovered that the Alpha—Nolan's dad—was banished from his old pack on suspicion of laundering drug money. People weren't too pleased to hear that the Alpha had such a colorful past, and many wanted him to step down. Nolan blamed Roni for the whole mess. That's not even the worst of what he did."

"Go on."

Eli flexed his fingers, unable to revisit the memories without wanting to punch the fuck out of someone. "The recording of the humans trying to rape Roni was used as evidence in the trial to show that Nick acted in his and Roni's defense. Nolan later got hold of it, and he posted it online. The twisted website was run by a jackal pack and allowed its subscribers to upload videos of shifter fights, sexual assaults, and even murders."

Casey swore. "Tell me Nolan paid for that."

"Oh, he paid." Eli, Nick, and Marcus had made Nolan pay *dearly*. As for Roni's human attackers … Eli had hunted them down after they served their sentences. It hadn't been easy, since they'd been given new identities, but he'd found and obliterated them. He also hadn't told anyone about it, but he was quite certain that Roni suspected they'd died at his hands.

"And the website?"

"We crashed it and destroyed the jackal pack."

"Good. Bastards deserved to die." She paused. "So, Nolan's father was forced to step down from Alpha?"

"Yes. But it didn't happen until me, Roni, and Kathy had transferred to another pack."

She tilted her head. "Why do I get the feeling that the bad shit didn't end there?"

"Because it didn't. Things were okay at the new pack until another Alpha was appointed. Floyd was a pure bastard. Nick took over after he left juvie."

"In what sense was Floyd a bastard?"

Eli rubbed his jaw. "There was something missing in him. I never thought I'd question if someone had a soul, but he sure made me wonder."

"Was he one of your trainers?"

"No." He'd never taught Eli a single move. He'd just repeatedly forced him to fight to the death, keeping Eli under his control by threatening Roni's safety. She'd been through enough, and Eli had been determined that she wouldn't go through more pain.

Sensing that Casey was about to probe further, he said, "We've talked about enough shitty things today, baby. Let's not spoil the mood." He retrieved two bottles of water from the fridge and placed them on the table, meeting pale hazel eyes that had narrowed to slits.

"There's something you don't want to tell me," she accused.

"There are a lot of things I don't want to tell you."

"But you will tell me in time, won't you?" When he didn't answer, she pushed, "Eli?"

He sighed. "One day, yes. For now, let's just say I've done some very bad things." He held his breath, hoping she wouldn't question him.

She stared at him, her expression totally unreadable. "Did you enjoy doing them?"

"Sometimes." The things he'd done while battling at the illegal fighting ring? No, Eli had found no satisfaction in them. But the things he'd done afterward to those who'd wronged his family or pack? Well, that was different.

"Did you eat people?"

His head jerked back. "What?"

"Did you eat people?" she repeated calmly, as if it were an everyday question.

"No."

"Have sex with animals?"

"No."

"Go on Ted-Bundy-style killing sprees?"

"*No.*"

"Rape and pillage entire towns like a reincarnated Viking?"

Eli stared at her, at a loss. "What are you even talking about?"

"Hey, a girl needs some reassurance at times."

His mouth bopped open and closed. "I don't know what to say to you right now."

"That's easy. Say my dinner's almost ready, because I'm famished over here."

He almost snorted. "*That* I can do." After putting the spaghetti onto two plates, he added the sauce-covered meatballs. Taking the seat opposite her, he set both plates on the table.

Once they'd finished their meal and stacked the dishwasher, Eli spread out on the couch and then pulled her down with him, so she was draped over his chest. He handed her the remote control. "Pick what you want to watch." He snaked his hand up the back of her shirt and unclipped her sports bra, so he could pet and trace and stroke her to his heart's content.

"You really don't have to lie here with me, you know," she said, even as she snuggled into him with a contented sigh. "I know you're a busy guy, and I don't want you being bored."

"I'm exactly where I want to be. And trust me when I say that being with you is never boring." Really, there was something so utterly satisfying about simply lying there with his mate, doing something as normal as watching TV.

"Your pack mates don't resent how much time you spend with me? I mean, you have a position that involves a shit load of responsibilities, and you're supposed to also work security shifts at the club—"

"Baby, *you* are my priority. They all know that." But apparently, she didn't, and that pissed Eli off.

Not that he blamed her for it. She'd never been made to feel part of her family, and each of the people who'd loved her—or *should* have loved her—had all let her down in various ways. She'd never felt important to anyone. Never been made to feel *enough*. It was truly no wonder that she didn't expect to be his priority any more than she'd been theirs—she quite simply didn't associate close relationships of any kind with being first to anyone.

She'd soon see she was the most significant thing in his life—Eli would make sure of it. "If you want the truth, they always push me to go to you. Especially Shaya and Roni."

"Why?"

"Because I'm apparently a moody and highly irritating fucker when you're not around. My wolf's the same. We want to be with you, and so we are. Now sleep. You need your rest, baby, because I'll be fucking you into oblivion later."

"Sounds promising."

Eli kept on stroking her back, doodling the occasional circle here and there with his fingers. He knew she was asleep when her breathing evened out and her body completely melted into his. Satisfied that she was getting the rest she needed, he flicked through the channels until he found a movie that piqued his interest. He couldn't have been more than an hour into it when there was a brisk knock on Casey's front door.

Eli stilled. She didn't wake, thankfully—which was a testament to how tired she really was. But then another knock came; this one a little louder. Worried they'd try calling her cell and then wake her with the damn ringtone, he carefully slipped off the sofa and settled her in his spot.

Her eyelids swept open, and he cursed under his breath. "Go back to sleep, baby. There's a knock on the door—I'll get rid of whoever it is."

Crossing to the door, he opened it. A couple stood there. He recognized the broad, blond male as one of the coaching staff who'd stood at the sidelines during Casey's game. The curvy brunette was unfamiliar, but there was a "note" to her scent that told him she was related to Casey somehow.

Neither looked like they wanted to be there—particularly the male. Good. Because Eli did *not* want them there.

"You must be Casey's mate," said the brunette, eyeing him somewhat clinically.

"I am," confirmed Eli. "Look, this isn't a good time for her. She's had a hard day."

"I know. I wouldn't be here if she hadn't asked me to come."

He frowned. "She asked you to come?"

There was a rustling behind him. "Mallory?" Casey sounded both sleepy and surprised.

Grinding his teeth, Eli slowly stepped aside, allowing the couple to pass.

Mallory strolled into the apartment and stared at Casey, lips thinning. "God, you look awful."

She snorted. "Thanks. Eli, this is my cousin, Mallory, and her mate, Preston. Guys, this is Eli, my mate."

Preston tipped his chin at Eli while Mallory offered him a too-quick smile. Eli just stared at them, folding his arms across his chest.

Mallory glanced around the apartment, and her expression twisted into a look of distaste. "I really don't know how you live in this place." Putting her hands on her hips, she faced Casey. "Anyway, what do you want?"

Casey blinked. "Huh?"

"Sherryl told me that you wanted to speak with me, so here I am. And by the way, I can't believe you still talk to that bitch."

Casey shook her head. "I didn't tell her that I wanted to speak with you."

Preston grabbed his mate's hand. "See, I told you Sherryl was probably just messing with you."

Mallory weakly flapped her arm. "But why would she?"

"You know she didn't like that I imprinted on you." Preston tugged her closer. "It's not that she wanted me for herself, she just found it hard to see one of her friends settle down. Now Casey's mated, and so she's probably pissed about that, too. It's spite and jealousy, honey, that's all."

Mallory sighed, brow wrinkling. "I still don't get why she'd send me here."

"She probably just wanted someone to disturb Casey while she needs her rest," said Preston.

Mallory huffed. "Whatever. If you really don't need me for anything, Casey, I'm going." Without even a goodbye, she swanned out of the apartment with her mate in tow. Preston gave both Casey and Eli a nod before closing the door.

Eli looked at his mate. "That's really your cousin? She didn't even congratulate you on your win today."

"It would have been fake if she had." Casey braced her elbows on her thighs and plastered her hands to her face.

Eli crouched in front of her. "What is it, baby? You were good at hiding it from Mallory and her mate, but I could *feel* how anxious you were when she mentioned Sherryl. What's going on?"

Her fingers spread just enough for her to peek through them. "I don't think I could handle you being disappointed in me."

"I could never feel disappointed in you. Tell me."

With a deep breath, she dropped her hands to her lap and sat up straight. "Okay … Before he mated Mallory, Preston and I had a one-night stand." She bit down hard on her lip.

Even as jealousy rushed through him, Eli gently rubbed her thighs. "And Mallory doesn't know?"

"I would have told her if he hadn't pursued her in the hope of making me jealous."

"Ah. He thought sleeping with your cousin would spur you into giving him more."

"I know I should have said something to Mallory, but I didn't want to hurt her, and I wasn't sure she'd believe me anyway. As her relationships were always short and sweet, I figured she'd toss him aside pretty fast and so there was no great need for her to know. But instead, things got more and more serious between them.

"I won't lie, I'm not remotely close to Mallory. I don't even like her, and there's no love lost there. She's done some bitchy things to me over the years. But that doesn't mean I'd ever want to cause her pain. And she will be hurt if she finds out. I know I should tell her, I just don't know *how*. Go on, tell me how much of a horrible person I am."

He rubbed her upper arm. "You're not a horrible person. I can see why you didn't tell her, and I can see why you still haven't. Although some would preach how unethical it is to keep secrets like that, there would be nothing to gain from telling her. It would just make you feel less guilty because the secret's finally out, so you could even say it would be selfish to say something."

Casey gave a soft snort. "That's stretching things a little, but I'll go with it."

"What does this all have to do with Sherryl? Should I take it that she knows?"

"She knows, and she's threatening to tell Mallory." Casey told him everything—her broken sort-of-friendship with Sherryl, the female's history with Miles, and the conversation she and Casey had had that morning.

"Do you think Sherryl really will live up to her threat?"

"I don't know. I told Preston earlier that we should spill the truth to Mallory, but he said he'd keep Sherryl quiet."

Feeling his mate's shame, Eli squeezed her thighs. "The person in the wrong here is Preston. He tried to hurt you, and he used your cousin to do it. Then he kept it from her, and he's pressured you to do the same. You might be withholding a heavy truth from her, but you're not the one who should be feeling so ashamed of themselves." He pressed a kiss to her mouth. "I'd like a little chat with Sherryl."

Casey stilled. "No. Don't. Part of the reason she's being such a bitch right now is that she's hurting. Being face to face with my true mate—something she'll never have—will only make it worse. Plus, I really don't want her anywhere near you."

"Casey—"

"I accepted that you needed to have that man-to-man talk with Ignacio, so I let it slide that you didn't take me along. Now you need to respect that

I'm the one who needs to deal with Sherryl. I get that you want to cover me in bubble wrap and hide me in your man drawer, but you can't."

"Man drawer?"

"That place every guy has where he dumps receipts, chump change, batteries, light bulbs, screws, spare keys, and all manner of shit. You'd like to say you don't have one of those, but you do."

"Yeah, I do." Eli sighed. "Fine, I won't go looking for Sherryl. But if she ever comes at you when I'm there, I won't keep my mouth shut. There's no way I'd be able to stand back and say nothing while someone gave you shit— I don't have that restraint in me. And, honestly, I wouldn't want to restrain myself."

"At least you're honest." Leaning into him, she hooked her arms around his neck. "I'm never going to be able to sleep now. Want to help me burn off the calories I just ate?"

His cock jerked. "You need rest."

"I did rest. Now I need your dick in me. Get with the program."

"Baby—" He cursed as she whipped off her top and bra, baring her gorgeous breasts. All the blood in his body seemed to head south. "You're not being fair."

"You don't want me?" She slowly lowered the zipper of her jeans. "I guess I could just make myself come. But you *did* promise to fuck me into oblivion. I thought you were a man of your word."

He tossed her over his shoulder and stood. "Fine. I'll make you come with my mouth," he said, heading for the bedroom area. "Then you'll sleep."

She snorted. "You'll be inside me within minutes, Axton, and we both know it."

"No." He dumped her on the bed. "You're only getting my mouth."

"Yeah, yeah." She parted her thighs. "Let's see how long you can last before you thrust that cock inside me."

He didn't last long at all.

SHARDS OF FROST

CHAPTER SEVEN

Eli stopped off at the smoothie bar on his way to collect Casey later that week. He was hoping he could soften her into agreeing to stay at his lodge the whole weekend. He had plans. Mostly that they spent it naked.

Thinking of his mate all spread out on his bed, he wore a ghost of a smile as he walked back to his SUV … right up until four males slid out of the shadows of the parking lot. Even as everything in him shot to alertness, he almost grinned at the sight of the balaclavas. *Fucking ridiculous.*

Resting the smoothie on the hood of his SUV, Eli inhaled deeply, taking in the scents of car exhaust, warm pavement, motor oil, and *falcons.* His wolf peeled back his upper lip, bracing himself to spring.

Eli's skin tingled with the agitation heating his blood, but he remained calm. Brawling with multiple attackers at once was almost always a losing situation. He didn't suppose they'd kindly come at him one at a time. No, they'd swarm him as a group, hoping to take him down fast. And if they *did* take him to the pavement, it would all be over. He'd find himself being kicked, stomped on, and beaten into submission. *Not happening.*

Given how outnumbered he was, his odds weren't good. Technically. But what the falcons didn't know was that he'd trod this path many, many times; had been repeatedly thrown into a fighting pit with multiple opponents. He'd won, but he'd never won with ease. Injuries were inevitable. He could only aim to minimize them.

It was a shame his cell phone was tucked in the pocket of the jacket he'd left on the SUV's passenger seat. He could have discreetly pressed the panic button and alerted his pack mates. They'd not only have known he needed backup, they'd have known his location through the GPS tracker on his phone. He'd just have to hope that Ally had a premonition of the incident but, considering her gift was playing up, that hardly seemed likely.

Not that he *couldn't* take care of these bastards alone—in fact, he'd enjoy teaching them just how fucking stupid they'd been to target him. He'd just prefer to instead round them up and take them back to his territory for questioning. Maybe he'd leave one alive so that he could take him to be interrogated.

Eli identified the leader easily. Taller and broader than the rest, he stood just a few steps in front of the others. And Eli knew he'd need to attack him first, since that would be a blow to the rest of the mob. Luckily, the leader was also closest, which meant Eli wouldn't need to wade through the pathetic gang to reach him.

Eli planted his feet. "You really think this is wise?"

The leader shrugged. "It's nothing personal, Axton. We respect you and your pack. But someone's willing to pay good money for you to get your ass kicked, and we'd be fools to turn down that kind of money."

"I see. Just who hired you?"

"We can't say—it was part of the deal. We haven't been ordered to kill you, though; don't worry."

"I wasn't. You won't even show me your faces. That's pussy behavior right there." Anger thickened the air. He probably shouldn't antagonize them. They might not have been told to kill Eli, but people would go much further in a group than they would do when alone. It was that whole mob mentality. Still, fuck it.

"They also want us to record everything," added the leader. That was when one of the others pulled out a cell phone and held it up.

Eli stilled, and his wolf's claws sliced out.

Three would-be attackers, one male recording the attack … The whole thing echoed Roni's assault far too clearly. It couldn't be a coincidence. No, someone had hoped that reconstructing what she went through would anger him enough to knock him off-balance.

Well, they were wrong. He'd long ago learned to shut off his emotions while engaged in a fight. Even now, the familiar numbness was creeping up on him—it was pure instinct to let it settle in.

Sadly, he wouldn't have the luxury of giving each bastard a real beating. He'd need to finish each falcon off in record time. The longer he took to end the fight, the likelier chance they had of overpowering him. He'd have to incapacitate each of them fast with powerful, well-placed, explosive blows.

Eli sighed. "My mate's going to be pissed."

"Because you'll be beaten to a pulp?"

"No. Because she didn't get to punch you herself."

The leader cocked his head. "I'll give it to you, Axton, you're pretty calm for someone who's about to get their ass handed to them."

"You think you're stronger and safer because you're part of a group?" Eli shrugged. "It's all right. You won't be the first to make that mistake. You don't think you could kick my ass without the help of your friends here? It's big of you to admit that, I suppose."

Anger flashed in the leader's eyes, and his fingers retracted like claws. "I can take you, Axton," he bit out. "But I'm going to give our client what he paid for, which was to see you flattened by a group."

"Doesn't mean you can't come at me one at a time, does it? Come on, you first. Let's see how well you do. Or are you as much of a pussy as I'm sensing you are?"

Clenching his fists, the leader dropped his chin, angled his body, and shifted one foot slightly in front of the other—it was a fast, fluid move.

Eli was faster.

He ducked the fist that flew at his head and aimed a precise punch to the side of the falcon's knee joint, instantly dislocating it.

The others gaped at their leader as he collapsed to the pavement, his face creased in agony.

"You sure you want to do this?" Eli asked them.

The leader growled, pointing at Eli. "Get him! Now!" And, of course, they stupidly obeyed.

Eli backed away fast, positioning himself between two cars, forcing the falcons to form a line rather than come at him from different angles. The first lunged at him. With adrenaline surging through his veins, Eli struck hard and fast. Targeted the pressure points. Aimed for the weakest spots. Delivered maximum pain and damage.

The first falcon went down easy, out cold, but the second could sure take a punch. He flew at Eli with devastating kicks and cheap shots. Eli evaded most of them—ducking, dodging, and jumping backwards. Other shots hit him hard.

Flesh burned as it tore open. Wounds stung as his sweat dripped into them. His jaw and ribs throbbed like a bitch. If it wasn't for the adrenaline dimming the pain, he'd be feeling a whole lot worse.

Eli fought just as dirty as his opponent. Using his arsenal of teeth, claws, fists, palms, knees, elbows, and feet, he delivered bone-fracturing blows, clawed at the falcon's face through the balaclava, headbutted him hard enough to daze the fucker and split his eye open.

Growls, snarls, curses, and grunts rang through the air, but they were overridden by the car alarms that had started blaring when Eli and the falcon each accidentally banged into the vehicles, denting metal and smashing windows.

It was hard not to be distracted by the feel of his mate's anger and bone-chilling fear pulsing along their bond. Eli hated that she was experiencing his pain with him, but there wasn't a damn thing he could do about it.

Pushing it to the back of his mind, Eli kept on fighting hard and mercilessly. The scents of blood, anger, and fear tainted the air, feeding his wolf's thirst for vengeance.

It was while the second falcon was trying to recover from a punch to the windpipe that the first falcon—having rose from his unconscious state—rushed around the car, trying to come at Eli from behind.

Having expected the move, Eli pivoted on the spot, dodged the punch, grabbed the bastard's arm, and struck the elbow joint hard. The falcon's cry of pain faded into a gurgle as Eli stabbed his claws into the asshole's throat and twisted, severing arteries.

Just as the falcon dropped like a stone, thick arms wrapped around Eli from behind. *Son of a bitch.* Eli slammed the back of his head into the fucker's face and heard a telling *crack* that made his wolf bare his teeth in a feral grin.

The arms that were curled around him dropped. Eli spun. A little dazed, the falcon threw a wild punch that was so slow in coming it might as well have had a postcard on it. Eli blocked it with his arm and punched the bastard in the throat so hard that he doubled over, gasping for air. That was when Eli grabbed the falcon's head and twisted sharply, snapping his neck.

With a muffled curse, the male holding the phone backed away, hands shaking. Eli stalked toward him, evading the cell that was thrown at his head. Of course, the little shit tried to run.

"What's the rush?" asked Eli, fisting the falcon's shirt and dragging him backwards.

The falcon spun to face him and tried striking out with his talons. One swipe of Eli's claws slit open the bastard's throat. The male cupped his bleeding neck, eyes wide in disbelief, choking on his own blood, and dropped to his knees.

Satisfied, Eli turned and headed for the leader, who was now ridiculously trying to hop away. Then the male shifted in a flash, squawking as he awkwardly flew away in his falcon form. *Shit.*

Breathing hard, Eli stood there—jaw tight, muscles trembling, knuckles burning. He glanced at each of the falcons that were sprawled on the blood-spattered pavement. All were dead. It took a few moments for that thought to truly sink in. Once it did, the battle adrenaline began to fade, and the numbness started to clear from his mind.

He snatched the smartphone from the floor and looked at the screen. *Smashed.* He pressed the buttons, but it didn't power to life. Still, he'd take it home and see if Nick could get anything out of it.

He could feel eyes on him, knew there were plenty of spectators watching. Some were even snapping photos. He also knew none of them would have called the police—shifter business was shifter business. And anyone who'd seen how inhumanly fast Eli and the falcons had moved would have known instantly that they were shifters.

He whipped the balaclavas off the dead falcons, hoping he'd recognize at least one of their faces. It was a pointless hope.

A quick search of their pockets revealed that none had wallets or cell phones on their person. There was, however, a cheap-looking cell phone in the pocket of the jeans the leader had shredded when he shifted into his falcon form. It was most likely a burner phone, but it could have some info on it. He needed his wounds seeing to, so now wasn't the time to check.

Both cell phones in his hand, Eli grabbed the smoothie from the bonnet and jumped into his SUV. The move pulled at his wounds and sent pain rippling through his ribs. He cursed between his teeth, gripping the wheel hard.

Taking stock of himself, he figured he had a fractured wrist, puncture wounds in his sides, a few broken ribs, and ugly gashes along his chest, thighs, forehead, and arms. Awesome.

Letting out a deep sigh, he tossed the phones onto the front passenger seat and took his own ringing cell from the pocket of his jacket, unsurprised to see his mate's name on the screen. Her soul-deep panic raced along their bond and tightened his chest.

Placing the smoothie in the cupholder, he swiped his thumb across the screen of his cell and said, "I'm fine, baby."

"You're not fine! I can feel your pain!"

"I've had worse."

"That does not make me feel better! What happened? I would have come to you, but I have no idea where you are. I called Roni, but your pack have no clue either. Cassidy had had some sort of *knowing* but it hadn't given them anything to go on. Seriously, what happened?"

"Falcons." He switched on the engine, deciding not to tell her that driving would be painful, thanks to his fractured wrist. She'd insist that he remain where he was. The injury would begin to heal as he drove.

"Where are you?"

"Outside the little row of shops near the new movie theater." No need to yet spoil the surprise of the smoothie. In this mood, she'd only berate him for buying it, claiming he wouldn't have been attacked if he had just driven straight to her apartment.

"That's about fifteen minutes away from your territory, right? Go home, let Ally heal you. I'll meet you there."

"Baby—"

"Don't argue with me, canine, I'm not in the fucking mood!"

He couldn't help smiling. Apparently, she not only went quiet when she was pissed, she fumed when she was scared. Although he despised that she couldn't quite beat back that fear, he couldn't help feeling warmed by it.

"Don't think I don't know that you're smiling," she said. "Now drive. I'm staying on the line until you're home."

"Casey, you don't need to—"

"*Drive, canine, drive.*"

Lips twitching, he put the phone on speaker and set it in the second cupholder before driving out of the lot. "How was your day?"

"Don't talk to me right now."

His mouth quirked. "All right." He heard her speaking to someone in the background, asking them for a ride, and heard a female voice respond—the words were too muffled for him to make them out, though. When he finally crossed the border of pack territory, he said, "I'm home."

"I'll be there soon." The line went dead.

After parking the SUV, he headed into the main lodge. Many of his pack mates were pacing in the living area, looking various levels of panicked.

It was Bracken who saw him first. The enforcer gaped. "What in the holy blue fuck happened to you?"

"A gang of falcons decided to have some fun with me."

Roni let out a string of inventive curses that made her mate's eyebrows fly up.

"Oh God," muttered Ally. She pointed to a sofa. "Sit."

Eli obeyed, placing the phones on the seat beside him. She laid a hand on his arm, and her healing energy flowed into him and set to work on his injuries.

"We've been trying to call you," said Nick, jaw tight, "but the line was busy. I'm guessing it was Casey."

Eli nodded. "She wanted to stay on the line until I was home." He gave Ally a thankful nod when he felt his wounds close over.

Roni blew out a breath. "I'll bet she *freaked.*"

"She did," said Eli.

"Want me to pick her up and bring her to you?" asked Derren.

Eli shook his head. "Thanks, but she's already on her way. One of her pack mates are giving her a ride. Contact whoever's guarding the border; tell them to let her pass."

"Will do," said Derren, pulling out his phone. "Where exactly where you when you were attacked?" he asked, his thumbs flying across the screen of his cell as he no doubt texted the enforcer on duty.

"The parking lot outside the little row of shops near the new movie theater," said Eli. He looked at his sister. "Casey said she called you; said you told her that Cassidy had a *knowing.*"

"We couldn't make any sense of it," Roni told him.

Shaya rubbed her temple. "Cassidy said she just *knew* you shouldn't buy a smoothie. That you'd be hurt if you did. We called and called but your phone just kept ringing."

"I must have already stopped at the smoothie bar by then—I left my phone in my jacket pocket, so I wouldn't have known you were calling." Eli sat up a little straighter. "The falcons were clear that someone hired them. I'm guessing it was Ignacio. I think he did this to hurt Casey—that's what he does, he retaliates by going after the people you care for. He wants to punish her, so he did it through me. But as he did it using the falcons, we can't prove he had anything to do with it."

Nick dug his cell out of his pocket and tapped the screen a few times with his thumbs. Everyone heard the phone ring clearly, since his brother had placed the call on speakerphone.

"Ah, Nick," Ignacio greeted. "What a surprise."

Still furious, Eli's wolf snarled at the sound of the cat's voice and lashed out with his claws.

Nick's face hardened. "Tell me, Ignacio, why has my brother just been attacked by a group of falcons?"

There was a pause. "I'll take it by your tone that you think I had something to do with it," said Ignacio. "Now why would I send falcons after Eli—or anyone, for that matter—when I have cats to do my bidding for me?"

Nick's hand tightened around the phone. "Because you know damn well that sending your cats would lead to my pack and hundreds of minks seeking revenge on you. A strike at Eli is a strike at Casey—her pack wouldn't let that go."

"Well, I suppose that would be a good reason to operate under the radar. But I can assure you, Axton, I am not behind this attack."

"You expect me to believe that?"

"Truth be told, I don't care what you do or don't believe. I can only respond to your questions, which I have done. Pin the blame on me if you must. But be careful—if you don't take the time to consider other culprits, the true one will escape your notice."

Nick ended the call with a muffled curse. "It has to be him. *Has* to be."

Shaya frowned as he began furiously tapping the screen of his phone. "Who are you texting?"

"Donovan," said Nick. "I want him to call his contact within Ignacio's pride and see if said contact knows anything. All I need is confirmation of Ignacio's involvement."

Bracken looked at Eli. "If we can talk to the falcons that attacked you, we can make them tell us who sent them. I don't suppose you let any live."

"One. He shifted and flew away." Eli gestured at the phones on the sofa beside him. "I got them from the falcons. There were four males in total. Three came at me. The fourth was recording the whole thing—apparently, they'd been paid to do it."

Roni hissed, clearly coming to the same conclusion that Eli had. "That motherfucking cat needs to choke on his own motherfucking dick."

Marcus soothingly rubbed her back. "Couldn't have said it better myself."

Derren examined the damaged cell phone. "This is probably a goner, but there might be something saved into the memory card." He pulled open the cell, and his lips flattened. "There's no SIM. Looks like he removed it just in case you managed to wrestle the phone from him, or this could be something he uses purely for 'business.'"

"No personal info or call log on this burner either," said Bracken, holding up the leader's cheap cell. "There is, however, a text message."

"Saying what?" asked Shaya.

"'Don't disappoint me.'" Bracken placed the phone in Nick's outstretched hand, adding, "If there was an exchange of messages before that, they've been erased. The number hasn't been saved into the phone as a contact."

"We'll give the number to Donovan, see if he can find out who it belongs to," said Nick. "But I wouldn't be surprised to find out it's the number of yet another burner phone."

Eli pushed up from the sofa. "Need to clean myself up a little." Lethargic from the adrenaline crash, he headed to the bathroom at the end of the hall and wiped the blood from his exposed skin, but there was no ridding the stains from his clothes. He would have gone to his lodge and changed before Casey arrived, but he suspected she was almost at his territory.

Whipping out his cell, he called her and asked, "Where are you?"

"Nearly there," she replied. "Does my pack mate have permission to cross the border of your territory when we reach it?"

"That's a stupid question. Of course they do."

"I felt your pain fade. You're healed now?"

"I'm healed." Eli walked out of the lodge and sat on the porch step, intending to wait for her.

"Did Ignacio send the falcons?"

"Probably. But he's denying any culpability."

"Bastard," she spat.

"Yeah."

"What exactly happened?"

By the time he'd finished giving her a bullet-point version of the fight, excluding the ugliest aspects of it, he heard a car approaching. "I take it you're here."

"I'm here."

"Good. I'm sitting on the porch." He ended the call and waited.

Moments later, a car drove into the lot. He recognized the driver as one of the females who worked in the bakery beneath Casey's apartment. He gave the baker a nod of thanks, and she gave him a quick wave in return. Once Casey slipped out of the car and shut the door, her pack mate drove off.

Eli stood. "Come here, baby."

She walked into his open arms, buried her face in his chest, and fisted his shirt. "Sorry I yelled at you. I don't handle fear very well."

Hugging her tight, he nuzzled her hair and breathed her in, taking the scent of her into his lungs, letting it steady both him and his wolf. "You don't need to apologize."

"I could feel your pain, I had no idea what was happening or where you were or if you'd be okay."

The shake in her voice made his chest ache. Sliding one hand up her back to palm her nape, he pressed a kiss to her temple. "I wouldn't have done too well with that kind of fear either."

Casey drank in his scent, so fucking relieved he was okay. She'd known through their bond that he was fine, but she'd needed to *see* that for herself before she could fully believe it. Her *mink* had needed to see.

Earlier, Casey had felt his agitation at first but hadn't thought much of it. Then there'd been a spike of anger that was quickly buried under a strange numbness. And then there'd been nothing but pain, and she'd been so terrified for him that she couldn't see straight.

It had only made it worse that she had no way of knowing where he was. She'd felt utterly helpless. *Useless.* Even now, the fear clung to her like a bad smell. She just couldn't quite shake it off, though having him there with her—alive, well, and safe—was helping it slowly drain from her system.

With a growl, she pulled back a little. "I can smell *them* on you. My mink wants to go hunting."

"How about we shower instead?"

"You should be angrier than this."

"Believe me, baby, I'm thoroughly pissed, because this was a strike at *you.*" Eli was just set on burying his fury so that he didn't exacerbate her own. "I'd love to rip Ignacio's throat out, but we can't prove it was him who sent the falcons. And we need to be sure, because a battle means people will die. We need to be one-hundred percent certain that the people we're tearing into deserve it.

"When my old pack was at odds with coyotes, the pack's rival pack orchestrated on attack on our Betas, making it look like the coyotes were responsible and tricked them into going to war. They all realized too late that the people they were slaughtering were innocent of the crime. Pups became orphans. People lost their mates, friends, and family members."

She sighed. "Okay, yeah, I get that we can't just storm Ignacio's territory, but that doesn't mean I can't really, *really* want to."

He kissed her. "No, it doesn't."

"How will you get proof that it was Ignacio?"

"A confession from the falcons would have been nice, but the one I let live flew away. I figure they were mercenaries. They did leave cell phones behind." Leading her to his SUV, he retrieved the smoothie from the cupholder as he told her about the text message on the burner phone.

"Let's hope Donovan can find out who sent the text." She melted into him, settling as his own sense of calm moved through her. "Thanks for the smoothie."

"You're welcome." He rubbed his nose against hers. "Stay with me this weekend. All weekend."

"I didn't bring enough clothes."

"That's fine. You won't need them for what I have in mind."

Her mouth canted up just a little. "I had the feeling you'd say that."

Just then, the front door burst open and Kathy stepped onto the porch, her breaths coming hard and fast. She looked Eli up and down. "You're all right? I heard what happened."

"I'm fine," he told her.

Her gaze sliced to Casey and hardened. "I hope you're happy with yourself."

Casey's spine snapped straight. Oh, the bitch had *not* just said that. "Excuse me?"

"If you hadn't brought Ignacio into Eli's life, none of this would have happened."

Wow, she'd really gone there. Casey's mink lashed her tail, snarling. "Don't tempt my inner bitch to come out, Kathy—it doesn't play nice."

"Mom, back off," Eli warned through his teeth.

Kathy looked at him. "Everything was fine until she came here. *Fine.*"

"Except for the part where I was miserable, yeah, it was fine," he said.

Kathy flicked a dismissive hand. "Now you're just being dramatic."

"You'd know all about dramatic, wouldn't you?" Casey folded her arms. "Go on, say everything you've been itching to say to me since the day I came here. Let it out. Have your tantrum. See if anyone respects you for it. See if you can still respect *yourself* afterward. Because in your shoes, I sure as hell wouldn't be able to."

Some of the Mercury Pack members gathered on the porch, but Casey didn't give a single flying fuck if they'd come to defend Kathy. The woman needed to hear this shit.

"You know, people have told me to be patient with you; that you're scared of seeing Eli go through what you went through and that it's messing with your ability to be happy for him," said Casey. "But me? I think it's about more than that. You clung to your kids to get you through a difficult time. But you lost Nick to his mate, then you lost Roni to hers, and Eli was all you had left … until me. Now you're feeling adrift, aren't you? Like there's no one to hold you here anymore."

Kathy's eyes flickered, but she didn't confirm or deny it.

"I can sympathize with that. I can. I do. But I can still judge the everloving shit out of you for not putting your son's feelings before your own."

"You know nothing about me," clipped Kathy.

"Maybe not. But you know nothing about me either. Hasn't stopped you from passing judgment or being a passive-aggressive heifer, though, has it?"

"I am *not* passive-aggressive."

"And my tits are big."

"Nor am I a heifer."

"And my ass is small."

Kathy's eyes narrowed. "You have a hell of a mouth on you. Does your mother know you speak to people that way?"

"Probably not. I haven't seen her in over a decade."

The bluster left Kathy in a rush. "Oh." The tension began to leach out of her muscles, and she sighed. "Your inner bitch really *doesn't* play nice, does it?"

"Not even for a second. Now are you done with your boring, self-centered bullshit or what?"

Kathy looked at Eli. "You going to let her speak to me like that?"

Eli pursed his lips. "Yeah, as it happens, I am."

Kathy harrumphed, but she didn't seem angry. "Don't come crying to me when her mink kills you in your sleep." And then she stormed into the lodge.

Casey turned to Eli. "Does that mean it's over?"

He curled an arm around her and pulled her close. "It's over. Sad as it is, that's the closest to 'welcome to the family' that you're going to get from her."

Casey shrugged one shoulder. "I can live with that."

It was dark when Casey's eyes fluttered open in the very early hours of the morning, but her shifter night vision enabled her to see clearly. It hadn't been a noise that woke her. It was a sense of restlessness humming down the mating bond, so it didn't surprise her to see that Eli was lying on his back, staring at the ceiling, lost in his thoughts.

She snuggled closer to him. "What's wrong?" Her voice sounded thick with sleep.

Blinking, he looked down at her. "Nothing." He pressed a kiss to her forehead. "Go back to sleep."

Nothing? "Liar," she said softly. "I can practically feel you brooding through the bond." She let out a contented sigh as his fingers began exploring her back, even though she sensed he was *taking* comfort rather than offering it. "You're lying here seething about something. Is it the falcons? Or is it that Donovan's contact hasn't responded yet?" But he didn't answer. "Talk to me. Please." It seemed to be the plea that got to him.

He sighed. "It's not so much the attack that gets to me. I don't even care that I had to kill the falcons—and yeah, I am aware that that doesn't say good things about me. What really pisses me off is that they were told to record it."

Casey stiffened, anger rising inside her. "You didn't mention that part yesterday. Don't think I didn't notice how vague you were—" She broke off as it hit her. They'd tried to record it, just as one of the humans had tried to record the attack on Roni. "Motherfuckers."

"This shit has dredged up bad memories for Roni. My sister is one of the toughest people I've ever known, but her attack took something out of her. Not just because it was as traumatic as any assault could be, but because her brother had been forced to kill for her. It weighed on her, ate at her.

"It was hard for us to watch Nick change little by little over the years. Every time we visited him at juvie, he seemed harder. Colder. But he never regretted what he'd done. I think the thing that bothered him most about his actions was that he'd been able to kill so easily without feeling any remorse. He was only thirteen."

She doodled circles on his chest. "And how had you felt about the whole thing?"

"I wished I'd killed the other humans that were part of the assault."

Intuition pricked at her, but she still asked the question that she suspected she already knew the answer to. "Where are those humans now?" He didn't reply. Just looked at her, his face blank, and she sensed her suspicions were right. "Does Roni know you killed them?"

"Probably, but she's never said anything."

"Are they the 'bad things' you mentioned you'd done?"

"Some of them. But they're not things I regret. Those pricks deserved what they got. My sister didn't. If you'd seen her after the attack … She was pale. Shaking. So scared." And he'd felt like he'd let her down, because he hadn't been there to help defend her as Nick had.

"It's a measure of her strength that she got past it and became an enforcer, especially since any form of violence should have taken her back to that day." Casey genuinely admired her for it.

"About a year after her attack, she asked me to put her in a chokehold; said she wanted to learn how to escape one." Eli's blood had run ice-cold. The very last thing he'd ever wanted to do was make her feel helpless ever again in her life, but she'd pushed and pushed him until he agreed. "She panicked at first. It was fucking hard to hold her like that, but she'd made me swear that I wouldn't let go; that I'd give her the chance to beat back the panic and free herself. And she did. My sister's a fast learner."

"You taught her to fight?"

"I taught her to kill. Not defend herself, not just fight dirty, but to fight until she was the only one standing—to inflict as much pain as possible, and to do it without any mercy."

"Why are you looking at me like you think I should be judging you for that?"

"You've seen me at The Den, baby. You've seen how brutal and pitiless I can be. I've never killed there, but I could have done it within seconds if I'd wanted to. I made sure she could do the same."

"Then I'd say it wasn't so much that you taught her to kill, it was that you taught her to survive. You gave her the skills she needed to be confident that no one could ever put her through a trauma like that ever again."

"Someone did try it again. A jackal. There was a battle on our territory; it was all tied up with that fucked-up website I mentioned to you. She later thanked me. Said she felt like everything I'd taught her had prepared her for that night."

Casey stroked his chest. "Obviously, then, I'm right."

She wanted to ask him again where he'd learned to fight—mostly because she could sense he was expecting judgment from her about something related to the matter, and she wanted him to understand that she'd *never* judge him for anything. But pushing someone to reveal their secrets before they were ready to do so didn't help anyone. And it would mean more to Casey if he shared with her because he *wanted* to.

Plus, right then wasn't the time, and she really didn't want him falling any deeper into the dark memories he was wading through. She could practically see him slipping away.

Casey touched the side of his face and said softly, "Come back."

His eyes focused fully on her. "I'm here." Kissing her soft and slow, he rolled her onto her back, giving her his weight. "Need you again."

SHARDS OF FROST

CHAPTER EIGHT

"Eli! Eli!"

Hearing his pack mate call his name the next morning, Eli paused in making coffee. There was no panic or sense of urgency in Bracken's tone, so it seemed highly unlikely that there was a problem of some kind. Why Bracken hadn't just knocked on the door, though, Eli didn't know.

He strode through his lodge and pulled open the door. "What is it?"

Standing near the bottom step of the porch, Bracken said, "Tell her to move." His eyes dipped down to the mink who sat on the porch like a sentry, staring at the enforcer.

Having been on the receiving end of that disconcerting stare, Eli understood Bracken's unease. Still, amusement trickled through him. "Just step around her."

The male's eyes widened. "Do I look slow to you? I'm not turning my back on a mink—that shit's just not done."

"Come on, Brack, she's just an itty, bitty thing. You don't really think she's going to attack, did you?"

"Um, *yeah*."

"You should be used to vicious creatures. You have a pallas cat for a mate."

"Yeah, but she's nice to me. And she doesn't look at me with cold, empty eyes."

Eli sighed and stepped onto the porch. "There's nothing wrong with her eyes. Come here, gorgeous," he called out softly to his little mink. She glanced back at him and let out a low hiss. "Yes, I know he doesn't belong here and he's trespassing, but he won't stay long. Come here." She didn't. But she *did* move aside, clearing a path for the enforcer.

Eying the mink warily, Bracken slowly ascended the porch stairs and walked toward Eli. The mink matched the enforcer step for step, always watching him. Once Bracken came to a halt, she scrambled up Eli's body and perched herself on his shoulder.

Reaching up to stroke her, Eli asked his pack mate, "What brings you here?"

"Nick sent me," said Bracken. "He wanted you to know that Donovan checked out the number who texted 'Don't disappoint me,' and he confirmed what Nick suspected—it was another burner phone."

Eli cursed under his breath. "Has Donovan's contact within Ignacio's pride got back in touch with him yet?"

"Yes. He told Donovan that Ignacio is claiming he didn't send the falcons after you. But only the cougar's inner circle will know the truth. Donovan's contact isn't part of that."

"So we have nothing to go on."

"No." Bracken shoulders lowered. "I'd like to say I think the danger has passed. But if it was Ignacio who set up the falcon attack, he'll probably strike again, since the whole thing was a total failure."

Yeah, it seemed likely. "He'll probably also hire mercenaries again to do his dirty work." Just then, his little mink let out a tiny squeak. As she scurried down Eli's body, dashed off the porch, and disappeared into the bush, he blinked. "Apparently, she trusts that you won't harm me."

"Apparently." But Bracken didn't sound convinced. He glanced around, as if expecting her to suddenly jump out at him for fun. "Oh, Nick also wanted me to let you know that Donovan's having trouble locating your mate's brother; there's not a whisper of the guy anywhere. But he'll keep looking."

"Ignacio will probably renew his efforts to find Miles. As you pointed out, the falcon's attack on me was an epic failure. Ignacio might figure it will be easier to punish Casey through Miles—especially since he knows I'll now be more on my guard. She doesn't have any other important people in her life, so there's no one else for Ignacio to target."

"Has Miles had any combat training?"

"It's doubtful. He lived mostly as a human. Although he spent time on Craven Pack territory and even dated a female mink, he didn't live there at any point."

"Then he'll probably be easy pickings for whoever Ignacio sends after him," muttered Bracken with a weary sigh as he again gave the area a once over. Then he spotted the soccer ball at the far side of the porch. "You played a few games with Casey?"

Eli just grunted.

The other male grinned. "She beat your ass, didn't she?"

"Fuck, yeah, she did. If you'd seen her play, you'd get why."

"Shaya showed me a short video she'd recorded of Casey's last game. Your mate is hardcore ..." Trailing off, Bracken frowned and tilted his head.

"Is it just me, or is everything *way* too quiet?"

Tensing, Eli inhaled deeply. "I smell cat. *Your* cat."

Bracken's eyes widened. "Shit! They'll savage each other!"

Both males hurried off the porch and into the surrounding woods, following the scents of their mates. There was allegedly no way to sneak up on a pallas cat, but minks were fucking ninjas. If anyone could take a pallas cat off-guard, it was a mink shifter. And while Eli did not want Madisyn hurt or dead, he also didn't want his mate ripped apart by—

Eli and Bracken skidded to a halt near a tall oak as they almost literally stumbled upon their mates. Neither spoke. Really, Eli didn't know what *to* say. Several scenarios had flicked through his mind when he realized Bracken's mate had trespassed onto his land, but not this.

"No way," Bracken breathed. "That's just ... I'm without words."

Eli grunted, staring down at the two females. The pallas cat kicked a dead vole and sent it skidding along the ground to the mink, who batted it back to the cat. They did it again. And again. And again.

Bracken shook his head in disbelief. "They're playing soccer. With a dead vole. And they're *good* at it." He raked a hand through his hair. "I can so see this becoming a 'thing' with them. Is it just me *dreading* the trouble these two could cause together?"

"No. Maybe we should keep them apart."

"Sounds best." Bracken picked up his cat, smiling at her snarl of annoyance. "Sorry, kitty, but it's time to go home." He stilled as he caught sight of the mink's pile of dead carcasses a few feet away. He blinked hard and then looked at Eli. "I've decided I'm not going to comment."

Eli gave a short nod. "Good idea."

Nuzzling his cat, Bracken walked away, whispering to her, "No coming back here. You need to find friends who aren't psychotic."

Eli scowled. "Hey!"

Bracken gestured at the pile of bodies. "Hello, trophy killer."

Eli's lips thinned. "She's just tidy and has a place for things."

"Anyone who needs and reserves a special space for dead bodies is the definition of psychotic." Bracken spared the mink a brief look and then walked off.

Whatever. Eli bent over and carefully lifted his mate. "I'm guessing the only reason you didn't attack the cat is that you recognized a kindred spirit in those crazy eyes," he said, walking back to the lodge. "And yes, that does disturb me." He should have expected that the two vicious creatures would become fast friends.

Reaching the porch, he asked, "Are you going to shift back? You've been out here for hours." Okay, maybe not hours, but it felt that long.

She let out a hiss and jumped out of his arms.

He sighed down at her. "Come on, Casey, we said we'd have a relaxing day together. Come back to me."

The mink made a sound of irritation, but then bones cracked and popped as she shifted back to her human form.

Eli smiled at Casey. "There you are."

She curled her arms around his neck. "You say that like I've been gone half the day. I was forty minutes tops."

"Too long." He kissed her softly, flicking her tongue with his. "Damn, I've had far too many fantasies about this mouth. It's not fair that you won't give my cock a kiss. It'll give you one back."

"Ha. I'll bet it will." She pulled on the tee and shorts she'd left on the porch bench before she'd shifted. "By the way, Bracken wasn't the only one to come by. Don't know if Zander intended to go to your lodge, but he stopped when he saw my mink. He asked me to tell you that, yes, he'll cover your shift at the Velvet Lounge tonight. I don't want you to neglect your duties for me, Eli."

"I've covered for Zander countless times so that he can have quality time with his mate. He has no problem returning the favor. Gwen will probably go with him and then just hang at the bar with Madisyn while he works—it's what she normally does. You should come with me next time I work a shift at the club."

"And hang at the bar? I'd probably get bored and start a fight."

He chuckled. "Coming to the club with me would be a good way for you to meet the Phoenix Pack females. They keep pestering me to bring you to their territory, especially since Roni sang your praises to them—my sister doesn't like many people. But you might feel more comfortable meeting them on neutral territory."

"You mean *you'd* feel better if I met them at a place where you and your pack mates were there to defend me if anything went wrong."

Eli felt his mouth hitch up at the corner. "Busted."

She rolled her eyes. "I won't bother pointing out I don't need you to be so overprotective—it's not something you don't already know. Why don't you just invite the Phoenix Pack females to your territory one day while I'm here?"

"Because, in case you haven't noticed, I like having you all to myself when you're here."

"Considering we never linger at the main lodge after dinner, yeah, I've noticed. So, you want to spend the day relaxing?"

"Yeah. I want us to have time to ourselves. No interruptions, no meals with the pack. Just us."

"Doing what?"

Curling an arm around her, he pulled her close. "Relaxing. Fucking. Eating. Fucking. Binge-watching movies. F—"

"Fucking, yeah, I got it. So, what relaxing activity do we start with?"

Eli jerked back to avoid the fist that came swinging at his face. He didn't move fast enough. The fist slammed into his jaw so hard his head almost snapped to the side. "Fuck, that hurt."

Casey's mouth twitched. "Pussy."

He raised a brow as they circled each other. "Oh, it's like that, is it?"

"You said you wanted to spar with me. I get that sparring means pulling my punches and keeping my claws sheathed, but I didn't think you wanted me to go *easy* on you. I can if you want, though."

Eli smiled and invited, "Keep it coming."

She lunged. Just like when she'd fought against the fox at The Den, she moved with a blinding speed and deadly accuracy that he couldn't help admiring. She didn't put as much power behind her blows, keeping the spar light and fun, but Eli wasn't gonna lie—they still hurt.

He also wasn't going to whine like the pussy she'd accused him of being, though, so he kept the pained grunts to himself as he dodged and deflected. He also dealt his own blows. It wasn't always easy to land them, since she moved like goddamn lightning.

When he *did* land a decent blow, she smiled. Didn't grunt. Didn't curse. Didn't complain. She. Smiled. *Crazy bitch.*

Eli did what he did with every opponent—observed her style, watching for patterns. But her trainers had obviously taught her to be instinctively prepared for that, because the awkward mink didn't *have* patterns. She didn't repeat the same combinations, favor either fist, telegraph her moves, or consistently use the same defensive move against the same strike.

And when she clipped him with an uppercut that came close to dazing him, he knew his mate would clean his clock if she ever hit him full-force. Why that made him smile, he couldn't say.

"Careful, Grandpa. You're slow."

He rubbed at his throbbing jaw. "Everyone's slow compared to you. How the fuck do you move that fast? Seriously?" He dodged her fist, angled his hips, and clipped her side with a light kick. "It's good that you don't drive. I have a feeling you'd be a nightmare on the road."

"It's true that I have no patience for traffic." Punch. "Or other drivers." Kick. "Or traffic lights."

Eli slammed up his arm to block her next punch and pressed a kiss to her temple before darting out of range. "Looking at you all flushed and sweaty makes me want to pin you to the ground and have my way with you."

She smiled. "Aw, you think you could pin me to the ground? Well, ain't you cute."

They went at it again, exchanging blow after blow, until their breaths became labored and their pace began to slow.

Pulling a fancy move on her that she hadn't expected, he managed to get his arms tight around her body, her back to his chest, her arms pinned to her sides. "Got you," he said into her ear.

She pulled a fancy move of her own, and he suddenly found himself flat on his back with her straddling him. "Got *you*."

Humming, Eli smoothed his hands up her thighs. "Now I like this position. Yeah, I like it a lot. Come here. I want that mouth." She leaned over and gave it to him. He groaned as her taste sank into him. It was as addictive and potent as her scent, and it soothed and aroused both him and his wolf.

Breaking the kiss with a nip to her lip, he said, "Tell me a secret."

She slanted her head. "A secret?"

"Yeah. I'm not talking deep, dark secrets. I just want you to share a little something with me. Something you haven't told anyone else. Something that only you and I will then know."

Eyes drifting to the side, she pursed her lips. "When I was a kid, I put a crushed beetle into my father's stew."

Eli lifted his brows, mouth curling. "Did he realize it?"

"Nope. I remember him pausing mid-chew and making this weird face, and then he just kept on chewing. Now you go."

Gently drawing little patterns on her thighs, Eli said, "I think I was about seven when it happened. My mom was railing Nick because I'd opened a boardgame and found torn out pages of a women's catalogue stuffed in there—pictures from the lingerie section. Nick kept saying he didn't put them there; that Roni must have done it to get him in trouble." Eli lifted his head and whispered, "I did it."

Casey's mouth quirked. "You went to your mother and acted like you'd 'found' those catalogue pages in the box, knowing she'd blame Nick?"

"Yep," he said, smiling.

"Why?"

"He broke my computer console, and I didn't feel he'd apologized well enough. He still thinks it was Roni who put the pages in the box."

Casey shook her head in mock reprimand. "You're mean."

"So are you." Eli let his gaze slowly drift over her face, hot and possessive. It amazed him that anything could be this integral to him; that just the mere sight of her could bring him pure joy.

Every layer fascinated him—the single-minded athlete, the brutal fighter, the dedicated enforcer, the fiercely loyal sister, and the soft underbelly she'd only given him peeks of. There was a distinct softness about his mate that she allowed few people to see.

"You're staring."

"Can't help it. Sometimes, I look at you and can't quite believe you're mine. But you are," he rumbled, smug and proud in equal measures. He tilted his head. "Who do you get your eyes from?"

"My maternal grandmother. I look more like her than I do either of my parents."

"What were your grandparents like?"

"I've never met two more mismatched people in all my life. She was all quirky and fun whereas he was uber serious and full of bluster. But they adored each other, and they were absolutely solid. I mean, *nothing* could have shaken their relationship. I wanted that kind of connection for myself, so I suppose it's not surprising that I was able to pick up the frequency of our mating bond so fast, but it did take me by surprise. I didn't realize I was *that* open to mating."

His brows dipped. "Why not?"

"Well, knowing there's someone out there who was born just for you is a special thing, but it's also pressure. Maybe it's just me but … I don't know, I guess I worried that I wouldn't live up to whatever expectations my true mate had of me."

Because she hadn't met the expectations of her family, Eli thought. Fuck, he loathed those bastards. "Hear me when I say this, because I need you to get it; to *believe* it. To me, you are everything. There's nothing about you that I'd change. Nothing about you that needs to change. I know your family did a number on you, baby, but the lack was never in you, it was in them. I'm not going to say you're perfect—nobody is. But you're, like, imperfectly perfect, and you're perfect for me."

Casey felt a smile split her lips. Melting, she was melting. "Dude—"

"Don't even dare call me sweet." He smoothed his hands up her thighs again. "Such perfect skin. Soft. Bitable. Flawless."

She frowned. "Flawless? I've got scars here, there, and everywhere." Some from fighting, some from soccer. She wasn't self-conscious about them— they were just a pattern on her skin, really.

He frowned right back at her. "Scars are not flaws. They can be badges of honor. They can be marks of survival. They can be proof of a person's craft. But never flaws. All these scars you have speak of your drive, skill, resilience, and fierceness."

"Now you really are being sweet—don't even deny it."

"Woman, I don't do sweet." He rolled, pinning her beneath him, and began sliding down her body. "As for the things I plan on doing to you right here …" His mouth curved into a wicked smile. "No one could ever call them sweet."

CHAPTER NINE

The whistle was blown, signaling the end of the game. Along with the rest of the spectators, Eli jumped to his feet with a cheer. On the field, the Hounds hugged each other, patted backs, and slapped asses.

Adrian blew out a breath. "That was a close game. For just a few minutes there, I thought the Hounds might lose."

Eli tossed the last of the popcorn into his mouth. "Ye have so little faith."

Adrian narrowed his eyes. "You were counting on Casey to swoop in and save the day with a kick-ass goal."

"Which was exactly what she did." The Arizona Sharks had played exceptionally well and given her team a run for their money. The Hounds were simply better.

"Casey's team might have scored sooner if one of them hadn't been unfairly sent off the field," grumbled Roni. "That ref is a goddamn joke."

"Unfairly?" echoed Marcus. "The player in question rammed the goalkeeper's head against the goal post. Four times. While roaring 'bitch' at the top of her lungs. And her reason? The keeper stopped the ball from hitting the net, which is sort of her job."

Roni shrugged. "It's not as if the keeper passed out or anything. She only bled for, like, five minutes."

Marcus stared at his mate. "Then I guess that makes it okay."

Shaya snickered. "To be fair, the ref *is* a joke. It's amazing how many fouls he just overlooked. Some of the Sharks should have been red-carded."

"Yeah, but if he'd given a red card to every player who committed a foul, there'd have been no one left on the field before the game even reached half-time," said Nick.

"Yeah, that can't be denied," Shaya allowed. "It has to be said that watching minks play soccer truly is entertaining. Oh, here comes Casey."

Eli had already noticed her jogging across the field toward the bleachers.

109

As usual, he lifted her and pressed a kiss to her mouth. "Congrats, baby. You delivered yet again." He nuzzled her neck and breathed her in. "Hmm, there it is."

"What?" Casey asked.

"The scent I've been missing all day. I'd get a little whiff of it sometimes when my shirt rustled, but it would always fade too quickly." He studied the gash on her temple, and his wolf growled as he remembered one of the Sharks "accidentally" clawing her. Only two things had stopped Eli from losing his shit—one, it didn't bleed much; two, the ref gave the Shark a yellow card, since unsheathing claws was never overlooked. "How's your head?"

Casey flapped a hand. "Fine. I was more pissed by the blonde bitch that kicked my ankle so hard she almost broke it. The ref didn't even foul her."

A growl rattled Eli's chest. "Yeah, I saw that. For a minute there, I thought you were going to elbow the ref right in the face."

"He would have deserved it."

"I agree," said Adrian, patting her shoulder. "Good game, Casey."

She smiled. "Thanks." She looked at Eli's pack mates. "And thank you all for coming." Once they were done congratulating her and praising her performance, Casey turned to Eli and said, "Just need to go take a quick shower. Meet me in the parking lot?"

"Of course," Eli told her, setting her back on her feet. He said his goodbyes to his pack mates, who then headed off. But Eli didn't move until Casey was gone from the field. Maybe it was stupid that he needed to be sure she was safely inside the building before he was willing to leave the bleachers, but whatever.

"You know, she showed a natural aptitude for soccer even as a toddler," said Adrian as he and Eli headed for the exit. "Whenever she'd come here to visit her grandparents, she'd kick a ball around with her friends or grandfather. She's always loved playing, so I figured she'd end up on the team if she put in the hard work. She did. Casey never does anything by halves. I think the team gives her a sense of belonging." He sighed. "It'll be a shame to see her leave it."

Eli felt his brows draw together. "Why would she leave?"

Adrian tossed him an impatient look. "Come on, Axton, we both know you're hoping she'll agree to move to your pack."

"She could be part of my pack and still play for the Hounds."

"You're not considering every angle. You're thinking that, hey, the competitions only occur over a short period once a year. But there's also the ten weeks of training they do running up to the games. During the competition and run-up to it, she'd be coming here daily, neglecting other aspects of her life—including you and any pack duties she might have. And she'd be investing all that time, energy, and hard work into representing a pack she's not even part of anymore.

"Her loyalty would be divided during those times. I don't mean to say that you'd ever be anything other than her number one priority, Eli. But—and take it from someone who was once in a relationship with a female who used to play for the team—there will be times when she's so focused on the training and games that you won't *feel* her priority. Your wolf sure wouldn't like that. He'd begin to see the team as a threat to the mating bond. Tell me he isn't already jealous of the attention she gives to it."

Eli couldn't claim the wolf wasn't jealous, but ... "He's not resentful of it."

"Because she's part of my pack. But if she were part of his, he wouldn't be so understanding. He'd feel that the team had no right to her time or attention."

Possibly. "Doesn't matter. If she needs soccer and the team in her life, she'll have it. He'll deal."

"I admire your optimism, but I can't say I share it. Think on it some more. Ask yourself whether you and your wolf would really be okay with it in the long-run. Be sure of your answer, because Casey needs that certainty." He walked through the exit and then patted Eli on the back. "Now take her home, make her rest. I'm sure we'll see each other at the next game, if not before."

Eli gave the Alpha a nod and then stalked through the parking lot to where his SUV was parked. Leaning against the vehicle, he pulled out his phone and skimmed through the photos he'd snapped of Casey as she'd played on the field. Her passion for soccer was clear to see, and he admired how dedicated she was to her team.

He'd meant what he told Adrian: He'd be fine with Casey continuing to play for the Hounds if she moved to his pack. But the Alpha was right; Eli would need to be positive that he'd *stay* fine with it and—

The click of heels on the pavement.

Lifting his head, Eli saw a skeletal female with very short pink hair slowly striding toward him, casually swinging her arms forward and backward. The same female he'd once caught glaring at his mate from the bleachers. *Sherryl.*

Calling on every bit of self-control he possessed, Eli kept his expression neutral and his stance relaxed. He'd scanned the crowd of spectators earlier, but he hadn't spotted her among them, and he'd hoped she hadn't attended the game. Clearly, there was no such fucking luck.

"You're Eli, Casey's mate." She cocked her head. "It's cute that you come to her games. I'm Sherryl, by the way. A friend of hers. We go way back."

His wolf snarled, unsheathing his claws. Friend? The bitch had been anything but.

"She told me a lot about you and your pack," Sherryl went on. "I hear your territory sure is a beautiful place. She's not so keen on moving there and leaving her pack or team, but I figure it's the best thing for her. Preston might not like it, considering he's a little possessive of her, but that's his problem. You've met Preston, right? He's one of the coaching staff. She and him once had a—"

"I know who he is to Casey," Eli cut in, sensing where this was going and quite frankly pissed that she thought she could play little games with him. "More importantly, I know who he *isn't* to Casey. I also know all about you and the petty threats you've made. Not sure why you look so surprised that she told me."

Cheeks reddening, Sherryl took two steps toward him. "It doesn't bother you that she slept with her cousin's mate? You're okay with that?"

Eli pushed away from the SUV, gratified by the glint of unease in her eyes. She wasn't quite as sure of herself as she liked to appear. "What bothers me is that you think you can fuck with my mate. *Why* you'd think something so damn stupid, I haven't a clue. But if you have any sense of self-preservation, you'll quit your games and stay away from her."

Sherryl jutted out her chin. "You think you scare me? Touch me just once and I'll have my entire pack crawling all over your territory within the hour."

"I *know* I scare you. And I know Casey does, too."

Sherryl shook her head. "She might think she's hot shit, but she's a nobody."

"If you really thought that, you'd pity her, laugh at her. Instead, you feel compelled to fuck with her life and piss all over it—and you don't even care who might get hurt in the process. That's because you know that the 'nobody' is you."

Her face twisted into a bitter scowl. "Bastard."

"You reek of envy. Do you know that? It's true. You know Casey's better than you—a better player, a better person—and you hate her for it. You're rotting on the inside, and it shows on the outside."

They both stilled at the sound of footsteps coming toward them. Eli knew the rhythm of that purposeful walk; knew it was Casey. Apparently, so did Sherryl, because she grinned and tried to plant a kiss on his mouth. He shoved her away with a growl.

Laughing, she turned to Casey. "Sorry. I can't help wanting to get a taste of that mouth. I'll bet it's got some skills."

"She's baiting you, Casey," warned Eli. "She wants you to attack so she can go cry to her Alphas and set her pack on yours." He gave her a look that said, "Don't fall for it."

Sherryl laughed again. "Oh, she won't do that, Eli. No. Casey doesn't want my Alphas asking questions that might lead to me telling them about her night with Preston. That news would get back to dear ole Mallory. And oh, that would be bad. Very, very bad. Isn't that right, Casey?"

Eli watched his mate carefully, impressed she was able to leash the ferocious anger that rippled down their bond—especially since her mink was no doubt tugging at the reins, wanting to lunge and maul the female who'd touched her mate. Casey stood unnaturally still, her gaze eerily blank and so disturbingly cold it could chill a person right down to the bone. And that stare was fixed intently on Sherryl, whose smile began to slip from her face.

"Come on, Casey, I'm just having some fun," said Sherryl. "No need to be so serious. It's not like I haven't kissed any of your other boyfriends, jeez."

Again, Casey didn't respond. Just stared at the other female, utterly still. The air thickened with tension and suppressed anger.

"So serious," Sherryl mocked, but she nervously combed her fingers through her short hair.

Casey ever so slowly tilted her head. Her words came out just as slowly when she asked, voice flat, "This really seemed advisable to you? You didn't have a single moment where you thought, hey, trying to kiss someone else's mate will be the height of stupidity?"

"Well, it's not like I can kiss my own, is it?"

"You know, a part of me used to feel sorry for you. No one should have to bury their true mate—especially when they're just a kid. I wouldn't wish that on anyone."

Sherryl's nostrils flared. "Bitch, I don't need your sympathy."

"That's good, because you no longer have it." Wicked fast, Casey closed the gap between them and pushed into her space, going nose to nose with her. "I've had enough of your shit to last me a lifetime, and I'm absolutely done dealing with it. You don't get to mess with my life just because you hate your own—I'm no one's whipping boy. And if you think I'll tolerate you offloading your brand of bullshit onto *my mate,* you're out of your freaking mind. Never again, Sherryl," she snarled, eyes flashing mink. "You never again even *try* to touch him."

"Or what? You'll smack me down?" Sherryl snickered. "Like I told Eli, you won't risk me telling my Alphas your precious little secret."

"Since the dead can't talk, I won't have that worry."

Sherryl's eyes flickered, and she took a shaky, involuntary step back.

"You touch, bother, or fuck with Eli again," Casey went on, "I'll kill you. You go telling tales to Mallory and hurt her just to be a vindictive bitch, I'll kill you. I will, and I won't lose a second's sleep over it. That's not a threat, it's a promise. A promise you need to heed, because I won't just kill you, Sherryl, I will shit motherfucking fury all over your goddamn bony ass—and you won't even see me coming."

Sherryl swallowed and took another step back. Casey knew it wasn't so much the threat that had rattled her, it was that Casey had *dared* to threaten her. Sherryl hadn't been trying to bait her as Eli thought. No, she'd simply believed she could do whatever the fuck she liked, certain that Casey *wouldn't* attack. Sherryl had been sure she had the upper hand and that possessing Casey's secret gave her power. Now the bitch was realizing that that wasn't so true after all.

Her mink's muscles quivered as she glared at the other female, back arched, claws out, scraping the ground with her feet. She wanted to dive at the little bitch and rain fresh hell on her. "If you push this, Sherryl, it will only end one way," Casey cautioned.

"Yeah, with Mallory kicking your ass," Sherryl spat, backing up again.

"No, with you dead."

Sherryl shot both her and Eli a snarl before pivoting on her heel and striding away.

Once they were alone, Eli slowly crossed to Casey and splayed his hand on her back. "You okay?"

She took a long breath. "Yeah."

"I know you probably don't want to hear this, but I have the feeling that you *will* have to take her down one day—and not in a way where she gets back up."

"So do I." Rolling her shoulders, Casey turned to face him. "But I'm going to hold out hope, however pointless it may be, that she chooses to heed what I said."

"There's nothing wrong with hoping."

Casey gave his hand a little squeeze, silently thanking him for his support. "I appreciate that you stood back and let me deal with her—I know that wasn't easy for you." She'd sensed how hard his protective instincts had hammered at him to intervene.

"I won't lie, baby, if she'd made even *one* aggressive move toward you, I'd have been on the bitch before either of you could blink. You're thinking I never would have hurt her because she's female. You're wrong. I'm capable of more fucked-up things than that."

"You don't eat people, fuck animals, go on killing sprees, or rape and pillage—that's good enough for me."

"We're back to that?"

"It would seem so," she said, feeling her anger drain away. Just having her mate—so solid, dauntless, and unflappable—right there, filling her senses and emanating a warm yet dark protective energy, was enough to steady and soothe Casey. His supreme air of unshakable cool always rubbed off on her and settled her mink. "By the way, don't think I don't know you're hard as a rock right now."

A smile tugged at his mouth. "Watching you shoot that bitch's shit down, owning your strength and defending our mating … I ain't gonna lie, it was a total turn-on."

She rolled her eyes. "You ready to go?"

"I'm ready." He kissed her forehead, draped his arm over her shoulders, and led her toward his SUV. "Come on. I'm taking you back to my lodge so I can feed and fuss over you."

She *felt* his need to cosset and take care of her; to tuck her away somewhere safe, away from Sherryl and anyone else who might threaten her. And although her highly dominant nature bristled at the thought of being mollycoddled in any way, she didn't fight him. Knew he needed this. "What are you cooking this time?"

"You'll see."

As he drove them to his territory with one of his big hands splayed on her thigh, Casey found herself marveling over how quickly and effortlessly he'd become part of her everyday life. Really, he'd slotted into her world like an Eli-shaped spot had been waiting just for him to come along and fill it. Which was sort of the case.

Maybe it was because they had similar duties and responsibilities that their worlds seemed to just fit together seamlessly without disrupting the other's schedule. Of course, she didn't doubt that he'd take up more of her time if he could. She knew he didn't like sharing her attention with even a soccer ball. It was kind of cute.

She also knew they needed to have a long conversation about which of them would switch packs. But each time she broached the subject, he gave her that "there's no rush to decide" speech. She recognized it as a stalling tactic, of course. He was buying himself time, hoping he could make her fall for his territory. Her mate was sneaky that way.

She hadn't complained, though, because he'd also done things such as work enforcer-shifts with her on her territory and explored every inch of it, getting a taste of what his life would be like if he were to switch to her pack.

Although he seemed content enough while there and she believed he'd fit in her pack just fine, one thing bothered her—if he transferred there, he wouldn't be able to keep the position of Head Enforcer. Adrian had told her that he'd be more than happy to have Eli as an enforcer but that he couldn't bump aside his present Head Enforcer without good reason.

Eli wore his dominance in a very subtle way, but there was no missing how close to an alpha he was. Although he had no aspirations to lead a pack, he'd need a position in the hierarchy that provided him with some level of leadership and authority. His wolf would need it. They'd never have that in her pack, which meant she couldn't foresee either man or wolf being truly happy there.

The thought of transferring to another pack made her chest tighten, especially as it might mean leaving the Hounds. While she believed Adrian would allow her to remain part of the team, she wasn't so sure that Eli or his pack would like it.

She frowned as he grabbed his phone when they stopped at a red light. His thumbs were deft and fast as they tapped the screen. "Everything okay?" Because he had a very serious look on his face.

"Fine," he said, placing the phone back in the cupholder. "I was just texting Nick. My pack mates are now under strict orders not to call, text, or visit us tonight so you can get the rest you need. Don't tell me you're not that tired. I can sense how exhausted you are."

Chest warming, Casey smiled. "You're good for me, you know."

He squeezed her thigh. "Just as you're good for me."

"So … after I've eaten and rested, are you up for fucking me into oblivion again?"

"That can definitely be arranged."

Her nipples tight, her pussy throbbing, Casey eyed Eli warily as he stalked around the bed wearing nothing but a wicked smile. *Let's play a little game,* he'd said. *Whoever breaks first has to submit to the other,* he'd said.

And what had he meant by "break?" Well, they each had to sit in a chair and remain still for an entire minute while the other teased and tantalized them—if they *did* move, they lost the game. If no one moved, they kept on going until someone did.

Simple. Easy. Fun. She'd figured he'd break in no time at all.

During the first round, she'd not only kissed, licked, bit, and stroked every sensitive spot he possessed, she'd worked his cock with her hands and tongue … but she hadn't sucked him off, and she'd known the torture of that alone had killed him. But he'd held out, the bastard, and subjected her to some torture of his own.

She'd also held out, though, and so they'd moved on to the second round. And the third. And the fourth.

During the fifth, as she'd finger-fucked herself right in front of him, he'd looked so close to losing control and reaching out to touch her … but he hadn't, the awkward fucker. And when he'd then had his turn, she'd realized it had been completely dumb to finger-fuck herself, because she'd made her body so desperate to come that she hadn't been able to resist gripping his hair and pulling him closer when he fluttered his tongue *far* too lightly over her clit.

So, yeah, she'd lost. *Lost.* That was bad enough. Worse, as part of the whole submission thing, he'd wanted her wrists tied to the bed.

Every cell in her body had said, *hell, no.* Obeying him was one thing. Letting him tie her down and make her completely vulnerable to him was something else altogether.

But he'd given her that hurt face and asked, "Don't you trust me?"

"Well, yeah," she'd replied.

"Then lie on the bed, relax, and let me make you feel good. You know I'd never do anything you didn't want."

She *did* know that, which was why she'd conceded her loss of the game and done what he'd asked. To her surprise, it hadn't dampened her arousal in the slightest. In fact, there was something almost heady about being unable to move; about being able to take only what he chose to give her. Still ... "I feel like a pagan sacrifice."

"You look hot as hell." His gaze raked over her. "I am a lucky son of a bitch. So much to taste. Touch. Mark." He moved to kneel on the bed between her thighs. "There are so many things I could do to you right now."

Oh God, he was gonna drag this out, wasn't he? "Why do you want me tied up?" she asked as he planted his hands either side of her head, bracing himself over her.

He nipped at her lip. "I want you to feel owned. Helpless. *Mine.*" He traced her mouth with the tip of his tongue. "I want to use you. Like you're my very own personal toy."

And then he was kissing her. Hard. Wet. Rough. He consumed her mouth with so much hunger and possessiveness that it sent her thoughts scattering and wound her body even tighter.

He trailed kisses down her neck and then bit her claiming mark. "I'll bet I can make you come within five minutes."

"Obviously."

"But I'd be sitting all the way over there in that chair near the wall. I wouldn't be touching you."

Casey's brow creased. "What, you think you can *talk* me into coming?"

"Maybe."

She narrowed her eyes. "If it doesn't work, you have to let me go, and then I get to tie *you* up."

He thought about it for a few seconds. "All right. But if it *does* work, you stay right here like this ... and you suck me off."

Not seeing how he could possibly make her come without touching her, she said, "Go for it."

Smiling, he slid a hand between her breasts, along her stomach, and down to cup her pussy. "All mine."

She sighed happily as he slid two fingers inside her and ... Her eyes widened. "What's that? Seriously, what the hell is that?"

"Oh, yeah, I forgot to mention the vibrator. It's inside you now. Not sure if you can tell, but it's egg-shaped. And this here in my hand is a remote control. See, that little silicone device inside you pulses and vibrates at different levels of intensity and speed. So, yeah, this is gonna be fun."

"You are such a fucking asshole! This isn't fair!"

Eli's lips twitched. "I'll just be over there." He left the bed and repositioned the chair near the foot of the bed. He sank into the chair, humming at the perfect view he had of her pussy—so pretty and plump and pink, it glistened with her juices. His full, hard cock pulsed, aching to be inside her.

He switched on the vibrator and smiled as her body did a little jerk.

"Relax, baby, just enjoy it. Feel good?" He already knew the answer to that, because a throaty moan slipped out of her. And another. And another.

He played with the different vibration patterns until he found one that had her squirming, groaning, and struggling against her binds. All the while, he fisted his aching cock, wrestling with the urge to join her on that bed and suck on her clit. "We'd have so much fun with this in public. Maybe at a restaurant. I could make you come right there at the table, and no one would even have a clue."

Feeling that she was close to coming, he upped the intensity level on the vibrator. "Let me see you come, baby. Do it for me. *Now.*" She arched. Moaned. Shook. And then she imploded, and an echo of her orgasm hit him through their bond, making his dick impossibly harder. "That's my good girl."

Eli switched off the vibrator, rose from the chair, and placed the remote on the dresser. He kissed his way up her quivering body as he climbed on the bed, pausing to lash at her nipple with his tongue. "I figured you'd like this," he said, carefully pulling out the vibrator. "You came within five minutes. You know what that means."

Her eyes fluttered open. "Tricky little shit, aren't you?"

Chuckling, he pressed a kiss to her throat. "Yeah, I am."

"I'm gonna shove that thing up your ass one day, and then we'll see how much you still like it."

"My ass? Sorry. Doesn't appeal to me. But your ass? Ah, that could be interesting. Thanks for giving me that idea."

"Because your filthy mind would *never* have thought of it all on its own."

He chuckled again. "Well, you lost the bet. Now it's time for you to pay up." He shuffled up the bed until his cock bobbed in front of her face. Slipping his hand under her head, he lifted it just right. "Open your mouth."

Instead, she blew over the head of his cock. It twitched in response, and a tiny shiver wracked his spine.

Growling, he dug his fingers into her scalp. "Open." The moment she did, he surged forward and thrust into her gorgeously hot mouth, just as he'd been aching to do since the night he first found her. He groaned. It felt better than he'd imagined and, fuck, just the sight of her plump lips wrapped around his dick was enough to make his balls tighten.

He wasn't going to last long. Not when he was already so close to exploding, thanks to the game they'd played earlier. But he'd damn well relish every second he could hold out for.

"Now I'm going to fuck this pretty mouth I own. And I'm not going to stop until you can feel my come dripping down your throat."

He pumped his hips, riveted by the sight of his cock sliding in and out of her mouth. She kept the suction tight, gliding her tongue along the underside of his shaft. "Yeah, that's it, suck hard for me. Fucking beautiful, aren't you, baby? *My* baby." His cock hit the back of her throat, and he groaned. She didn't try to pull back, she swallowed him deeper. *Fuck.*

Feeling the light prick of his claws in her scalp, Casey moaned. He must have liked the sensation, because his cock throbbed in her mouth and he gave an extra hard thrust. She sucked even harder, determined that it would be the best blowjob he'd ever had.

Spike after spike of carnal pleasure rippled down her bond as she sucked and licked, tracing every ridge and vein with her tongue and swirling it around his long shaft. His whispered praise sank into her bones while every hungry growl hit her in her core.

"So fucking good," Eli rumbled, feeling his orgasm creep up on him. Her eyes—glazed over with need—locked with his, and he felt that sex-drunk look all the way to his balls.

Spiced with arousal, her potent scent twined around him and filled his lungs. He could almost taste it, and that only made him and his wolf more crazed for her. They needed to claim her mouth just as they'd claimed her pussy—it was a primal thing, and there was no fighting it.

Fisting her hair, he drove faster into her mouth and slipped his other hand around her neck. "I want to feel your throat work as you swallow my come." Tightening her lips, she sucked even harder, and the breath slammed out of his lungs. Then she hummed, and the vibration seemed to shoot along his dick and zip up his spine. And like that, he was gone.

Heart pounding, he exploded with a growl. "Fuck, yeah, take it." His thighs quivered as his dick pulsed inside his mate's mouth over and over, claiming it with his come. And, yeah, that had been the best blowjob of his fucking life.

Throat dry, Eli pulled back. "Open. Show me."

Understanding, Casey opened her mouth wide, showing him that she'd swallowed every drop. She wasn't gonna lie, she got a little kick out of how hard he was breathing. His eyes went all lazy with satisfaction, which never failed to make a delicious warmth bloom in her lower stomach.

He stroked the tips of his fingers down the column of her throat. "Good girl. Now you get rewarded."

"Untie me first."

He gave her a mock frown, sliding down her body. "You said you trust me."

"I do."

"Then just lie back and enjoy."

His mouth clamped around her pussy, and Casey arched into him with a gasp. His fingers dug into her hips as he held her still, feasting and growling and making her burn from the inside out.

"I don't like that other men have had your taste on their tongue," he rumbled. "Don't like that they've played with my pussy. And it *is* mine. It was always mine." He went back to eating her out. That blessed tongue licked, flicked, lapped, and thrust, driving her higher and higher.

She didn't know why being tied up made it all so much hotter, but it did. Feeling so vulnerable … Something about that seemed to make every nerve ending in her body so much more sensitive. "*Eli.*"

"Right here, baby." He pumped his tongue inside her and closed his hands around her breasts. He gave them a possessive squeeze that was just shy of painful—that rough touch was all it took. Her pussy rippled around his tongue and she came with a choked cry.

Eli draped his body over hers, pressing his throbbing cock against her clit, and almost shuddered at just the feel of his skin settling over hers. "Can't seem to get enough of your taste." He scooped some of her cream out of her pussy and idly painted her nipple with it.

"Eli—"

"You know what I want," he said. She gave him her throat. "Good girl." He sucked her wet nipple into his mouth and slammed his cock into her pussy, forcing his way past swollen muscles that rippled and contracted around him. "*Fuck,* baby."

Casey wrapped her legs tight around him as he rode her hard. "Rode her" wasn't really the best term. Exuding pure male power, he ferociously rammed in and out of her like he was caught in a frenzy. Brutal. Frantic. So impossibly deep she should have felt him in her throat.

After so many orgasms, her body should have been spent. It wasn't. The friction began to build again fast, making her arch and writhe and pull half-heartedly at her bindings—there was no give in them, which only fired the carnal need coursing through her.

He groaned. "Every time you struggle, your pussy squeezes my cock." He paused, hooked her legs over his shoulders, and started slamming into her again. "You ready to come for me?"

She moaned her assent, more than ready.

He slipped his thumb between her folds and circled her clit. "Then come."

Her body, trained to respond to him, gave him exactly what he wanted. Casey's back bowed, and a hoarse scream tore out of her throat, almost drowning out his growl. He sank his teeth into her shoulder as he slammed home once more and exploded deep inside her.

Casey lay there, shuddering, her eyes closed, drifting in a blissful fog … until her mink started shoving at her, demanding her attention; demanding she acknowledge something important. Opening her eyes, Casey took in a deep breath. And froze. "You smell that?"

Eli's nostrils flared. "Our scents have mixed."

"The bond … it's more intense. More *there.*"

"It's progressing," he said, feeling a smile tug at his mouth. His satisfaction ran soul-deep.

"What do you think triggered it?"

Eli thought about it for a moment. "Maybe it was that you trusted me and submitted, despite how hard it was for you." She hadn't just allowed him to tie her up, she'd sucked him off and swallowed his come, which furthered his claim on her on a sheer primitive level.

Speaking of her being tied up … Eli withdrew his cock, intending to release her, not wanting her uncomfortable. "I don't like seeing my come leak out of you. I want it to stay inside you. Want it to mark what's mine." Maybe even put a baby in her, though it might be considered too soon. He freed her wrists and then massaged her arms until they were as loose and languid as the rest of her.

As they then lay on their sides facing each other, he pulled her close. "Love that you wear me on your skin now. Love that everyone will know just by your scent alone that you're taken."

Casey might have rolled her eyes if she wasn't feeling the same way. She'd never been possessive until Eli. Hadn't known she could *be* this possessive of anything or anyone. Maybe the intensity of it would tone down once their bond fully snapped into place and made her feel more settled and secure in their mating. Then again, maybe not.

"My mink is very happy with this new development, by the way."

"So is my wolf." Little bumps rose on Eli's skin as she nuzzled his neck. He held her tighter. She smelled of him, sex, and their bed. Smelled of home.

She'd appeared in his life when he'd least expected it and, in no time at all, had become an integral part of it. He hadn't had to adjust to her presence, because it was like she'd always been there. Everything had clicked into place the moment they mated.

Despite that they'd never met prior to that night, there had never been any awkwardness between them or any hesitation to invade the other's space. In fact, they were so perfectly in tune with each other that it should have been scary.

Bringing her into his life had been effortless. It was like she was written into his soul and inscribed into his bones. And it gave him a whole new understanding of just what his mother had gone through.

Staring at his mate, Eli genuinely didn't think he'd be able to survive losing her. He wouldn't care to. Wouldn't want to exist without her. Wasn't even sure if he could. And he knew for a fact that if he *did* somehow manage to survive the loss of her, he'd be a shell of a man. An absolute fucking wreck. He wouldn't be able to find any enjoyment in life, because his world would lose color and warmth and vibrancy.

"Nothing can ever happen to you," he said.

She splayed her hand on his chest. "Nothing will, because you'd never let it."

Damn fucking straight. Pulling her closer, he kissed her forehead. "Sleep, baby," he said softly. "Dream of me. Then you'll be nice and wet when you wake up, ready for me to take you again."

She smiled. "I'll see what I can do."

CHAPTER TEN

"Closer."

"Dude, I'm practically fused to the side of your body."

"Not close enough." Eli pulled her onto his lap and settled his chin at the crook of her neck. "Better." Using the heel of his foot, he rocked the porch swing, enjoying the small solitude he'd have with his mate before the day officially began.

They'd already been for their morning run—he'd actually grown to enjoy their jogs, although that was mostly because he liked seeing her delectable ass encased in the little running shorts she wore. More, he liked whipping off the shorts afterward so he could take her against the tiled wall of the shower.

Sunlight peeked through the towering, weathered trees and glimmered off the long grass. The breeze was light but cool. The birds perched in the nearby tree chirped and fluttered their wings. Wolves playfully barked in the distance.

Nuzzling his mate, Eli breathed in their combined scent, letting it override the smells of pine needles, clean air, and moss. His wolf rubbed up against her, more secure in their mating now that their scents had mixed and she wore him on her skin. The beast wasn't happy that she'd soon be leaving them, though—he'd no doubt sulk until she returned, just as he usually did.

Eli slid his hand under her shirt and danced his fingers up her belly. "Damn, I love it when you're not wearing a bra." It meant he could now idly pet, cup, and doodle patterns on her soft, creamy breasts.

"You know," began Casey, "I don't understand how the human race can invent AI, endless NASA shit, and do all kinds of other weird and wonderful stuff … but they can't invent a bra that's comfortable. It's like they haven't even tried."

"They don't have their priorities right."

"Exactly, thank you." Sighing, she went back to admiring their surroundings. "It's a real pretty view you have here, Eli."

It was. Especially with the faint mist that had gathered around the mountains, hazing the trees, river, and meadow. "It could be your view. *Our* view."

She tensed. "Eli—"

"Just hear me out a sec." He turned her so that she was straddling him. Now that their bond had progressed a step, it was time they had this conversation. He'd already rehearsed it in his head several times. "I won't push you to transfer to my pack if you don't think you can be happy here. But let me just say a few things."

She gave a slow nod.

Eli tucked a loose strand of her hair behind her ear. "I know you love your territory. I get that it was the only place you ever felt safe growing up. And I understand that it would be hard for you to leave the people who gave you refuge when you needed it. But, baby, you don't need that refuge anymore. *I'm* your point of safety now.

"There's your soccer team to consider, yes. But Adrian will let you continue playing for the Hounds no matter where you are. I'd never try to interfere with that or ask you leave the team. *Never.* Soccer is all tied up in who you are.

"You love being an enforcer, I know. But you could be an enforcer here. You're *needed* here. We don't have as many enforcers as Adrian does, and our pack will keep on growing, so it needs more people to guard it. I won't lie, I'd feel like I was deserting my pack mates if I left, but I will leave if it's what you want."

She touched the side of his face. "I know you will, but you don't need to."

Eli blinked. "You'll move here?" His wolf went completely still, waiting on her answer. "Seriously?"

"Seriously," said Casey. "You'd never be content in my pack, since you'd have to be demoted to an enforcer. You'd also miss your family, and I know how important they are to you. I don't have family who'd miss me at the Craven Pack, so there's no one holding me there. Other than my teammates, of course. I hope you mean it when you say you wouldn't ask me to leave the Hounds, because it would hurt like hell to do it."

"You think I would do anything that would cause you pain?"

"No."

He caught her hand and kissed her palm. "Then you know I meant what I said."

She bit her lip. "Do you think Nick would take me on as an enforcer? I'd need a position, Eli. I wouldn't cope without one."

"You don't have to tell me that. And yes, I do think he would." Eli played with the end of her braid, tempted to untie it so he could run his fingers through that sleek hair. "He'd be stupid not to, given how strong, capable, and fierce you are. My brother is a lot of things, but not stupid."

She took a deep breath. "Well then, if Nick is truly okay with appointing me as an enforcer and nobody insists on me leaving the Hounds, I'll switch to your pack."

As both satisfaction and relief settled over him and his wolf, Eli rested his forehead against hers. "Thank you, baby."

"Thank you for being willing to put my happiness before yours."

"I'll always do that. Always." Eli pulled her close and pressed a long, lingering kiss to her mouth. "When?"

"Hmm?"

"When will you move here?"

"After the games are over. Don't pout. There are only two left to go."

"I know. But I'm selfish, I want you close." He rubbed his nose against hers. "I want you here with me. I've wanted it since I first found you."

"And you'll have it once the games are over." Casey almost laughed at his frown. He always seemed confused and surprised when she didn't let him have his way. Her mink found it sort of cute. The animal had no issues with switching packs; her loyalty was to Eli, not the Craven minks. Plus, the animal liked Eli's land and preferred his lodge to her apartment.

"I want us sharing the same space," Eli went on. "I want your things mixed with mine."

Casey almost rolled her eyes. He was so spoiled. "And they will be, just not yet."

"I don't like the idea that if you ever need me throughout the day, it would take me time to reach you."

"That could apply even if we were living together," Casey pointed out. There would be times when she'd bend, but there would also be times when she'd dig her heels in and refuse to budge. He'd walk all over her otherwise. "Look, leaving isn't going to be easy for me, Eli. As you said, Craven Pack territory was my refuge, the only place I felt safe and accepted growing up. I already have plenty of things distracting me from the games—Miles, Ignacio, Sherryl. I don't want anything else shaking my focus.

"You know this isn't a simple hobby for me. I didn't train this hard and long to fuck it up at the last minute and let my teammates down by not being at my best."

Eli squeezed her nape, getting it. "All right."

"You need to talk this over with your Alphas first and be sure they're okay with me joining your pack."

He snorted. "Are you kidding? They keep bugging me to ask you to move here."

Casey suspected that was mostly because they didn't want *him* moving to *her* territory, but it was still nice that they wanted her there, whatever the reason. "You sure they'll be fine with it? I know Shaya's happy for you, but sometimes I get the feeling that our mating makes her ... not sad exactly, but

... I don't know, I can't really describe it."

Eli rubbed her thigh. "It's not about us. You know it's not common for true mates to recognize each other at first sight, right? Many things can block the frequency of the bond, which means some people can go a long time without sensing it. But Nick and Shaya recognized each other straight off. The thing is ... Nick initially walked away from her."

Casey blinked. "Walked ... he walked away?"

"Yes. It's a long story, which I'll share with you another time because we've got a busy morning ahead of us. He did it thinking it was best for her. Months later, he realized his mistake, tracked her down, and did what was necessary to fix his fuckup. Luckily, she forgave him. You've seen for yourself how happy they are. But hearing that I claimed you instantly, with no hesitation whatsoever, must remind her of the simple and painful fact that he didn't do that with her."

"Ah. If you'd walked away from me that night, I think it would have killed something in me. I think I also might have killed you. I'm not as forgiving as Shaya."

"You say that as if I *could* have walked away from you." He cupped her jaw and breezed his thumb over her lower lip. "From the second I realized you were mine, you became the most important thing to me. I honestly don't know where Nick found the will to stay away from Shaya. If what he told me was true, she did initially try to take his head off with a bat."

"Can't say I blame her. I'd have done a lot worse in her position. But then, I'm not as good a person as she is."

Eli smoothed his hand up her back and tugged her closer. "You might be a proper badass, but you're all soft and squishy on the inside. Don't think I haven't seen you passing candy to the pups when you think no one's paying attention. Adrian told me about some of the things you take upon yourself to do for your pack mates, like checking on or doing favors for the elderly or pregnant members." He almost smiled at her blush.

"Until you came into my life, I had spare time—it was no biggie to spend some of that time helping the more vulnerable members."

"Soft and squishy," he repeated in a whisper.

"Whatever."

He chuckled. "Back to what we were talking about earlier ... If you need time before moving here, I'll give it to you, but I can't promise I won't grumble about it when the mood strikes me."

"Knowing you as well as I do, I wouldn't expect anything different."

Eli kissed her. "Let's tell Nick and Shaya about your decision, and then we'll need to tell Adrian."

"Okay."

He smiled. "Okay."

A short while later, Eli and Casey sat opposite the Alpha pair in Nick's office. Eli could almost feel his brother's relief when she revealed that she was willing to switch to their pack. He also felt Casey's surprise when Shaya pumped her fist and hissed, "Yes!" Nick only rolled his eyes at his mate.

"We really appreciate you agreeing to join our pack, Casey," said Shaya. "We know it can't have been an easy decision to make, and we hope you know that we don't just want you here so that we can keep Eli with us. You're our family now, and family is important to us."

Casey swallowed. "Thank you. I will be continuing to play for the Hounds—I hope you can support that."

"It's not a problem for us," Nick told her, hooking his arm over the back of his mate's chair.

"There will be times when my pack commitments might collide with my training sessions or the games themselves," Casey pointed out.

"We'll make it work." Nick held up a hand, adding, "And before you say it, yes, I do know you'll need a place in the hierarchy. Adrian told me about the skills you possess and the amount of training and experience you've had. He said I'd be a complete fool not to welcome you into my ranks as an enforcer. The things I've heard about you from Eli supports that theory. My brother's Head Enforcer; I trust his judgement. If he says you have what it takes to be an enforcer here—and no, he wouldn't say that simply because you're his mate—I believe him."

The Alpha pair weren't so happy to hear that Casey wouldn't *immediately* join the pack, and Eli figured they worried she'd change her mind at some point. But they claimed to understand her reasons, and he highly suspected Shaya would still arrange a "welcome to the pack" party—if for no other reason than to communicate to Casey that she was wanted there.

After the meeting was over, Eli drove Casey to Adrian's house, which was located deep in Craven Pack territory. The Alpha welcomed them inside with an easy smile, but that smile faded when Casey shared the reason for the visit.

Settled in an armchair, Adrian blew out a breath. "I can't say this is a surprise. I'll be sorry to lose you, Casey. You're one of my best enforcers, and this will be a heavy loss to the others. I can proudly say that, collectively, my enforcers function like a well-oiled machine. Taking away a piece of that machinery will rock them. But I can see why you've decided to leave, and I can't disapprove of you putting your mate first." His gaze cut to Eli. "You're a lucky man, Axton. I hope you know that."

"I do," said Eli, his arm draped over the back of the sofa, where she sat beside him.

"I also hope your pack will see her value. Casey's meant for better things than hanging around, seeing to this and that. She's an enforcer straight down to the bone."

"I know that better than anyone."

"Yes, I suppose you do."

"I want to continue playing for the Hounds," Casey told the Alpha. "Eli has promised to be supportive of that, and Nick has assured me that it won't be an issue. I'm hoping it won't be one for you either."

Adrian looked at Eli. "You and your brother are *both* certain you can fully support this in the long-run?"

"We're sure," said Eli.

"Good." Adrian slid his gaze back to Casey. "I have no problems with it. I suspect your team would go on strike if I didn't allow you to remain part of it anyway."

Smiling, she gave a short nod. "Thank you."

"When will you be packing up?" Adrian asked.

"Not until after the games are over."

"Ah. You don't want the emotional upheaval to throw you off your game—no pun intended."

"Exactly."

The Alpha shrugged. "Well, there's no rush on my end."

"Until I officially leave the pack, I want to continue working my enforcer shifts."

"You think I'd stop you? I'll be happy to—" Adrian frowned as a fist hammered on the front door. He stood. "Excuse me."

The fist pounded on it twice more before the Alpha even stepped out into the hallway. Casey exchanged a look with Eli.

The hinges of the front door creaked, and then Adrian snapped, "What the fuck is your—?"

"*Where is the little bitch?*"

Hearing Mallory's voice, Casey glanced at Eli again. She was sure they were both thinking the same thing: *she knows.* Fuck, fuck, fuck.

"Calm down, honey," urged Preston.

"Don't you tell me to calm the fuck down, asshole!" Mallory yelled. "I know she's here—the wolf's SUV is outside!"

Adrian cursed, and then high heels click-clacked down the hardwood floor of the hallway, getting louder and louder.

Squaring her shoulders, Casey stood, readying herself. She'd let her cousin get one hit in, she decided. Just one. After all, the other female had a right to her wrath.

Mallory stormed into the room, and her eyes blazed as they fixed on Casey. "You *bitch*," she spat, closing in on her fast. "You fucking, fucking, *fucking* bitch."

Growling, Eli slid in front of Casey, shielding her. "No," he told Mallory, who stumbled to a halt.

Mallory bared her teeth. "Step aside."

"It's fine, Eli," said Casey with a sigh. "Let her pass."

"No," he told Casey, though his eyes remained on the female in front of him, "because I know you'll let her hit you, even though you don't deserve it."

Mallory fisted her hands. "She'll *totally* deserve it."

"What the hell is this all about?" demanded Adrian, sidling up to her.

"Oh, you don't know?" Mallory let out a bitter, humorless laugh. "Well then, let me tell you." She jabbed her finger at Casey. "That bitch *fucked my mate!*"

Standing behind Mallory, Preston rubbed at his temple. "It was one night," he told the Alpha. "It happened before Mallory and I started dating."

"*Days* before." Mallory's eyes narrowed to little slits of fury. "Bitch, you should've told me! I had to hear about it from Sherryl. *Sherryl.*"

"That's *my* fault; I asked Casey not to say anything," said Preston. He grabbed his mate's arm, but she shook him off. "It's not Casey you should be pissed at. It's me. This whole thing is on me."

"Oh, is that right?"

"Yes. I put her in an impossible situation. If I'd thought for even a second that I'd come to feel even *half* of what I feel for you now, I'd have told you about the one-night stand in the very beginning. But I didn't, and then I was scared to tell you because *I didn't want to lose you.*"

"You think that makes it okay?" Mallory propped her clenched hands on her hips. "Tell me the truth. Did you love her?"

"No. My ego was bruised, even though I knew she was right that it would be a bad idea for a member of the team to get involved with one of the Hounds' staff. That's all it was."

"Then how come Sherryl told me you were so determined to change Casey's mind that you thought you'd try making her jealous? If it had worked, you'd have left me for her, wouldn't you? *Wouldn't you?*"

Preston shoved his hand into his hair. "I'd like to think not. Honestly, I didn't really believe it would change her mind—she's more stubborn than anyone I've ever met."

"But you wanted to hurt her, and so you used me to do it."

Adrian stepped between the couple and shot her a pointed look. "Not sure you're in a position to judge him too harshly on that one, Mallory. How many times have you done such a thing to others? Seems like karma came knocking on your door."

She gaped at her Alpha. "Now hang on a minute—"

"You've tested the endurance of your bedsprings with a lot of males in this pack," Adrian forged on. "Do you think that's any easier for Preston to live with than this will be for you? I don't recollect any of those males being his cousins, but I know that at least one of them is his friend."

Mallory winced. "He still should have told me. *She* should have told me."

"Like you told Casey about the times you slept with her ex-boyfriends? And what about the times you lured males away from her?"

Mallory's mouth bobbed open and closed. "That's different. None of them were her mate."

"Just as Preston wasn't your mate back then. He was a single male, free to do as he pleased. He didn't betray you."

"But he did lie to me. They both did."

As his mate's guilt traveled down their bond, Eli cut in, glaring at Mallory, "You do realize all this is fucking pointless, don't you? What he did was an asshole-move—I'm with you on that one. But you're both exactly where you want to be. If Casey *had* originally told you about what happened, you would've broken things off with him—presuming you even believed her— and you wouldn't be mated to him now. You might be pissed at him, but you wouldn't want to undo that even if you could."

"Eli's right," said Adrian. "It's *Sherryl* you should be angry with."

Some of the staunch leached out of Mallory, who suddenly looked unbelievably sad. "She was laughing when she told me. *Laughing.*"

No doubt *feeling* the extent of his mate's pain, Preston squeezed his eyes tightly shut for a moment. "She doesn't find any of it funny, Mallory. She's bitter and angry and it's twisting her up inside. She laughed because she wanted to get you all riled up and itching for a fight."

"Well, it worked." Mallory looked at Eli. "I noticed you don't seem surprised by any of this. Casey told you?"

"She told me," Eli confirmed. "At the time, she was agonizing about the fact that she hadn't told *you.* I'll say to you what I said to her—there was nothing to gain from her telling you. All it would have done was hurt you, which was the one thing she wanted to avoid. *Everything* she's done or hasn't done was all in an effort not to cause you any pain. Going by the shit you've done to her in the past, I don't think you'd have been so concerned about *her* feelings if the situation were reversed."

Shoulders slumping, Mallory averted her gaze and swallowed hard. Preston put his hand on her shoulder, offering his silent support. She didn't shake him off this time, but she did stiffen.

Sensing that her cousin was no longer on the verge of snapping, Casey said, "For what little it's worth, I *am* sorry that you're hurting. You're a real bitch, but I still wouldn't purposely hurt you." Much. Most of the time.

Preston stroked his mate's hair. "And I'm sorry, honey. So fucking sorry."

"But I'm certain Sherryl's *not,*" Adrian cut in. "And she needs to be dealt with."

"She will be," said Casey, face hardening. "I warned her to back off and she hasn't. I don't think she has any intention of doing so. There's only one thing for me to do now—I'll have to challenge her. But not until after the games are over."

"Why wait?" asked Eli.

"If I do it before then and I end up killing her, there'll be so much rage circulating among her pack and mine that it will filter over onto the teams and then there'll be a bloodbath on the damn field." That sort of thing had happened before, and Casey didn't want to see it happen again.

"You'll only get to play the Seals in the final if you defeat the Washington Weasels—and I'm sorry, but that's a dumb name for a soccer team—in the semi-finals," Adrian pointed out.

"We'll make it to the finals." Casey *had* to believe that. "And we'll annihilate the heifers. If we *don't* make it, I'll challenge Sherryl once my team has been eliminated from the competition."

Adrian gave a satisfied nod. "She'll be expecting you to wait, though. She'll fuck with you in any way she can in the meantime, hoping to provoke you."

"Oh, I know," said Casey. "And I'm not saying I won't smack the bitch down if she comes at me. Just that I'll postpone issuing the challenge."

"All right," said Adrian. "In the meantime, she's banned from our territory. She doesn't get to visit her family here, she doesn't get to attend any games."

Preston's brow puckered. "What about the cemetery? You intend to keep her from it? Her mate is buried here. She visits his grave at least once a month."

"Not anymore she doesn't." Adrian lifted his chin, his mouth set into a determined slash. "A ban is a ban. I'll negotiate an arrangement with her coach that allows her to come here *only* to play with her team, but nothing else—and she'll be followed the entire time by one of my enforcers."

"She'll probably run crying to her Alphas and try to sic them on you," said Eli.

"If they contact me, I'll inform them that I'll lift the ban if she apologizes to Mallory, Casey, and Preston. If I come across as fair and not cruel, her Alphas will have no reason to take this further. They'll simply tell Sherryl to swallow her pride and apologize, which she won't do—it's not in her nature."

"She'd rather swallow glass," agreed Preston.

Adrian's shoulders lowered. "It pains me to have to ban her from coming here—she was one of my minks once. But it seems that that doesn't mean much to her now, and so I won't let it mean shit to me."

SHARDS OF FROST

CHAPTER ELEVEN

"I'm just saying it's odd that there are no 'B' batteries," said Frankie, smoothing her rose-gold bangs away from her face. "Don't you think so, Casey?"

Casey nodded at the tipsy she-wolf, who was a member of the Phoenix Pack. "Oh yeah, definitely." She put her bottle to her mouth and tipped it back. The cold beer slid down her parched throat.

She'd gone out on "girls' nights" with her teammates, so she wasn't new to the act of sitting at a table full of rowdy females. Normally, though, she'd be itching to leave. She wasn't a big fan of nightclubs. They were too loud and crowded, and her mink despised the strobe lights and stench of cigarette smoke. But there were no such issues in the Velvet Lounge, so it was easy enough to relax, have fun, and get buzzed.

The girls' night was Shaya's idea, since the females of her pack had complained that Eli always "hogged" Casey, giving them no time with her. Only Ally had stayed at home, although that was because she'd fallen asleep on the sofa. No one had wanted to disturb her, so Shaya had simply told Marcus to drive the Seer to the club if she woke before they returned.

Eli wasn't particularly happy about the girls' night, so it hadn't come as a surprise to Casey when he suddenly announced that Derren "needed" Eli to work the Beta's security shift at the club for him. She'd simply rolled her eyes.

She wasn't sure whose idea it was for the Phoenix Pack females to meet them there, but now they were all gathered around the VIP table, listening to Mila sing on stage while Harley played on the electric violin beside her. Most at the table were also mouthing the lyrics and doing weird hand actions, to which Roni was crossing her eyes. Sucking on a lollipop, the female enforcer looked the height of uncomfortable. Casey had come to learn that social situations weren't Roni's thing.

Of course, some of the Phoenix Pack males had come along to watch over their mates—and damn if they weren't very healthy specimens. But the guys had no sooner said their hellos to Casey than their females had shooed them off to the bar, insisting on having "alone time" with the other girls. The males were *not* pleased about it at all.

She couldn't really snicker at the males' overprotective behavior, given that Eli was patrolling the perimeter of the club just so that he could keep a close watch on her.

In the past week, since she'd first told him that she'd switch to his pack, he'd been sneakily moving her things from her place to his. Small things at first, like little knickknacks and framed photos from her shelves. Then some of her clothes had gravitated to his lodge, along with a lamp and two of her plants. He'd also whined occasionally that he didn't want to have a separate home from his mate, but she'd just stared at him until he threw up his hands and let it go.

Given how close the packs were, Casey had expected the Phoenix Pack females to make her run a gauntlet; to question her as they decided whether she was good enough for Eli. Instead, they'd been friendly and warm since the second Shaya introduced them to Casey. Oh, they'd asked her questions, but none had been rude or invasive.

They were also quite fascinated by her being a mink, since none of them had ever met one before. Casey could honestly say she liked them all, and she didn't take to people easily. It often took her time to warm up to others. But, like the Mercury Pack females, they were just impossible to dislike.

The table broke out into applause as the song tapered off. But then Mila quickly launched into another song.

"God, Mila's just amazing." Jaime, the Phoenix Beta female, let out a wistful sigh. "I really wish I could sing like that."

"I just wish I was a pallas cat," said Taryn. The blonde she-wolf was a teeny little thing, but she was *all* Alpha. She looked even tinier when stood beside her mate, Trey, who was built like an overgrown linebacker. He was also scowling at Taryn from his position at the bar.

"You're crazy enough to be one," Shaya told Taryn. Apparently, the two Alpha females had been best friends since they were kids.

Taryn smiled and nudged Shaya. "Aw, thanks."

"It's in here somewhere, I know it is," Makenna muttered to herself, rummaging through her purse as she piled the contents onto the table one at a time.

Gwen frowned. "Why do you have an acorn in your purse?"

Makenna stared at Gwen as if she'd asked the most absurd question. "Duh. Same reason everyone carries an acorn around with them."

Gwen exchanged confused looks with everyone at the table. "Yeah, I don't think anyone else here does that."

"Carrying an acorn around brings you good luck and ensures a long life.

Come on, people, you should know this shit." Makenna shook her head, as if they were all utterly hopeless, and went back to rooting through her bag.

Madisyn smiled at Casey. "You've never in your life met a more superstitious person than Makenna."

"How much longer before we leave?" asked Roni, peeling the label from her bottle.

Riley, a raven shifter, watched the she-wolf curiously. "You realize that peeling labels is a sign of sexual frustration, right? What's the matter, you not getting it regular these days?"

Roni barely glanced at the raven. "I'm not sexually frustrated, I'm freaking bored."

Shaya rolled her eyes. "It's a club, Roni, not a knitting group."

"A knitting group would be more fun," grumbled Roni. She guzzled down some beer from her bottle. While the other females went back to singing, Roni turned to Casey and asked, "Have you heard anything from Sherryl?"

"Not a peep," replied Casey. She'd agreed with Eli that the pack should know about the Sherryl situation, especially since Casey intended to challenge her. "I spoke briefly to her aunt a few days back. Sherryl's apparently distraught that she can't visit her mate's grave." And Casey couldn't help feeling sorry for her.

"But not distraught enough to apologize, or she'd have done it by now," Roni pointed out, scrunching up the label.

"That's what I said. Her aunt even agreed. But we have to talk about something else, because if your brother senses my mood plummeting, he'll come right over here to ask me what's wrong."

Mouth quirking, Roni nodded. "It's exactly what he'll do. Dominant male wolves can be annoyingly nosy and overprotective. Eli's pushier than most, but you seem to deal with him just fine. He positively *loathes* being away from you, you know," Roni added, a twinkle in her eye. "He gets all grumpy and snippy. I tease him that he has separation anxiety issues, but he's yet to lunge at me. Though he did throw a box of tissues at my head last time I said it." And she seemed delighted by that.

A shadow fell across their table. Looking up, Casey saw a blond, immensely hot male.

"Ladies," he greeted, smooth as glass, but his eyes were on Mila—who was currently bowing, now that her song was over—and glimmered with pride.

"It's a *girls' night*, Dominic," Taryn told him, shooing him away with her hands.

"I know," he said, "but Trey just told me that Eli's mate is here. I came to say hi." His eyes swept the table and landed on Casey. His mouth curved into a killer smile. "You must be Casey. I'm Dominic."

"Mila's mate," Casey remembered. "She mentioned you earlier. It's good to meet you."

"Likewise," said Dominic with a nod. Then he scowled as another male body literally bumped him out of the way. "Hey!"

Moving to stand behind Casey's chair, Eli glared at him. "Don't smile at my mate; I don't like it."

Dominic laughed. "Dude, you're such a goner, it's not even funny. Your mink is safe from me. I don't use cheesy lines on people's mates anymore."

"Only because Mila would remove your eyes with an ice cream scooper," said Eli.

"Hell, yeah, she would—my mate's a mean little thing." That only seemed to make him proud.

Taryn groaned as the other Phoenix Pack males fanned out behind Dominic. "*Now* look what you did. If one comes over, they all follow."

Of course, each of the males had every excuse in the world why they'd needed to come over—they thought someone called their name; they just wanted to speak to Dominic; they were checking no one needed another drink; they thought Taryn had waved them over.

Madisyn groaned as her own mate approached with Zander. "Seriously, guys, we're fine over here."

Gwen sighed at Zander. "You do realize I'm armed and quite capable of—"

"You're *armed?*" Zander gaped. "Tell me you're joking."

"Guns are no joking matter," said Gwen.

"Hey, why's everyone gathered around?" asked Harley just as she and Mila returned to the table.

Before Mila had a chance to sit, Dominic curled his arm around his mate and hauled her close before planting a hot kiss on her mouth.

Mila huffed at him. "You long ago delivered the message that I'm taken, GQ—it's not necessary to keep on reiterating it."

Dominic kissed her again. "I disagree."

"You were great up there, Mila," said Trick, another Phoenix Pack enforcer. His brow furrowed. "Hey, did you put your cell in your back pocket? Because that ass is calling me."

Mouth tightening, Dominic glared at Trick. "Funny."

"Yeah, I thought so," said Trick. "It's just a little payback for the times you used lines on my Frankie."

Dominic narrowed his eyes. "Whatever, asshole."

"Anyone know who that is?" Riley asked, flicking her blue-black hair over her shoulder.

Casey tracked the raven's gaze to a corner table where a bunch of females sat—one of whom was staring right at Casey. Her mink puffed up, affronted. Hearing Eli curse, she looked up at him and said, "Tell me that's not your ex or something."

"Not an ex," he said, jaw hard. "That is Ignacio's mate, Dahlia."

"The bitch has some nerve showing up here," growled Shaya, straightening in her seat. "If I'd thought she'd dare to come, I'd have showed a picture of her to the doormen and instructed them to turn her away."

"Why?" asked Casey. "Because if it's just that she's Ignacio's mate, I've heard they aren't a real couple and seem to each go their own way, so she might not have anything to do with the crap he's pulling."

Shaya looked at Eli. "You didn't tell her?"

Casey tensed. "Tell me what?"

Rubbing at his nape, Eli exhaled heavily. "When we met up with her and Ignacio, she ... expressed a belief that you should be punished for putting a blade to his throat. I disagreed and made it clear you'd wipe the floor with her. Ignacio didn't contradict me on that."

He didn't need to feel her anger humming down their bond to know that his mate was *pissed*. Not when she'd gone so eerily silent and still, glaring at him through blank eyes. *Shit.* Eli was a grown man who'd faced down numerous dangerous people in his life, but when his mate looked at him like that, he honestly felt the need to squirm.

"What you're saying is," began Casey, her words coming out slow and without emotion, "she basically told you that she intended to come at me ... and you didn't think to tell me this?"

"The only reason I didn't mention it was that I didn't take it seriously. She and Ignacio aren't real mates; they're more like business associates. She has no emotional drive to avenge any slights to him, and she's hardly going to attack a female of a lower rank than her if she knows that said female can kick her ass."

"Oh," said Casey, her tone still flat. "Well that makes it okay."

"The bitch is making her way over," said Taryn. "Bold as brass, this one."

"I'll get rid of her." Eli stalked over to the set of three steps that led to the VIP area, intending to block the cats' path to his mate. So when he found himself flanked by Shaya and Casey, he growled, "*I'll* deal with this." Both females ignored him.

Sensing his pack mates were among those who'd gathered behind him, Eli said, "Zander." He didn't need to say more. Knew the enforcer would understand what he wanted.

Zander snorted. "If you think I'm going to even *try* to manhandle a mink, you're out of your mind."

Bastard.

Just then, the cougars reached the bottom step, but none attempted to ascend them. They also didn't look the slightest bit intimidated by the number of people they were facing.

Dahlia inclined her head at the Mercury Alpha female. "Shaya."

"You shouldn't have come here," said Shaya.

Dahlia's gaze sliced to Eli. "I heard about your attack. Ignacio had nothing to do with it."

Like Eli would believe a single word that came out of her mouth. His wolf snarled at the cat, raring to pounce and defend his mate. "You need to leave."

"You're worried I'll attack your little mink here?" Dahlia snickered. "If I was going to hurt her, I'd have done it by now. It would have been simple enough."

Anger whipped through Eli, tightening his muscles. Some of that anger belonged to his mate.

"Oh, she did not just say that," Roni hissed behind him.

"This is not gonna end well for the cougar," Bracken muttered quietly.

No, it wasn't, because Eli had felt the spike of battle adrenaline surge through his mate. She hadn't yet said a word, but she was staring at Dahlia in a way that made the cougar bristle. She might be taller than Casey, but she wasn't stronger.

"You got something to say?" Dahlia snapped at Casey, who just continued to stare at her.

"I really recommend you leave now while you can still walk on your own steam," Shaya said to the feline.

Dahlia didn't. Instead, she curled back her upper lip and leaned toward Casey. "What the fuck are you staring at, bitch?"

"Just you, Darla," said Casey.

"It's *Dahlia.*" The cougar's claws sliced out.

Eli slipped in front of his mate. But said mate somehow skirted around him, lunged at the cougar—covering the three steps in a single jump—gripped Dahlia by the throat, and slammed her onto an empty table. It happened so fast, Eli double-blinked in surprise.

Before Dahlia's cats could even think to intervene, Eli and his pack mates were there, blocking their path. Fights occasionally broke out in the club—it was nothing new. But plenty of people still gathered around to gawk.

Dahlia didn't struggle. She just stared up at Casey, her eyes wide, her lips parted. But then, maybe her stillness had something to do with the hand snapped tight around her neck or the claws that were threateningly pressed above her heart.

Casey leaned over the feline, smiling at the hint of fear in the cougar's scent. "Ah, you see now that you made a mistake. Shame for you that you didn't sense that a little earlier." Her mink bared her teeth and lashed her tail.

Dahlia's nostrils flared. "You wouldn't dare harm me. My mate—"

"Has already targeted mine," Casey finished. "Why shouldn't I have some fun with his?"

"It wasn't Ignacio!" She squirmed slightly. "Get the fuck off me."

"Ask nicely."

Dahlia's mouth fell open. "You have to be kidding."

"Do I look like I am?" Because Casey wasn't kidding. Not even a little. The bitch didn't get to come at her like that, try to humiliate and goad her in front of all those people—including her mate—and think that Casey would let it go so easily. "You want me to let you up, ask nicely. Bitch, I can do this all night—it won't bother me in the slightest."

Upper lip quivering, Dahlia kicked hard at Casey and tried lashing out with her claws.

Casey used her grip on the cat's throat to slam her head on the table. "Ask. Nicely." She let her claws pierce the flesh above Dahlia's heart. "Note that each time you hit out at me, I'll thrust these a little deeper into your chest."

Lips tremoring, breaths coming a little faster, Dahlia glared up at the ceiling. "Let me up, *please*," she hissed in the same tone someone might say "fuck you."

"If you insist." Casey released her and took a slow step back.

Dahlia scrambled off the table and righted her clothes, trying for dignity when she had to feel the height of embarrassed.

"Don't say something dumb and cliché like 'you'll regret this.' Just go."

"And have more sense than to come back," added Eli.

Rubbing at her throat, Dahlia shot all the gawkers a glare as she stalked away with her cats trailing close behind.

Eli took a step toward his mate. "Casey?" Ever so slowly, she turned her head and looked at him. The intensity in her eyes acted like an electric charge to his senses.

"It would have been nice if you've shared with me that she was out for my blood, Eli."

Marveling over how she could sound so deceptively calm, he held up his hands. "I didn't consciously keep it from you. I just dismissed it, the same as I would dismiss a fly buzzing in my face. It never occurred to me to tell you because I hadn't taken it seriously, and I'm sorry for that. I won't make that mistake again."

She flexed her fingers. "I don't like it when people keep things from me."

"I don't like it that I need to fuck you but we're surrounded by so many people I can't do shit about it." He wasn't kidding; he was hard as a rock after that little display of dominance.

One corner of her mouth ever so slightly twitched. "I'm not finding you funny."

"Yes, you are."

"There's nothing amusing about this."

"And yet, you're fighting a smile." Risking his eyes, he crossed to her. "I swear, baby, this wasn't me keeping secrets from you. If I thought there was a threat to you, you'd be the first person to know about it. I'd *never* hold back something like that from you. Never. I'd want you to be alert and prepared." Slowly, he reached up to stroke her hair. "I'd never risk you,

Casey. You know that. You're my everything."

She took a deep breath, and the tension seeped away from her shoulders. "You make it hard for me to stay mad at you."

"Don't be mad." He brushed his nose against hers. "I messed up, but I'll make it up to you."

"Oh yeah? How?"

He knew his smile was nothing short of wicked. "You'll find out when we get home." She might not have moved in with him yet, but his lodge was still *their* home as far as he was concerned. "You forgive me?"

She sighed. "I guess so."

He pulled her close and kissed her. He was just about to try luring her into leaving early, but then Shaya sidled up to him and gestured for him to go.

"Not sure why male wolves have a problem understanding that girls' nights don't include them, but you need to leave us to enjoy the rest of our evening," said the redhead. "No way are we ending it early because of some cougar bitch."

Eli frowned. "Casey was almost attacked—"

"Oh no, don't try using that 'all my protective instincts are telling me I have to stay close to her, it isn't my fault' bullshit," said Shaya.

Damn, that was exactly what he'd meant to do. It was no surprise that she'd seen it coming—she was mated to an Alpha who was just as overprotective as Eli.

"Go on now, go patrol the club and we'll pretend you're not doing it just so that you can keep tabs on Casey." Shaya looked at her. "I don't know how you deal so well with it. Nick drives me crazy when he gets like this, which is why he never comes along to girls' nights."

Casey shrugged. "To be fair, Eli did warn me that he'd be clingy."

Eli's brows snapped together. "I said I'd be all up in your space and want more of your time and attention than I was entitled to."

"All I heard was 'clingy.'"

He nipped her lower lip in punishment. He wasn't clingy, it was just that … "I waited a long time for you. I like having you close. I see no reason to fight that."

Shaya's expression softened. "Aw, that was sweet. But you still can't have her back yet." She snatched Casey's hand and dragged her away, laughing at his growl.

Bracken and Zander crossed to him, their mouths tight and their bodies tense.

"I don't know why they have such a problem with us sitting at their table," said Bracken. "It's downright unsocial. Not to mention discriminating against the male gender. And I don't care what Madisyn says, I don't monopolize her time. I just don't like being excluded. I think that's natural."

"Gwen accused me of being unreasonable, if you can believe that." Zander shook his head. "She's a human in a place full of shifters. *Of course* I'd want to be at her side. The only saving grace is that she'll be hammered soon—drunk sex is always fun."

Bracken's brows lifted. "Yeah, there is that."

Eli hummed. Normal sex with Casey was phenomenal. Drunk sex would be out-of-this-world. "I guess we should buy them more drinks. Maybe send over a tray of shots."

Zander pointed at him. "I like the way you think. Shots it is."

Later that night, Eli learned that drunk sex with his mate was as outfuckingstanding as he'd anticipated.

Eli stormed into the living area of the main lodge the next morning, his fists clenched. "Do you have to be such a fucking child, Roni? Really?"

His sister didn't even look up at him. She was busy playing a game on her phone.

Kathy sighed. "Will the pranks never end?"

"I'd say it's unlikely," said Marcus, who then turned to Eli. "What did she do?"

"She duct-taped a fucking air horn to the wall behind my bathroom door," said Eli. "I got up in the night to take a piss. The door hit the horn and, fuck, the noise was a *bitch*."

Roni finally looked at him. "What did you expect? You removed my showerhead and poured grape Kool-Aid in it! I was not imfuckingpressed when I had myself a purple shower."

Kathy looked at her daughter. "Ah, so that's why I keep smelling grapes."

Just then, Nick strolled into the room and nodded at Eli. "You're here. Good. Shaya wants to go to the outdoor mall to buy the pups new shoes. I want you and Zander to come with us."

Ally sat up straight. "The mall? I am *so* there. I love the—"

"No fucking way," Derren clipped.

Ally arched a brow at her mate. "This is not up for debate, sunshine. I'm going."

He shook his head. "Not happening, baby. Malls are crowded. It would be too difficult to protect you there."

"Protect me from what? Bar code scanners? You need to stop being so overbearing. I'm pregnant, not ill. Derren, *I need to get air.* Me and my wolf are going *crazy* being cooped up here. I love our territory, but it's starting to feel like a prison."

"I'm sorry to hear that, but you're still not going."

And on and on it went.

Roni crossed to Eli and whispered, "My money's on Ally. She's good at getting her way."

Eli grimaced. "Yeah, but Derren's a stubborn bastard who won't back down for anyone."

"True. But my money's still on Ally."

Eli nodded. "If she turns on those fake tears, Derren will be a goner—he can't take them."

And that was exactly what Ally did, so the Betas joined them on the shopping trip. A trip that should have been short, since the objective was to buy shoes for the kids, but neither Shaya nor Ally saw any harm in stopping at practically every store they came across.

As they strolled around the mall, Eli stayed ahead of his Alphas, Betas, and the pups while Zander covered the rear, ever vigilant. The whole time, Eli's wolf sulked. The animal didn't like the crowds, how exposed they all were, or the feel of the sun beating down on them. Mostly, he didn't like being away from Casey. Neither did Eli. It made him ... antsy.

Eli suspected that would cease happening once their bond had fully snapped into place. Both he and his beast would then feel much more secure in their mating. The edginess might even calm a little when she finally moved in with him—he'd soon find out.

"Ooh, can we go in there, Mommy? *Please?*" begged Willow.

Eli pivoted on his heel to see the pup pointing at a toy store. He suspected it was the array of plush animals that had caught her attention. Willow was a sucker for them.

"Pleeeeaaaase!" she again begged.

Cassidy peeked in the store. "Look, they have bracelets with—" She stilled, her eyes briefly flashing white, and then those eyes widened. "Cain's coming to visit!" she declared excitedly, referring to Ally's foster brother who'd joined The Movement—a group of shifters that retaliated against the human anti-shifter extremists.

Ally blinked. "What? When?"

Cassidy's brow wrinkled. "Not sure, but he's gonna be really, *really* mad about something."

"I like it when Cain comes," said Willow. "He brings me and Cassidy presents. Good ones. Can we go in the store now?"

Shaya looked from one pup to the other, both of whom were wearing pitiful expressions. "Since you've been so well-behaved, I don't see why you can't have a little treat."

The girls let out happy little squeals and followed Shaya into the store. Nick and the Betas trailed behind them while Eli and Zander stood outside, on guard.

For what felt like the hundredth time that day, Eli glanced at his watch, as if it would make the time tick by faster. 3:30pm. Not long left to go before Casey's enforcer shift would be over.

"You know," began Zander, "I've occasionally wondered if maybe Cain and Cassidy are true mates."

Eli sighed. "I've asked myself the same thing." Cain was a hard bastard who'd long ago lost his moral compass, but he was good with Cassidy. Gave her his undivided attention. Treated her as if she were important. Very few things truly seemed to have any importance to Cain Holt.

"It wouldn't surprise me if Nick and Shaya suspect it, too."

"I can't say I like the idea of little Cassidy being bound to someone as messed up as Cain, but if anyone needs their true mate, it's him. So while I'd worry that he wouldn't be good for her, I'd find it hard to begrudge him that happiness."

"I'm not sure he'd ever take a mate. Cain doesn't like vulnerabilities." Zander rubbed at his jaw. "I guess time will tell. So … how are things going with you and Casey?"

"Amazing. The only thing that could make it better would be if our bond finally snapped into place."

"Any idea what's stopping that from happening?"

"I have a few theories. Her father is an asshole, Z. Made her feel inferior all her life. Her mother never defended her, and her sister … well, she was no sister. I believe her brother loves her, but he also cut contact with her after he separated from his girlfriend. None of them made Casey feel truly important. I wonder if maybe—even if it's only on a subconscious level— she struggles to trust that she's my priority."

Zander pursed his lips. "Could be that. You're sure it's nothing on your end?"

Eli shook his head. "There's nothing I want more than to be fully bound to her. I hate that I'm not."

"That doesn't mean the problem isn't you. Secrets can block the bond. So can fears and insecurities—we don't always consciously know we have them. Think on it some more, be sure it's not you."

Eli nodded, though he was quite certain that it wasn't him.

He and Zander talked about general things until the Alphas, Betas, and pups finally filed out of the store.

Cassidy held up her wrist, flashing Eli a look at her sparkly bracelet. "What do you think?" she asked.

He smiled. "I think—"

A loud crack split the air. Cassidy's body jerked. Her eyes went wide with shock and pain. The scent of blood crashed into Eli.

Everyone moved fast.

Heart slamming against his ribs, Eli grabbed Cassidy and, like the others, dropped to a low crouch. Shielding her with his body, he scrambled into the store with his pack mates, dodging the other bullets.

Eli's stomach lurched as he cradled the pup. She trembled in his arms, her breath hitching, her little face creased in pain and draining of color. A chill swept over his body and settled in his bones as he saw the red stain blooming over the front of her dress. "Ally!"

The Beta female crawled to them. "Did the bullet go straight through, Eli?" she asked, remarkably all business.

He checked. Nodded. Fought to think through the fury that thudded through him.

Cassidy clutched at his shirt. "I don't want to die."

"You're not going to, baby," said Shaya, taking the little girl's hand in hers while Ally healed the wound. The redhead's face hardened as she looked from Zander to Derren. "Find the fucker," she hissed.

"I want him alive," Nick bit out, holding a sobbing Willow close. "But kill him if you have to."

Nodding, the two males left. No more bullets were fired, so the shooter had to be on the run.

Even as Eli could see the pain begin to leach from Cassidy's face, blind terror clawed at him and coated his tongue. She was just a baby. *A baby.* And she'd been shot. Shot on *his* watch. A sense of failure snaked over him and his beast, who let out a mournful howl.

Ally finally sat back, pale. "You'll be okay, sweetie."

Shaya set the pup on her lap and held her tight, rocking her from side to side and making soothing noises. Cassidy's shoulders shook, but her tears were silent. Nick crouched beside them and stroked Cassidy's hair, whispering reassuring words to her while Willow held her hand.

Seeing Ally sway a little, Eli curved his arm around her, keeping her steady and upright. Healing wounds always took a little something out of her. "Are you okay?"

Ally nodded. "Just … shocked. I mean, it happened so fast. Did anyone else get hit?"

The others all shook their heads.

Eli's cell began to ring. He whipped out his phone, unsurprised to see his mate's name on the screen. He answered, "Baby—"

"*Please* tell me you're okay," said Casey. "I'm not feeling any pain from you through the bond, but I know you're pissed and scared."

His chest squeezed at the shake in her voice. "I'm fine," he assured her, surprised at how calm he sounded while his insides were being ravished by sheer panic. "Some shit went down but it's over now. I'm okay. Everyone's okay."

"Define 'shit.'"

He hesitated. Decided against it. "I can't really talk right now, but I'll fill you in later, I promise."

"Where are you?"

"The mall. As soon as I get back to my territory, I'll call you, I swear."

144

"You'd better, canine, I mean it."

"I will. I have to go now. Stay safe for me." He ended the call and pocketed his cell.

"Why didn't you tell her what happened?" asked Ally.

"For one thing, I don't think I can get the words out without losing my shit." He was barely holding it together. Especially while the scent of Cassidy's blood clogged his nostrils. "Also, Casey adores the pups. She'll lose her mind when she hears what happened. The first thing she'll want to do is go after Ignacio."

Nick narrowed his eyes. "You think he sent someone after Cassidy?"

"I don't know," said Eli. "It's possible that the bullet was meant for me. Maybe the shooter kept on firing because they hadn't hit me. But we have to consider that they didn't shoot until you all left the store, so there's a chance I wasn't the target.

"It won't matter to Casey, though, if she's in a blind fury. She won't be rational. And if I'm not there to keep her calm when I tell her what happened, she might do something dumb like go confront Ignacio herself and demand to know if he had anything to do with it."

"We need to get Cassidy home," Shaya said to Nick, nuzzling the pup's hair.

"We will," Nick told her. "As soon as Derren and Zander comes back, we're out of here."

A human crawled from behind the counter. "Is everyone all right? I called 911. Help should be here soon."

By then, Eli and his pack mates would be gone. The police wouldn't help anyway once they realized it was shifter business.

Hearing the mish-mash of voices, Eli flicked his gaze to the shop doorway. A bunch of fucking idiots were so desperate to snap a photo that they were coming close. "We need to leave sooner rather than later," he told Nick. "We don't know what the shooter looks like—they could walk in here, acting like a gawker, and we wouldn't know any different."

Cassidy's head snapped up, and her eyes went wide with fear. "They could come back? We have to go."

"Do you have a rear exit?" Nick asked the shopkeeper.

The human blinked. "Y-yes."

"Good, we'll need to use it," said Nick. "I'll call Derren and—" He broke off as his cell rang and then he pulled it out of his pocket. "Speak of the devil …" He answered, "Tell me you have him, Derren."

The look that twisted Nick's face was enough to tell Eli that the answer was no.

Deep inside him, Eli's wolf howled his fury.

SHARDS OF FROST

CHAPTER TWELVE

Eli stood as a familiar car drove into the lot. Like last time, he'd sat on the porch step of the main lodge as he'd waited for Casey to arrive. He'd texted her the moment he crossed the border of his territory, asking her to come to him. Despite that Cassidy was tucked up in bed, completely fine, his stomach was still in knots, and the chill hadn't yet fully left him.

His wolf hadn't calmed either. He kept pacing, snarling, and raking at the ground with his claws.

She slipped out of the car and said goodbye to the baker who'd given her a ride. Eli gave a brief nod to the driver and then cut his gaze back to his mate, who was ascending the porch steps. "Over here, baby," he said. "Need to hold you right now."

He closed his arms around her and breathed her in, letting the feel and scent of her settle into his system and chase away the chill. Slowly, the knots in his gut fell away, and the fury lost its sharp grip on him. His wolf pushed up against his skin, wanting to be nearer to her.

"What happened?" she asked. "I've been imagining all kinds of messed up scenarios."

Guilt twisted his gut. Pulling back only slightly, he told her of the shooting. With every word he spoke, she got stiffer and stiffer in his arms. By the time he was done, she looked ready to burn shit down.

"I'll kill him," she said softly, her voice vibrating with suppressed rage. Then she was gone from his arms and pacing up and down, her neck corded, her nostrils flaring. "We need to go pay that motherfucker a visit *now*."

Yeah, he'd been right not to tell her over the phone. "We don't know for sure that Ignacio is behind this," said Eli, knowing it was who she meant.

"It has to be him. You must have been the real target."

"From what Derren gathered, someone got themselves comfortable on the rooftop opposite the store we were at, and then they took their shot. But

147

they didn't take it until *after* the others filed out of the shop. That tells us there's a strong possibility that Cassidy was *deliberately* targeted."

Pausing in her pacing, Casey licked her lower lip. "Ignacio wouldn't try striking out at me through the pups."

"No, he wouldn't. He played the innocent card when Nick called him. The bastard truly did sound pissed that Cassidy had been shot—apparently, he doesn't like kids being hurt. Also, according to the contact that Nick's friend has within the pride, Ignacio's also maintaining that innocence to his pride. Maybe it's an act, maybe it's not. But if we follow the theory that Cassidy was in fact the real target, we can't ignore the possibility that one of Nick's enemies was striking out at him through her."

"But you said the shooter kept on firing. Why would he do that if he'd hit his target?"

"Maybe he was also supposed to shoot Willow." Crossing to Casey, Eli relaxed her fists and massaged her palms with his thumbs. "There are a lot of maybes. We have to be positive that Ignacio is responsible before we go invading his territory, Casey—you know that."

She ground her teeth. "So how do we find out if it was him?"

"That I don't know. We have no clue who the shooter was. Derren said he smelled fox on the rooftop—that's all we've got. The scent led him to the mall's parking lot, where it abruptly disappeared." Eli slid his hands up her arms and then began to massage her shoulders. "It was probably a lone shifter acting as an assassin-for-hire."

"I get that there are other suspects to consider, but it seems far too coincidental to me that this would happen now, while shit's going down between us and Ignacio. *Especially* when I had a little altercation with his mate last night. Did he mention that to Nick on the phone?"

"Only to apologize on Dahlia's behalf, calling her indirect challenge a 'drunken mishap.'" Eli had growled at that. "Zander quite rightly pointed out that an enemy of Nick's might have found out about that little scene between you and Dahlia and then decided to act on their own grudge now, assuming we'd blame Dahlia. That kind of thing happens."

Eli kept on rubbing her shoulders until the tension finally ebbed out of them. Her anger hadn't yet left her, but it was no longer burning so hot that she wasn't thinking straight.

"Now I get why you didn't tell me this on the phone. You were worried I'd storm over to Ignacio's territory with the intention of slitting his throat, weren't you?"

"Something like that," Eli admitted, tugging her close. His wolf rubbed against her again, *giving* comfort this time.

"Tell me the truth. Are any of your pack mates angry with me?"

He frowned, jerking his head back slightly. "Why would they be angry at you?"

"Because what Kathy said a few weeks ago was right: *I* brought Ignacio into your life. It would be easy for someone to blame me for this when their emotions are running high."

Eli narrowed his eyes. Ah, so that was the reason for the niggle of guilt he could feel pecking at their bond. "You hold no blame whatsoever in this, and you know better than to take any responsibility for another person's actions. To answer your question, no. None of their anger is directed at you." Or if it was, nobody had voiced it. He'd chew a metaphorical chunk out of the ass of anyone who dared to.

Casey rubbed a hand down her face. Intellectually, she knew he was right; knew the blame belonged solely to whoever the culprit might be—and she was leaning toward Ignacio, despite that Eli's points were valid. But the guilt was there all the same.

"I'm not the only one feeling guilty, though, am I?" she challenged without heat. "It was faint at first, so I didn't pick it up through the bond until your anger, shock, and fear faded." The emotions were still there, but they were no longer so intense.

He exhaled heavily. "She was shot on my watch, Casey."

"Not just your watch. It was Zander's, too. In total, you had five other adults with you. Granted, Derren's attention would have been mostly on Ally. But he's a Beta—his instincts will have had him sweeping rooftops with his eyes and constantly studying his surroundings, watching out for threats. Nick will have been doing the same, even though his attention will have also been divided between his mate and pups."

Eli's jaw hardened. "He trusted that I'd protect them."

"You did exactly what you were supposed to do. You acted fast. You got Cassidy out of harm's way. You have nothing to feel guilty about. And if anyone tells you differently, I'll shatter their fucking kneecaps."

His mouth twitched. "You will, huh?"

"I will." Casey puffed out a breath. "God, this has been one weird day."

"What do you mean?"

"Adrian called me when I was on my way here. He spoke with Sherryl's aunt. It seems that Sherryl was attacked last night."

Eli blinked. "She was attacked, or she just *claimed* she was attacked?"

"She was attacked. Her aunt visited her. Said she's in a bad way. Vera wouldn't lie—especially about something like that."

"Adrian thought you did it, didn't he?"

"*That* or you sent someone to hurt her on my behalf. But I told him that you promised to let me deal with her."

"I'd never undermine you by sending somebody else as if you couldn't deal with the bitch yourself."

"I know. I just don't know who did hurt her."

Eli rubbed at his jaw. "It could have been Mallory. Maybe even Preston."

"Possibly. Adrian said he'd speak to them about it. Right now, it's Cassidy I'm worried about. I don't mind admitting I was scared when I felt your fear. It rushed down the bond so hard and fast it almost knocked me on my ass. Seriously, if I hadn't been on my knees at the time, I probably would have lost my footing."

"You were on your knees?"

"Yeah, I dropped my bottle of lotion on the floor. It burst."

"Burst?"

"Just erupted. Like a fountain. Spurted cream everywhere. I had it all over me—even in my hair. A big dollop of it landed on my lip—if my mouth had been open, I'd have had to spit it ..." Seeing his mouth kick up into a smile, Casey pressed her lips together. "Forget I said anything."

The front door opened, and Kathy stuck her head out. She frowned. "What are you two doing out here? Come in, I'm making sandwiches." She disappeared into the lodge.

Casey looked at Eli and echoed, "Sandwiches?"

"Mom makes them when she's mad or anxious. It's just her outlet, I guess." He kissed Casey's head, curved his arm around her shoulders, and steered her toward the door. "Come on. Quick warning: the mood is not good inside. Cassidy's in bed. Willow and Shaya are in her room with her. I think most of the other females would be up there too if they weren't busy trying to keep their mates calm."

Walking into the living area a few moments later, Casey saw what he meant. Gwen was hugging Zander tight as he stared out of the window. Ally was leaning into a rigid Derren on the sofa, stroking his thigh. Madisyn was sitting behind a scowling Bracken on the armchair, massaging his neck and shoulders. Caleb and Kent were holding hands as they watched Nick pace up and down in front of the fireplace. The Alpha looked close to exploding.

Marcus seemed less tense than the others, but perhaps that was because Roni was perched on his lap, rubbing his chest. The only person speaking was Harley, who was snuggled into Jesse's side, sifting her fingers through his hair. But the margay was talking so quietly to him that Casey couldn't make out the words.

The males weren't so caught up in their own anger that they weren't aware of their mates' fury, though. They were touching the females just as affectionately—stroking their hair, giving their hands a comforting squeeze, or pressing a kiss to their temple.

"You're going to wear a hole in that rug," Kathy told Nick as she brought in a tray piled with sandwiches. Instead of setting it on the coffee table and leaving people to help themselves, she circled the room, stuffing sandwiches into people's hands and insisting that they eat.

Everyone offered Casey faint smiles, nods, or quiet hellos as she and Eli sat on one of the sofas. If any held her to blame, none showed it.

"Have you and Derren finished writing your list of potential suspects?" Eli asked Nick.

The Alpha gave a curt nod. "It's not a short one. We wanted to be thorough, so we didn't just note the people we've warred with over the years such as the jackals, black bears, and Miranda's pack. I made enemies in juvie. I made some when I challenged and drove out the Alpha of our old pack. I made more each time I backed one of our allies in a battle."

He'd also made enemies when he helped crush the illegal fighting ring that Eli was forced to fight in, but Eli didn't mention that. He hadn't yet told Casey about it, and he wasn't looking forward to doing so. "Is your gut pointing you in any particular direction?"

Grinding his teeth, Nick shook his head. "Given that the people we most recently had problems with were the black bears, I might have leaned toward them if we hadn't wiped out the whole clan and its allies. Claudia's pack could be seeking retribution for her father's death," he added, referring to a male who'd partnered with the bear clan to fuck over Bracken, "though I highly doubt the new Alpha would do so—he'd never liked her father, from what he told me."

"We also have to consider that shifters are renowned for biding their time," said Derren. "That's why we included Nick's enemies from juvie. Someone might have wanted to wait until he had something to lose before they pounced. Those bullets could have been meant for Shaya, Willow, *and* Cassidy."

"Shouldn't we also be considering the possibility that the anti-shifter extremists could be behind this?" asked Gwen. "It wouldn't be the first time they'd hired shifters to do their dirty work for them."

"And we know just how far the sick fuckers are willing to go," added Bracken, balling up his hands. Casey wondered if he was recalling what had happened to his family. Pretty much all shifters had heard the story of how his family died and what he did to avenge them.

"It's possible that—" Nick frowned and cocked his head. "I hear an engine."

"It might be some of the Phoenix wolves," said Harley. "I'll be surprised if Shaya hasn't already called Taryn."

But if the male who came stalking through the house and into the living room without first knocking on the front door was in fact a Phoenix wolf, it was one who Casey hadn't met before. He was a good-looking guy, she noted absently. He was also thoroughly *pissed.* Even as he appeared coldly composed, there was a manic energy about him.

Lips clamped shut, the male glanced around the room and then looked at Nick. "Where's Cassidy?" It was a demand, and it clearly rubbed Nick the wrong way.

Bristling, Nick narrowed his eyes. "I'm guessing you know what happened. *How* do you know?"

"I called him," said Shaya, trudging into the room. She gave the visitor a weak smile. "Hi, Cain."

Ally huffed at him. "I don't even get a hello?"

Cain only inclined his head at her, though his expression did soften slightly.

Confused, Casey raised a questioning brow at Eli, who said quietly into her ear, "It's Ally's foster brother."

"Where's Cassidy?" Cain asked Shaya.

It was Nick who answered. "She's in her room, resting."

Cain's gaze sliced back to Nick. "I need to see her."

The Alpha male stiffened from head to toe, and the tension in the air strangely quadrupled. "Why?" The question was a whip.

"You know why," said Cain, meeting his gaze head-on, not in the least bit intimidated by the vibes of menace radiating from the Alpha.

"And how long have *you* known?" Nick asked him.

A muscle in Cain's cheek ticked. "A while."

Nick cursed and raked a hand through his hair.

"You're thinking she deserves better than me, and you're right," said Cain. "But it changes nothing. Cassidy was meant for me. She's mine."

Ah, *now* Casey understood.

"You could walk away," Nick said to him.

Cain snorted. "Like you walked away from Shaya? Remind me again how that worked out for you."

Shaya winced.

Nick clenched his fists. "You can't take Cassidy—can't take *anyone*—as your mate, Cain. You're a member of the fucking Movement."

"When she's old enough for me to claim her, I'll leave the group and take her to live with me and my pack."

Nick's spine snapped straight, and he bared his teeth. "You're not taking my daughter *anywhere*."

"She can't stay here with you indefinitely. In seven years, she'll be eighteen. Two adult Seers can't exist within the same pack. You'd have to choose between your adopted child and a Beta female who has bled for you and your pack. You know that, Nick. You've always known that."

Muscles bunched, the Alpha scrubbed at his jaw.

"But it won't come to that, because I will claim Cassidy when she's old enough. You won't keep me away from her in the meantime, Nick, so don't even try it."

Shaya held up her hands. "No one intends to do that, Cain. We trust that you'd never hurt her. Plus, she'd only hate us for it—she loves you. We're all just a little on edge, so it's hard for us to be rational." She waved a hand toward the hall. "Come in, I'll take you to her." When Nick looked as if he'd object, Shaya shook her head and said, "He has every right to see her. Don't be an ass." She and Cain then left the room.

Nick cursed again and turned to face the window.

"Well, I guess that confirms what I think most of us suspected," said Zander.

"*I* never suspected it." Kent put his hand to his throat. "She's just a little girl. She shouldn't have to worry about keeping a sociopath stable."

Ally frowned. "Hey, it's not like he's a serial killer or something."

"But he's not exactly *good*," said Kent, his voice gentle.

Caleb put a hand on his mate's thigh. "I think what Kent's trying to say is that Cain is someone who … lost his way."

"That doesn't mean he doesn't deserve a mate like everybody else," said Ally. "Juvie messed him up, but he's not cruel or sadistic."

"We know that, baby," Derren softly assured her. "Everyone's just feeling hyper-protective of Cassidy right now."

Ally looked at the Alpha. "I can tell you one thing, Nick: Cain might not be your first choice for Cassidy, but you'll never have to worry about her safety when she's with him. He'll never let a single thing harm her. Knowing that she was shot … this will have hit him hard. He'll want blood as much as you do."

A short while later, Cain and Shaya returned to the living area. Eli studied the male carefully. Cain's expression was hard, and his eyes were like glaciers, but he seemed slightly … well, not calmer exactly. But it was like his anger had switched from hot and manic to cold and controlled. As if seeing that his mate was alive and well had eased his fury just enough for Cain to find some reason and rationality.

"Is Cassidy sleeping?" asked Eli.

"No, she said she's bored of sleeping," said Shaya, one corner of her mouth kicking up slightly. "She's watching a movie with Willow."

"I'll go sit with the girls while you all talk," said Kathy, who then swanned out of the room.

Cain looked at his foster sister, his eyes still glacier cold. "Thank you for healing Cassidy."

Ally rolled her eyes. "You don't have to thank me, dumbass."

Cain's gaze cut to Eli. "And thank you for shielding her and getting her to safety. I didn't realize you'd met your mate," he added, his eyes flitting from Eli to Casey. "Your bond is strong. Congratulations."

Eli inclined his head. The latter word might have been tightly spoken, but there was sincerity behind it. "Thank you."

Cain turned to Nick. "Shaya gave me a brief summary of what happened. I want the whole story."

So Nick gave it to him. "We have a list of suspects, but none stick out at me."

"I'd say Ignacio is the likeliest culprit," said Jesse, to which many people nodded.

Cain's brow furrowed. "Ignacio?"

"Ignacio Rodriguez," Jesse expanded. "The Alpha of—"

"The Rotunda Pride," finished Cain. "I've met him."

"Eli's mate, Casey, has been having trouble with him." Nick brought Cain up to speed on the matter, including the altercation between Casey and Dahlia. "Considering someone hired a bunch of falcons to attack Eli not so long ago, it wouldn't be a stretch to conclude that that same person also contacted a hired gun to take care of him. It's possible that the bullet accidentally hit Cassidy, but we're not sure."

Cain's lips pulled back slightly, baring his teeth, as his jaw clenched so hard it had to hurt. But then a cold calm seemed to once more descend on him. "The shooter probably followed you around the mall, though they may have stuck to the rooftops. I'm guessing you kept the children shielded at all times."

Derren nodded. "The rest of us gathered around the pups and Ally as we walked."

"Yet, the shooter didn't open fire until the pups were exposed," said Cain, his voice carefully controlled. "I can see why you doubt Ignacio's guilt. He targets people's loved ones. The pups are technically Casey's nieces, but I'm not sure he'd consider that good enough. Then again, this whole thing could have been an attempt to strike at Eli through Cassidy. After all, he's no doubt pissed Ignacio off purely by protecting Casey."

Shaya's brows lifted. "That's true. I never thought of that."

"We need to have a little talk with Ignacio," said Cain, and Eli sensed that there would be nothing civil about that "talk."

"I already have." Nick told him about the phone call, adding, "Not that I believed he'd admit to any involvement even if he was responsible for it. I can only tell you what he told me."

Eli wasn't in the least bit surprised that his brother didn't mention Donovan's contact. Cain would demand to know the name of the source so that he could go question him—which he wouldn't do calmly or cleanly, since torturous interrogations were more Cain's style—and there was no way that Donovan would reveal the source's name anyway.

"We need to arrange a face-to-face chat with Ignacio." Cain licked his front teeth. "I want to look into his eyes when he says that he has no connection to the shooting."

Nick gave a slow shake of the head. "You can't, Cain. You're known as a person who only gives a shit about The Movement. If you confront Ignacio about what happened to Cassidy, he'll suspect that she's someone to you. If that somehow becomes common knowledge, your enemies will target her. We can't risk that."

Nostrils flaring, Cain spat a curse. "You can't ask me to sit back and do nothing."

"I don't like it any more than you do. But we have no proof that he's behind the shooting. I have plenty of enemies, Cain. You know that."

"You don't want to start a war with someone unless you're positive they bear guilt in the situation. Understandable," said Cain, though he didn't sound as though it would particularly bother him if he accidentally targeted the wrong person. "But I won't stand back and do *nothing*."

"Neither will I, which is why Derren and I made a list of potential suspects. We'll have Donovan help us look into each of them and see where they are and what's going on in their lives. It might help, it might not, but at least we'd be doing *something*. Focusing too much on Ignacio would be a mistake when we have no proof that he's the culprit."

"But like I said, it would make sense that it's Ignacio if the whole thing was a bid to get at Eli."

"There is another angle to consider," said Casey. "The loss of a pup impacts everyone. You would all have been an emotional mess if you lost Cassidy, and you'd have been looking for someone to blame. You might have pointed the finger at me. Might have wanted me gone from your pack and your lives. That could have been what Ignacio had hoped for."

Frowning, Shaya shook her head vigorously. "We would never have blamed you."

"Damn fucking straight," rumbled Eli.

Casey gave a wan smile. "You can't know that. Not for sure. People aren't always rational when they're grieving. They say things they don't mean, and they look for someone to blame so that they have an outlet for all the anger and grief. As someone who brought Ignacio into your lives, I'd have been the most obvious target."

Madisyn sighed. "Casey's right. I'm not saying *I* would have felt that way," she hurried to add. "But I've seen a lot of grieving people at the shelter. They're not always in their right mind. Their grief clouds the situation, stopping them from seeing it clearly."

Jaw clenched, Eli shook his head. "I would never have turned on you, Casey. *Never.* You have to know that. You have to know you come first to me."

"I do know that," Casey assured him. "But Ignacio isn't properly mated to Dahlia. He's never experienced the depth of loyalty that mated pairs have toward each other. He can't conceive of the kind of bond you and I have or how firmly it connects us. It would be easy for him to misjudge how you would react in such a situation."

"It's a good point," said Cain. He turned to Nick. "You need to up your security ten-fold and close the motel until this is over. I'll stay here—no, don't tell me to leave. I have a right to be here to protect my mate. You won't stop me, so let's not waste time with bullshit. Besides which, I promised her I'd stay—I won't break that promise."

Nick swore. "Fine."

"Run me through your list of other suspects, tell me about them," said Cain.

"It's a long list, so it could take a while."

"I have time."

"Dude, you really have to stop brooding."

Eli did a slow blink and looked down at his mate, who was lying on the sofa with her head pillowed on his thigh. "I don't brood."

"Then what have you been doing for the past half hour?" she challenged.

"Watching TV with you."

"You've been lost in your own thoughts. You didn't even notice when I pressed mute." She sat up and straddled him, her far-too-knowing eyes raking over his face. "Talk to me."

He settled his hands on her hips and shrugged. "You can already sense what I'm feeling."

"Your emotions only hint at what's going through your mind." She tilted her head. "The guilt you were feeling earlier is heavier now. Like a weight on your shoulders. Please tell me you're not tormenting yourself with what *could* have happened earlier. That doesn't help."

He sighed. "I know. I know it's senseless. But I just keep thinking that if Ally hadn't been there at the mall—and she almost wasn't, because Derren tried ordering her to stay behind—Cassidy would be dead right now."

"You don't know that for sure."

"I do. I saw the wound. It was fatal, Casey. The bastard shot to kill. If it weren't for Ally, my niece would be gone. She would have died in my arms."

"But she didn't. She's tucked up in bed, safe and well. *Because you shielded her from the other bullets and got her to safety.* If you hadn't done that, it wouldn't have mattered that Ally was there. You didn't fail Cassidy, Eli. Just like you didn't fail Roni, despite what you tell yourself."

He scrubbed a hand down his face. "Fuck, I let Roni down in too many ways to count."

"It's hardly your fault that you weren't there the day those humans tried assaulting her."

"Maybe not, but …" God, he did not want to talk about this. He really didn't. But Zander was right that secrets could block the mating bond. What if Eli *was* the reason the bond was incomplete? In any case, she deserved to know everything. She'd been honest and open with him from the start; she was entitled to that same courtesy.

Eli took a deep breath. "Just before Nick left for juvie, he told me to look after Roni. I didn't even manage to make sure she had the time and space to heal from the attack."

"She *did* heal. Well, she's about as healed as anyone who's been through that kind of hell *could* be."

"That's mostly thanks to Marcus." Eli slipped his hands under his mate's shirt, needing the feel of her skin beneath his palms. "I mentioned my old Alpha, Floyd, to you."

"You did. You said he was an asshole."

That had been an understatement. "Floyd didn't have a mate. He had a harem. And if someone didn't do as he asked, he'd threaten to add one of their female relatives to his harem."

"And he wanted you to do something for him?"

"He wanted me to duel in an illegal fighting ring. It didn't matter to him that I was only a juvenile. He threw me in that pit over and over. Every battle was a fight to the death. There were no rules, referees, or healers. They didn't give you weapons. Not even when you were pitted against multiple opponents." He ground his teeth, preparing himself for the pity that would no doubt ripple down their bond. But it wasn't an echo of pity that touched him. It was sheer rage.

"*That motherfucker.*" His mate looked ready to go on a killing spree.

To Eli's shock, he almost found himself smiling. "Floyd kept Roni in the main house with him as 'insurance,' just as he did the relatives of others he had do 'favors' for him. That's what he'd call it. A favor. He only forced the most dominant young males in the pack to fight in the ring, but it wasn't because we were the toughest."

"It was a twisted form of domination," Casey guessed. "He was keeping you all in line by using your love for your relatives against you. Making you feel helpless. Making you feel powerless against him."

Eli nodded. "I hated that I couldn't get to her; that I couldn't protect her." His sister had been through enough.

"You did protect her. It can't have been fun for her to live in his house, but I'm damn well sure that life would have been a waking nightmare for her if she'd been part of his harem. I'm just so sorry that you were put in that position, Eli."

"Each time I fought, I hated myself and Floyd a little bit more. I tried rallying the other fighters into banding against him, but they were afraid of their loved ones being hurt. It was a relief when Nick took over and helped us fix the pack."

Casey caught his face in her hands. "You didn't let Roni down. My guess is she feels guilty that you were forced to fight in that ring just to keep her safe from further trauma. You'd tell her that was dumb, and she'd call you that very same thing if she could hear you now." He only shrugged. "You didn't tell me about the fighting ring earlier because you thought I'd judge you for the things you'd done, didn't you?"

"Who wouldn't?"

She exhaled heavily. "Eli, you didn't duel in the fighting ring because you wanted to."

"Doesn't matter. I hurt a lot of people, Casey. Hurt them bad before I killed them. Real bad. None died easily. Not all of them wanted to be there. I could tell when, like me, they were being forced to fight. But I couldn't let that matter. Couldn't help them. Couldn't even help myself or my sister."

"You were just a juvenile, Eli, you couldn't have gone up against him. You did what you had to do to survive, just like the other boys in your pack did, and no one could ever blame or judge you for that."

Maybe. Maybe not. "Even when life got better, I was as bad as my mom and Nick for assuming I knew what Roni was feeling and what she needed. She used to disappear in her wolf form for months at a time to escape how suffocated we made her feel."

Casey put her face closer to his. "She loves you. She does, Eli. I see it in every crazy interaction that you guys have." She slid her hands from his face into his hair. "If you'd really let her down, she wouldn't feel safe with you. Wouldn't feel safe enough to tease you, wouldn't trust that you'd never take the pranks so far that you crossed a line for her. I'm telling you, your sister loves you. How could she not? You're rather loveable."

Eli sucked in a breath and swallowed hard. "Yeah?"

"Yeah," she said, her voice soft.

"You love me?"

"*Duh.*"

He smiled. "That's good. It's very, very good. Because I love you more than I've ever loved anything. I genuinely don't know how I functioned without you."

"You told your mom you were miserable before me."

"I was. The night I found you, I'd just heard that my cousin from another pack had found his mate. I couldn't even be happy for him. I wanted to be, but I was too envious. It just seemed like everyone around me was moving on to the next stage of their lives while I was alone. So I was …"

"Brooding," she supplied.

He shot her a mock glare. "Contemplating life." He ignored her little snort. "And then there you were. Even now, when I'm feeling like shit, I'm happier than I've ever been purely because I have you. It never matters how much I have on my mind, you're always up here." He tapped his temple. "Distracting me. Calming me. Reminding me that I'm a lucky fucker. Making me look forward to getting the day over with so I can get back to you."

Casey swallowed. "And yet, you kept all that stuff from me because you thought I'd judge you. Such a dumbass."

A startled laugh bubbled out of him. "A dumbass? I tell you that you make me the happiest I've ever been, and you call me a dumbass. I feel so loved."

"You are loved, which is why it makes me mad when you put yourself through the ringer and start brooding—"

"I don't brood."

"I'd ask you to promise that you won't mentally beat yourself up like that again, but I don't suppose you will."

He made a speculative sound. "I don't know, baby. When you set to work on my cock and do that thing with your tongue … yeah, I reckon you could get me to promise you just about anything."

Her lips curled. "You're kind of easy for my mouth."

"I *love* your mouth." He gave her a slow, deep kiss, smoothing his hands up her back.

Breaking the kiss, she flashed him an impish smile. "So … want to help me with something in the bedroom?"

He hummed. "What kind of help do you need?"

"Oh, it'll be a very hands-on job. The kind you're best at."

Chuckling, he stood with her in his arms. "I'm always happy to give you a helping hand. Tell me more about what this job entails," he said as he headed for the bedroom.

"Well …"

CHAPTER THIRTEEN

Casey kept her eye on the ball as a striker for the opposing team positioned herself to take a free kick. With no clouds to ease the brightness of the sun, she found herself constantly squinting to avoid the sharp rays of light. Sweat trickled down her flushed skin and stung the graze on her cheek that was courtesy of an "accidental" foul.

The Washington Weasels—God, Adrian was *so* right about it being a dumb name—had sure kept the Hounds on their toes. The Weasels were focused and highly skilled, and their teamwork was faultless.

Each team had scored two goals so far, and there were twenty minutes left before the final whistle would blow. Both teams were so desperate to score another goal that they'd been trying a little *too* hard, which was why they were repeatedly slipping up and committing more fouls than usual. And now the Weasels had been awarded yet *another* free kick. That wouldn't have made her so nervous if the free kick wasn't happening so close to the goal area.

Blowing out a breath, Casey rolled back her shoulders. Adrenaline pumped through her, keeping her sharp even as tiredness began to settle in. They were *all* tiring, and that lethargy was made worse by the baking heat. The air was so dry and humid that it seemed to saw at her dry throat like sandpaper.

She almost winced as a foot stepped on hers. The line of players that had formed in front of the goal nudged and jostled each other, all jockeying to— depending on which team they were playing for—either block the ball or help it pass and hit the net.

Casey's eyes narrowed as the striker up ahead of them ran on her toes toward the ball, speeding up as she got closer to it. Then, executing one hell of an impressive kick, she sent the ball sailing through the air toward the net.

Heart beating hard in her chest, Casey jumped to block it. Missed. *Shit.* But then a hard headbutt from Kristin redirected the ball and sent it hurtling toward another Hound.

Fucking yes! Adrenaline once more spiking through her, Casey sprinted toward the opposition's goal. Her teammate passed the ball to her without hesitance and, with a clear shot to the net, Casey brought her leg back and volleyed the ball hard … only a second before a foot mercilessly slammed into her outstretched leg. *Son of a bitch!*

Casey sucked in a breath as white-hot pain streaked up her leg. She felt and heard a nauseating crack, and her stomach rolled. She landed awkwardly on her hurt leg, and a blinding pain *exploded* in her ankle. Stars burst behind her eyelids, and her knees would have given way from the agony alone if she hadn't already been sprawled on the turf.

She blinked, trying to clear the spots from her vision. "Fuck, fuck, *fuck.*"

She was distantly aware that Kristin and Emma were yelling at one of the Weasels while the other Hounds gathered around Casey protectively. The spectators on her team's side of the bleachers were booing and roaring angry insults at the offending player. Casey knew Eli would be one of them. She could *feel* his fury as if it were her own.

"Out of the way!" ordered Donahue as she and Dennis shouldered through the crowd.

"Did I score?" asked Casey, her voice thick with pain.

"Yes—and it was a beautiful shot." Crouching beside her, Dennis winced as he examined her leg. "That ankle's broken for sure."

Donahue cursed. "You're gonna have to sit the rest of the game out, Frost."

It was automatic for Casey to try voicing a protest—she did it without thinking.

"Don't tell me you can still play," said Donahue. "There's no way you can hobble around on that field with this injury. Dennis will get you healed, and then you can watch from the bench. I'm sorry, Frost, but that's the way it has to be." She turned to the ref, who was gazing down at Casey's leg. "If you don't red-card the shit out of this situation, you're gonna have a riot on your hands."

His mouth tightened. He spun without a word and stalked away.

Emma appeared. "Fuck, that looks really bad." She bent over and whispered, "We'll get the bitch for you, Case, if she's not sent off the field."

Gritting her teeth against the agony still racking her, Casey gave her teammate a solemn nod. Dennis soothing energy moved through her, healing the injury, but it didn't entirely ease the pain. That was the annoying thing about being a mink—for some unknown reason, the pain of their injuries lingered a little after they were healed.

"You played well," said Dennis as he helped her stand. "At least you have the comfort that you scored."

Casey only grunted, flexing her ankle, her nostrils flaring at the throbbing ache. Satisfied that she was fine, her teammates gave her nods and pats on the back—all looked hungry for vengeance. And she knew they'd target the bitch who'd hurt Casey if the ref didn't do *something*.

Her mink certainly wanted to do something. Hissing and lashing her tail, the animal demanded freedom so that she could hunt down and maul her attacker.

Just then, there was a distinct *shift* in the spectators. The boos turned to contended cheers, but the other half of the spectators jumped to their feet and yelled their displeasure.

Kristin jogged over to Casey. "The heifer's been sent off the field, and the ref has awarded us a penalty kick, since the foul happened so close to the goal area."

Casey's brows shot up. "Who's taking the PK?"

"Emma."

Casey smiled. "Then we have this." Because no one was better at penalty kicks than Emma.

Kristin nodded, mouth curling. "Yeah, we fucking do."

Casey did her best not to limp her way off the field, but it was hard. It only pissed her off more that some of the Weasels shot her smug looks. They wouldn't look so fucking smug when Emma booted the ball into the net—which she damn well would.

As Casey slumped on the bench behind the sidelines, Dennis shoved a water bottle into her hand. "Thanks," she mumbled. She tipped her head back and closed her eyes as she gulped down the water.

A familiar scent swamped her just as a heavy weight settled beside her on the bench. She looked at Eli in surprise. "How did you get down here?" Not that she wasn't terribly glad to see him, especially since his very presence distracted her raging mink.

Straddling the bench and bracketing the side of her body with his thighs, he snorted. "Like anyone was going to stop me from getting to you. I needed to check you were okay."

"I'm fine, just pissed." But her assurance didn't lessen the anger she could feel radiating through him.

"Then why were you hobbling off the field, even though you seem to be healed? I can feel an echo of your pain." His voice sounded faintly accusatory, and she had the feeling that he thought Dennis had deliberately failed to fully heal her.

"It's a mink-thing. When our injuries are healed, the pain hangs around a little. It's fading now."

"Really? I didn't know that about your kind. Weird."

Weird, and fucking annoying. As he curled his arm around her, she said,

163

"I'm all sweaty."

"Don't care."

A shadow fell over them, and they looked up to see Preston.

"I wanted to check you were okay," Preston told her.

"She's fine," said Eli, splaying a possessive hand on her thigh.

Casey nudged him. "Look, they're getting ready for the penalty kick. I'm kind of surprised the ref awarded one."

Eli's eyes flared. "The Weasel went for you on purpose. It was a calculated act."

Preston nodded. "You're the best player and the best scorer; she knew the loss of you would make a huge difference to your team and to the game itself. You'll probably have to deal with this type of crap again if you go up against Sherryl's team."

"Have you heard from Sherryl?" Eli asked him.

Preston sighed. "No. I thought she might call me and ask me to appeal to have the ban lifted—we were friends for a long time. But she hasn't bothered."

"She probably figured it would be a waste of time, given that she almost ruined your relationship with your mate," Eli mused.

Casey took another swig of water. "How are things with you and Mallory?" she asked Preston.

He rubbed at his nape. "She let me move back into the house. I'm in the guest room, but that's better than sofa surfing while I wait for her to calm down."

Casey suspected Mallory was holding onto her anger merely for the sake of it at this point, but she said nothing. She shifted her gaze to Emma, who placed the ball on the grass a short distance from the goal. "Here we go," said Casey, anticipation buzzing through her.

Emma took five steps back, just as she always did before taking a PK. And then a hush fell over the field. It seemed like minutes later that the ref blew his whistle, and then Emma burst to life. She moved fast, which seemed to take the goalkeeper off-guard. She took a short, straight run and kicked the ball hard and low.

The ball shot through the air like a bullet. The keeper dived, swiping out with an arm to block it. She missed. The ball sank into the net like it was its job.

Beaming from the inside out, Casey jumped to her feet with a loud, war cry. Ignoring the smarting in her ankle, she bounced on her feet like a crazed kangaroo. Emma took off at an elated run, her face glowing. And then the other Hounds were crowding and lifting her.

"We're winning 4-to-2," Casey gloated.

"You realize that the Weasels are going to go at your team even more aggressively now, right?" asked Eli once the noise had died down.

Casey parked her butt back on the bench. "Oh, I know." And she had to admit, it made her nervous.

She braced her elbows on her thighs as she watched the game, silently encouraging and praising her teammates. She also cursed and snarled at the Weasels, who upped their aggression ten-fold, just as Eli had predicted.

She almost charged onto the field twice after the Weasels committed two shitty fouls on Emma, as if they were aiming to punish her for the PK. Only the arm that Eli had wrapped tight around Casey kept her ass on the bench.

He kissed her temple. "I know it's hard for you to sit back and watch, but you did your bit, baby. You scored two of the four goals. They'll take care of the rest."

She had complete confidence in her team. But it still felt wrong to be watching when she could be *helping*. It was so stomach-twistingly nerve-racking that she almost couldn't watch at all. She would have bitten her nails if she'd had any.

Her stomach plummeted when one of the Weasels scored—she could sense that it gave the heifers a sort of spiritual *lift*; gave them hope that they could close the gap and, at the very least, end the game with 4-to-4. And it filled Casey with dread that their hope would pay off.

The Weasels created several opportunities to score, but the Hounds were there every time; intercepting and redirecting the ball. Just as they reached the last minute of the game, two minutes of extra time were added. *Great.* To be fair to the Weasels, they didn't resign themselves to a loss. They kept on playing, and they didn't let up the pressure.

Casey bit hard into her lip as a Weasel intercepted a kick from a Hound, regained possession of the ball, and volleyed it straight at the goal. The Hound's goalkeeper tried catching it. The ball skimmed over her fingertips … and hit the goal post. Relief poured through Casey as it bounced away from the net. The keeper scooped it up and booted it downfield.

Then the whistle blew.

Casey and Eli shot to their feet, cheering. Donahue and the rest of the staff just about lost their minds, as did the Hounds on the field.

Eli hugged her tight. "Congratulations, baby, you're through to the final. How does it feel?"

"It feels fucking amazing." She exchanged hugs and ass-pats with each of her teammates as they filed off the field, beaming in pure delight.

"I told you we'd win this season, Frost," said Kristin.

Casey smiled. "We haven't won yet. The bitches of Eastwick won't make it easy."

Emma looked at her ankle. "Are you doing okay?"

"Fine," said Casey, stretching her foot. "The pain's gone." She turned to Eli, ready to tell him she needed to go shower. "Why are you frowning at your cell?"

He looked up, his expression unreadable. "Nick just texted me."

"And?"

Eli cupped her hip. "We have your brother's location."

Her mink stiffened. Casey almost jerked in surprise. "Where is he?"

Cradling a cup of tepid, untouched coffee in her hands, Casey could only sit and stare at her brother. He'd lost a *lot* of weight since she'd last seen him. His dark stubble didn't help hide his sallow, gaunt face, just as his plain clothes didn't hide how stick-thin he was. The guy didn't seem to have even an ounce of muscle on him.

Her mink was saddened by what she saw. Miles had always had a spark. A spark that lit his eyes, energy, and lifeforce. That spark had all but gone.

Casey had honestly never seen a person look so dejected and hopeless. And as she drank in the sight of him, she felt a deep shame. She'd never thought to look for her brother in a place like this, and how shitty of her was that?

Eli squeezed her thigh in comfort. He hadn't spoken much; seemed content to just observe as she and Miles made what could only be described as awkward small-talk. She just didn't really know what to say to him, and he seemed to be having that same issue.

She swallowed. "I don't understand why you didn't call me."

Miles looked at the plain white walls of the reception area. "This isn't the first time I've checked into rehab, Case. I always mean to stay. Always. But the process always kicks my ass after a couple of months." He sniffed. "I never saw the sense in contacting anyone unless I thought I could stick it out."

"You also didn't want to see me."

He grimaced at the soft accusation. "It's not that. You tell your teammates practically everything. If *you* knew where I was, *Sherryl* would know where I was, and she's the last person I—"

"Sherryl's not part of my team, Miles. She left the pack over a year ago. Until recently, I hadn't seen her since then."

He gaped, blinking hard. "What happened recently?"

"I found Eli. She didn't take it too well."

Miles grunted. "She'd rather wallow over the loss of her true mate than heal and be happy. She's her own worst enemy. I told her that a thousand times."

"I'd have to agree with you." But as she suspected that Sherryl wasn't the safest topic to discuss with him, Casey changed the subject. "How's your mink doing?" she asked, placing her cup on the table.

"He hates this place. He wants out."

Which undoubtedly made it even harder for Miles to stay committed to the rehabilitation process. She fisted her hands, hating that there was literally nothing she could do to help her brother. Nothing. He had to help himself. All she could do was support him. "Have you seen or heard from Mom or Emily?"

"Not since before I split from Sherryl. Last time I spoke to Emily on the phone, she told me that she was engaged to Theo Marsden."

The son of their father's close friend, Casey remembered. Theo was also a university lecturer and, unlike other lecturers she'd met in the past, unbelievably boring.

"She said the wedding would take place this year," said Miles. "It's pure shit to think that my sister could be married by now … and I'll have missed it. Not that Dad would have let me into the church anyway." He forced a smile, his eyes darting from her to Eli. "So, where did you meet?"

"We met at The Den, a fight club for shifters," said Eli.

"I remember you once told me about it," Miles said to her. "Not surprised you'd gravitate to a place like that."

She shrugged. "I like to keep my skills sharp. People are always too careful when they spar."

Eli drummed his fingers on her thigh. "She wiped the floor with a fox, and I knew I had to have her. I followed her outside, and that was when I saw her talking to Ignacio Rodriguez."

Casey gritted her teeth. She'd told Eli before they entered the rehab center that she wanted to keep the conversation light and easy—no stressful topics, no mention of Ignacio or any of the crap going on in her life. He'd only nodded. She should have known he wouldn't keep his mouth shut.

"Ignacio?" echoed Miles, straightening in his seat, clearly alarmed. "I told him to stop hounding you, Casey."

"You can't be all that surprised that he ignored you," said Eli, his voice empty of the anger she could sense bubbling inside him. "You knew he'd go to her for the cash if you didn't pay him—don't pretend differently."

"But I *did* pay him. I even paid the fucking *interest* he adds on, because I didn't want him going near Casey again." Miles looked her up and down. "Did he hurt you?"

She quickly shook her head. "No—"

"He whipped out a blade," Eli cut in. "Thankfully, she wrestled it from him and put it to his throat."

Casey rounded on him, eyes wide. "Eli, would you please exercise your right to remain silent? And I mean *now*."

Ignoring that, Eli went on, "I paid the debt you owed Ignacio. But I need to be clear on something, Miles: It won't be something I'll do again. I made that very clear to him, too. I want him out of Casey's life, not nipping at her heels every now and then, looking for cash. I don't think you want that for her either. I know she doesn't want it for you."

She hissed out a breath. "*Eli.*"

"No," Miles said to her. "He's right to defend you. Protect you. I'm glad you have that. But I swear to you both, *I paid him.* There've been times when I haven't, sure, but that was in the past." His Adam's apple bobbed. "I have tried to get clean, Casey. I've tried it so many times. But the cleaner I got, the more I could feel the loose connection I had to *her.*

"It's not as strong now. Not as intense. And the depression … it doesn't have that same hold on me that it once did. I wish I could tell you that I'm going to be fine, that I'll stay clean. I can't promise you that. I can only promise that I'll give it my best shot."

She licked her lips. "That's all I can ask."

"This is the best place for you," Eli told him. "Not just because of your addiction, but because you'll be in danger out there. Ignacio will be looking for you. So far, he obviously hasn't thought to look for you at rehab centers. Maybe that will give you added motivation to stay where you are and see this through to the end."

"I want to see this through," said Miles. "But I won't lie to Casey about whether I will. I won't give her false assurances."

Eli inclined his head. "If you won't do it for you, do it for the female that's somewhere out there, waiting for you to find and claim her."

Miles' smile was somewhat bitter and self-depreciating. "My true mate would be better off without a latent, pack-less shifter who comes with my kind of baggage. She'd be ashamed if she could see me now."

"You're an unofficial member of the Craven Pack, so you're not exactly a lone shifter," Eli pointed out. "Unless you can tell me that you'd turn away from your mate simply because she's latent, I can't imagine that she'd do the same to you. As for her being ashamed of you? I doubt she would be, because she'll understand you in a way that no one else ever can. She'll never judge or reject you. She'll accept every part of you—even your flaws and whatever baggage you bring. So do her proud, put her first, and get your shit together for her sake."

So much for keeping the conversation light and easy, Casey silently grumbled to herself. Miles didn't respond, but she could see that Eli had given her brother something to think about.

She and Miles talked a little more about normal, everyday things until, finally, the visitation was over. Tears stung her eyes when his arms wrapped around her. She'd missed him so much, and she hated that he was going through this alone. Absolutely fucking hated it. "I'll come back."

His arms flexed around her. He slowly let her go before shaking Eli's hand and saying, "Take care of her."

Drawing her neatly to his side, Eli nodded. "Look after yourself, Miles. We'll come see you again soon."

The minute they were out of the center, Casey tossed a harsh glare at Eli.

"You were an asshole in there. The last thing he needs right now in that frame of mind is a lecture."

Maybe, thought Eli, but … "He needed to know that he had more to lose by leaving than he did by staying. He needed to know that he wouldn't have you as his safety cushion anymore." Because Eli wouldn't fucking tolerate it.

"He needed to know he has my support," she countered.

"And he does. But part of the rehab process is facing the shit you've done. He's been out of contact with you for a long time, Casey, so he's never really *seen* the effect his addiction had on you. Now he knows."

"Yeah, but now he'll be worrying about me instead of concentrating on helping himself. He said he paid his most recent debts to Ignacio, which means the fucker was just playing with me for his own amusement and personal gain."

"Or Miles hasn't been able to keep track of his debts because he was high as a fucking kite most of the time." For Eli, that was the likeliest scenario. Another possibility was that Miles was too ashamed to admit to his sister that he'd, basically, fucked her over.

Eli caught her arm as they reached the SUV. "I know you love your brother, I know it's important to you that he recovers. But *you're* important to *me*. I love you. I want you safe. And, like it or not, Miles is the reason you haven't been safe in a while. He needed to be faced with that truth. If he's the good person you say he is, it might motivate him to stick with rehab and get his life together." Her anger was so fierce that Eli wasn't prepared for how quickly she just … deflated—shoulders slumping, lips trembling, eyes watering.

She swallowed so hard it was audible. "I never even thought to look for him at a rehab center. Not even once."

And then Eli realized that most of her anger was directed at herself. Heart squeezing, he pulled her close. "Baby …"

"I gave up on him, Eli. I didn't know that I had, but—"

Eli squeezed her nape. "Stop. You had no reason to assume he'd try to get clean."

"But it should have at least occurred to me that just maybe I couldn't find him because he was trying to get well, *not* because he was hiding."

"Why would it have occurred to you? His dealer came to you time after time, expecting you to pay Miles' debts. By all accounts, it looked like he was so deep in that lifestyle he had no interest in trying to crawl his way out of it."

Eli thumbed her tears away. "You saw him in there looking all vulnerable and lost and fragile, and now you have this idea in your head that you let him down. *You didn't*. You're the only person who hasn't. Don't try to take on the weight of his fuck-ups—it's stupid and pointless and doesn't help anyone, especially not him. He has to accept and own his mistakes, Casey, if he's going to get through this."

She let out a shaky breath. "You're right. I know you're right. It's just hard to see him that way."

"I know." Eli held her tighter, tucking her face into the crook of his neck. "But it's better than not seeing him at all, right?"

Her tears were killing him. *Killing* him. He wanted to scoop her up, take her to their lodge, run her a bath, fuck her soft and slow, and then hold her while she slept. Seeing her this way put knots in his gut.

His wolf let out a low whine, nudging her with his head. He wanted to take away the source of her pain, and it angered the beast that he couldn't.

"I know you planned to go out with your team to celebrate getting through to the semi-finals but let me take you home." Eli pressed a kiss to her temple and slid his hand up her spine. "Text Emma and tell her about Miles—she'll understand why you won't be in the mood for a night out clubbing."

Casey gave a weak, soft snort. "You'd try to talk me into staying with you even if I wasn't upset."

Busted, he thought with a smile. "I don't like being away from you, true, but I will *loathe* being away from you while you're so sad." He just wanted to fix it. Wanted to comfort and cosset her. "Come on, let me take you home, get you settled, and take care of you. I need it, and so do you."

She took a deep breath. "Okay."

The knots in his gut fell away. "Okay."

"But I have to ask, will there be orgasms involved?"

"Multiple."

White-hot pleasure spiraled through Casey, stealing the breath from her lungs and making her eyes go blind. Eli's tongue didn't let up. It kept on licking and stabbing and swirling as she rode out her orgasm.

Eyes closed, body trembling, heart pounding, Casey melted into the mattress. Contentedly floating on a cloud of bliss as, seemingly in no rush whatsoever, Eli idly kissed and nipped his way up her body. He suckled hard here and there, renewing little marks that were fading. The pads of his fingers traced and stroked her skin, blatantly possessive.

Her eyes snapped open as one hand pinned both her wrists above her head. Eli was draped over her, his eyes hot, his face cold. A shiver raced down her spine. And then her lips parted on a gasp as she felt his thick cock push inside her, stretching the quaking walls of her pussy.

"That's it, keep your eyes on mine." In one smooth territorial thrust, Eli drove himself deep. He groaned. "Fuck, you feel good. Wrap your legs around me, Casey. Good girl."

He eased his hips back and then thrust forward, surging deep. His grip on her wrists flexed as he lazily withdrew again, leaving only the head of his dick inside. Then he slammed home. "Did you know that your pussy strangles my cock whenever I pin you down?" He fucked her slow and hard, ignoring her orders to move faster. "Do you want my come in you, baby?"

"Every last drop."

His cock throbbed at that answer. "Hmm, you'll get it. But not in your pussy." He held his finger to her mouth. "Suck it."

And then she understood. "Eli—"

"Your ass is the only part of you I haven't claimed, Casey. I want it. It's mine." If Eli thought for a second that she didn't want this, however, he wouldn't push it. But he could sense that she was curious, and she'd enjoyed every bit of anal play they'd done so far. "We've been readying you for this, we know you can take me—your body was made for me." He put his finger closer to her mouth. "Now suck it."

Defiance flashed in her eyes and buzzed down their bond. But then she took a deep breath, and the emotion faded.

He hummed, slamming his cock deep again. "That's my girl."

She sucked his finger and swirled her tongue around it, just as she often did to his cock. Which almost made him abandon his current plan and fuck her mouth instead. Almost.

Eli kept on fucking her slow and hard as he gently worked his wet finger into her ass, just as he'd done many times before. Each time he buried his dick in her pussy, he sank his finger into her ass. Only when he sensed sexual frustration hum through her did he add another finger, growling at how hot and tight she was. "Fuck, I can't wait to get my cock in here."

"I need you to move faster."

And he needed her to come, so he gave her what she wanted, his pace feverish as he rammed hard again and again. She went wild beneath him, groaning, bucking her hips, struggling against his tight grip on her wrists. He drove a third finger into her ass, stretching her even more, satisfied when she didn't wince or flinch.

"I'm not going to take you from behind, Casey. I'm going to take your ass while you're like this, so I can see your face when you come." He loved watching that moment when her pleasure took her. Just thinking about it made his balls tighten.

He rode her harder, literally feeling it as she wound tighter and tighter. God, she was so fucking wet and snug it was a strain not to let go of his control and just power into her. Especially when her pussy turned inferno hot and began to tighten around him even more. Yeah, she was close.

"Come for me, Casey." Knowing what would knock her over the edge, he bit down hard on her neck. She came apart around him with a scream.

Gritting his teeth against the urge to explode right then, Eli withdrew his dick, angled her hips and—while she was still coming hard—replaced his fingers with the head of his cock. "Push out," he clipped, steadily pushing his way in. Even half out of it, she did as he asked.

Battling the drive to slam deep, he slowly sank inside her ass, loving every fucking second of it. He growled deep in his throat. "Jesus, you're so tight and hot." And knowing he'd claimed a part of her that nobody else had ever had only fired his need and made his cock ache like a bitch.

Buried as deep as he could go, Eli flexed his hips. "Ready?"

Casey licked her lips. "Yes. I'm good. You need to move."

Taking her at her word, Eli smoothly withdrew his cock until only the head was inside her. Then, just as smoothly, he sank back into her ass. The sight alone made his dick throb, and he knew he wouldn't last long.

Each slow, deep thrust ate at his control until all he could think of doing was hammering into her ass. But he didn't. He kept his pace slow and his thrusts nice and easy.

"Look at the pretty picture you make beneath me," he rumbled. "Eyes sex-drunk. Mouth swollen. Nipples tight. Skin flushed. Your ass squeezing my cock as I sink in and out."

She hissed out a breath. "Harder. I'm not fucking fragile."

"You sure you can take it?"

Her glazed eyes flared. "I can take it."

He pumped his hips harder, faster, driving balls-deep with each thrust. He kept a mental eye on her through their bond, making sure she wasn't feeling any pain. All he could sense was raw hunger and a desperate need to come.

"You have such a tight, perfect little ass. I own it, don't I?" He slapped said ass hard, and then a fierce orgasm whipped up and consumed her, taking them both by surprise. The pleasure poured into him through their mating bond and dragged him under.

Biting out a harsh curse, he pounded into her as her tight inner muscles squeezed him tight, shooting rope after rope of come inside her, *finally* claiming her ass as his own. And then, as satisfaction settled deep into his bones, they both collapsed.

CHAPTER FOURTEEN

Since she'd missed her celebratory night out with her teammates, Eli proposed they go on a date the following evening to make up for it—somewhere they could relax, wind down, and have fun. So, of course, they went to The Den. If that made them weird, Casey didn't care.

It was packed, as usual. Some stood around the combat ring while others sat at tables or hung out at the bar. The scents of beer, sweat, blood, and various breeds of shifter filled the warm air. Beneath the cheering and shouting, she could hear pained grunts, angry growls, and flesh hitting flesh.

Walking around The Den with Eli was something of an experience. Everyone knew and respected him, so they nodded, waved, or said their hellos—they were also sure to get a good look at the female whose hand he was holding. She'd competed there many times, so a lot of people recognized and greeted her, too. Quite a few of the females, however, shot her dirty looks. Yeah, well, if she'd seen Eli breezing around the place with another female, Casey wouldn't have been too pleased about it either.

For the first hour, she and Eli watched fights and placed bets on who'd win. Most of those bets paid off. Casey later hopped into the ring with a female hyena. Eli shouted words of praise and encouragement as she let loose on the hyena. The two females exchanged blows, kicks, bites, and scratches—it was an ugly fight, but it was over halfway into the first round after Casey knocked the hyena clean-out.

As people once again cheered, Casey slid out of the ring and right into Eli's arms. "I've got blood on me," she warned.

"Don't care." He held her tight and gave her a quick kiss. "Well done, baby. You were ruthless."

"Is that why you're hard as a rock?" She could feel his cock pressed against her lower stomach.

"Oh, yeah. It has to make me twisted that I want you so badly when you've got someone else's blood splattered on you. But seeing you let loose in that ring never fails to fire me up." He set her on her feet. "Come on, let's get you cleaned up."

Not in the least bit bothered that it was the women's restroom, he followed her inside and helped wash the blood from her skin. Satisfied that her wounds were shallow and would heal within the hour, Eli said, "Now it's my turn."

She smiled. "Good. Watching you fight is always a treat—especially since you take off your shirt. I often find myself objectifying you when you're half-dressed or naked."

He chuckled. "As it's you, I'll let it go."

Taking her hand in his, Eli led her out of the restroom. They were a few feet away from the ring when he felt Casey tense. He looked down at her. "What's wrong?" He tracked her gaze. A growl rumbled up his chest and out of his throat—one that came from both Eli and his wolf. Ignacio and four of his cats were sat in the corner, and the Alpha's eyes were locked on Casey.

"We should go," she said.

Eli frowned. "Because he's here? Fuck that."

"Not because he's here. But because he'll probably take this chance to play mind games with you."

"Probably," Eli agreed. "But I'm not going to let anyone chase me out of here." There wasn't a chance in hell that Eli would jump in the combat ring, though. He wasn't going to leave her side for even a second.

"Half an hour," she said. "You promised me you'd fuck me silly later—I expect you to deliver."

Eli smiled. "Oh, I'll deliver."

Just as they'd done earlier, he and Casey watched fights and placed bets. It was just when two polar bears started their second round that the scents of cougar drifted toward Eli. That might not have made his wolf lunge to the surface, wanting to maul and kill, if one of those scents hadn't belonged to Ignacio.

Keeping his body slightly in front of his mate, Eli turned to face the Alpha, his expression carefully blank.

Ignacio smiled at them as he greeted, "Eli, Casey." His gaze danced between them. "Mated life suits you. Although ... I cannot help but notice that your bond hasn't yet snapped into place," he said with false sympathy. "Hmm. That must be driving your animals insane."

"Is there a point to this conversation?" asked Casey, sounding bored.

Ignacio tilted his head. "Still smarting after that unnecessary business with Dahlia?"

"*And* the attack on Eli," she said. "*And* the shooting. *And* the fact that you breathe."

Tension coiled in Eli's muscles, readying him to spring. The cougar would surely lunge at Casey for that remark. Surely.

But he didn't. The corners of Ignacio's mouth tipped up. "As I've said before: Balls of steel." His gaze shifted to Eli. "I am sorry to hear your pack has had such problems recently. I take it there have been no more incidents, since I've had no other accusatory calls from your Alpha. I suppose it's fortunate that I'm not easily offended. If I were, I might take exception to his insistence in pointing the finger of blame my way."

"I think we can safely say that, no, there is no point to this conversation," Casey decided, turning to Eli. "Let's just go."

"Have you seen anything of Miles, Casey?" Ignacio asked.

She lifted a brow. "You think I'd really tell you if I had?"

"Perhaps not," said Ignacio. "If I were you, I'd be worried. He's disappeared several times in the past, but never for this long. Yes, in your shoes, I'd be on tender hooks, dreading that I might get a call to say he's been found in a gutter somewhere."

"And if I were in your shoes, I'd cut off that ponytail and just face the fact that it didn't look good on me."

Once again, Eli braced himself to intervene, expecting the Alpha to try pouncing on her for the derogatory remark. But Ignacio's smile didn't even falter. And, wait, had the cougar's eyes just … *softened*? Hell, yeah, they had. Not much, but a little. Something wasn't right. Unease slithered through Eli as a dark suspicion pricked at him.

"It's touching that you have such a vested interest in my appearance," the Alpha said to her.

"Go back to your table, Ignacio," said Eli, wanting the male away from his mate *yesterday*.

"At least let me buy you both a drink first. Call it a congratulations on your mating." There was the slightest edge to his voice as the cougar spoke the latter word, and it made Eli's wolf bare his teeth.

"I only drink with people I respect," Eli told him. "And how can I respect a man who has lone shifters do his dirty work?"

The cougar's face hardened. "I can assure you, Eli, I do my own dirty work. Mostly because I enjoy it. There's something about watching the life leave a person's eyes that is almost … invigorating."

"Is that comment supposed to spook me?" Eli snickered. "I've met plenty of people in my time who were sick in the head. It didn't keep them conscious when I beat the shit out of them."

"Yes, yes, you're a big, tough guy," said Ignacio with a bored sigh. "We're all very afraid."

"You should be," Casey told him. "Come on, Eli, we have plans." The sexual implication was clear.

Ignacio tensed. "Leaving so soon, Casey? I was going to propose that you and my enforcer, Brenna, have a duel in the ring."

And there he was, trying to snag Casey's attention again. Narrowing his eyes, Eli cocked his head. "Why is it that you feel the need to toy with Casey? It's like you just can't help yourself. You see her, and your first instinct is to pit your personality against hers; to needle and goad her into reacting to you … almost in an attention-seeking way. Why would you want my mate's attention?" That dark suspicion pricked at him again. "You don't think she's your true mate, do you?"

Ignacio's expression didn't alter in the slightest. "Dahlia is my mate."

"But not your true mate. Do you think it's Casey?" It would explain a lot of things—why Ignacio had repeatedly sought her out rather than punishing Miles for not paying his debts; why Ignacio had never hurt her, not even when she held a knife to his throat; why he'd never insisted on retribution for her hurting and embarrassing Dahlia.

Miles had said that he'd paid his most recent debts to Ignacio. Eli hadn't believed him at the time, but what if it were true? What if the reason Ignacio came to her again and again looking for cash to cover Miles' habit, was very simply that he wanted to see her?

Ignacio could even have been responsible for the attack on Sherryl. He wasn't the type of person who'd claim their true mate—he'd consider her and the bond itself a weakness. But he probably wouldn't keep his distance, and he'd likely want some form of attention from her. He'd also avenge her if he felt the need to.

"No, I do not," said the cougar.

"Yeah? I'm not buying it. As I recall it, you questioned that day at the marina whether I was sure she was mine. You didn't seem convinced."

Ignacio gave a careless shrug. "It just seems rather coincidental to me that you didn't like me confronting her, wanted me to leave her be, and then the very next day you claim you're her mate. Naturally I wondered if you made that claim purely to protect her."

"Well I can assure you that she's mine," said Eli, his voice thick with possessiveness. "You know, I originally thought you targeted me to strike at her. But it wasn't that, was it? You targeted me because you don't like that I have her." The more Eli thought about it, the more it all made sense … and the more he wanted to slit Ignacio's throat.

"That's quite an elaborate theory you have there. Even if I were single and had my eye on Casey, I'm not the jealous type, Eli. Rest assured, I have no designs on her, just as I have no wish to do you harm. I'm also not in the habit of hiring loners. As I said, I do my own dirty work. I wish you luck in finding the real culprit." Ignacio gave a courteous nod. "Enjoy the rest of your evening."

As they watched the cougar walk away, Casey spoke. "I don't think he ever thought he and I were true mates, Eli."

"I think we're both too close to the situation to really be sure," said Eli. "We need an outsider's opinion."

A short while later, Eli stood near the fireplace while most of his pack mates were scattered around the living area of the main lodge. Casey and Cain were also present. She sat on the sofa, her legs crossed, her arms folded, her gaze focused inward. She'd been quiet on the drive home, and she hadn't spoken much since arriving at the lodge, which was why some were casting her concerned looks that she totally missed.

Although the pack often headed to their own homes after dinner, they'd lingered to attend the meeting that Eli had called for. He was just waiting on his mother and Gwen—both of whom were cleaning the kitchen. Eli could hear cutlery clinking and the faucet running, so he knew the females weren't done yet. The only people absent from the room were the two pups, who were playing in Cassidy's room upstairs.

"Can you give us a hint about what this relates to, Eli?" asked Shaya. "My imagination is coming up with all sorts of dark scenarios."

"It's about Ignacio," he replied. "He hasn't attacked again, before you ask. But we did see him tonight."

"So nothing bad has happened?" asked Ally, nibbling on her nail. "There wasn't another incident that I failed to foresee?"

Derren squeezed his mate's thigh. "You haven't failed anyone. Don't use that word again."

"There hasn't been another incident, no," Eli told her. "And Derren's right: You haven't failed us."

He heard the click of heels on the hardwood floor moments before Kathy walked inside closely followed by Gwen. The human female headed straight to Zander and let him pull her onto his lap.

As soon as his mother had taken a seat, Eli said, "I'll get straight down to it. Casey and I saw Ignacio at The Den earlier. Some of the things he said and did make me wonder if he believes that Casey is his true mate." Just speaking the words was enough to make Eli's stomach harden. He didn't want *anyone* coveting her. "She disagrees with my theory. I wanted to run it by all of you."

There was a boom of silence, and some of his pack mates exchanged uneasy looks.

Nick rubbed his jaw. "He didn't seem happy at the marina when he realized you'd mated with Casey. He also wasn't convinced it was real, and I could see he didn't want to heed your warning to keep his distance from her. But I never got the sense that he thinks she's his."

"Ignacio isn't a person who'd stand back and deny himself what belonged to him," said Marcus as he pulled open a pack of potato chips—the guy never stopped eating.

"He also isn't a person who'd claim his true mate," said Eli, sure he was onto something here. *Despising* that he was onto something. "I've met guys like him before—they see a true-mate bond as a weakness."

Bracken gave a slow nod. "One of my old pack mates had that attitude. He claimed that having a mate made a man vulnerable; that by binding yourself to another person in such a way that their death could cause your own, you were giving them the ultimate power over you. 'Fate won't control my life,' he used to say, 'I choose my own path.'"

"Ignacio has certainly chosen his own path," said Madisyn, sitting cross-legged on the rug, absentmindedly tracing the little scorch marks on it that were courtesy of the log fire. "He wanted to be an Alpha more than he wanted his true mate. He proved that when he claimed Dahlia."

"But it's not a real mating," Caleb pointed out. "It's just a façade. He could walk away from her at any time."

"Not without giving up his position of Alpha," said Zander, stroking Gwen's thigh. "He won't want to do that. He wouldn't have forsaken his true mate in the first place if having the position wasn't so important to him."

Nick leaned forward in his seat and braced his elbows on his thighs. "Let's consider what we know about Ignacio. His life's goal was simple: become what his father always wanted to be and then use his position of Alpha to cut his old pride off from their alliances, which he's been very successful at so far."

"Yes," said Shaya. "He wants power. Wants to isolate his old pack. Wants all the right connections so he has pawns to play in his games. And those wants won't just go away, because they're motivated by his own personal demons—the powerlessness he felt as a kid, the hatred he feels for his father, his disgust in his old pride. He probably planned his revenge very carefully. It no doubt gave him purpose."

Eli nodded. "He made sacrifices, bound himself to someone he doesn't care for. If he doesn't get his revenge, all that will have been for nothing. He also can't afford to lose his power. If his true mate was to then come along, he wouldn't abandon his plans for her. But I think he'd want to watch over her."

"He'd need to be very careful about it, though," mused Cain. "He wouldn't want to risk that anyone would even begin to assume she was his. Wouldn't want her to be targeted by his enemies, and he wouldn't want it to be known that he has a vulnerability. People would use her to get to him, just as he strikes at people's loved ones to hurt them."

"And given the way he's acted toward Casey, who'd ever think he believes she's his?" Eli folded his arms. "I don't like that I could be right, but I do believe I am."

Casey sighed, *so* done with this conversation. The cougar had never given her *any* indication that he saw her as anything but a pain in his ass. She'd certainly never done anything other than *be* a pain. Surely he'd have treated her much differently or, at the very least, left her well alone if he believed she was his mate.

"I can see why your thoughts have taken you down this road, Eli." Sort of. "But come on, he harasses me for money. He plays little mind games with me. He even tried blackmailing me into throwing a fight at The Den. Who would do shitty stuff like that to someone they thought was their true mate?"

"I don't think he did those things to hurt you," said Eli. "I think that was about control. You said yourself that you got the feeling he likes pushing and cornering you."

"Control," echoed Cain with a nod. "That would make sense. He's all about control, and he'd want to have some form of it over her."

"I saw for myself that he enjoys playing with her," said Eli. "But what if he wasn't toying with her to be cruel? What if he did it because it was the only form of interaction that he'd allow himself to have with her?"

Casey scooted forward in her seat, still unconvinced. "But—"

"You held a blade to his throat, Casey," Eli reminded her. "A *blade.* He didn't retaliate. Didn't even demand vengeance, although Dahlia did. My guess is he knew you'd wrestle it from him."

Casey felt her face scrunch up. "You think he wanted me to hold that knife to his throat? Seriously? I mean, I'm trying to be open to what you're saying, but it's just not adding up for me."

"Because you don't want it to. Think about it, baby. Ignacio is very well-known for dishing out some real ugly punishments. He never once hurt you as a message to Miles. Never once punished you for any of the things you did or said to him. That has never made sense to me."

"He didn't harm me because my pack would have decimated his pride."

"I think it suited him to let you assume that. But I don't think it's truly why he never hurt you. He could have harmed you in a way that never implicated him; could have hired loners to do it for him. But you've never once been randomly attacked, have you?"

Casey's lips thinned. "Well, no, but—"

"Do you have a reason whatsoever that would explain why he never went after you, other than your belief that he feared how your pack would react?"

"He said I remind him of his sister; that he admires the loyalty I show to Miles."

"I'm sure he does admire your loyalty—it's not exactly something that his family or old pride members showed him much of. But that wouldn't be enough for him to ignore the need to punish Miles through you."

"Okay then, how about this? Miles said that he paid his recent debts, and I think he was telling the truth. If that's the case, it stands to reason that Ignacio wouldn't really feel a huge need to punish him."

"And yet, he went back to you again and again. Why would he do that?"

"Because he's an asshole? Because it amuses him? Because he's bored shitless and gets a kick out of manipulating someone as dominant as me? As Cain said, he's all about power."

"Yes, he is. And since I came along and blocked his access to you, he lost whatever power he thought he had over you. He wants me gone." Eli swept his gaze across the room as he went on, "I think he sent the falcons after me. I think he sent the hired gun after me. But I don't think Cassidy's bullet was meant for me. I think me, Nick, Shaya, and the pups were all targets."

"It wouldn't be the first time that Ignacio wiped out a family as a punishment," said Cain. "I can tell you of at least three families he slaughtered."

"I think he also sent someone after Sherryl," said Eli. "I think he was punishing her for threatening Casey."

"But there's no way he could even know about the trouble I'm having with her," Casey told him.

"Unless he has a mole on your territory," said Eli. He felt her denial slam into their bond. "If he believes he's your mate, he'll want to know what's happening in your life—knowledge is power, baby. The mole might not be someone from your pack. It could be one of the people who work in the stores that your pack own. They'd hear plenty about what goes on."

Nick straightened in his seat. "It might be a good idea to run that theory by Adrian."

"I intend to," said Eli.

Shaya sighed. "I really do hate to say this, but your theory has weight, Eli. There were some things that didn't add up for me. But now, looking at it all from this angle, they come together."

Casey shook her head. "After seeing us tonight, he'll know he was wrong because our scents have mixed, Eli."

"That sometimes happens with imprinted couples," said Jesse, setting his mug on the table beside the lamp. "Usually, they just wear each other's scent. But mine and Harley's have started to mix ever so slightly. Ignacio might just think you two have imprinted on each other."

Roni nodded. "Originally, he probably just thought you lied about being her mate to protect her, Eli. That will have pissed him off, because he'll think protecting her is *his* job. Now he'll see you as someone who's stealing what's his from right under his nose. It won't matter to him that he has no intention of claiming her. He won't want you to have her."

"No, he won't." Eli shifted his gaze to Nick. "I'll call Adrian and suggest he talk to his employees. If one of them is leaking info to Ignacio, it's something Adrian needs to know."

"I don't think any of them would do that," said Casey.

Eli looked back at her, hating the pain he saw in her eyes. "I hope you're right." But he didn't believe that she was.

CHAPTER FIFTEEN

Opening the front door of his lodge the next morning, Eli found Bracken standing on the porch, his mouth set into a thin slash. "What's with the scowl?"

Bracken's nostrils flared. "Your mink has corrupted my mate!"

"Corrupted? What are you talking about?"

The enforcer held up his phone. "Look!"

Peering at the photograph on the screen of the cell, Eli felt his lips twitch. Jesus Christ.

"My cat now has her *own* little collection of corpses, all neatly piled on top of each other behind her rockery."

It was probably wrong that Eli found this so amusing. "To be fair, Brack, that cat of yours has always been crazy."

"But not a murderous psychopath!"

"My mate is not a psychopath." The mink was, however, silently skittering up the porch rail behind an oblivious Bracken, her nose twitching as she glared at the visitor's back.

"Casey's not, no," allowed Bracken. "But her mink sure is. And she's grooming my cat to be her partner in crime!"

Tipping his head to the side, Eli pursed his lips. "I wouldn't say partner. More like 'apprentice.'"

In a blur of movement, the mink leaped onto Bracken's nape with a little snarl, and then jumped onto Eli's shoulder.

Bracken slapped the back of his neck. "Ow! She just bit me!"

"She did not."

"Look!" The enforcer twisted only slightly, not letting the mink out of his sight. Sure enough, there was a mark and a few dots of blood, but nothing like the kind of bite a mink could deliver with those formidable teeth.

181

"It was just a little nip."

Bracken's brows shot up. "A *nip?*"

"You're on her territory, yelling at her mate. What did you think she'd do? Come on, don't be a pussy." The mink licked at Eli's face, making him smile. He gently lifted her from his shoulder and held her against his chest as he stroked her. Just as she always did, she snuggled into him with a little purr. "See, she's harmless."

"Harmless? You have to be kidding."

"She's as playful as a pup." Most of the time. She'd bitten Eli once, but that was only because he'd tried bathing her after she came into the lodge covered in mud. Honestly, that small bite had brought tears to his eyes.

As she lay in his arms quite content, Eli scratched and rubbed her belly. "It's okay, gorgeous. The big, mean, whiny wolf is just a little scared of you, that's all."

"I'm not scared of her, I'm damn well *disturbed* by her. And I'd say I have reason to be, considering she just tried to kill me. That's how minks kill, you know. They bite the nape of their prey, puncturing the skull or spinal cord like a freaking jaguar."

"And where's the wrong in that?" Eli asked. Hearing the rustling of grass in the distance, his wolf's ears perked up. "We have company."

Soon, Roni and Madisyn came into sight.

Madisyn's brow furrowed as she spotted Bracken. "I thought I heard you yelling. What's going on?"

His mouth thinned. "I showed him the photo I snapped of your cat's little collection of dead bodies."

Madisyn rolled her eyes. "You make it sound like she killed some hitchhikers and kept their corpses as trophies."

Climbing the porch steps, Roni gasped. "Oh, Mads, look how cute she is!"

Madisyn's face went all soft. "And she lets him cradle her like a baby." The feline put a hand to her chest. "My heart can't take how utterly adorable this is."

"You hear that?" asked Roni. "She's purring like a little kitten. And now she's licking my hand. Oh, she's so sweet."

"She is *not* sweet," snapped Bracken. "She just bit me!"

"Where?" Madisyn studied the spot he pointed at. "It's just a little nip. What did you do to her?"

Bracken's eyes widened. "*I* didn't do anything. She has it in for me."

"Has it in for you," the feline repeated. "Right."

Eli was surprised when the mink let out a contented clucking sound and crawled up Roni's arm. Then again, the mink probably felt comfortable around her given that the she-wolf's scent was like his own.

"Hey, cutie." His sister very carefully shifted the mink so that she was pressed against her chest, her little head peeking over Roni's shoulder.

Madisyn clasped her hands. "Can I hold her, Eli?"

"No!" Bracken shook his head wildly. "No holding her."

Madisyn frowned. "Why not?"

"Because I don't want to carry home your severed fingers."

Again, Madisyn rolled her eyes at her mate and then turned back to Eli. "Do you think she'll let me hold her?"

Eli shrugged. "She should be okay with you, since she's friends with your cat."

"You can have your turn in a minute, Mads," said Roni. "Here, stroke her back, let her get used to you and your scent." Roni turned toward Madisyn, inadvertently giving the mink a clear view of Bracken.

The enforcer jerked back slightly. "She just snarled at me!"

Madisyn shot him an exasperated look. "Stop being an idiot. She's too busy purring to be snarling."

"I saw her," insisted Bracken.

So had Eli, but he clamped his lips shut and said nothing.

"*Now* she's glaring at me over Roni's shoulder." Bracken perched his hands on his hips. "I'm telling you, she's thinking of launching herself right at me."

Madisyn shook her head. "God, you can be such a drama queen. And stop shouting, you're going to scare her." Like the mink was a sensitive, nervous fawn or something.

The enforcer slashed a hand through the air. "That's it, I'm done here." Bracken stalked off, muttering to himself.

Eli turned to his female visitors. "So, what brings you two here?"

"We came to make sure that Casey hadn't sneakily split," said Roni. "I know she's not exactly looking forward to the party."

Casey had initially talked Shaya into waiting until Casey had moved in before throwing the welcome party, but Shaya had brought the date forward, figuring it would be good for Cassidy to be part of a celebration and be surrounded by her closest friends. The pup had been a little subdued since the shooting, although having Cain around did seem to reassure her.

"It's not that Casey doesn't want to attend the party," said Eli. "She just doesn't think she deserves to be thrown a welcome party when she hasn't officially joined the pack yet."

Madisyn shrugged one shoulder. "Shaya threw mine before I joined—it's no biggie."

"That's what I told her."

"How's she doing this morning?"

"All right. She still won't accept that Ignacio might believe she's his mate, but she informed me earlier that she intends to put him out of her mind today. That works for me. I want her to enjoy the party, not be distracted by thoughts of him." Eli smiled as the mink leaped onto his shoulder, apparently done being fussed over. "Hey, gorgeous, you ready to go inside?"

"We'll head to the lodge and see if Shaya needs any help setting things up. See ya soon." Roni waved at the mink. "Bye, cutie."

Eli walked into the lodge, closed the door behind him, and looked up at his little mink. "Enjoyed fucking with Bracken, did you?" She clucked, and he nodded. "So did I."

"I just don't understand why anyone would want to lick an ass hole," said Casey. "I mean ... it's an ass hole—enough said."

Eli chuckled. They'd been firing lighthearted questions at each other as they traipsed through the trees toward the main lodge, hand in hand, and he'd just asked what sexual practice she simply didn't understand the appeal of.

"What do you prefer—thongs or panties?" she asked.

"Thongs," he replied without hesitation. "They're easier to snap off." Eli smiled when her pupils dilated. He pitched his voice low as he asked, "What's your biggest sexual fantasy?"

"Hmm, I can't say I have sexual fantasies, really. I did think a few little scenarios might be hot, though, like being seduced in my sleep—something you've already done. It *was* hot." She tilted her head. "Would you rather give oral or get oral?"

"Ah, that's a tricky one. Normally I'd say I like to be on the receiving end—what guy doesn't love a blowjob? But eating your pussy has become my favorite hobby." He put his mouth to her ear and whispered, "Love the little noises you make when I fuck you with my tongue."

"Stop that, you'll make me wet!"

He just laughed.

"Ever had a girl take you with a strap-on?" she asked just as they stepped out of the trees and the main lodge came into view. The party was being held inside, since the weather forecast had predicted rain.

Eli grimaced at her question. "Not interested in having anything up my ass, baby. But your ass? Yeah, I love having a piece of that."

"Favorite sex position?"

He pursed his lips. "Depends if you're sober, baby. My favorite is definitely girl-on-top when you're drunk. No woman has ever ridden me as hard as you do when you're blitzed." Eli was kind of hoping he could get her to do the same tonight.

"Least favorite sex position?"

"Depends if you're sober. I love taking you from behind, but not while you're drunk—you always sneakily try playing with your clit and get us both off too soon." He made a mental note to tie her hands behind her back next time.

"What's your favorite—oral, anal, or regular sex?"

He blew out a breath. "Depends if you're sober—"

"Oh my God, forget it."

He chuckled again.

Entering the lodge, they found that the living, dining, and kitchen areas were packed with people. All turned at the sight of Casey. He squeezed her hand. "Come on, I want to introduce you to everyone. You met a lot of them at the Velvet Lounge."

Half an hour later, Casey *still* hadn't yet met everybody—none were satisfied to simply say hi and let her move along, which surprised her. They asked her questions, told her a little about themselves, and quizzed her about mink shifters.

Even with the many lawn chairs that Shaya had brought inside, there wasn't enough seating for everyone. Some had perched themselves on the kitchen counter or the arms of the sofas. Others sat on their mate's lap or on the rug near the fireplace.

People chatted and laughed, overriding the sounds of food crunching, bottles clinking, and cans popping open. The breeze occasionally swept through the open windows, swirling the scents of beer, hard liquor, and the various foods that were spread over the dining table.

Kathy and Gwen took turns brushing the crumbs and bits of food that had fallen from paper plates. They also occasionally circled the large open-space, collecting disposable kitchenware and empty bottles and cans.

Casey suspected that Eli would consider it hectic. But compared to the parties she'd attended with her many, *many* pack mates, it was pretty tame. Still, being in such a small, crowded space never made her mink happy, and Casey wasn't too fond of it either. She did like the guests she'd met so far, though.

The Phoenix Pack kids were a riot, especially the Alpha pair's son, Kye. He seemed to feel compelled to try staring down Nick, which irritated the Mercury Alpha male to no end.

It was just as a Phoenix Pack she-wolf, Grace, was chatting with her in the kitchen that two unfamiliar people approached, paper cups in hand.

The elderly woman gave Casey a gracious nod. "I've been waiting for Eli to bring you my way, but he was taking too long. I'm Greta, Trey's grandmother. This is a good friend of mine, Allen."

Casey smiled at them both. "Hi, I'm Casey. It's really nice to meet you both."

Greta returned the smile. "My Roni and Mila told me all about you. They're *lovely* girls." She lifted her chin slightly. "They think the world of me, just as my boys do."

"Aw, that's nice."

"Roni says you're a mink. I knew a mink once. He ..." Greta averted her gaze, blushing. "Well, he was a very nice man. And very sweet to me."

Oh, so she'd once had a little fling with a mink.

Greta touched her arm. "Roni also says you're perfect for Eli. I'm glad."

Allen nodded. "It's good to see him smile a *real* smile."

Casey peeked up at her mate, who was staring at Greta in what looked like bemusement. "It is," Casey agreed.

"I wish you and Eli every happiness." Greta patted her hand. "I'm sure we'll talk again later." And then she and Allen were gone.

Casey turned to Eli. "She seems really nice."

"Well, she's not," said Grace, frowning. "I don't know what that was. Then again, she often puts on an act in front of Allen."

Eli shrugged, pulled Casey closer, and tipped his chin toward the cooler. "Beer? Soda? Water?"

"I haven't finished this beer yet." Casey took a long swig from her bottle, noticing that Eli's eyes—glittering with heat—were glued to her throat as it worked to swallow the beer. She spoke in a low voice as she said, "You're thinking some really filthy things right now, aren't you?"

"Put it this way," he said quietly. "If we weren't in public, you'd be on your knees with your mouth wrapped around my dick."

"It's *my* dick."

His mouth kicked up into a smile. "Possessive little thing. I like it."

"I know you do." She grazed his ear with her lips as she whispered, "Just thought you should know … I'm not wearing panties."

He groaned. "You're going to pay for that later."

"Oh, I do hope so."

With her mate close behind her, Mila sidled up to them. "Hi, Casey, it's good to see you again. Before I forget, I want to say thanks for getting me a ticket to your last game. It was awesome."

"You're welcome," Casey told her.

"It was the best fun I've had in ages," said Mila. "I would totally have smacked the shit out of the bitch who broke your ankle if Dominic hadn't held me back."

"And then you would have been banned from future games," Dominic pointed out.

Just then, Jesse, Trick, and Marcus approached. They dug beers out of the cooler.

Jesse's smile was somewhat impish. "Hey, Mila." He put a hand to his chest. "Is there an airport near here or is that my heart taking off?"

"Speaking of hearts," said Trick, "mine's been stolen since I first saw you. Can I have yours?"

Dominic glared at them. "Ha. Fucking. Ha."

Marcus leaned toward her. "You know, Mila, I've heard it said that a kiss is actually the language of love. Want to go to my lodge and have a conversation?"

Dominic's nostrils flared. "Do we have to go through this shit every fucking time? Really?"

Marcus pursed his lips. "Honestly, I don't foresee it stopping any time soon. If ever."

Leaving Dominic and the other males to argue, Eli led Casey into the living area. There were no empty seats, but Jaime shuffled along the sofa to make room for Casey to fit on the end. Eli perched himself on the armrest, content so long as he was close to his mate.

Sitting on his mother's lap, Jaime's infant son, Hendrix, reached for Casey with both arms and grunted, "Uh."

Jaime sighed. "He makes that sound when he wants something. Or when he doesn't. Or when he's hungry. Or when he likes something he sees. Basically, it's all we get out of him."

Casey drained her bottle, set it on the table, and then carefully took the infant and set him on her own lap. "Hey, mister. Don't you look smart." She blew raspberries on his neck, loving his contagious giggle.

As Eli dropped a kiss on her head, Hendrix frowned at him and said, "Uh."

Jaime tried stifling a smile. "I don't think he wants to share Casey's attention."

"Tough luck, kid," Eli told him.

Chuckling, Shaya looked at Nick, as if expecting him to be doing the same. But he was too busy glaring at someone on the far side of the room. Shaya poked his shoulder. "Would you stop having stare-outs with Kye?"

Nick frowned at her. "*He* started it."

"Cassidy seems to be doing fine," Jaime cut in.

Shaya's gaze shifted to the little girl, who was holding hands with Cain in the dining area. "She's had a few nightmares since the shooting, but she doesn't seem to remember them afterward."

"I heard that Cain admitted he's her true mate," said Dante, the Phoenix Pack's Beta male.

"Yeah." Shaya's eyes narrowed slightly on Dante. "You suspected it?"

"I doubt that it will come as a surprise to many people," the Beta told her.

"He's so good with her," said Jaime, watching as Cain spun the pup in a circle. "Does she know he's hers?"

It was Nick who responded. "She hasn't mentioned it, and we haven't said anything because we're not sure how she'd react."

"I think the knowledge would be a comfort to her," said Casey. "I mean, it's clear she adores him."

"I don't like the idea that she'd be moving to another pack when she's older, but not many are lucky enough to have their children stay within their pack." Shaya slid her gaze to the couple approaching them, who were arguing over a plate of chocolate cake.

Roni whacked Marcus' chin with her cutlery. "If I'd wanted to share it, I'd have gotten two forks. My God, do you ever stop eating?"

"I have a fast metabolism," Marcus defended himself.

"You have a bottomless stomach." Roni shoved a forkful of cake in her mouth, shooting him a look that dared him to try to take the dessert from her.

"*He's* no different," Frankie said to her, gesturing at Trick as he crossed to her. "I asked him to watch over my food while I went to speak to Kathy. All that was left when I got back was a blob of potato salad."

Sighing, Trick offered his mate his cake. "Here, have that."

Frankie sniffed, folding her arms across her chest. "No, thank you," she clipped.

Trick sighed again. "Don't cut off your nose to spite your face."

Frankie frowned. "Why would I ever want to cut off my nose? And that would be masochistic, not spiteful."

His lips thinned. "*It's just a turn of—*"

"Yeah, yeah." Frankie looked at Shaya. "Ally seems kind of quiet." She tipped her chin at the Beta female, who was talking with Taryn and Riley at the dining table.

"She's feeling guilty," said Nick. "Her Seer gifts are playing up, so she didn't foresee Eli's attack or the shooting. I've told her she has nothing to feel guilty about, but it's like talking to a brick wall. The words just aren't penetrating."

"Derren won't let her wallow for long," said Frankie. "It's cute how he stands behind her chair like a sentry, looking all serious."

Shaya's mouth curled. "He's been in such a crazily overprotective mood since she got pregnant that I half-expected him to be weird about welcoming a newcomer to the pack, especially since minks are rather … interesting … but he's been great."

Holding a bowl of chips to her chest, Madisyn smiled. "Casey's mink is so amazingly sweet."

Bracken stared at his mate, incredulous. "Sweet? Seriously?"

Madisyn gave him a bored look. "You're not still whining about that little nip, are you?"

"It wasn't just a little nip," Bracken snapped. "I'm telling you, she wants me dead."

"I can't possibly imagine why she would." Madisyn's words were dry as a bone.

Bracken twisted in his seat to face her. "Oh, is that so? Well, I can't possibly imagine why someone would start waving their arms when they're asleep, calling out, 'that's not how you do the Hokey Cokey, get it together, people!'"

Licking salt from her fingertips, Madisyn flushed a deep red. "I did not do that."

"Lies." Bracken turned to Casey. "Be honest, your mink would totally add my body to her collection if she could, right?"

Casey tilted her head. "I think she'd rather just scalp you."

Madisyn gave him a pointed look. "See, you're just being a drama queen."

Bracken gaped at his mate. "Like scalping me would be nothing?"

Exchanging an amused smile with Casey, Eli squeezed her nape, asking, "Want another beer, baby?"

"That would be great, thanks," said Casey.

"Make it worth my while, then." Eli sank into the kiss she gave him, though he kept it PG since Hendrix was watching like a hawk. "Hmm. Best taste ever."

Casey watched him head to the kitchen. Okay, she watched his *ass* as he walked to the kitchen. It was a rather delicious sight.

Leaning forward, Shaya smiled at Casey. "He's so totally gone for you— I love it. I was worried about him for a long time. It's nice that I don't have to worry anymore. I was so surprised that he recognized you as his mate so fast, given that Kathy's experiences had to have left him with some issues. Nick and I recognized each other at first glance, you know."

Casey widened her eyes, going for clueless. "Really?"

Shaya stared at her for a long moment. "Eli told you, huh?"

"Only some of it," said Casey. "I noticed you seemed sad sometimes when you saw me and him together. He just wanted to assure me that it wasn't personal."

"It's really not personal. It hurt when Nick walked away from me. I've never felt pain like it before or since. It would be easy to be bitter about it, but I'm not. I mean, think of this: If he hadn't turned his back on me, I wouldn't have moved to Arizona. And if I hadn't moved there, I wouldn't have met Bracken, Jesse, Zander, or Kent. We wouldn't have later all come back here with Nick and formed the Mercury pack. Caleb might never have known Kent, just like Bracken might never have found Madisyn, and Eli might never have met you, and so on and so on. We're all where we need to be, and that's what's important."

Casey wished she could say that she'd be able to look back on such a painful time and spin it in a positive way, but she'd be lying through her wisdom teeth. "God, Shaya, you're so nice."

Shaya just chuckled.

"What's funny?" Eli asked as he returned. His mate just shook her head.

Although all the food was consumed within a couple of hours, the guests stayed—drinking, telling stories, teasing each other. Eli relaxed more and more as the evening went on, purely because his mate relaxed. Everyone was kind and welcoming toward her, just as he'd hoped they'd be.

He doodled patterns on her nape with his finger, wishing he knew why their bond hadn't snapped into place. He'd claimed every part of her. There were no secrets between them, no protective walls, no doubts about mating or about each other. And yet, their bond remained incomplete. He just didn't get it, but he didn't let himself dwell on it right then, knowing she'd pick up on his change of mood. He didn't want to spoil what was supposed to be a fun evening.

It was dark when the tipsy guests finally began staggering out of the lodge—most were humming merrily as the sober, designated drivers guided them to the crowded parking lot. Eli and Casey joined some of his pack mates in following the guests to the door to wave them off.

Just as Riley was about to leave, Gwen grabbed her arm. "Hey, Riley, what can I get Savannah for her birthday?" she asked quietly, referring to the young viper who the Phoenix Pack had adopted.

Riley raised her hands, swaying slightly. "Don't ask me, I'm genuinely stuck on what to get her. She's not an easy kid to buy gifts for. There are things I would have thought she'd *love*, but she's barely paid them a glance when they pop up in a TV commercial. If anyone has ideas, that would be great."

Casey shrugged. "All I ever wanted were balls."

Eli barely managed to hold back a smile as all eyes, twinkling with amusement, landed on his mate.

Riley cleared her throat, her lips twitching slightly. "Balls?"

Casey nodded. "I'd play with them all day, working and improving on my technique."

Almost groaning, Eli wished he had a pretzel or something to shove in her mouth.

"Technique?" echoed Riley.

"Yeah," Casey went on, oblivious. "But I was picky about size. I didn't like them too small—you don't get as much use out of them then. Hardness, pressure, and diameter are important. They're no good if they're going to …" And then realization seemed to dawn on her, because her cheeks reddened. She sighed. "Yeah, I'll shut up now."

Eli chuckled, which earned him a pinch to the side from his mate. After waving off the Phoenix Pack, they helped clean up the mess in the lodge. Noticing his mate stumbling a little drunkenly, he spoke into her ear. "You okay? You look like you need to go and lie down. It's probably best if you spread your legs while you're at it."

Casey's mouth quirked. "I'm kind of tired. Maybe we could just cuddle tonight."

Knowing she was teasing him, he nibbled on her earlobe as he whispered, "We can cuddle after I've taken you."

"But I'm feeling really sleepy."

"Come on, I'll only take five minutes. You won't even know I was there."

She chuckled. "Fine, fine. But you have to do all the work."

"I don't have a problem with that." Eli kissed her, sipping from her mouth and sifting her hair through his fingers as she melted into him.

Breezing past them, Bracken said, "You'd better hope she doesn't shift into her animal form when drunk. A mink under the influence of alcohol will be one unstable creature. Then you'll learn what her *nips* feel like."

Madisyn groaned. "Oh my God. Would you let it go already!"

Bracken's spine snapped straight. "Her psychopathic mink wants me dead, and you're asking me to let it go?"

"Stop picking on the poor thing and calling her names, you're gonna hurt her feelings."

"What feelings? She's a stone-cold killer."

"Then why piss her off?" Madisyn picked up the garbage bag and hauled it outside, ignoring Bracken as he trailed behind her, muttering under his breath.

Casey turned to Eli. "I can't tell whether she's messing with him or not."

"Oh, she's messing with him," said Eli. "Madisyn likes dicking with people in general, but she persistently does it to him. We all love it, because it brings out some of the old Bracken; the parts we thought died along with his family. She probably teases him so often because he hogs so much of her time and gives her very little space. You think I'm bad—he's ten times worse. If Madisyn was on a soccer team, he'd observe every practice and possibly even insist on hanging with the coaching staff during games."

Casey snorted, scrubbing sticky stains from the kitchen countertop. "Like you haven't thought of doing both those things."

Of course Eli had. "Only because I like watching you play and want to be close in case you need me." Hearing his phone ring, he pulled it out of his pocket. Eli felt his brows draw together as he saw Adrian's name on the screen. "Hello," he greeted. What the Alpha said next made Eli grind his teeth. "Yeah, I'll tell her."

Ending the call, he pocketed his cell and turned to Casey. "That was Adrian. The young girl working at the bakery beneath your apartment has been dating one of Ignacio's cats. She claims he did ask questions about the Hounds and that your name cropped up a lot in the conversations. It was all disguised as pillow talk but, yeah, I'd say she was being milked for information on you."

Casey cursed and slapped the wet cloth on the counter.

"*Now* will you consider that just maybe I'm right and he believes you're his true mate?"

She shoved a hand into her hair. "I just don't know why he'd ever think that. I never came onto him or—"

Eli caught her face in his hands. "I am not for one second suggesting that you did anything to make him believe it. He got the idea in his head somehow. It could be that he just didn't know how else to explain why you drew him."

"Drew him?"

"You're a very compelling person, Casey. And you'd be ten times more compelling to someone with the kind of demons he possesses. You're everything that the people who let him down, including his mother, aren't— strong, protective, loyal, caring. It makes sense that you'd be a temptation to him; that he'd want to possess you."

"If you're right about that, he'll try to kill you."

"I know. But I'll be ready when he does. Although I might not have to wait until he comes to me. You remember the falcon I let live?"

"Yes."

"Cain thinks he might have an idea of just who it was—apparently, there was a particular group of falcons he knew who were also hired thugs. He's having some of his associates from The Movement check it out." Eli stroked her bangs away from her face. "This could all be over soon. When it is, we can forget about that fucker and get on with our lives. Move in together. Have our mating ceremony. Maybe have a pup or two. Or a mink—I'm not fussed so long as they're healthy."

"You have it all planned out, huh?"

Bracken followed Madisyn back into the lodge, saying, "Well, when you find my scalp pinned to our front door, you'll feel like a bitch for not taking me seriously."

Madisyn scratched her cheek. "I don't see how a mink could hammer a nail into a door. She'd be more likely to just use your hair to feather a nest or something, so there's really no need for the drama. Honestly, you always insist on making a mountain out of a molehill."

Bracken threw up his arms. "I give up."

CHAPTER SIXTEEN

"You are evil, Roni," Eli hissed, marching into the dining area of the main lodge the next morning. "Totally. Fucking. Evil. What the hell did you put in my toothpaste?"

Fighting a smile, Casey sidled up to him. Did she like that the siblings pranked each other so often? No. Especially since it was only a matter of time before she got caught in the crossfire—something Marcus had warned her of. But Casey couldn't deny that the pranks could be entertaining at times.

Sitting at the table, Roni lifted one shoulder. "It might have been a numbing oral gel. I know it had 'maximum strength' printed on the tube."

Casey had figured as much. The she-wolf was ruthless.

He gaped at his sister. "Are you fucking kidding me right now?"

Roni's eyes flared. "What I did was tame compared to *your* little stunt."

Eli curled an arm around Casey's shoulders. "Casey could just as easily have used the toothpaste, Roni—did you think of that?"

"Yes, but I also knew she'd forgive me when I told her that you gave me a box of truffles that were actually *sprouts covered in chocolate*. Sacrilege!"

Casey sighed at him. "Oh, Eli." His sister was a sucker for all things that contained chocolate, which he knew full well. "Is there no chance of you two easing up on each other?"

Both Eli and Roni snorted.

"That was pretty much what I thought," said Casey.

Marcus looked at her. "I wish I could say they'll stop with this shit one day, but I can't see that happening. It's been an ongoing war for far too long. Trying to talk them out of doing it or attempting to rationalize their bond only leads to frustration—trust me on that."

Shaya nodded. "Marcus is right, unfortunately." She tilted her head. "You look tired, Casey."

She didn't look tired, she looked rough as hell. Of course, if her mate hadn't had a restless sleep that involved a lot of tossing, turning, and nudging, she'd have slept perfectly well. "Eli kept poking me all night. Worst wake-up calls ever." Realizing what she'd said, Casey winced. It didn't help matters that her mate didn't bother to smother a chuckle, even though he knew she was embarrassed. "Anyone want coffee? I'll make coffee."

Pulling on her jeans later that day, Casey frowned as she heard … well, she couldn't really term it someone *knocking* on the front door of her apartment. It sounded more like two fists were pounding on it. The fuck?

Having fastened her fly, she dragged on her tee and strode out of the bedroom area. Sherryl, she thought, flexing her fists. It had to be fucking Sherryl, didn't it? So far, the bitch hadn't done anything else to provoke or annoy her. In fact, the other mink had wisely stayed off her radar. But Casey had known it would only be a matter of time before the bitch resurfaced.

Her mink stood, alert and ready. Adrenaline pumped through both her and Casey, preparing them for the confrontation.

Given that Sherryl had been banned from Craven Pack territory, it was dumb of her to turn up there. Showing up at Casey's home was even dumber. But then, Sherryl hadn't been acting smart for a while now.

Reaching the front door, Casey flicked her hair—still wet from her shower—out of her collar and yanked the door open. Her lips parted at the sight she found, and she almost rocked back on her heels. *Not* Sherryl. Not even close.

Anger and shock unfurled inside Casey, making her palms tingle and her hackles rise. The same emotions blasted through her mink, who coiled with a hiss, prepared to strike.

Just what in the holy hell was *he* doing here? More, how had he gotten her address?

His tall, lean figure stiff with tension, Ira Frost glared at her through his sharp blue eyes. A muscle in his drawn, stubbly cheek ticked. "Where is she?"

Casey blinked at her father. "Huh?"

"Emily. Where is she?"

Lashing her tail like a whip, her mink hissed again. She wasn't a fan of Ira's, and she did *not* like his harsh tone or grating voice at all. The animal particularly didn't like him showing up at her home. "How would I know?"

He jabbed a blunt finger at her. "Don't play games with me, Casey. I've looked everywhere, spoken to every one of her friends—none of them have seen her. If she really wanted to hide from me, this would be the place to come."

"And why would she hide from you?" Casey folded her arms across her chest. "What's going on?"

"Like you don't already know."

"I truly have no idea what's happening. But I won't lie and say that I *would* tell you where she was if she asked me not to. Craven territory is probably the last place she'd ever choose to hide."

"Which is why she *has* come to you—she thought I wouldn't think to look for her here. Well, she was wrong. I'm not as stupid as she seems to think I am."

"That's debatable."

His flushed face hardened. "She's in there, isn't she? She's with you. *Emily!*" He tried to barge inside, the fucker. *Oh, the hell no.*

Planting her hand on his chest, Casey shoved him back a step. "No," she clipped. "You don't get to come into my apartment. You're not welcome here. Never will be." She held up her palm when he tried objecting. "You can piss and moan about it all you want—it's not like I'm not used to that shit. But you are not getting inside."

"Because you're hiding her here."

"Because you're an asshole."

He took an aggressive step toward her, his hands fisted, his jaw hard. And her mink just about lost her mind—hissing, arching her back, baring her teeth, whipping her tail from side to side.

"Careful, Ira. My mink would *really* like to slash your face again, and I'm pretty sure she'd leave permanent marks this time."

Fear flickered in his eyes. Casey knew it wasn't just the prospect of tangling with her mink that spooked him. Like any playground bully, his confidence was shaken when anyone stood up to him.

Ira was a very rigid, authoritarian, anal retentive person who came across as somewhat invincible. But that was the surface. Scratch it just a little, and you'd find he was riddled with self-doubt and a deep sense of inadequacy that he chose not to acknowledge.

His finger shook slightly as he held it up. "You touch me, I'll sue you."

That was the best he had? Really? She almost rolled her eyes. "Right. Because the human authorities will *totally* go up against shifters. They'll just tell you that you knew the risks when you stepped onto shifter territory and confronted me—we both know that, Ira, so don't think to threaten me. Now get the hell away from my apartment. I don't want you here."

"I'm not interested in what you want. I'm not interested in you. I'm not *here* for you. I just want to speak to my daughter. My *only* daughter. My only child, for that matter."

That should have hurt, shouldn't it? He was her father, after all. But it seemed that her defenses against him were hard as steel, because his words just had no emotional impact on her. "Well, it seems like your only child doesn't want to speak to you or she wouldn't be lying low, would she?"

He peered over her head, trying to see inside the apartment. "Emily! Get out here! You can't skip your own damn wedding and then think—"

"Whoa, wait, she missed her wedding? Seriously?"

His eyes tightened around the edges. "You know damn well that she did. I'm not sure what reason she gave *you* for doing it, but she told your mother that her mink wouldn't accept Theo. That's a lie. She has no mink."

Now he was just being deliberately obtuse. "That's not true. You know perfectly well that her being 'latent' simply means her mink has never surfaced. It doesn't mean her mink isn't a presence within her."

"Well if that's true, the damn animal has just ruined everything for her. But then, I wouldn't expect any different from such sly creatures. If you care about Emily at all, you'll send her out here so that she can fix things with Theo and return to her life—a life that doesn't include *shifters*."

Casey slanted her head and stared at him. "It must be weird to live in a fictional reality. Like it or not, neither Emily's life nor yours has *ever* been free of shifters. My mother—your *mate*—is a shifter. All three of your children are half shifter. It doesn't matter whether they're latent or not, that doesn't change what they are. And if you refuse to accept Emily for who she is, and if you insist on ignoring what her current dilemma is, you're going to lose her. Then you'll have none of your kids in your life. Is that really what you want?"

He sneered. "Like I care that you and Miles aren't around. You and that boy brought shame upon the family—the pair of you are an utter disgrace."

She planted a hand on her hip. "I have no idea what in the world makes you think you're so superior and perfect, but I have news for you—you're nothing but a pathetic little man who feels threatened by anyone stronger than him. You hated that you couldn't control me, so you tried to make me feel worthless and inferior to you. Then I would have been easier for you to manipulate, wouldn't I? Only it never worked."

"You think I see you as stronger than me?" he scoffed. "Emily and Miles were special. But you? No. You were always selfish. Ungrateful. *Weak.* Unfit to be a Frost—"

"And too outspoken and argumentative and not feminine enough—yeah, yeah, you've told me all this already. Multiple times, as it happens."

"Because it's the truth. If Miles had just kept his distance from you and this pack, he'd never have met the bitch who hurt him, and he wouldn't have become an addict. Though I have to say that having heroin in his veins is a lot better than the shifter blood coursing through them—that stuff is pure poison. And I'm not about to let it ruin Emily's life the way it did his."

Casey studied him curiously. "You know, you were always bigoted against shifters, but you never used to sound so hateful, bitter, and twisted when you spoke of them. And it makes me wonder if you don't really look down on the shifter DNA your mate and children share. No, you see that it makes us strong, enhances our senses, and helps heal our wounds faster. We make you feel inferior, don't we?" Oh God, how hadn't she seen that before? "Knowing your mate could wipe the floor with you if she chose to do so … yeah, you resent that in a big way, don't you, Ira?"

A flush swept across his cheeks, and the tips of his ears reddened. He didn't speak. He pressed his lips tight together and ground his teeth. Yeah, she'd hit the nail right on the fucking head.

"I don't know why you're here and what you want," said a new voice, "but I think it's about time you left."

Ira whirled on the spot and jerked back at the sight of Eli. Her mate had moved silently as he'd ascended the iron staircase, but she'd sensed his presence and growing irritation. She could also sense that his wolf was very close to the surface, no doubt raring to pounce on the human male.

"Who the hell are you?" demanded Ira, thrusting his chest out.

"Someone who won't tolerate that tone you're using," said Eli. "You speak to Casey with respect, or you don't speak to her at all. Choose."

Ira jutted out his chin. "I'm her father, I'll speak to her however I damn well please."

"Father? I'd have to dispute that. You sure never *acted* like a father, and you're not doing it now either." Eli took a prowling step toward him. "The last person who should have *ever* spoken to her like that is her father, which just goes to prove my point."

Ira made a sound of disgust. "Shifters always think they're so damn superior."

Casey's brows shot up. Um, pot, kettle, *black.* The guy truly had such a complete lack of self-awareness it was astonishing.

"Get going," said Ira, tipping his chin at the stairs, all false bravado. "This is not your business."

"Casey's my mate, which makes this very much my business." Eli stalked toward him, nostrils flaring. Her father was tall, but Eli towered over him. "You know what my wolf has always been good at scenting? Weakness. You're just riddled with weaknesses, aren't you? It's no wonder you feel so intimidated by Casey."

Ira spluttered. "Intimidated? You know *nothing*."

"I know that Casey doesn't want you here. Which means *I* don't want you here."

"And I'll be more than happy to leave, but not without Emily."

Eli looked at Casey and flicked up his eyebrow. "Emily?"

Casey shrugged. "I've told him she's not here, but he refuses to listen."

Ira half-turned and shot Casey a glare. "I know she's here. There's nowhere else for her to go."

"Yeah, because there's a real shortage of hotels, motels, and places to rent out there," said Casey, voice dry. She waved a dismissive hand. "Just go, Ira. You're wasting our time and making yourself look even more stupid than you actually are."

Hands curling, he made a move toward Casey—bad idea.

Eli fisted his collar and dragged him backwards, barely resisting the urge to shove him down the iron staircase. "You're done here."

"I want—"

"I could give less of a shit what you want." Adrenaline and anger pumping through him, Eli crowded the human who was singlehandedly responsible for making Casey feel like an outsider in her own family. "Do the smart thing and get the fuck out of here. I don't want you even breathing Casey's air, let alone being anywhere near her."

Eyes blazing, Ira straightened his jacket as he stared at her. "Tell your sister I expect to see her soon."

Casey sighed. "I'd tell you once again that she's not here, but you're clearly not willing to listen. There's something I will tell you: If you really want Emily in your life, you need to back off for a while. She'll surface when she's ready. And if you have any sense, you won't jump down her throat when she does or try forcing her to marry a man she doesn't want—you'll only drive her away if you do."

Ira didn't respond. He just shot Eli one last glare and then made his way down the stairs.

Eli kept his gaze locked on the human, who hopped into a car that was parked outside the bakery and slammed the door shut behind him. Only when the car disappeared did Eli turn to look at his mate. His gut clenched at the lines of strain carved into her face. That little scene had taken something out of her.

Eli gently herded her into the apartment and closed the door behind them. He slid his hand under her curtain of wet hair and squeezed her nape. "You all right?"

She puffed out a breath. "Yeah. That's the first time I've seen him in over a decade. He hasn't changed a bit."

Drawing her close, Eli stroked his hand up and down her back. "He was looking for your sister?"

"Yep. It turns out that Emily left her fiancé, Theo, standing at the altar."

"She stood him up?" Eli let out a low whistle.

"Apparently, her mink wouldn't accept him. I'm not sure if the animal withdrew from the relationship or never approved of it to begin with."

"It's not uncommon for our inner animals to withdraw like that if they're not fully satisfied with their partner." Leading her into the living area, Eli settled on the sofa and pulled her onto his lap. "Pretending to be human every day of her life may have gotten tiring for your sister after a while."

Casey nodded. "Her mink has probably gotten angrier and angrier at how hard Emily tried to deny she existed." Propping her elbow on his shoulder, she combed her fingers through his hair, smiling at the low growl of contentment that vibrated his chest. "I sometimes wonder if part of the reason Emily acts human and ignores her mink's needs is that she's irrationally angry with the animal for not surfacing. Whatever the case, she's not ignoring her mink so much now."

"Do you think Emily might come here at some point?"

"I doubt it. She loves Ira. It's sad that she can't see that it's only a one-sided relationship with him. You don't get emotional feedback from people like Ira. Maybe she just *chooses* not to see it. Whatever the case, it would break something in their relationship if she came here. He'd see it as a betrayal so, no, I don't think she'd come to me."

Eli rubbed her thigh, trying to pet the tension out of her. "Why would she literally hide from him? Is she afraid of him?"

"No, she's afraid of his disapproval—always has been. Which is why I'm genuinely shocked that she left Theo."

Toying with her wet hair, Eli kissed her temple. "I'm pissed that he came here, and I don't trust that he won't come back. The sooner you move into my lodge, the better. Today would work." And no, he didn't feel bad using this situation to try convincing her to move in with him before she'd originally planned. Not just because he wanted her living with him, but because her father wouldn't be able to reach her there.

"When I finally *do* move in, will I find my photo albums? Because I've searched this place from top to bottom, and I can't find them anywhere. I'm just wondering if, like many of my other possessions, they've mysteriously migrated to your lodge."

Stifling a smile, Eli shrugged. "It's possible. I can't say for sure."

Casey snickered. "It's a good thing I love you, Eli Axton."

"Yeah, it is." Because he'd be a miserable bastard without her. Needed her like he needed air to breathe. Despite that their bond wasn't yet complete, they were so closely bound that it almost felt like she was an extension of him at times.

He'd never felt part of anything the way he did this mating. Never knew it was possible to feel so connected and at ease with someone. He didn't need to hold back with her. Didn't need to guard parts of himself or ever worry that he'd be anything other than her number one priority, just as she'd always be his. Which was why it continued to baffle him that their bond hadn't snapped into place yet.

"Speaking of your possessions, they should all be boxed up by now." He glanced around, noticing that quite a few cardboard boxes had been packed and taped shut, but she had plenty more to do. "You said you'd move in with me after the games were over. The final is tomorrow."

"I got started this morning. I don't have a lot more stuff that I need to take with me. Your lodge is fully furnished, and I don't have any real attachment to any of the furniture here. It's not all mine anyway. Some of it was already in the apartment when I moved in. I'm sorry, but my focus can't be on packing right now. It has to be on the game tomorrow."

Unable to deny or grumble about that—at least not out loud—Eli asked, "You nervous about the game?"

"A little, yeah. And I'm not ashamed to admit it. The Seals are super good. We'll need whatever edge we can get."

"Sherryl will probably do her best to provoke you tomorrow," he warned, nuzzling her hair, inhaling the scent of her coconut shampoo. "What better way to have you sent off the field than by goading you into a fight?"

"I'll be ready for that. When I first heard Ira pounding on the door, I thought he was Sherryl. Like Adrian, I expected her to spend the past couple of weeks hassling me, but I haven't heard a peep out of her. Neither has Adrian. Her team's coach spoke with him and negotiated for the ban to be lifted for a single day to allow her to partake in the final game, but that's all. Maybe the attack spooked her, though she's not the kind of person to back down after something like that. It would only make her angrier."

"I don't think it was the attack that rattled her." Eli tucked her hair behind her ear. "The last time you talked to her, when you threatened to kill her if she didn't back off, you scared her. More, it shook her that you were *able* to scare her—she wasn't expecting that."

"Hmm, maybe."

"I don't think that will stop her from bitching at you tomorrow, though. She'll feel safe surrounded by her teammates. When will you challenge her?"

"Outside my team's headquarters after the game. Why, you want to watch?"

He smiled. "As if I'd miss watching you kick someone's ass. I have every intention of being there to support you. *And* to make sure that none of her team get the dumb idea to jump into the fight and help her."

"I don't think they would, but I suppose it's possible. *Especially* if they lose the game."

"They will. Your team is fucking spectacular. And I've yet to see another player perform anywhere near as well as you do."

Casey's mouth curved. "You would say that—as my mate, you're biased."

"Biased, sure, but I'm also being serious here." He pressed a kiss to her neck. "Your team has every chance of winning. My pack mates have been taking bets on how many goals you'll score."

Her smile shrunk a little. "Miles used to do that. Before he dated Sherryl and went down a bad path, he used to go to every one of my games without fail—he was always my biggest supporter."

"Did your sister or mother ever go?"

Casey shook her head. "The only reason they even know I play for the Hounds is that he told them. He'd say to me, 'oh, I told Mom and Emily about your game; they said congrats on your win,' but I don't think they really did. I doubt they even care."

Eli truly didn't understand how they could turn their backs on Casey, but he figured she was better off without them. "Your sister doesn't deserve the worry you're putting yourself through for her."

"Maybe not, but I can't help worrying. I don't think Ira will back off and give her time, or that he'll be anything less than a complete asshole when she finally comes out of hiding. He'd never be sorry if he drove her away. To feel remorse, you have to acknowledge that you fucked up. Ira Frost is *always* right, and he *never* makes mistakes."

Eli snorted. "He's a fucking prick. I'd say the best thing you ever did was leave your childhood home and move here."

"Nah. That was the second-best thing." She lightly stroked his hair. "The best thing I ever did was find you."

Warmth filled his gut and flowed out to fill every part of him. He didn't know how to handle it when she said stuff like that. The sweet, raw honesty with which she spoke always reached deep inside him; made his blood heat and pool low.

He caught her earlobe with his teeth but didn't bite it. Instead, he let it slowly slide out of his mouth, grazing it with the edges of his teeth as he did so. "Saying things like that will get you bent over the arm of this sofa."

"Sounds like fun."

"In that case …" He snapped open her fly and shoved his hand in her panties. "Let's get you nice and wet for me."

CHAPTER SEVENTEEN

Watching Casey fuss with her smoothie the next morning, Eli reached across her small dining table and gave her hand a supportive squeeze. "Your team will win, baby."

She put down her glass. "I know."

Eli sensed that she fully believed the Hounds would be victorious—she was always that way before a game. Always filled herself with a bold assurance that they'd win, no matter how good the other team were. Well, self-belief was a powerful thing. "Then stop worrying."

"I'm not worrying … per se. I'm—"

"Thinking too much. You're focused, but you're not in your usual zone." His wolf was worried about her. Eli tipped his head to the side. "Is it because you know you'll be challenging Sherryl later?"

"Not really. I hate that the game will be tainted by the shit going on between me and her, though. I want it to be about soccer, nothing else. I want both teams to strive to *win,* not to hurt each other out of spite."

"I get it." He took a sip of his coffee. "It might be that way in the beginning, but you can bet your ass the focus will shift to the need to win as soon as the first goal is scored. That's when everyone's competitive streak will flare." But none would ever burn as bright as hers. Eli never would have thought he'd meet anyone more competitive than him or his sister, but Casey had them both beat.

"You look good in my jersey," she said.

His mouth kicked up into a smile. He'd insisted that she get him one, determined to wear it at her game. The moment his pack mates saw it, they'd all whined that they didn't have one. His mate had seemed somewhat befuddled by it all, but she'd agreed to their request to get them each a jersey of their own.

"Not as good as you look in my shirts and tees," he told her.

She snorted. "There's never any sense in me wearing them. You just take them off."

"Only because you look so hot in them that I have to have you right then."

"Well, since I want to ride you while you're wearing my jersey, I can't really judge."

Like that, his dick went hard. "Little witch. You can't say stuff like that when you have a no-sex-before-games rule. It's just plain mean."

"But fun." She polished off the rest of her smoothie and stood. "Need to use the bathroom. I'll be back in a sec."

He swatted her ass as she passed, smirking at her mock cry of outrage. Hearing his cell chime, he placed his mug on the coaster and pulled out his phone. *Nick.* Eli swiped his thumb across the screen and greeted, "Hey."

"I have an update for you," said Nick. "But you're not gonna like it."

Eli stilled. "Go on."

"Remember Cain said he might know who the falcon was that led the attack on you?"

"Yeah, he told me that one of his associates from The Movement would check it out."

"Well, Cain just got a call from said associate. The guy had a long chat with a certain lone falcon, who apparently played dumb for a while. But when the *chat* got a little too intense, the avian admitted he was part of the attack on you. He also confessed that Ignacio was the person who hired him."

Eli's upper lip curled, and his wolf sliced out his claws. "Fucker."

"Yeah." There was a wealth of fury in that one word.

Taking a deep breath, Eli scrubbed a hand down his face. "I can't do anything about this right now."

"Today is about Casey, I know. We'll all be there for her, cheering her on—both at the game and during the challenge. Ignacio can wait until tomorrow. It's not like he's going anywhere."

Tomorrow, Eli promised himself, taking a long breath. He'd deal with the bastard tomorrow. Right then, he needed to concentrate on staying calm so that he didn't alert Casey that something was wrong. He'd wait until later before sharing Cain's news.

"How is Casey?" Nick asked.

"Nervous but focused."

"Good. Tell her not to let Sherryl draw her into a fight. She *will* try it."

"Casey knows that." Eli lifted his mug and took another sip of his coffee. "She won't fall for it."

"Sherryl knows her well, which means she'll know how to get under her skin," Nick pointed out.

"Doesn't matter. Casey's ready for it. She won't snap." She was smarter than that.

"Let's hope not." With that, Nick rang off.

Eli pocketed his phone just as she returned to the kitchen. "Nick called to check how you were doing. He's worried that Sherryl will manage to goad you into attacking her on the field. As he said, she knows you well, so she knows how to get under your skin."

"Yeah, but that works both ways. I don't want to start shit on the field, though. I'll bide my time and wait until after the game."

Eli snatched her hand and tugged her onto his lap. "No matter what happens today, I'm proud of you." Proud to have her as his mate. Any male would be. It was little wonder that she'd caught Ignacio's attention—Eli should have seen right off that the cougar wanted her. Just the mere thought of Ignacio made his jaw clench.

"Everything okay with you?" she asked, her far-too-perceptive eyes sweeping over his face. "Something's bothering you. What is it?"

"I don't like that I have to sit on the bleachers while you play today." It was true, just not the entire truth. "Donahue vetoed me sitting with the coaching staff; said she'd only allow it if you needed to be benched. If Sherryl and her teammates go at you—"

"There'd be nothing you could do about it anyway," she finished. "The Seals will commit a few fouls, but they'll be careful not to go too far. They won't risk getting sent off the field." Well, Casey *hoped* they wouldn't. It really all depended on how much Sherryl had succeeded in riling them up— something the bitch was quite good at. She'd certainly wound Mallory up tight.

Casey traced the stubble on his jaw. "I'll be fine. You just concentrate on helping Marcus keep Roni in her seat. She's pissed at Sherryl, and I don't think it would take much to make your sister charge onto that field and try to deal with the bitch herself."

"Baby, all the females of the pack want to get their hands on Sherryl. Honestly, I won't be surprised if they pull out pom-poms when you're beating the shit out of her outside the Hounds' headquarters later."

Casey's mouth quirked. "Yeah, well, Roni in particular has a real hard-on for Sherryl."

"Roni's very protective of you. Plus, any insult to you is an insult to me— she won't tolerate that. Marcus will keep her calm, though. If you ask me, it's Madisyn we need to worry about. That female is crazy. There's no warning with her. One minute she's looking at you, the next minute her cat is latched onto your face."

"I like her." Casey interlocked her fingers behind his neck. "I like her cat, too. She's awesome."

"You would say that—she brings your mink dead rodents as gifts. Rodents they both then often play soccer with."

"That's partially because both the cat and Madisyn like to torment Bracken." And Casey had to admit, it was always fun to watch the enforcer lose all patience with his mate. Her mink found it highly entertaining.

Combing her fingers through Eli's hair, Casey tugged lightly. "You're staring."

"Why wouldn't I? You're beautiful." He kissed her. "And mine. So very, very mine."

"Yours," she agreed. His mouth took hers again, all lazy and languid, kissing her until she felt like her bones would melt. Yeah, her mate knew how to make every bit of edginess drain from her system.

Pulling back, she flicked a look at the wall clock. "I have to go."

"I know." He tapped her ass. "Come on, let's get you to the headquarters."

A short while later, he parked outside the building and asked, "You ready for this, baby?"

She took a slow breath. "Ready."

His eyes roamed over her face, and whatever he saw there made him nod in approval. "I won't say good luck, because you don't need it. Just do what you always do and give it your all—no one can ever ask more of you than that."

"I will."

"Remember what I said earlier: I'm proud of you, no matter what happens today." He reached out, cupped her chin, and breezed his thumb over her jaw. "I love you."

"Right back atcha."

He let out a playful growl, tightening his hold on her chin. "I want the words."

Amused, Casey forced a sigh. "God, you're annoying."

"*Casey.*"

"I love you."

He slowly released her. "Now you can go."

"Why, thank you."

"You're welcome. Now get out there, annihilate the Seals, and deal with Sherryl so I can take you home and fuss over you. Then, after you've rested, we'll move your things to *our* lodge, and then I'll be fucking you until you scream in *our* bed."

"Hmm, sounds promising." Casey grimaced as she slid out of the SUV and into the baking heat. Seriously, it was sweltering hot with only a very mild breeze. Not great weather for a soccer game. "See you later," she told Eli, throwing her duffel over her shoulder.

As she walked inside the building, she felt that familiar acute sense of purpose settle in and fill every part of her, so there was no room for anything else—not doubt, not nerves, not outside issues. She exchanged nods with each of the staff as she prowled to the locker room. All eyes looked her way when she pushed open the door. In various states of undress, her teammates called out greetings.

Sitting on the bench tying her cleats, Emma smiled. "Ooh, Case, you have that bloodthirsty look on your face. Good. That means you're in your zone."

Securing her curly hair into a tight, messy ponytail, Kristin bumped Casey's shoulder with hers. "We'll win this, Frost, I'm telling you."

Casey plopped her duffel on the bench. "Fuck, yeah, we will."

She pulled on her uniform and put her things in her locker, not allowing her thoughts to drift from anything other than the upcoming game. It was as she was tugging her socks up over her shin guards that their coach clapped her hands to get everyone's attention.

"Ladies, now that you're all dressed, the ref would like a quick word." Donahue stepped aside.

A tall, gangly male stepped forward, his face set into a hard mask. "I've been made aware that there's bad blood between the two teams," said the ref, settling his fists on his narrow hips. "I don't want this bleeding over onto the field. I want a clean game. If I see any indication that anything other than soccer is going on out there, I'll act on it immediately. Be professional and keep your personal matters out of it. I'll be issuing the same warning to the Seals." On that note, he left.

"I wasn't expecting that," said Emma. "I'm guessing he doesn't want a repeat of what happened in Arizona years ago when a fight broke out on the field."

Kristin turned to Casey. "The Seals will still come at you. They'll just be sneaky and subtle about it."

"Yeah, they will," Casey agreed. "And while their attention is divided between me and the ball, you'll all take advantage of it, won't you?"

Emma's smile was a little feral. "We sure as hell will."

Outside, after Donahue gave them her usual pep talk, the Hounds jogged onto the field and took up their positions.

Stomach fluttering, Casey inhaled the familiar earthy scents that always filled her with calm. Adrenaline pumped through her veins, heightening her awareness, readying her mind and body, and making her "fight" instinct kick in. In many ways, the game *was* a fight. A fight to win and prevail.

Anticipation. Aggression. Eagerness. Determination. All of it hummed in her blood. As always, knowing Eli was out there, watching and supporting her, gave her that extra incentive to *kick ass.*

Soon enough, the Orlando Seals jogged onto the turf. Feeling the weight of someone's gaze, she looked to see Sherryl glaring at her so hard it was a wonder there weren't lasers shooting out of her eyes. Casey's mink swiped out with her claws, her body all puffed up. But Casey only quirked an eyebrow before glancing away, dismissing her. She wasn't going to give the bitch any warning of what was to come after the game.

Putting all thoughts of the challenge away, Casey rolled back her shoulders.

Bouncing lightly in place, Emma caught her eye and mouthed, "We got this."

Yeah, they damn well did.

"There's the little bitch," Roni snarled as the Seals took up their positions.

"Sherryl?" Madisyn looked around. "Where? Which one?"

Roni pointed at her. "That one with the mop of pink hair."

Madisyn's nose wrinkled. "Casey can take her."

"See how smug and superior the Seals look?" asked Mila, sitting directly behind Eli. "They think this is in the bag."

"They've won more competitions than any other team has," Eli pointed out. "They're dumb to be cocky, though."

Rubbing her arm, Kathy glanced around the bleachers. "Is it always this packed?"

Nick's hand dived into Shaya's popcorn. "There's normally a lot of spectators, but there's way more than usual today. I guess no one wants to miss the final."

There wasn't an empty seat in sight. Many of Eli's pack mates were there—his Alphas, Kathy, Roni, Marcus, Madisyn, Bracken, Gwen, and Zander. The others had needed to remain behind to guard their territory and pups, but they hadn't been happy about it, which was why Shaya promised she'd record the whole game with her cell phone. As they were sitting in their usual seats on the front row, she had an unobstructed view.

Some of the Phoenix Pack had also come along, including Taryn, Mila, Jaime—none of whom were pleased that they didn't have jerseys of their own—Dante, and Dominic. They were sitting in the row behind Eli.

The atmosphere buzzed with the same anticipation that Eli could feel swelling within his mate. It was the first game his mother had attended, and he was glad she was there; understood she was making the gesture that she considered Casey to be part of the family. *About damn time.*

"Casey looks good, Eli," said Clare, sitting further down the row with Adrian. "Composed. Alert. Ready for battle."

She did, thought Eli. The picture of pure focus, she stood solid and at the ready, her eyes bright with vigilance and bloodthirst. His wolf approved.

"I'm kind of worried the Seals will purposely injure Casey to get her out of the game." Shaya rubbed her thighs. "Not just to please Sherryl, but because Casey's the best player—if the Hounds lose her, it would dampen their confidence and lessen their chances of winning."

"Quite a few of the Seals are slanting glares at Casey," said Gwen.

"I noticed that, too," said Taryn. "I also noticed that it's making a few of the other Seals uneasy. I'd say that if there's a plan of some kind to target Casey, not all of the Seals are comfortable with it."

Eli had made the same observation. "Any type of divide in the team is good. It's a weakness. The Hounds will see it." They'd also exploit it.

Bracken grunted. "If Sherryl's teammates are so protective of her that they'll target Casey on the field during *the final*, they might not be prepared to stand back when Casey challenges her."

Madisyn patted her mate's knee. "No need to worry about that. Us girls have that covered." Her tone was neutral, but Eli heard the menace there.

"Not if they shift into their mink forms to fight," said Dante. "They might be small, but *I* wouldn't try getting in the middle of them."

"Random question," began Gwen, her tone ever so casual, "will bullets do much to slow down a group of raging minks?"

Zander turned to his mate and hissed under his breath, "Tell me you're not armed."

"I'm not armed," said Gwen.

The whistle sounded, making Eli's pulse spike. Both teams went at it.

Within minutes of the game, Eli saw why the Seals had such an impressive record. They were quick. Sharp. Far more skilled than any of the other teams he'd seen the Hounds compete against.

Fierce and determined, Casey's team played well and kept up the pressure. Nonetheless, the Seals were in possession of the ball pretty much seventy percent of the time. When the Hounds did manage to gain possession of it, the Seals had little problem intercepting the ball.

As time ticked by and no goals were scored, his gut churned. The Seals were indisputably dominating the game, and that only seemed to feed their confidence and surety that they'd win.

The Seals created several scoring chances, but the Hounds were there each time, redirecting the ball. It was something they were exceptionally good at. He wondered if the coach had had them work hard at it, anticipating that the Hounds would find themselves in this very situation.

The defender marking his mate was fast and fluid. She made it hard for Casey to have enough space to get off a shot. But she was nowhere near as good a player as his mate. Casey, able to go from a slow walk to a purposeful run in a second, repeatedly left the defender in the dust as she tackled, sprinted, chased, and blocked.

Casey also did a lot of subtle, simple feints that consistently fooled the Seals. As such, she almost scored four times. Sadly for her, the Seals' goalkeeper was exceptionally good.

When another of Casey's shots were blocked, Roni spat a vicious curse. "It's only a matter of time before she scores so long as she keeps piling on the pressure."

Maybe the Seals had that same thought, or maybe it had been their plan all along to wait until they were midway through the first half of the game before targeting Casey, but many of them turned their attention to her. And since the Seals were easily dominating the game, they could afford to redirect their attention that way.

Sherryl kept her distance from Casey, but the others didn't. And as he felt a dark fury begin to build within his mate, Eli worried that it wouldn't be long before she'd retaliate and find herself red-carded. *Shit.*

Picking herself up off the ground yet again, Casey wiped the grass and dirt from her hands onto her jersey. These bitches needed to burn in the ninth circle of hell.

They'd been making a nuisance of themselves since minute one. At first, they'd been happy to simply hiss little insults at her—bitch, whore, heifer, slut. Like she'd cared. The dirty bitches even spat at her, their bodies always angled in a way that prevented the ref from seeing.

Ignoring them, Casey kept on kicking, passing, heading, dribbling, and shooting. And then the Seals *really* got down to it. Elbows jabbed into her ribs *hard.* Fingers subtly pinched sensitive parts of her skin. Feet stomped on her own and grazed her legs with their heels, or "accidentally" tripped her.

Eli must have felt an echo of her pain each time she was fouled, because anger spiked down their bond again and again. That anger fed her own and intensified that of her mink, making it difficult for Casey to ignore the urge to lunge at the little bitches—which was just what the Seals wanted. Instead, she continued to play, even as several parts of her body throbbed, stung, and ached.

The baking heat only served to agitate her more. Her throat was parched, and her skin was hot and damp with sweat. She repeatedly flapped the front of her jersey, trying to cool down. She'd just love some rain right about now.

The ref would no doubt have pounced on the fouls if the Seals weren't being so subtle. She didn't once appeal to him. The Seals might not realize it, but they were playing into her hands. Because the more they got away with their little sneak attacks, the bolder they got—it was only a matter of time before they fucked up and a Seal got themselves sent off the field.

Also, they were paying less and less attention to the ball itself whenever they came at her; more intent on causing her pain than regaining possession of the ball. Determined to take advantage of that, she bided her time, waiting for just the right moment. Sadly, that opportunity didn't come before the whistle blew to signal the end of the first half of the game.

As she began to walk off the field during half-time, Sherryl shouldered her hard and said quietly, "Oh, the talented Casey Frost fails to score. Then again, 'failure' runs in your family, doesn't it? How *is* your junkie brother, by the way?"

Balling up her hands, Casey ground her teeth. She'd *love* to send one of her fists crashing into this heifer's jaw. "You know, I can't help but get the feeling that the smartest thing that ever escaped your mouth was a dick."

Sherryl hissed, and then one of the other Seals slid between them and urged her to calm down.

Leaving them to it, Casey headed into the building. As the Hounds sat in the locker room, Dennis healed people's wounds while Donahue gave them yet another pep talk—telling them not to lose hope, rallying their spirits, and dishing out her own brand of tough love.

Donahue then looked at Casey. "I noticed the Seals were targeting you and—"

"Taking risks that are going to backfire on them," Casey finished. Mouth so dry it felt sticky, she gulped down water from her bottle. "Let them keep on thinking they're being sneaky and clever. They'll slip up."

Kristin stuck her chin out. "And we'll all be ready when they do."

Soon, the teams were once again positioning themselves on the field. Casey sensed that Sherryl was doing her best to catch her eye, but Casey paid her zero attention. The whistle sounded, and all the players sprung to life.

Again, the Seals hogged the ball. Again, they also had their sick fun with Casey; did more pinching, elbowing, spitting, and tripping her up so often that her skin tingled with turf burns.

A Seal midfielder cockily committed a foul right under the ref's nose. Even though Casey's knees and palms burned from the fall, she inwardly smiled as the ref issued the midfielder a yellow card. Some of the Seals surrounded him and tried appealing his decision, but no amount of whining from them made any difference.

Really, you'd have thought the Seals would then have decided to be more careful. They didn't. And then the opening that Casey had been waiting for finally came.

Powering past the bitches trying to crowd her, she intercepted a kick from one of the Seals. Heart beating rapidly in her chest, Casey rocketed up the field, steering the ball with her instep. Most of the Hounds seemed to stampede toward the opposition's goal, and hardly any of them were covered by Seals because the bitches were too busy descending on Casey.

Undeterred, she kept moving, feinting, and dribbling. Mere seconds before a Seal defender tripped her, she kicked the ball, passing it to Kristin. Casey went down hard, and pain streaked up the back of her leg. She ignored it, her eyes locked on the ball as Kristin booted it hard. It zipped through the air and straight into the low, right corner of the net.

The Hounds roared. Kristin let out a war-cry. Cheers and hoots sounded from the spectators.

Casey jumped to her feet, ignoring the twinge of pain in her leg, and ran to her teammate. She and Kristin collided, hugging each other tightly. Some of the other Hounds surrounded them, roaring in triumph.

Glancing around, Casey could see that the Seals were *beyond* shocked. Maybe they'd just figured it would be an easy win, maybe they just had a whole lot of confidence in their goalkeeper, or maybe they'd thought that making it hard for Casey to play would be enough to stop the Hounds from scoring—she didn't know.

As for Sherryl … her face was twisted into a mask of pure fury.

Moments later, the teams were playing once more. Just as Eli had predicted, everyone's focus seemed to snap onto the game, as if the Seals finally remembered why they were there. But, shockingly, they began to play like crap. They were totally invested in the game, but they couldn't seem to get their shit together. The Hounds, on the other hand, had never played better—no doubt partly because the goal had lifted their spirits.

Casey's leg was still smarting from her awkward fall. She knew it would give her some grief throughout the rest of the game, but she'd be *damned* if she'd show it. The Seals would pounce on that weakness and target her leg again and again.

The defender marking Casey ceased trying to foul her and instead threw all her energy into trying to block her shots. The bitch was good, so she often succeeded. But not always.

At one point, Casey spun, using her body to shield the ball from the defender. Timing it just right, Casey abruptly swerved and then volleyed the ball hard. It sank into the net. Joy lifted her heart. She smiled as Eli's pride and elation hummed down their bond like a congratulatory hug.

The Seals then seemed to get desperate, because they were committing fouls here, there, and everyfuckingwhere.

One Seal crashed into Kristin with such force that she knocked the midfielder down. The side of Kristin's head smacked hard into the ground. The harsh *whack* made Casey wince. She would have been surprised that her teammate hadn't passed out if it had been anyone other than Kristin—the girl had a hard head.

The captain bounced to her feet, seething as her infamous temper kicked in, and went nose to nose with the offending Seal. *Oh, shit.*

Casey and Emma quickly dashed over and slipped between the two players. The ref hadn't seen the foul, so he didn't act on it. That only pissed Kristin off more, so it wasn't easy to talk her down from punching the ref in the throat—something she vowed she'd do to him the moment the game was over, which made him swallow hard.

Red splotches covering her damp face, Kristin shoved at her short sleeve and settled for spitting at the offending Seal's feet. "Bitch."

Panting, throat raw, Casey guided her away and said, "She went after you on purpose, knowing you were likely to snap. We can't afford for you to get sent off the field. Keep it locked down, yeah?"

Wheezing, Kristin nodded. "Yeah," she bit out. "For now."

Casey patted her back. "Good girl."

A faint breeze whispered over her, dancing across her damp skin like caressing fingers. That small respite from the glare of the sun was most welcome. There was still twenty minutes left of the game to go and, *God*, she was tired. Tired and aching and sore as hell from the many fouls.

She wasn't the only one who was exhausted, she thought, as the players resumed the game. All around her people panted and dragged their feet, clearly digging deep for the strength to keep moving.

Although the Seals were losing, they eventually managed to get their act together. And then they were pursuing the ball like it held the secret to immortal life. A few players almost scored a shot, but the Hounds' keeper caught the ball each time and hurled it downfield.

When the keeper did it a fourth time, a Seal intercepted the ball and passed it to Sherryl, who managed to nail a kick that sent the ball careening into the Hounds' net.

Well, fuck.

SHARDS OF FROST

CHAPTER EIGHTEEN

Slapping her hands to her head, Casey gritted her teeth as the Seals went *wild*. Like seriously wild. Honestly, you'd have thought they'd won the game, not merely scored a goal. But then, they probably believed it wouldn't be so hard at this moment to—at the very least—equalize.

Casey glanced at her teammates, all of whom seemed varying degrees of anxious. Yeah, they knew the Seals could still win this game if they really threw themselves into it. As such, she'd expected the goal to fuck with her team's positivity. It didn't. In fact, they played even more aggressively than before.

As time ticked by and the Seals didn't score again, the bitches began to get desperate. Careless. Reckless. They again committed fouls left, right, and center. And they weren't even being subtle about it. The ref dished out more than five yellow cards.

During the final minute of the game, Casey swiftly dribbled the ball downfield, ready to pass it to her teammate … when Sherryl careened into her out of fucking nowhere. Casey landed hard on her arm, *felt* as something broke. Pain radiated up her limb, and her stomach curdled so badly she thought she'd vomit.

Cradling her arm, Casey sat upright and kept her head bowed as she breathed through the pain. Just as when she'd broken her ankle, her teammates crowded her while also yelling at Sherryl and demanding that the ref act.

Boos and outraged yells came from the bleachers. Casey just knew one of the people raging would be Eli. She could *feel* his fury.

Just as furious, her mink was going *insane.* It didn't care for rules; couldn't give a sliver of a fuck that it would affect the team if Casey retaliated. The mink wanted Sherryl to suffer, bleed, and cry out in pain.

Later, Casey promised her mink. They'd get to that later.

Dennis hunkered down beside her. "That's it, breathe nice and slow." He checked out her arm. "Broken," he told Donahue and the ref.

"I gotta sit on the bench, I know," said Casey. "But something better be done about what just happened, because that was *personal*, and we all know it."

The ref didn't comment. Just spun and disappeared into the crowd.

As Dennis touched her shoulder, his healing energy flowed through her, fixing the break and tackling the other wounds and turf burns. Her arm continued to throb with pain, but she still pushed to her feet … just in time to see the ref thrust a red card into the air. She smiled.

Sherry lost her shit in a spectacular fashion—screeching, swearing, and raving at the ref. Casey's teammates saluted or grinned at her as she walked off the field with Dennis. The injury had hurt like a motherfucker, but the pain was worth it if it meant Sherryl got sent off the field. She just *hadn't* been able to resist fouling Casey, had she?

Casey smiled as she saw Eli waiting for her on the sidelines—hell, he'd moved fast. Every muscle in her body sore and tight with exhaustion, she melted against him and gratefully took the bottle of water he held out.

"You okay? I wanted to kill that fucking bitch," he hissed, easing her onto the bench as if she were fragile.

"Dennis healed me, I'm fine." She guzzled down water, her throat unbelievably raw. "Look, they've added four minutes of extra time. Damn."

Anything could happen in four minutes. Hell, she'd seen teams win during extra time. As such, she was a nervous wreck as she watched the two teams play. Aside from the player who'd substituted Casey, the Hounds were tired. They were also on their guard, though.

The Seals … it was like they'd just given up. Like every one of them mentally checked out. None tried to even create an opportunity to score, and they made little effort to intercept the ball.

Still, it wasn't until the whistle sounded, signaling the end of the game, that Casey stopped chewing on her finger. "Fuck me, we won," she whispered, so stunned that it took a moment for elation to settle in.

Eli hugged her tight. "Congrats, baby, you and your team fucking did it. Get out there, celebrate with them."

So she did. There were hugs, high fives, and butt pats. Some of the Seals shook hands with them, but most shot glares at any Hound that came too close.

Laughing with Emma, Casey headed back to the benches where Eli waited for her. She was sore. Tired. Sweaty. Hungry. Just wanted to get washed and dressed so she could go home and let him cook her a meal and fuss over her the way he liked. But that wouldn't happen yet because—

Her instincts screamed at her. Casey sharply moved sideways, evading

Sherryl as the bitch leaped at her. "The fuck?"

Planting her feet, Sherryl pointed at the ground, her eyes blazing. "You. Me. Right now."

Emma gaped at Sherryl. "You're really gonna throw down here? Seriously?"

"Hmm, *someone's* a little bitter that they lost, huh?" muttered Kristin.

Sherryl ignored them; her attention was firmly on Casey. "Well, Frost?"

"Not here," Casey told her. "Outside the headquarters."

"*Here,*" Sherryl hissed.

"You really want the entire stadium to watch me smack the shit out of you?" It was an appealing thought, but the turf was sacred to her team; Casey wouldn't sully it with this shit.

"No. I want them to watch while I rip you apart." Sherryl stepped forward, her fists clenched. Her eyes slid to something over Casey's shoulder, and her mouth set into a bitter twist. "Oh, look, your wolf is here. Touching. Just make sure his wolf-friends don't get any ideas like jumping in to save you."

One of the Seals reached out to touch her arm. "Sherryl, you—"

"*Back off!*" Sherryl snarled at the female. Her gaze sliced back to Casey. "Do you accept the challenge?"

"Oh, it's accepted," said Casey, conscious that Eli now stood behind her. "But I won't do this on the field."

Sherryl's upper lip curled back. "Bitch—"

"Outside," declared Adrian, entering the circle. "You'll do it outside the headquarters."

Sherryl whirled on him. "I want—"

"*Outside,*" the Alpha growled, baring his teeth at the female. "Don't expect me to care what the fuck you want."

Eyes flickering, Sherryl turned away from him. "Let's do this, Casey." She pivoted on her heel and then stormed off the field and into the building with her teammates hot on her heels.

Casey walked at a slower pace with Eli at her side, wanting to give the pain from her healed injuries a chance to fade away. Certain spots on her body still burned and throbbed, and pain streaked up the back of her leg each time she put weight on it. Worse, her arm still ached as if it were broken, but she'd fought in the past while in worse agony than this.

No one spoke as she and Eli stalked through the headquarters with Adrian, Clare, Donahue, and the Hounds close behind them. Stepping outside, Casey saw that the Seals had formed a circle around Sherryl. Eli's pack mates and allies were also there, and they all looked ready to commit murder.

As Casey and Eli reached the edge of the circle, he turned to her and said, "You're not going to take her down fast, are you?"

Hell, no. "I warned her that I'd shit fury all over her ass."

Approval flashed in his eyes. "Then go do exactly that."

Madisyn sidled up to her. "Don't worry about the Seals jumping to her defense—we'll make sure they stay out of it."

"If they don't, *my* teammates will jump in, so you'll have company."

"Hey, Frost, we gonna do this or what?" Sherryl called out, cocky and eager.

"Wow," said Madisyn. "The bitch really thinks she stands a chance of winning, doesn't she?"

"Sherryl hasn't been thinking clearly for a while." Casey gave Eli a too-quick smile. "See you soon." She strode into the circle, adrenaline pulsing through her body, and met Sherryl's glare head-on.

Sherryl stood tall with her chest thrust out, clenching and unclenching her hands, looking mighty confident. "About time you joined me. I was beginning to think you'd changed your mind."

Casey didn't respond. She just stood solidly with her shoulders back and her expression neutral. Her sore muscles threatened to tighten from the tension, but she kept them loose and relaxed, even as her very spirit seemed coiled to strike.

Her mink stood very still, bracing herself to shift and pounce if needed. The animal didn't like being surrounded by so many, but she wasn't worried. No, she was confident that Casey could take their opponent down.

Sherryl grinned. "Shame Miles couldn't be here for this."

Oh, Casey was *so* gonna enjoy smacking the shit out of this heifer. It wasn't just about the injury Sherryl had caused her on the field. This bitch had stabbed her in the back countless times. She'd tried to kiss Eli and play dumb games with him, hoping to drive a wedge between him and Casey. She'd hurt Casey's cousin and, in doing so, almost wrecked Mallory's relationship with Preston just because she could. Worse, she'd hurt Miles so badly he'd literally unraveled.

Was Sherryl to blame for his drug addiction? No. But she'd convinced him that he could trust, confide in, and count on her. And then she'd shit all over him.

"Speaking of your brother ... I always intended to dump him, you know," said Sherryl. "The plan was to hurt you through him. And it worked."

Fury blazed through Casey. Sherryl had faked caring for him just as surely as she'd faked being a friend to Casey. "You didn't expect to *really* grow to care for him, though, did you?" Just as Preston hadn't expected to care for Mallory. The difference was that Preston had stayed with Mallory and built something with her. Sherryl had walked away from Miles.

"Your brother's a nice guy and a sweet fuck, but he's not 'mate' material. I told him that right before I tossed his latent ass out of my home. Hey, it's not nice to snarl. Save that for the duel. I suppose we should begin that now."

"Works for me."

"I can see that you think you have this in the bag," said Sherryl, a smirk playing around the edges of her mouth. "But since joining my new pack, I've been put through enforcer training. I'm faster and stronger than I used to be."

"How awesome for you."

Sherryl twisted her mouth. "You know, I've been meaning to ask you … do you have to work hard at being a hoe, or does it just come naturally to you?"

Oh, she thought she could get Casey to rush at her in anger? How dumb. "I'd probably find that insulting if I cared about your opinion but, yeah, I just don't."

"Your problem is that you think you're—"

Casey snapped out her fist and punched the bitch hard in the jaw, making Sherryl's head snap to the side. "Yep, that felt as good as I thought it would." Casey exploded into action. She went at Sherryl from each angle with her fists, knees, feet, and elbows. She fought with everything in her—always did. It was just her way.

She put raw power behind every strike and mercilessly targeted every weak spot. She didn't want to fight Sherryl, didn't want to merely neutralize her. She wanted to make her hurt. *Badly.*

Having sparred with her in the past, Casey had gotten a good sense of her strength. Sherryl hadn't been lying when she said that she was stronger and faster now. Hell, yeah, she'd learned some good moves. She'd also learned some dirty moves, and she didn't hesitate to use them.

Fists flew at Casey's temples, jaw, and nose. Feet kicked out at her knees, thighs, and sides. But Casey was always in motion, making herself a difficult target.

Casey sharply weaved and ducked, but she didn't evade every blow. Some connected, and there was some serious power behind them. Worse, the bitch repeatedly targeted Casey's recently healed arm—punched, kicked, and yanked at it, making it throb like a motherfucker.

The spectators were loud as they cheered, booed, and egged on whoever they were supporting, overriding Sherryl's curses and snarls.

A palm strike to the solar plexus sent Casey's breath whooshing out of her lungs. Growling, she thrust her claws into Sherryl's breast, smiling grimly as the female hissed through her teeth.

Casey didn't give her a chance to retaliate; she went in hard and fast, inflicting maximum pain and damage. Sherryl was careful to defend her vulnerable areas—particularly her head, neck, and face. But she wasn't careful enough. Bruises and scratches soon marred her gaunt face, which delighted Casey's mink.

Pain rippled through her body as a fist crashed into her ribs almost hard enough to break bone. She might have doubled over if that reflex hadn't long ago been trained out of her. Instead, she swiped out her claws, carving into Sherryl's chest, tearing open her jersey.

"Bitch," hissed Sherryl.

"You think? Your dad used to call me 'sweet' when dry humping my leg."

Sherryl's eyes narrowed into slits of fury. She charged and tried grappling Casey to take her to the ground. That move failed, so the bitch lashed out with her claws, and a burning heat blazed along the side of Casey's face.

Sherryl inhaled sharply and gave her a smile of mock sympathy. "Ooh, sweetie, that looks sore. We can stop if you need your mate to kiss it better."

Ignoring the blood trickling down her face, Casey smiled. "Bless your little gangrene heart." She went at Sherryl again. Fought hard, fast, and smart, making each strike count.

A hard jab of an elbow to Casey's throat sent pain slicing through her and stole her breath. But she didn't ease up. She swung her hips and snapped out her leg, ramming the heel of her shoe into Sherryl's thigh, who spat a harsh curse.

Sherryl went to grab her ankle but failed—Casey had predicted the move and was able to pull her leg back in time. Snarling in fury, Sherryl lunged again, slashing and striking. Casey dodged, ducked, and jerked backwards to evade each move, but claws stabbed deep into her side and twisted. *Son of a bitch.* Then Sherryl punched her in the tit and, *fuck*, that hurt so much it almost brought tears to her eyes.

Okay, enough was enough.

Casey whipped up her arm to block a punch—the same arm that was pulsing with pain after Sherryl went at it so aggressively. The lingering pain from the soccer injury would have faded by now if it hadn't been for that. "I'm done going easy on you."

Sherryl snorted. "Easy?"

"Yeah. I won't lie, this is gonna hurt really bad."

Eli smiled as his mate ceased holding back and finally engaged in her own brutal art of kicking ass. She was fluid, efficient, and smooth as she punched, blocked, parried, deflected, and kicked, incorporating her whole body into the brawl. Every strike was powerful and perfectly timed. Her footwork was faultless, and her speed was *blinding*.

Like his pack mates, he cheered her on and yelled encouragements. Shaya occasionally slung curses at Sherryl even as she gave Harley a move-by-move commentary of the fight via her cell phone.

"How the fuck can anyone move *that* fast?" asked Nick. "I mean, I thought Ally was fast. This … this is something else."

"Casey goes from move to move without pausing," said Dante, his voice filled with respect. "And yet, every strike is incredibly precise."

Pride snaked through Eli. He loved the savage, gritty, hardcore way with which his mate fought. Loved that she could tear a person to shreds with little effort. But a part of him still hated to see her partaking in a real duel. He enjoyed watching her fight at The Den, but that was different—her opponents weren't trying to fatally wound her. Sherryl, however, would do her best to kill Casey. She'd also fail.

Sherryl was fast—he'd give her that much. But she was nowhere near as fast, strong, or skilled as Casey, and it was clear that she'd now come to that realization. Fear flickered in her eyes as she tried fending Casey off with little success.

Nonetheless, his wolf paced up and down, peeling back his upper lip. He felt his mate's pain as clearly as Eli did, and he did *not* like seeing her bruised and bleeding. The scents of blood, pain, anger, and fear were prodding at his composure, making him want to shift and attack.

"Yeah, fuck that bitch up, Casey!" Mila shouted. She put a hand on her mate's arm. "God, if Sherryl hasn't yet realized she's outmatched, I can't fathom why and—*oh my God, she just kicked Casey right between her legs!* Oh, now that's low."

"Literally," said Taryn.

Eli flinched as Sherryl's teeth sank into Casey's upper arm. Worse, the little bitch sharply twisted her head, trying to bite a chunk out of Casey. With a feral grin, his mate dealt Sherryl a solid punch to the windpipe that sent her staggering backwards, gasping for breath. She topped it off by swiftly carving a perfect 'C' into Sherryl's cheek.

"Yeah, I don't think I'll be making Casey my sparring partner," said Roni.

Eli would have laughed if a fist hadn't then clipped his mate's jaw. "Come on, Casey, be done playing with her!"

Eyes swollen and tearing from Casey's bone-crunching strike to the nose, Sherryl angled her hips and whipped out her leg, landing a kick on Casey's side. His mate only smiled. It was a satisfied, cocky, you're-so-dead smile. Then she sent her fist smashing into Sherryl's jaw and, yep, down the bitch went.

Dazed, Sherryl curled up on the blood-spattered ground, her face a mask of pain.

"Yield, Sherryl, or she'll kill you!" one of the Seals yelled. "For God's sake, *yield!*"

But Sherryl did something else instead.

Perched on the edge of the armchair, Harley gaped at the cell she'd put on speakerphone. "She *shifted?*"

"Yes," replied Shaya on the other end of the line. "And now Casey has too! Oh God, this could be bad."

Bad, but no doubt entertaining, which was why Harley was mega bummed that she was unable to watch Sherryl get her ass handed to her.

"Next year, I am *so* going to these games," declared Ally, leaning forward on the sofa.

"Me, too," insisted Makenna. She and her mate, Ryan, had come to visit, along with another mated couple from the Phoenix Pack, Riley and Tao. Everyone other than the pups—who were both playing upstairs—had gathered in the living area of the main lodge to listen to Shaya's live commentary.

"So what's happening now, Shaya?" asked Harley.

The Alpha female blew out a breath. "Well, the minks have jumped out of their clothes and they're ... oh God, this is getting weird. They're doing that war dance thing that weasels do."

"I've heard of that," said Riley. "What's it like?"

"Um, well, they're sort of glaring at each other while twisting, hopping, rolling, and darting from left to right," replied Shaya. "Ooh, Casey's mink just pounced on Sherryl's!"

Makenna's eyes lit up. "Awesome!"

They all jerked back at the sounds of screeching, hissing, and growling.

Riley grimaced. "That's a *whole* lot of noise they're making."

"Tell me about it," said Shaya. "They sound like Tasmanian devils or something. I can't even give you a good description of the fight, they're moving too fast. There's a lot of pouncing, rolling, and each trying to wrap their body around the other. Basically, they're going crazy on each other's ass."

"Ask Madisyn to take some photos," urged Harley.

"She's doing one better—she's recording the fight with her cell phone."

And that was why Madisyn was Harley's favorite pallas cat ever.

Harley looked up as the pups hurried into the room. She stiffened from head to toe as she took in Cassidy's pale face.

Cain pushed out of his chair. "Cassidy, what's wrong?"

The little girl blinked up at him, her eyes wide as saucers. "Cats are coming," she whispered. "Lots of cats. Big ones. I think they're already here."

Everyone jumped to their feet, and the air snapped taut with tension.

"Shit!" Harley hissed.

"What's going on? What's the matter?" demanded Shaya.

"Cassidy says cats are coming," Harley told her.

"*What?*" the Alpha female fairly shrieked.

People instantly sprung to action—Tao called his Alphas to request backup, Jesse pulled up the CCTV footage on his laptop, Caleb and Kent tried leading the pups out of the room to the basement. Cassidy reached back for Cain, but he insisted she leave and then joined Derren in coaxing Ally into following Caleb, Kent, and the pups into the basement.

"Do *not* get hurt, Derren Hudson!" Ally shouted as she left the room.

"What's going on?" asked Nick, who'd obviously taken the phone from Shaya. "My phone alarms haven't gone off, which means no one has crossed the border."

"They're trying, though," announced Jesse, his eyes on the screen of his laptop. "They're near the border of the land behind the motel, running right for the electric fence in their cougar form. There's a lot of them, so I think Ignacio brought some of his allies along for the ride."

"Fuck," spat Nick. "The pups—"

"Are heading to the basement with Ally, Kent, and Caleb," Derren assured him. "We've activated the traps and landmines around our territory, before you ask."

"Good," said Nick. "We're leaving now. Well, everyone except for Casey and Eli." With that, Nick rung off, so Harley pocketed her phone.

"That fence near the motel is a good twenty-minute run from here, right?" asked Cain, to which Jesse nodded. "And even if they pass *this* fence, they'll also have to pass the electric fence that stands between that land *and* this land, correct?"

"Yes," said Jesse. "But the fences won't keep them out for long. Not when there are so many of them. The voltages are strong enough to daze someone or even put them into shock, but not enough to kill."

Tao pointed at the laptop screen. "Look, some are actually trying to use the fallen bodies of the dazed cougars as stepping stones to hop the fucking fence."

"Not that it'll do the cats much good—most will fall straight into the hidden ditch behind it that's embedded with wooden spikes," said Harley, her stomach in knots. "But others will learn from their mistakes, and they'll soon pass."

"Thanks to the landmines and traps, Ignacio's number will have taken a hit by the time they get here, but they *will* get here," said Jesse. "And not before the rest of our pack mates arrive."

"Ours will make it here before them, though," said Riley. "Ignacio has probably come for Eli."

"No, I don't think so." Cain rubbed at his jaw. "Ignacio keeps track of Casey. He'll know about her game, and he'll know that Eli will be there to support her. My guess is that he's using the game as a distraction; he came to attack the people that Eli cares for."

And then the alarms sounded.

CHAPTER NINETEEN

"What's wrong?" Eli demanded the moment his brother ended his call. "What's happening?"

Nick looked at him, his jaw hard. "Ignacio and his pride are invading our territory as we speak."

Eli's stomach bottomed out, and his wolf froze. Curses and gasps flew out of his other pack mates and allies, who gathered closer.

"The rest of us have to leave, but you should stay with Casey," Nick told him, urgency in every syllable. "Join us when you can." And then they all rushed off.

Fisting his hands, Eli looked at his mate. The dark brown mink was still tearing into her opponent like a crazy critter from hell. They repeatedly lunged, pounced, and leaped at each other, always trying to grab the other's legs, tail, or nose. Small tufts of fur flew as they rolled and twisted and flipped while wrestling for control, leaving yet more blood on the pavement.

He couldn't—*wouldn't*—leave Casey. But, fuck, it hurt not to follow his pack mates and join the battle that lay ahead of them.

"Your brother's having trouble with Ignacio Rodriguez?" Adrian asked.

"Not Nick," Eli told the Alpha. "Ignacio's issue is with me and, to an extent, Casey. To cut a long story short, he believes that she's his true mate. He wants me to suffer for claiming her, which means he probably intends to kill the people I love—it's his MO." Eli cursed a blue streak, hating how powerless he was to help them.

"I see." Adrian looked at his Beta, who'd been eavesdropping. "Clare."

Whatever the Beta female saw on his face made her nod and melt away.

Adrian turned back to Eli. "Until Casey moves to your pack later today, she's one of mine. And I don't take kindly to anyone targeting her mate. Clare will see to it that your brother has plenty of backup from my pack."

225

"What kind of backup?" asked Eli, hope flickering to life in his belly. He'd take *any* aid at this point. The assistance of a mink pack was no small thing.

"Oh, approximately one hundred minks. Trust me, Eli—Ignacio won't get out of this attack alive, and nor will any of his cats. Now wipe that worried look off your face and enjoy what's left of this duel. Casey's mink is just about done with Sherryl's."

Scrubbing at his jaw, Eli turned back to the fight just in time to see his mate tear a strip off the fawn-colored mink's scalp. He winced. Fuck, that had to hurt. But he felt no sympathy for his mate's opponent.

Panting heavily, the fawn mink looked tired and disoriented. It was no surprise, considering she was bleeding from too many injuries to count.

His mate had a lot of wounds of her own, and Eli could *feel* that she was in real pain. But, apparently, his little mink was much like Casey and had an impressive tolerance for pain, because she was still fighting hard and dirty.

Claws unsheathed, his mate latched onto the neck of the other mink, who twisted and slashed at her with sharp claws. And then ... honestly, they moved at such a dizzying speed that it was truly hard to follow exactly what was happening.

The whole time they fought, they shrieked and hissed and snarled so loud that he was surprised his ears didn't bleed.

They had seriously fast reflexes, which was good, or his mate's skull would have been punctured long ago by her opponent's sharp teeth. The fawn mink was a vicious little shit, always trying to bite his mate's head or claw at her eyes and throat.

The alarm on his phone chimed, alerting him that the border of his territory had been breached. *Fuck.* Despite knowing that his pack mates would soon have plenty of backup, panic rode him so hard that his heart was racing. "End it, Casey!" Because they needed to fucking leave *yesterday.*

Just then, the two minks backed away a moment, glaring at each other. They growled, scraping at the ground, preparing to lunge.

It was his mate who moved first. Back arched, tail whipping from side to side, she pitched forward and slashed at the fawn mink's face. Then they were at it again—pouncing, rolling, and biting.

His mate finally got a firm grip on the fawn mink, who frantically spun and writhed as she tried to wriggle free. But his mate spun and writhed along with her, holding her tight. Then his mate sank her sharp teeth into the base of the other mink's skull. She didn't let her go. Just held her in that bone-crushing bite.

"Yield or she'll kill you!" a Seal shouted. Her teammates echoed her, their eyes gleaming with horror.

The Seals' coach leaned forward and shouted, *"Yield, Sherryl!"*

But the critter didn't. It twisted again, pointlessly trying to claw at his mate, who then bit harder into her opponent's skull.

Everyone sucked in a breath.

Eli watched as the fawn mink's struggles slowed until, finally, it went limp. *Dead.* He let out a long breath, and his wolf almost sagged with relief.

Eli expected his mink to try playing with the corpse—she did that often at his territory. Instead, she backed away from the body and shifted.

Muscles quivering, Casey rose to her feet and stared down at the dead mink. Eli rushed to his mate and curled his arms around her, careful not to press on her injuries—she was covered in vicious bites and rake marks.

Knowing she needed a moment to gather her composure and have her injuries healed, he fought back his eagerness to leave and palmed the back of her neck. "You did good."

She rested her forehead on his chest. And then Dennis was there, placing his hand on her shoulder. Eli *felt* the male's warm healing energy flood her body. Unlike Ally's healing energy, however, it didn't soothe her pain. But her injuries were healed—that was what mattered.

She looked up at Eli. "I can feel anxiety and panic racing through you. I'm fine, the duel's over."

He grabbed her upper arms. "We need to leave now. I'm sorry, baby, but I can't wait for you to wash away the blood—we have to go."

She stiffened. "What's going on? And where are the rest of your pack mates?"

Adrian appeared at her side. "Here are your clothes, Casey."

"Eli, tell me what's wrong," she insisted, even as she pulled on her clothes.

Eli licked his lips. "Ignacio and his cats are invading my territory right now."

"What? Shit! You should have left without me!"

"Fuck that, I'd never leave you while you were in the middle of a damn duel."

"You bitch!" A Seal made a fast beeline for Casey. Kristin crashed into the bitch and took her down. A second Seal jumped into the fray, followed by another Hound. Then the two teams shifted into their mink forms and began ripping into each other.

"I should have seen that coming," said Adrian before turning back to Casey, who was now fully dressed. "I've sent backup to Mercury Pack territory. Ignacio won't survive this attack."

"That doesn't mean he won't take out some of my pack mates before then." Cupping her elbow, Eli led her out of the crowd—most of whom gave her nods of respect or pats on the back—and over to the SUV.

Inside, she snapped on her seatbelt. "You're going to kill Ignacio, aren't you?"

Eli switched on the engine. "No."

"No?"

"I want to," he said, reversing fast out of the parking space. "I want to fucking dismember the bastard. But I'm not the only guy whose mate he targeted. And there's someone in Nick's lodge who wants Ignacio as dead as I do." Once he'd driven out of the lot, Eli slammed his foot on the accelerator. "I'll be surprised if Ignacio is still alive when we get there."

For Cain, an advantage of being a sociopath was that you could accurately predict what other sociopaths would do. You knew how their minds worked, how they operated, how essential control was to them, and just how badly they'd react when they lost said control. You could also anticipate their next move. And so, Cain wasn't outside the lodge, helping the others fight off the cougars. He was standing near the basement door, waiting for Ignacio, knowing he'd come.

The Alpha had deceived, manipulated, and blackmailed Casey in order to get into her head and gain control of her. In molding her reality, making her believe that her brother wasn't paying his debts and that she was the only thing standing between Miles and sadistic punishments, Ignacio had gotten a firm grip on her. He'd become someone she was forced to interact and toe the line with. That had satisfied Ignacio's need for power and dominance; had made him feel that she was under his control.

And then Eli had pushed him out of the picture, ripping that control away from him.

Ignacio's attempts to punish him via the lone shifters had failed. He'd be determined to put that right. Determined to prevail over Eli and win at all costs—it was probably something only another sociopath would really understand.

Cain knew Ignacio hadn't invaded Mercury Pack territory purely for a war. No, Ignacio had come to fix his failures. The abrupt attack on the pack had been a diversion. A way for Ignacio to get on the land and keep the strongest members occupied while he hunted down the pups he'd marked for death, trusting the cougars outside to eliminate Eli's other closest relatives. Ignacio would want *every* single one of them dead. And he'd want to kill the pups himself because he knew it was their loss that would hurt Eli most.

More Phoenix wolves had appeared before the cats had the chance to launch their attack, so the cougars weren't finding the battle an easy one. Cain doubted that Ignacio would care much if he lost pride mates or allies to this battle, though. People were often interchangeable to those like Ignacio and Cain.

One counsellor at juvie had told Cain that he was a "stable sociopath," if there was even such a thing. By that, she'd meant he wasn't self-delusional and hadn't let himself become a slave to his impulses.

Cain was no slave to anything. He was always fully in control of himself.

Ally constantly told him that he wasn't "bad," just lost. She didn't want to face the cold truth. Didn't want to acknowledge what he'd become.

By his own admission, he didn't care for society's definition of right and wrong. He put his own needs and wants first, and he felt zero empathy for others—something he was glad of since, from what he'd seen, it seemed to weaken a person. The only people who held any value to him were Ally, his uncles, and Cassidy.

If asked, he would have said he'd have no problem walking away from his true mate. He didn't bond with people. He was loyal to those that mattered to him. What he did feel for them … he wouldn't term it "love." The feeling was fifty percent respect, forty percent possessiveness, and ten percent of something that was close to adoration—an odd brew that was intense but selfish, because he didn't prioritize those people over himself.

He'd been fascinated by Eli's telling of how he recognized Casey as his mate so fast. Cain hadn't felt an instant emotional pull toward Cassidy. Hadn't quite simply *known* she was his mate. But he'd felt *something* on first meeting her. Something he hadn't been able to name; something that had tickled his instincts in a way he couldn't explain. It had grown with each interaction they had, until he'd finally recognized it for what it was: a primitive sense of ownership.

Cassidy … when he looked at her, Cain saw someone that belonged to him. Someone he had innate rights to. It was the "someone" part that surprised him. He tended to view people as tools to be used, but he didn't regard her as some*thing* that he owned.

He didn't want her the way he imagined a person would want their mate—he wasn't a fucking pervert, for Christ's sake. He just wanted her to be safe. Healthy. Happy. He'd want that for any child. With Cassidy, it was *vital* to him that she was all those things, and he'd do whatever it took to make that happen. Lie. Cheat. Kill. Die. It was the latter part that was a telling point, because there was nothing self-sacrificing about Cain.

She brought him a sense of … something that quietened all the chaos inside him. He selfishly drank in whatever it was, giving nothing back because he didn't *have* anything to give.

The best thing he could do for his true mate would be to walk away—he knew that. Really, Cain saw no logic in making a place for himself in her life, waiting for her to grow old enough to be claimed, when the reality was that he was probably incapable of forming a mating bond with anyone. And that was why, just a few months ago, he'd made the official decision to leave Cassidy's life.

His uncles had tried to talk him out of it; had insisted he was a good guy "deep down." They were wrong. He wasn't unfeeling or callous, true. He felt emotions, but they were more like flickers of feelings—never anything deep or meaningful.

Regret? Yeah, he felt it … when his actions hadn't gotten him the result he wanted. But guilt? No. Shame? No. Remorse? No. A wish that he hadn't caused someone pain? Only if said person's pain then impeded him in some way. He would never harm the people he valued—that was as close to a "good guy" as Cain got.

He'd intended to stay away from Cassidy and cut all contact between them. But when he'd heard she'd been shot … he couldn't describe what he'd felt that day. It had been dark. Irrational. Turbulent. Violent. An all-consuming rage he hadn't experienced since his years at juvie.

There was no way he could have stood back and let Nick take care of it. Cassidy wasn't Nick's to protect or avenge, she was Cain's, and so he'd intended to be at her side until the threat was eradicated. And he'd realized he'd been bullshitting himself when he thought he could leave her life. It would never happen.

Cain could never have remained in the shadows, watching over her—he was too selfish for that. He might not be able to give her the emotional feedback that another male would, but he'd never let a thing harm her. Never violate her trust, allow anyone to exploit her gift, or risk her safety. That had to count for something. And if it didn't, well, she was welcome to try fighting his claim to her when she was old enough. It wouldn't work, though.

The scent of cougar drifted to Cain mere moments before Ignacio appeared in the hallway. He'd clearly followed the pups' scents, just as Cain had anticipated.

Surprise briefly flared in Ignacio's eyes. "Ah, Cain Holt. So you *are* in contact with your foster sister, after all. Well, since you're here instead of participating in the battle, I'm assuming she's behind that door over there."

"You made a mistake coming here," said Cain. "But I'm glad you did. It saves me the bother of hunting you."

"For what, exactly? I have done nothing to your foster sister or uncles, nor have I done anything to hinder the actions of The Movement. I would imagine very little else matters to you."

"But you *are* responsible for all the recent trouble that this pack has been having. An associate of mine had a long talk with the falcon who survived the attack on Eli; he named you as the person who'd hired him and the other falcons. So, it seems highly likely to me that you also hired whoever shot his niece. *That* I have a real issue with."

"Since when did you have a soft spot for children?" Ignacio raised a hand. "I have no beef with you, Cain, so I'm going to give you a chance to leave and let me deal with this matter. If you like, you can take your foster sister with you. But the others will stay."

"So that you can kill every last one of them?"

Ignacio shrugged. "It won't be long before Eli returns. I like the thought of him arriving to find sheer carnage."

"But you also mean to kill Eli, don't you? You mean to finish the job that the falcons barely started."

"It's true that if you want something done right you should do it yourself."

"If you kill him, you'll kill Casey."

Something flashed in Ignacio's eyes. "And why should I care if anything happened to her?"

"Considering you believe she's your mate, I'd say she's probably the only person on this planet who matters to you. I get why you want Eli dead. If someone not only imprinted on my mate, they convinced her that *they* were her true mate—that she was born for *them*, that she belonged with them, that she was no one whatsoever to me—I'd want him dead. Dead and buried.

"If I couldn't have her, I'd at least want her to acknowledge that she was meant for me. But Casey hasn't acknowledged that she's yours, has she? Eli has her utterly convinced that you're no one to her. Maybe you are, maybe you aren't. In any case, they're mated now. And like I said, killing him would kill her."

Ignacio's jaw hardened. "Their bond is incomplete."

"But not fragile."

"She'd survive his death. Casey is too strong to do anything but survive. She and I are very much alike, you know. Driven. Resilient. Ambitious. She understands how achieving what you want in life can mean making sacrifices you might resent."

Cain wouldn't say that she and Ignacio were alike at all, but whatever. "That doesn't mean she's your mate."

Ignacio's face darkened. "She is mine." The words were spoken flatly, but there was a wealth of possession there that was almost child-like in its simplicity.

A normal person might have questioned how Ignacio could ever have mistakenly thought that she was his mate. But people like him and Cain couldn't rely on feeling the pull of the mating bond, since they didn't *feel* in the same way that normal people did. They just didn't have the emotional capacity to.

It was clear that Ignacio was drawn to Casey, and Cain could understand it. She was strong, loyal, full of life, and fairly brimmed with positive energy. She was everything Ignacio could never be; everything that the people around him had never been. For him, she'd be like a lone bulb in a dark room.

Given the cougar's nature and past, it was not at all surprising that he'd want to own her. And that was all it was—Ignacio wanted to possess her. Not because she was born for him, but because she appealed to him on a level that no other female had done before, and he'd mistaken that for the pull of a true-mate bond.

"I don't believe she's yours, Ignacio. And I don't just say that because I've seen her and Eli together. I say it because you see her as a thing that belongs to you, not a person—I can hear it in the way you speak of her. You'd never prioritize her needs over yours, would you? Having the position of Alpha is more important to you than she is, which tells you everything you need to know."

Ignacio snapped his teeth together. "Think what you like, Holt. But facts are facts. Casey Frost is mine."

"Here's a real fact for you." Cain took a step toward him. "You're going to die today, Ignacio. See, you're right that very little matters to me other than my family and the Movement. But there *is* a little someone who matters above all else to me. A little someone who's safe behind that door you want to get through. A little someone *you had shot.*" Cain felt his nostrils flare. "I almost lost my mate because of you, Ignacio."

The cougar went very, very still. "I didn't know she was yours."

"I don't care."

"If I'd known—"

"It wouldn't have made a difference to you." Cain tilted his head. "Men like us ... we live with dark, violent, destructive thoughts and urges, don't we? They poke at us. Prod us to act. And we have to make a conscious decision every day *not* to act on them, even though we see no real reason why we shouldn't.

"Me personally? I don't understand why I should be so concerned about following what's 'right' when the lines of morality are blurry at best. Morality is objective. Ethics can be twisted to suit a person's agenda. For example, I can argue that I'm justified in killing you, considering you'll kill a whole lot of people today if I don't. But that's not why I'm going to kill you, Ignacio. I'm going to do it because the thought pleases me. Because you tried to take the thing that matters most from me. Because I'm a cruel, vindictive bastard who likes to hurt people sometimes."

Ignacio lifted his chin. "You won't find me easy to kill, Cain."

"You're already dead. You were dead the moment that bullet sank into my mate."

Eli had no sooner switched off the engine than he was hopping out of the SUV. Following the growls, snarls, shrieks, and hisses that rang through the air, he ran out of the parking lot, dashed around the main lodge, and onto the clearing near the play area. There, he skidded to a halt. His wolf ceased panicking and blinked in surprise.

Dozens of dead cougars littered the field. Many of his pack mates and allies were working in teams to bring the live cougars down, and they were taking their time about it, since there weren't many foes left standing. The rest of his pack mates and allies stood aside, watching while Taryn healed their wounds.

But what grabbed Eli's attention was that some of the live cougars were covered from almost head to toe in a mass of writhing, clawing minks. More of the little critters surrounded them, hissing *in tune* as their pack mates savaged the felines.

"That beat sounds oddly familiar," Eli said to his mate, who didn't look whatsoever surprised by the sight in front of them.

Clearing her throat, Casey shrugged. "It's Queen's *Another One Bites the Dust.*"

Eli stared at her. He'd have said she couldn't possibly be serious that the damn minks were, essentially, singing while slaughtering fellow shifters. But, yeah, he recognized the song now. "They do this a lot when they're in battle?"

"I want to say 'no, of course not,' but you'd know I was lying. Look, they don't get to battle like this often—they're just making the most of it."

"Making the most of it," he echoed.

Just then, a cougar staggered past them with a pallas cat wrapped around its face and a second pallas cat curled around its hindleg. Of course, the sight wouldn't have been so weird if there wasn't a long of minks following, each clinging to the tail of the mink in front of them while the leader clung to the cougar's tail with its teeth. It was like they were doing the fucking Conga dance or something.

"I see you judging them," said Casey.

"How can I not judge that?"

A yelp made Eli's head snap to the right. Zander's wolf jerk away from a cougar who'd torn a strip out of his flank.

A loud curse burst out of Gwen, who was stood amongst the spectators. "For God's sake, Zander, stop playing with the fucker!" She aimed her gun and fired. Instantly, the cat slumped to the ground. "There," she said to her mate. "See how easy that was?"

Shaya snorted a laugh and turned to speak to Taryn, but then she noticed Eli and Casey. Shaya beamed at them. "Hey, you're here."

Eli crossed to her. "Doesn't look like our help is needed."

"Oh, it's not." Shaya smiled at Casey. "Glad to see you're okay after the Sherryl-thing. Your mink friends made *all* the difference here."

Gwen nodded. "Don't know how they got on our territory without setting off any motion sensors, but they came out of *nowhere*. And then they were just everywhere."

"Some were scrambling up trees and then dropping onto the backs of cougars, puncturing spinal cords with their teeth," said Taryn. "Some just jumped onto the cougars and scalped the fuckers. Other minks were latching onto cat-jugulars while their furry little friends swarmed the body of their prey until you couldn't even *see* the cougar anymore. In fact, some are still doing that."

"Ooh, and a bunch of them circled a cougar and did that weird war dance," Gwen added. "But it was more like they were just playing with it for messed-up fun … and then they all just lunged at once—it was *amazing*."

"I wish we could have recorded it all with our phones," said Shaya. "I've heard it said that minks go into killing frenzies, but … yeah, I guess I just didn't expect them to decimate the cougars' numbers so fast."

Eli glanced at the cats. "Which one of them is Ignacio? I'm hoping you're going to tell me he's among the dead bodies."

"I spoke to Jesse a minute ago when Taryn healed his wounds before he threw himself back into the battle," said Shaya. "He said he hadn't scented Ignacio out there, but that doesn't mean the asshole isn't among them."

Brow furrowing, Eli gave the area another once-over. "Where's Cain?"

"According to Ally, who calls me every five minutes to check that Derren's okay, Cain insisted on guarding the basement," said Shaya.

Eli exchanged a look with Casey, and then he took her hand. "Let's go have a chat with Cain." He kept his body slightly in front of hers as he led her into the main lodge. They'd only made it a few steps inside when a familiar scent reached his nostrils, making his wolf bristle. Eli bared his teeth. "Ignacio's here."

"Bastard," she hissed.

Adrenaline pumping through him, Eli followed the scent trail, which took them to the hallway near the basement. It was empty. No Ignacio. No Cain.

"Look," said Casey, pointing at the floor.

His jaw hardened as he noticed a few specks of blood there. Eli's nostrils flared as he drew in the scents around them. "That's Ignacio's blood. And he went that way," Eli added, gesturing toward the back door. "Cain's scent is tangled with his, so it looks like they went outside together."

Eli again walked slightly in front of Casey as they tracked the two males. The scents took them out of the lodge and into the surrounding woods. Usually, he'd hear birds chirping and animals moving around in the underbrush. But right then, the only sounds were that of leaves rustling and the tree branches creaking in the breeze. It was almost eerie.

The smells of pine, moss, and wild mint were heavy in the forest, but Eli didn't let them distract his senses from the scents of Cain and Ignacio. Dead leaves and pine needles littered the ground, but he and Casey moved soundlessly through the woods, thanks to their enforcer training. Their targets' scents took them deeper and deeper into the maze of tall trees.

Eli's step faltered as another strong smell slammed into him. *Blood.* He hastened his pace as he followed the thick coppery scent, aware that Casey was close behind him and—

He halted as the two males finally came into view. Eli sucked in a shocked breath, and his wolf stopped pacing. Ignacio was sprawled on the ground and … shit, there was *so* much blood. It looked like he'd been attacked by Jack the fucking Ripper. Deep gouges crisscrossed his body. Organs were spilling out. His face had been smashed to a pulp. The meaty parts of his thighs and arms lay beside him.

And Cain, well, he was standing over the body, holding what looked like a heart. He wasn't panting with rage or glaring at the remains of Ignacio with hatred. He was just … looking.

"I guess I don't need to ask if he's dead," said Eli.

Cain's gaze sliced to him, utterly devoid of emotion. "I know you wanted the pleasure of ending him, but I won't apologize for stealing that pleasure from you. He coveted your mate, but he tried to have mine killed. He would have killed her tonight if I hadn't been here. I had more of a right to execute him than you did."

Execute? Eli wouldn't have used that word to describe what Cain had done to Ignacio. No, it was more like the guy had *butchered* him. Not that Eli had any complaints about it. Yeah, he'd longed to tear Ignacio into tiny little pieces, and he wished he'd had the satisfaction of watching him die. But Eli couldn't regret that Cain had taken care of the matter—not when he'd made the cougar suffer in such a spectacularly brutal, albeit slightly sickening, fashion. His wolf very much approved.

Also, Eli couldn't deny that Cain had the right to wipe Ignacio from the Earth—he'd avenged his mate, just as any shifter would. "Did you chase him out here?"

"No," replied Cain, sliding his gaze back to Ignacio. "He tracked the pups to the basement; he was going after them. I didn't want to kill him in the lodge, so I brought him out here."

"You knew he'd go after the pups, didn't you?"

Cain shrugged. "I know Ignacio's brand of logic." He tossed the heart on the ground as if it was a ball that he was bored of playing with. "Is the battle over?"

"Probably. Only one way to find out." Eli headed back to the clearing with Casey. His pack mates and the Phoenix Pack members were all stood aside in their human form, staring open-mouthed at the cougar-littered field, watching the minks in sheer fascination. Eli felt his brows fly up in surprise.

Nick spared him a brief glance and said, "Um … I'm not really sure what's happening."

"That looks … wrong," said Trey.

Shaya nodded. "I mean, the minks are so small and yet they're actually dragging dead bodies along the ground. Bodies that are a *lot* bigger than they are. And they don't even seem to be struggling."

"It's the whole piling-the-bodies-on-top-of-each-other thing that has my attention," said Zander. "The minks are also lining other carcasses neatly in a row."

Derren rubbed his nape. "For me, what's even weirder is that they're rolling the severed heads over to the stacks of corpses."

"At least they're tidying up after themselves," said Mila.

"They're not tidying up, they're gathering their kills together so they can gloat over their successes." Bracken nudged Madisyn. "Can you honestly tell me you *still* think those furry little beasts aren't stone-cold trophy killers?"

Kathy heaved a sigh of exasperation. "Honestly, Bracken, you can be so dramatic."

The wolf gaped at her. " *You're* the one that called minks the psychopaths of the shifter kingdom."

Kathy put her hands on her hips. "Why are you bringing up old crap?"

"Wait, is it just me or is their number shrinking before my eyes?" asked Harley. "It's like they're just … melting out of sight."

"Damn, that's eerie," said Gwen.

Eli suspected they were all disappearing through whatever burrows in the ground they'd used as an entrance. Minks could easily fit through tiny nooks and crannies, including mouse holes. He looked down at his mate. "Am I right in thinking they probably would have taken some of the carcasses home if the cougars weren't too big to fit through the burrows?"

Lips pursed, Casey nodded. "It's a likely scenario."

Smiling, Jaime took a long breath. "Man, I want to be a mink."

Dante sighed at his mate. "I don't know what bothers me more. That you're weird enough to declare something like that, or that you truly mean it."

Nick took a step forward. "Well, this will make disposing of the bodies a quicker job. I suppose we'd better get started."

CHAPTER TWENTY

That evening, Eli lay in bed, staring up at the ceiling while playing his fingers through his mate's hair. She'd crashed hard, just as he'd expected she would.

After the minks had slinked away—they hadn't tripped any alarms, proving there really wasn't a way to mink-proof your territory—and the dead cougars were disposed of, the Phoenix Pack members left and then everyone headed to their respective lodges.

Eli and Casey had taken a long shower before sliding into bed. He'd fucked her soft and slow before rolling onto his back and hauling her close. No sooner had she pillowed her head on his chest than she slipped into a deep sleep.

Although he was dog tired, Eli found himself wide-awake. The day's events just kept replaying in his head over and over and over. He couldn't relax. Couldn't unwind. Not even with the feel of his mate pressed against him, safe and healed and sound asleep.

At least he didn't have to worry that his mental restlessness would wake her. No, she was out cold. The soccer game had taken a lot out of her. Dueling with Sherryl straight after the game had all but exhausted her. It was only the adrenaline and worry for his pack mates that kept her alert throughout the whole Ignacio mess.

Pride trickled through him. His mate was fearless. Never backed down or showed weakness. She stood her ground, and she gave no quarter. There was no denying that Casey Frost was tough as hell. Which was a damn good thing, because if she'd needed him today to boost her strength through their bond while she dueled, he'd have been fucking useless to her.

He couldn't understand why their mating bond hadn't yet fully formed. It made no sense to him. None.

She'd struggled to believe she was his priority at first, but that was no longer the case. They were both fully open to one another. They had no doubts about mating, kept no secrets, and had complete trust in each other. And fuck if she wasn't wrapped around his heart. He knew she loved him just as deeply; he *felt* it. He couldn't possibly doubt the depth of her commitment—she'd moved to his fucking pack, for Christ's sake.

They were tight. Solid. *Happy.* There was nothing he wanted more than to be fully bound to her. He knew she wanted the exact same thing just as badly. And yet, their bond remained incomplete—something that pained him and his wolf every day.

He just didn't fucking get it.

Eli was missing something for sure. What he needed was an outsider's perspective. He was too close to the situation. And, since sleep eluded him, there was no time like the present to go talk to someone. So, leaving Casey to rest, he headed back to the main lodge.

He knew his brother would be awake, relaxing on the porch swing. Nick always did it after a battle, as if some part of him was paranoid that the family or allies of their intruders would come for revenge.

Using the heel of his foot to still the swing, Nick tipped his chin in greeting. "Thought you'd be in bed with your mate."

Eli sat on the swing beside him. "Shaya and the girls okay?"

"Fine. How's Casey?"

"Exhausted. She went out like a light."

"I'm not surprised, given how eventful her day has been. The adrenaline crash will have hit her hard, too." Nick eyed him curiously. "So, why are you here instead of lying beside your mate?"

"You're one of the most perceptive people I've ever met. You know me better than anyone except Casey. If I …" Eli trailed off, struggling to put his thoughts into words.

"You don't understand why your mating bond hasn't fully formed yet," Nick guessed.

"I've looked at it from every angle. I can't work it out."

"Neither can I," Nick grumbled. "Your bond with Casey might not be complete yet, but it's damn strong. It's easy to see just how much you two care for each other. You meshed your lives so easily. Connected so well. Honestly, I don't think any couple here became so solid so fast—it's probably because neither of you held back.

"Initially, I thought your bond would snap fully into place very quickly. I truly don't get what could be standing in the way. One of you must be blocking it on a subconscious level. Do you fear the fact that it's completely irrevocable? That there's no way out that doesn't involve one or both of you potentially turning rogue?"

Eli shook his head. "Not at all. And neither does she—I know that for certain. I know *her.*"

"Maybe it's not fear, then. Maybe it's just hard for her to trust that you won't betray or hurt her the way others did before you."

"I see why your thoughts have taken you in that direction, considering her family let her down so badly, but it's not that. She trusts me one hundred percent. I know that all the way down to my bones. She wouldn't hold back from this; she wants what her grandparents had—a mating that's strong and true."

Nick shrugged. "Then I don't get it, E. I wish I did. Look, the bond will fully form in time. You just have to be patient. I know that's easy for me to say. I know this must be killing you and your wolf. But it'll be worth the wait—trust me on that."

Hinges creaked as the door swung open. Kathy stepped onto the porch and gave them both a tentative smile. Knowing his mother as well as he did, Eli had no doubt she'd done a little eavesdropping.

"Sorry to interrupt," she said. "Willow had a nightmare. Shaya's checking on her, but Willow's asking to see you as well, Nick."

His brother rose. "Give me a few minutes, E." With that, he disappeared inside.

Crossing to the swing, Kathy slowly settled onto the spot that Nick had vacated. "How are you doing?"

"I'm good," replied Eli. "You?"

"Better now that Ignacio no longer walks the Earth. How's Casey? She was covered in blood earlier, so I'm guessing her duel with Sherryl was brutal."

"Her team's healer took care of her wounds before we came here—we just didn't take time to wash away the blood. She's okay. Just tired."

"Must have been hard for you to see her so hurt." Kathy looked off into the distance. "Your father fought alongside his Alpha many times. He'd come home covered in wounds—there's not a lot worse than seeing someone you love injured and in pain. Of course, losing them definitely beats all. That's an agony like no other. An agony every shifter is terrified they'll one day feel. It's one of the main issues that block mating bonds."

Eli's forehead wrinkled. "If you think I haven't bonded with Casey because I'm holding back out of fear that I'll lose her—"

"That's not what I think at all. I know you, Eli. You wouldn't hold back from your mate to protect yourself. That's not who you are."

Mollified, Eli nodded.

"It's your father's birthday next week, you know," she said, fingering the necklace her mate had once given her.

"I know."

"I miss him every day. But you know, even if a Seer had told me long before I met your father that I'd lose him, I'd still have mated with him. I don't regret it, never have."

"Not even when you were at your lowest?"

She raised a brow. "Would you ever regret mating with Casey?"

"Never," he said without hesitation.

"Then you understand. And although losing him is something I'll never recover from, I have never once wished I'd let myself die along with him. I'm not unhappy, Eli. My three children are now all mated, and I have grandchildren to spoil—hopefully, I'll have more of them soon. It is a pleasure and a privilege to see.

"What I do regret is that he and I didn't always make the most of what time we had together. Sometimes we let life get in the way, or we took it for granted that we'd have forever together. It doesn't always work that way." Kathy gave him a quivery smile. "Make the most of every single moment you have with Casey. Never let her doubt how special she is to you. Celebrate the small things, not just the big things."

"So you've fully accepted her, then?"

"I was worried at first. You might not be a born alpha, but you're so close to it that you could easily lead your own pack. You need someone who won't crumble under the weight of your personality. Take Shaya, for example. She's a submissive wolf, but she has the inner strength to push back when Nick pushes too hard. I should have trusted that fate would give you what you needed, but I still worried—that's what it is to be a mother."

"Casey's exactly what I need."

Kathy nodded. "She suits you. She's strong, focused, and has her shit together. She's not afraid to give you all of her or to show others just how much you mean to her, which takes a whole other type of strength. There's only one thing that can break a person so resilient, and that's the loss of a mate. But you already know that, don't you? And it scares the life out of you."

His mother twisted to fully face him. "I meant what I said before—you'd never hold back from Casey to protect yourself. But I believe you'd do it to protect *her*." Kathy rested her hand on top of his. "We can't dictate how the future will go, but we can damn well enjoy the present. So let that fear go. Shove all that negativity aside. Live and laugh and be happy. That's all any of us can do."

She patted his hand, pushed to her feet, and then retreated into the lodge, leaving Eli alone with his thoughts.

Feeling like he'd been hit by a two-by-four, he could only sit limply in his seat. Shit, fuck, shit, his mother was right. She'd seen what he himself had been unable to see. The truth was really very simple. Deep inside, Eli worried that fully bonding with Casey meant—should he ever die, causing the mating bond to shatter—he might one day inadvertently kill her.

No, it wasn't a worry. It was a fear. A cold, stomach-churning fear.

People had more chance of surviving the loss of their mate if they only shared a partial bond. The moment Eli dropped that last wall between him and Casey, he could very well be condemning her to death or to the half-life his mother had been living all these years, depending on what the future had in store for them.

It wasn't rare for a person's mate to die. Plenty of the cougars had died tonight—many, if not all of them, could have been mated. He didn't want Casey to experience that loss. He *never* wanted to cause her any pain. He wanted to protect, cosset, and shield her.

But, really, holding back wouldn't protect her, would it? It would only eat at them both; would only peck away at their bond and create a tremendous amount of bitterness between them. It might also be pointless, considering there was every chance they could live a long, happy life together … if he'd only let go of this fear.

He wanted to. He did. But he couldn't. He'd never stop fearing that they'd one day be torn apart. Never.

That was all part and parcel of loving someone, though, wasn't it? Really, it didn't seem logical to *not* fear losing someone you loved. So, no, he couldn't do what his mother had asked and let said fear go.

But he could do the other things she'd asked of him. He could shove the negativity aside and enjoy the present rather than overthinking what the future might bring. He could treasure the happiness he'd found with Casey and—

A sharp pain slammed into his head and chest, disorienting him. He double-blinked as his vision darkened around the edges. But then the pain faded little by little … and he realized that the mating bond had fully snapped into place.

A smile touched his mouth, and a deep warmth spread through his body. Eli closed his eyes for a moment, relishing the elation and peacefulness that settled over him. His chest felt light … as if a weight had been lifted from it. Inside him, his wolf did a languid stretch, feeling fulfilled all the way from his head to his paws.

Opening his eyes, Eli took a deep, contented breath. He *felt* Casey so much more strongly now … like his whole being was fully tuned into the metaphysical frequency of hers. He could sense that she was awake, which was no surprise.

Wanting nothing more than to share this moment with her, Eli pushed off the swing and headed back home, breathing easier than he had in what felt like years. Inside their lodge, he went straight to the bedroom and found her sitting on the bed, looking adorably flustered. He had to smile.

Peering up at him through heavy-lidded eyes, she shoved her hair out of her face. "Okay, what happened? I mean, I know the bond snapped into place. It woke me up. I'm just wondering what led to it."

Eli lay on his side on the mattress and planted his elbow on the pillow. "I had a talk with my mother, and she made me see a few things." He danced his fingertips along her bare arm. "It was my fault the bond hadn't fully snapped into place."

Casey lay down next to him, mirroring his posture. "Your fault how?"

"My mother was in a terrible state after my father died. It was hard to see her that way. I could tell how easy it would have been for her to just slip away. I wouldn't even have blamed her for it. She was just in so much pain. So depressed and devastated."

Casey swallowed, all too able to imagine just how hard it had been for Kathy. The woman had been through all nine circles of hell. And it was a hell she'd never leave, because she'd always be without her mate.

"Losing him wrecked her. Changed her. It's not right that she'll grow old alone and then die alone." He combed his fingers through her hair. "I don't want that for you. One of my biggest fears is that you'll suffer the same fate as her. Because of that, I subconsciously held back from the bond."

Getting it, Casey gave a slow nod. Really, she should have guessed that was the issue. "I understand."

"You're not pissed at me?"

She snorted. "Why would I be? You didn't hold back to be an asshole; you weren't caught up in how *you'd* feel if the unthinkable happened. You desperately wanted us to be fully bound, but you were so worried about what that might one day do to me that you denied yourself what you needed." She splayed her hand on his chest. "I'm just glad you're done with that. My mink is glad." The animal was curled up in a ball of utter contentment.

"So is my wolf, and so am I." He pressed a long kiss to her mouth. "Love you, baby."

"Love you right back," she whispered, delighted that they were finally fully mated, loving that she could bolster his strength if he needed her to.

It was amazing how much clearer his emotions were to her now. She couldn't help but wonder if she'd feel his orgasms more strongly now, too. "You tired? Because I have a few ideas for how we can spend the next hour."

Twisting his mouth, he traced her collarbone with one finger. "I'm not tired, but I can think of a few ways I can tire myself out."

Her mouth canted up. "It's like one mind."

CHAPTER TWENTY-ONE

Eight years later

Putting his hand on the doorjamb, Eli knocked on the open door. "Come on, little man, time to go."

Sitting on the rug among hundreds of colored, plastic bricks, seven-year-old Curtis lifted his head. Big brown eyes so like Eli's own narrowed on him. "But I'm building a weapon of mass destruction."

"You'll have gifts to open at the main lodge," Eli reminded the pup. It was the pack's Christmas tradition to gather there at noon. Just thinking about the large dinner that awaited them made his stomach rumble. "Someone might have bought you something that will improve your weapon."

Curtis' nose wrinkled. "I don't want to open the presents at the lodge. You'll make me share with the other kids."

Eli's lips twitched, and he felt his wolf's amusement. His boy was extremely possessive. "Christmas is a time for sharing."

"I never learned how to share. I'm an only child."

"No, you're not. Now hurry up. Your mom and sister are waiting."

With a long, suffering sigh, Curtis abandoned his toys and preceded Eli down the stairs. In the hallway, he pulled on his coat, gloves, and hat—frowning at Eli when he tried to give him a hand. His son was just as independent as he was possessive.

"Is Uncle Miles coming to visit later?" Rubie asked her mother as Casey zipped up the five-year-old's coat. She'd shocked everyone when she popped out of Casey with a little mop of ruby-red curls—the color didn't run in either side of the family.

Eli thought his daughter bore a strong resemblance to Roni, but she had her mother's pale hazel eyes. Eyes that could make your stomach twist when she concentrated that mink-unblinking stare on you. His wolf liked that, though.

"Yep," replied Casey with a smile. "He'll be here after dinner."

Rubie pumped her fist in the air. "Uncle Miles buys good presents." She smirked at her brother. "I'm his favorite."

Slipping on his boots, Curtis sniffed. "He just feels sorry for you because you were adopted."

Rubie's lips thinned. "Mommy, Curtis is telling lies again!"

Casey sighed. "Curtis, stop telling her she was adopted. And can we please have one day where you two don't argue?"

Both kids just looked at their mother in a way that said, "can't promise nothing."

It wasn't so much that they didn't get along, it was that they were very different. Curtis was an indoor kid whereas Rubie was very physically active and liked to be outdoors. She'd play soccer all day long if she could. Like her mother, she had an innate talent for it.

Casey had retired from the Hounds a year ago, but she still got together with her old teammates to play for fun now and then. She often took Rubie with her.

Eli clapped his hands. "Come on, let's go, I'm hungry." Once everyone was all bundled up, he grabbed the bulging gift sack from beside the door and gestured for all three of them to file out the lodge first.

Stepping onto the porch, Casey inhaled deeply, drinking in the ozone scent of snow. The fresh, crisp air filled her lungs and made her shiver just a little. A thick, white blanket had covered the forest; frosting bushes, branches, and dead logs. It really was a beautiful sight.

The kids walked on ahead as they all traipsed through the snow. Casey loved the sound of it crunching beneath her feet. She was glad it was no longer snowing. She liked snow, she just didn't like being outside while it was snowing. Having flakes of it pelt her face, chap her skin, and cling to her clothes and hair was not Casey's idea of fun at all. But she'd enjoyed making a snow fort with Eli and the kids the previous day.

"Walk in front of me," Eli said to her. "I like staring at your ass while you walk—it's one of the best parts of my day."

She snickered. "You're so full of it."

"Hey, that was a heart-felt compliment." He threaded his gloved fingers through hers. "Did you hear from Adrian this morning?"

"Yes. He and Clare are planning to come by one day this week." The mated mink-pair had initially wanted to drop by tomorrow, but it was tradition for the Mercury and Phoenix Pack to have a huge get-together on Boxing Day since, due to the number of visitors each pack received, they weren't able to meet up on Christmas Day.

"I also got a 'Merry Christmas' call from Emily when you were in the shower," Casey added. "My mom was with her, so she spoke to me for a few minutes, too. They're planning to visit soon."

Casey couldn't say she had a solid relationship with them, but it wasn't awkward. They'd started speaking again seven and a half years ago, when she'd gone to visit Miles at rehab. Emily and their mother had been there and … well, Gayle had collapsed into heart-wrenching sobs the minute she'd spotted Casey.

It was when Ira tried forcing Emily to marry his friend's son that Gayle had finally snapped out of her bullshit "I must follow my mate's lead" state. You didn't follow someone who was a complete asshole.

Gayle had rebuilt a relationship with each of her children, despite that Ira wildly disapproved. It had helped Miles a lot with overcoming his addiction, so Casey was glad of it. It had taken a while for her mink to accept Gayle and Emily's presence in her life, though; she still didn't trust them.

"Damn, it's cold," Casey said with a little shudder. "One thing I hate about winter is how dry it makes my skin."

"I'll give you a facial later."

She gave the dirty-minded wolf the side-eye.

He put his mouth to her ear. "I love it when you swallow my come, baby, but blowing my load all over your pretty face is always a pleasure. Come on, let me. I'll make sure you have a happy ending."

She chuckled. "You're an idiot."

A small breeze came along, rustling branches and causing a few clumps of snow to cascade down.

"Will you two stop!" a male voice burst out.

Turning, Casey glimpsed Bracken through the trees. He was glaring down at two little dark-haired girls who could pass for identical twins.

The oldest, Regan, jabbed her finger at her sibling. "The Thing started it!"

"Stop calling me that!" Yasmin yelled.

Casey exchanged an amused smile with Eli. The cute pallas cats were only a year apart in age, and they could play together beautifully. They shared, laughed, and constantly made up weird songs. But it was never long before one was trying to choke the other to death, and it could be over the most menial stuff.

Madisyn strode up behind her mate. "What are you two demons whining about this time?" Her frown melted away when she noticed Casey and Eli. "Hey, guys! Merry Christmas!"

"Same to you!" Casey called out. She smiled at the pallas kits. "Did Santa bring you all the stuff you asked for?"

"He didn't bring me the tarantula, which is a bummer," said Regan. "I was gonna put it in The Thing's bed."

And then Yasmin launched herself at her sibling, taking her to the ground.

Bracken let his head fall back. "This is what I get for ignoring Vinnie's advice to have them decades apart."

Madisyn laughed. "We'll catch up in a minute, Case."

"Sure." Casey gave them a quick wave and then headed to the main lodge. Kathy must have noticed them out of the window, because she opened the door before Casey had a chance to knock.

Kathy beamed at them. "There you all are!" She gave a hug to Eli and Casey and then made a huge fuss of the kids, peppering their little faces with kisses.

After removing their coats, gloves, and hats, they all walked into the living area. Casey wiggled her cold fingers. The room was gorgeously warm, thanks to the crackling fire. Most of the pack were already there, and she found herself quickly swept up in hug after hug after hug.

"Uncle Eli!" The Alpha's son dashed over and wrapped himself around Eli's leg.

Eli ruffled his nephew's ash-blond hair. "Merry Christmas, Kellen."

"Dad said the kids can open their gifts before dinner this year so that he doesn't have to deal with my pouting and whining while he's eating."

"Good thinking on his part."

Kellen released Eli's leg. "What did ya bring me?"

"It might be in this sack." Eli dumped it on the floor. "Take a look."

"Presents!" yelled Kellen, and every kid in the room descended on the sack.

Ally and Derren's take-charge son tried making the others line up, insisting he'd take out the gifts one at a time and call out whoever's name was on the tag. He usually managed to make the other kids dance to his tune, since he was the oldest, but today they were all too high on excitement to give a hot shit what he wanted. It didn't help his cause that his two little sisters were advising the others to "ignore Mr. Bossy Pants."

Hearing her daughter giggle, Casey turned to see that Roni had balanced the little girl on her hip and was twirling in circles. But then Roni abruptly halted, and her eyes narrowed on the boy standing by Curtis. "What have you been eating, Cody?" she asked the eldest of her three sons.

The mini version of Marcus froze and then batted his eyelashes, all innocence. "Nothing."

"So why do you have a chocolate mustache?" Roni challenged.

A loud gasp came from the kitchen. "Who opened the chocolate trifle?" demanded Kathy.

Roni groaned. "Oh, for heaven's sake!"

Cody pointed at his youngest brother. "It was his idea!"

Dash scowled at him. "Snitch!" And then they were grappling with each other, which wasn't an uncommon sight. Marcus quickly broke up the fight and tossed the youngest to Zander, who caught him easily, making Dash laugh like a loon.

Roni and Marcus' middle child, Keane—who was an absolute genius like his mother—sighed and said, "This is why I don't like children."

Casey felt a tug on her pants and looked down to see Curtis holding up a gift-wrapped box.

"Can you guard it for me?" he asked.

She almost laughed at his word choice. "Guard it?"

He handed her the gift sack they'd brought along, which was now empty. "You can put it in that."

"Aren't you gonna open it?" asked Ally, crouched beside him as she dumped all the torn wrapping paper into a garbage bag.

"Later," said Curtis. "For now, I want to enjoy time with my pack mates."

Ally's face went all soft. "Aw, that's the sweetest damn thing I ever heard."

It was Curtis' problem with sharing, that was what it was. And so each time one of the pack handed him a gift, he politely thanked them and chucked it in the sack.

Derren shook his head. "At his age, I wouldn't have been able to wait for even five minutes before opening—" He flinched. "Jesus Christ." The Beta growled down at the margay cub that was chomping on his ankle.

Sighing at his son, Jesse lifted him by the scruff of his neck. "Dude, we've been over this, you can't shift and—ow, dammit, that was my finger!"

Casey bit back a smile, and her mink twitched her tail in amusement. Unlike most breeds of shifter, margay cats could shift as children. Harley and Jesse had two gorgeous boys. The oldest was polite, placid, and as musical as his mother. The youngest was freaking nuts, and he spent a lot of time in his cat form.

"Cassidy's here!" Caleb bellowed.

Striding into the room, Cassidy laughed as the kids swarmed her like ants. She'd been part of Cain's pack since they mated six months ago, so people were still getting used to not having her constantly around. It hadn't been an easy adjustment for Willow, since the two girls were so close.

Being mated hadn't changed Cain, but he was different with Cassidy than he was with others. He took care of her and protected her fiercely. Even now, he stood infinitely close to her, as if he might shove her behind him at any moment to shield her from a threat.

He'd left The Movement, just as he'd sworn that he would, and now all his focus was on her. And he hadn't complained about her wanting to spend Christmas dinner with the Mercury Pack every other year—Casey liked him for that alone.

Eli pulled his niece into a hug. "Merry Christmas, sweetheart." He and Casey exchanged nods with Cain.

"Right back atcha, Eli," the she-wolf said, her smile bright.

"How's life at your new pack?" asked Casey, rubbing her upper arm. "Are they being good to you?"

"Oh, yeah," Cassidy assured her. "They like having a Seer, so they've been very welcoming. Although I think that's partly because they fear that Cain will hang them by their own intestines if they're not."

Casey chuckled. "Good point."

"Dinner's ready!" Gwen sang, a hand resting on her pregnant belly.

The pack headed into the dining area and settled at the long table, disregarding Kathy's seating plan like they always did. She hovered and fussed and poured drinks while everyone piled ridiculous amounts of food on their plates and whined at Marcus for hogging the gravy.

In between eating, drinking, and bantering, people snapped photos and pulled apart Christmas crackers. Kellen collected all the little jokes and read them aloud while the other kids traded the small toys. Kathy tried peer-pressuring everyone into donning the paper crowns. It didn't work with Cain or little Keane, but the others obliged her.

Later, once the table had been cleared, Casey sank into her chair with a sigh. Dammit, she was bloated. And tipsy. Very, very tipsy. Most of the pack looked ready to fall into a food coma. Honestly, she didn't think she had room for dessert, but she smiled when Kathy set it in front of her.

Shaya sighed at her daughter. "Willow, will you please get off your phone? It's rude to use it at the dinner table."

The pretty teenager held up a finger, her gaze still on her cell. "One sec, Mom, just one … There, done." Willow pocketed the phone and turned to her chocolate trifle. Noticing her father was staring at her, she blinked. "What?"

"Tell me you weren't talking to that punk again," said Nick.

"I wasn't talking to that punk again." She pointed her spoon at him. "And Kye is not a punk. He's my friend. Leave him alone."

Instead, Nick continued to grumble about her friendship with Kye, earning him huffs and eye rolls from Willow.

Eli draped an arm over the back of Casey's chair and kissed her temple. "You full, baby?"

"Unbearably," she replied. "And now I can't stand the feel of my waistband. Is anyone going to wake up Kent, or should we just let him rest?" she asked no one in particular. The poor guy was slumped in his chair, his eyes closed, his mouth slack.

Smiling, Caleb flicked a hand. "He's fine."

Playing his fingers through his mate's hair, Zander eyed Bracken. "You look like you could just as easily doze off."

"Had a crap night's sleep," said Bracken, spooning some trifle. "The girls took hours to settle last night because they were so excited. They woke up, like, three times, asking to go check if Santa had been. And Madisyn woke me up at one point, snarking in her sleep, 'You smell like feet, Morpheus, where the fuck's the blue pill?'"

Madisyn's cheeks pinkened. "I did not say that."

Bracken snickered. "Trust me, you did."

"Eli, Casey—one of you make her stop," said Nick.

Looking at her daughter, Casey had to stifle a smile. Rubie's eyes were locked on Nick's, unnervingly blank in a way that could give even an Alpha a chill. "Rubie." The single word was a warning.

Her gaze slid to Casey. "My mink wants to bite his jugular."

Bracken shook his head. "I love you, Rubes, but you minks are vicious creatures. Your mom's mink bit me again right on the back of the—Don't you dare, Regan!"

But Regan dared. Ignoring her father's warning, she splattered her sibling's face with a handful of trifle. Predictably, a fight commenced that included Regan getting repeatedly smacked over the head with an empty dessert bowl by Yasmin.

Dash tapped Harley on the arm and asked, "Can I have the rest of your trifle?"

Harley raised her brow. "What's the magic word?"

Dash's face scrunched up, and he lifted one shoulder. "Bibbidi-Bobbidi-Boo?"

Shaking his head at his son, Marcus burst out laughing. "Kid, you crack me up."

The little boy was a hoot. He was also pure trouble, which Casey's mink really liked about him—typical, really.

Eli kissed her neck, inhaling deeply. "I really should stop doing that," he whispered.

Casey frowned. "What?"

"Breathing in your scent in public," replied Eli, still whispering. "It goes straight to my cock, which has no sense of decorum—it doesn't matter where we are or how many people are around, it gets rock hard for you."

She smiled. "You can show me just how hard later."

"Oh, I plan to."

That night, Casey flexed her grip on the rungs of the headboard as her mate's tongue stabbed deep into her pussy. Yes, this was what she needed. He'd teased her mercilessly—licking, lapping, nipping, and rubbing his tongue up and down the side of her clit. Each time a little growl rumbled out of him, she all but shivered.

Flooded with feel-good chemicals and covered in a fine sheen of sweat, her body twisted, writhed, and bucked as he pumped his tongue inside her. Her pussy spasmed, aching for more, tightening as her orgasm crept closer and closer.

Eli's fingertips bit into the globes of her ass, holding her to him as he devoured and tortured her. God, she was wound so damn tight, she felt like she'd burst any second. He knew every sensitive spot she possessed, knew how to drive her into a fever pitch of pure need—something she appreciated when he wasn't taunting her this way.

"Eli," she rasped, feeling her release hurtling toward her. "I'm gonna—"

"No." He nuzzled her folds. "You're not coming until I'm inside you."

She bared her teeth at him. "Asshole."

Getting to his knees, he fisted his cock, looking so sure and in command. "I want you riding me tonight."

That she was good with. They switched positions, and she took a moment to drink him in—to admire that rugged face, powerfully built body, and that very fine cock. And he was all hers.

Eli looked up at her, his eyes smoldering with so much carnal hunger it took her breath away. "Come on, baby, wrap that pussy around my dick."

More than happy to do so, Casey straddled him and curled her fingers around the base of his cock. She lowered herself onto him, sucking in a breath as—

He punched up his hips, and she found herself impaled on his hard, oh so thick shaft.

Her lips parted in shock. "Jesus, Eli."

"I needed to be in you. You were taking too long."

Splaying her hands on that warm, solid chest that was packed with muscle, she slowly rose until only the head of his cock was inside her. Then she sank back down. His groan of masculine appreciation went straight to her core.

"Fuck yourself, baby. Ride me hard. That's it." Eli slid his hands up her smooth thighs and grabbed her hips. Possessiveness pounded through his blood as he took in the sight of her rising and falling on his cock, her eyes glazed, her breasts jiggling. "Love your body. Soft and strong and perfect."

He filled his hands with her breasts, shaping and squeezing. Teased her nipples into hard little buds that looked painfully tight. "Harder, baby."

She dug her nails into his chest as she rode him harder, scoring his flesh. After so many years, he had a countless number of teeth marks and scratches scarring his skin, and he loved every fucking one of them.

"Come here," he ordered. She leaned over, and he splayed his hand over her throat as he kissed her hard. Savored her taste. Drowned in her scent. All the while, he punched up his hips, drilling her pussy hard with his cock. But when he sensed she was ready to come, he stopped. "No."

Ignoring her curses, Eli rolled them over. "Shh, you'll get what you need. But not yet. You don't come until I say." He hooked her legs over his shoulders, groaning as he slid even deeper inside her. "Not until I say, Casey," he reminded her.

"What-the-fuck-ever," she snarked, but he knew she'd hold on for him.

Eli pulled his hips back in a slow, smooth movement, loving how her pussy tried sucking him back in. And then he slammed so deep the breath stuttered out of her. He ground his teeth as her tight inner muscles clamped around him. *So damn hot.*

He grazed her cheek with his mouth. "Breathe."

The whisper feathered over Casey's skin and made her stomach flutter. She hadn't even realized she'd been holding her breath until then.

"Grab the headboard again. Good girl. Now *I* fuck *you*."

And that was exactly what he did. Casey dug her heels into his back as he powered into her. Fast. Brutal. Ramming deep over and over, his eyes locked on where their bodies joined.

"Love the sound of my cock slamming into you while you're so wet."

Casey *was* unbelievably wet. She was also hot and desperate for release. Her orgasm was brewing inside her, making her skin flush and her muscles tighten. So many sensations were sweeping her under—his thickness stretching her, his balls slapping her ass, his fingertips digging into her hips, his cock throbbing inside her.

His eyes flicked to hers, hot and dark. A growl rumbled out of him. "Yeah, you love my dick, don't you?" Covering her hands with his on the headboard, he jackhammered in and out of her pussy so hard and savage she knew she'd be sore. Then he shifted his angle so that he was hitting her sweet spot with each powerful thrust.

"Make me come, Casey. Make me blow my load inside your pussy *right now.*"

He bit her shoulder. Waves of white-hot bliss fired through her blood, arching her spine and trapping a scream in her throat. Eli growled as he pounded harder and faster. When she reared up and bit into his shoulder, he exploded with a snarl of her name. His cock throbbed and pulsed as jet after jet of hot come splashed her inner walls. Then the strength left them both.

Fine tremors racked her body as she lay there, struggling to catch her breath. She felt all sated and warm and deliciously sore. Her mink was dozing off, just as content.

Panting, Eli dropped on the bed beside her, flat on his back. He dragged her to him so that she was burrowed into his side. She loved the way he held her so close, like he hated even the slightest bit of space between them.

He stared down at her through glazed, heavy-lidded eyes. "You okay?"

She hummed. "Fine. Did you have a good Christmas?"

"I had an amazing Christmas, as always. What about you?"

"I'm kinda sorry that it's over." After losing her grandparents, she'd stopped looking forward to Christmas. Miles had rarely been around, so she'd been relatively alone. Oh, she'd had her pack mates, sure, but they'd been busy celebrating with their families—just as it should be. Then she found Eli, and everything changed.

Now, she was *never* alone at Christmas. It was a time that made her feel all warm and fuzzy inside, especially with how excited the kids were.

Eli was so good with them. A devoted Dad who protected, encouraged, and supported them; who made sure they knew they were loved. He was also careful to treat them both the same, and she figured it was because his own mother wasn't as affectionate with Roni as she was with Eli and Nick.

Casey remembered how much he'd worried about her throughout her pregnancies—he was just a worrier when it came to those he loved. Probably because he'd already lost one of them and knew just how easily it could happen.

She also remembered how proud and elated he'd been when holding both his babies for the first time. He'd been a hands-on father from the start. Whenever he'd fed them during the night, she'd heard him talking softly to them—sometimes it was utter nonsense, sometimes it was a story they were far too young to understand, but he seemed to have loved it.

He'd once confessed that some part of him worried that he'd be taken from them when they were young, just as his own father had been taken from him. As such, he made the most of every moment he had with them—particularly since he wanted them to have nothing but fond memories of him.

Tracing circles on his chest, she looked up at him. He was wearing a pensive expression. "What're you thinking?" she asked.

"That I'm a lucky bastard." He palmed the side of her face. "Thank you."

She blinked. "For what?"

"For being mine. For moving to my pack. For giving me two amazing kids. For just being you." Eli sipped from her mouth. She was his little powder keg. The person who made every single shitty thing he'd been through worth it. His wolf plain fucking adored her; would do literally anything for her. He was just as gone for her mink.

Their mating ceremony—which had taken place a month after the Ignacio business was over—had been, hands down, one of the best days of Eli's life. She'd already fully committed to him by that point, yes, but he'd loved that they could finally celebrate it without the cloud of danger lingering over their heads.

All her teammates had attended the ceremony, so it hadn't been a surprise that a "friendly" game of soccer commenced at one point—the Hounds vs. the Mercury Pack males.

Yeah, his pack mates had lost in a dramatic fashion.

"I used to think that fate was cruel," he told her. "Don't get me wrong, I was thankful that I had a true mate out there somewhere and I was determined to find you. But it still seemed shitty that the universe would predestine two people to be together, that it would make them two halves of a whole, if one of those people was fated to die a lot sooner than the other."

She nodded. "I get it."

"But fate's far from cruel. It gave me you, and nothing on the fucking planet could make me regret finding you, even if—God forbid—our time together was cut short. You're by far the best thing that ever happened to me. Every single one of my all-time favorite moments have you in them. The only thing I regret is that I didn't find you sooner. When it comes to you, it's the only regret I'll ever have."

She swallowed and bit her lip. "You're gonna make me cry. And then I'll have to hurt you."

He spoke against her mouth, "You can take a few compliments—you're tough. I love that about you. Love all that spirit and fire and grit inside you. Love that you've passed it all onto our kids."

"Nah, I think they get it from you."

"No, they got that whole 'them being a trial at times' thing from me."

"Oh, there are times when you can be a real handful," Casey conceded.

Eli's lips twitched at the unintended inuendo. "A real handful?"

"Yep. You push and push, and you're not gentle about it. But I can take it, I know how to push back. And it's not like you're too hard to handle or you expect me to bend all the time. Or that we're always going back and forth over the same—" Casey broke off when his lips curled into a wide smile. She felt her face heat. "Okay, I'm shutting up."

Shaking with silent laughter, he put a hand over his eyes.

She poked his side. "You can stop laughing any second now, Chuckles." But he just laughed harder, the bastard. "Seriously, stop. You're making the bed rock, idiot. It's like the more I tell you to stop, the harder and harder you do it. What's worse is that you do it in public, too, even though you know it makes me all flustered. Believe me, I don't like that this stuff comes out of my mouth. If I could swallow it back, I would. Especially since you always erupt into—" And then she realized she'd done it again. "Oh, shut up."

SHARDS OF FROST

ACKNOWLEDGMENTS

So many people to thank ...

My husband, my kids, my sister/assistant—all of you are amazing and I seriously couldn't do this without your support and encouragement. Thank you for being awesome.

The team at Montlake Romance, because although I self-published this title, they have given me so much guidance throughout the series. I can't thank them enough for that.

All my readers, because you're just the most fabulous people *ever*. Every single one of you—it doesn't matter whether you only read one book, whether you read a few, whether you've been a faithful fan of the entire series, I'm so thankful for you all.

Love the whole bunch of you!

S :)

Suzanne Wright lives in England with her husband, two children, and two Bengal cats. When she's not spending time with her family, she's writing, reading, or doing her version of housework—sweeping the house with a look.

TITLES BY SUZANNE WRIGHT

The Deep in Your Veins Series
Here Be Sexist Vampires
The Bite That Binds
Taste of Torment
Consumed
Fractured

The Phoenix Pack Series
Feral Sins
Wicked Cravings
Carnal Secrets
Dark Instincts
Savage Urges
Fierce Obsessions
Wild Hunger
Untamed Delights

The Dark in You Series
Burn
Blaze
Ashes
Embers

The Mercury Pack Series
Spiral of Need
Force of Temptation
Lure of Oblivion
Echoes of Fire
Shards of Frost

Standalones
From Rags
Shiver

SHARDS OF FROST